WESTERN

Rugged men looking for love...

A Haven For His Twins
April Arrington

A Country Christmas
Lisa Carter

MILLS & BOON

A HAVEN FOR HIS TWINS
© 2023 by April Standard
Philippine Copyright 2023
Australian Copyright 2023
New Zealand Copyright 2023

First Published 2023
First Australian Paperback Edition 2023
ISBN 978 1 867 29823 6

A COUNTRY CHRISTMAS
© 2023 by Lisa Carter
Philippine Copyright 2023
Australian Copyright 2023
New Zealand Copyright 2023

First Published 2023
First Australian Paperback Edition 2023
ISBN 978 1 867 29823 6

MIX
Paper | Supporting
responsible forestry
FSC® C001695

Published by
Harlequin Mills & Boon
An imprint of Harlequin Enterprises (Australia) Pty Limited
(ABN 47 001 180 918), a subsidiary of HarperCollins
Publishers Australia Pty Limited
(ABN 36 009 913 517)
Level 19, 201 Elizabeth Street
SYDNEY NSW 2000 AUSTRALIA

Cover art used by arrangement with Harlequin Books S.A.. All rights reserved.

Printed and bound in Australia by McPherson's Printing Group

A Haven For His Twins
April Arrington

MILLS & BOON

April Arrington grew up in a small town and developed a love for books at an early age. Emotionally moving stories have always held a special place in her heart. April enjoys collecting pottery and soaking up the Georgia sun on her front porch.

Visit the Author Profile page
at millsandboon.com.au.

And we know that all things work together for good to them that love God, to them who are the called according to his purpose.
—*Romans* 8:28

DEDICATION

For Him. Thank You for giving me
a new purpose and a better life.

CHAPTER ONE

HOLT WILLIAMS HAD never been a perfect man—most people would say he'd never even been a good one—but he was proud of having worked hard for seven long years to become a decent one. He was proud of having stuck it out. Of having resisted the tempting pull of the old life he'd led. But that warm swell of confidence in his chest vanished the moment the front door of the small cabin across the street opened.

A woman walked out onto the porch, leaned her left hip against the rustic porch rail in a graceful pose and sipped from a coffee mug she cradled between both hands. Auburn hair shining beneath the sun that slowly rose above the Blue Ridge Mountains, she made the perfect picture of cozy, rural contentment. The type of guilt-free, peaceful existence Holt hadn't experienced in years.

She lifted her head and fixed her gaze on the windshield of his truck, which was parked on the side of the dirt road in front of her cabin.

Inside the cab, Holt shifted uncomfortably in the driver's seat. She couldn't possibly see him. The windows were tinted and the pickup he drove now was a different make and model than the one he'd driven up her driveway seven years ago.

Still, his heart kicked against his ribs, and he curled his clammy palms tighter around the leather steering wheel. She'd met him back then—seven years ago, when he'd been twenty-nine years old and at his lowest. So low, his cheeks blazed even now with the memory of how he had approached her that night.

But the bright side was that she knew very little about him other than the fact that he'd been desperate at the time. And the kind, empathetic look in her eyes that night made him believe she might be inclined to forgive him and offer a second chance.

He held his breath as she continued staring, her eyes narrowed as though she saw past the thick tinted glass, recognized his features and read his expression. But after a moment her expression relaxed, and she returned inside, slowly pushing the door closed behind her.

Holt exhaled, ran his fingers through his hair and smoothed his palm over his T-shirt, ensuring he looked presentable despite yesterday's long drive and a fitful night in a motel bed. It was time to face her; he couldn't put it off any longer. Not if he wanted to find his sons.

He exited the truck and strode slowly across the dirt road toward the cabin. Though it'd been seven years since he'd traversed the driveway to her home, his feet—and heart—remembered the path. Each painful step he'd taken toward her that night seven years ago had been imprinted into every cell of his being. He could still feel the warm weight of his infant sons in his arms, their wide eyes blinking up at him, their soft breaths seeming to beg him to reconsider.

His eyes burned, his step faltering. Spring rain had fallen for hours last night, and small muddy clods of Georgia clay coated the toes of his boots and sucked at his heels. The misty coolness of the morning air hit his bare forearms and he shivered slightly but pressed on, clenching his fists at his sides as he reached the steps leading to the cabin's front porch.

The same ornate hummingbird sculpture he recalled from seven years ago remained nailed to one of the thick columns at the top of the porch steps. *Hummingbird Haven*, the place was called, if he remembered correctly. He hadn't focused on the name the last time he'd visited… just the woman's face, her voice and the gentleness in her arms as she'd held his sons. He'd heard from locals she was exceptionally skilled at placing children in happy foster homes and that the cabins on her property served as the best shelter in the area.

He hadn't known what to say when he'd shown up at her door that night. Though he'd spent most of his adult years living a fast, carefree life on the rodeo circuit, enjoying days and nights filled with the sport, liquor and women, he'd slowed his pace when his sons were born, had given up the reckless excesses of the bachelor life he'd lived and tried his best to be a good father. Alone, ill equipped and inexperienced in childcare, it shouldn't have come as a surprise to him when he'd failed. But it had. And he'd never been more disappointed in himself.

It'd taken all the strength he'd had left to place his one-month-old sons in her arms that night and choke back the hot tears that had threatened to make him crumble. He'd wanted so much to gather his sons back against his chest, hug them close and leave again...even though he'd known he wasn't worthy of being their father.

She must've seen the desperation in his eyes and known how close he'd been to breaking down. She'd accepted his sons silently and taken them inside. Then she'd returned, had gently slid the straps of their diaper bags off his shoulders and asked one question. He hadn't been able to answer her, but instead of disdain, he'd only seen compassion in her eyes. For him—that night especially—she'd been nothing short of a hero and a better person than he'd ever been.

Now he hesitated, eyeing the hummingbird sculpture then the front door and large windows. The door stayed closed and the white lace curtains on each window remained still.

Unfurling one fist, he gripped the rustic porch rail and ascended the steps until he reached the front door. He knocked immediately, lifted his chin and straightened his six-foot-four-inch frame to its full height despite feeling smaller—and more unworthy—than he ever had.

Footsteps shuffled across the floor, a lock clicked as it released, then the door opened. And there she was—*Jessie Alden*. Three feet in front of him. Close enough to touch.

His memory of her—which had lingered in his mind for years—had been exact. Long auburn hair a unique shade of which he'd never seen before or since, dark brown eyes that could see right into the soul of a man and a curvy pink mouth made for smiling. Though Holt hadn't done anything worthy of earning her smile and hadn't had the good fortune of seeing it that night seven years ago.

She didn't smile now, either.

Instead, her mouth parted, and her eyes widened up at him, much in the same way as they had that night when he'd stood in front of her in the very same spot with two infants in his arms.

He focused on her eyes. "I have an answer to your question now." His voice sounded strained, even to his own ears. He cleared his throat and said in a steadier voice, "My sons matter most to me."

She frowned up at him but remained silent, her gaze pinned to his, emotions flickering through her expression, most too fast to identify save for one: *fear*.

He quickly took a step back. "Do you remember me?"

He'd felt sure she would recognize his face, even after all this time, and the last thing he'd ever want to do would be to frighten her. Though her reaction didn't surprise him—he was a big guy and his stature alone intimidated others more often than he liked. "I came here seven years ago. I had my... Well, I had two babies with me. My name is H—"

"I remember."

He stilled, letting her soft voice wash over him, pleased to discover he'd remembered the sound of it accurately over the years. Her tone was as gentle and patient as it had been that night. Forgiving, too? He hoped so. She was his only chance of discovering the whereabouts of his sons and, hopefully, reclaiming them.

"You asked me a question that night," he said. "You asked what mattered most to me."

Her gaze drifted lower, studying his lips intently as they moved.

"I didn't answer you then." He grimaced at the memory of the flawed, lost person he'd been years ago. "Because I didn't really know. But I do now. My sons matter most to me."

Her eyes met his again and her mouth tightened into a thin line. "Why now?"

Why not seven years ago? His cheeks burned. She hadn't said the words, but the question was right there in her defensive posture and guarded gaze. He didn't blame her for being suspicious of his presence...or less than welcoming.

He rubbed his hands over the jeans covering his thighs and ducked his head. "I was a different man then." He raised his head, met her eyes again. "My focus was on my own self-interests rather than my sons. But I've changed. I want to let you know who I am now, and I wanted to thank you in person. It wasn't something I thought I could do justice over the phone, but now that I'm here, 'thank you' doesn't do the job, either."

She returned his gaze, her posture relaxing just a bit.

"What you did that night—" he spread his hands, words escaping him "—taking in my sons and caring for them as you did. No criticism, no judgment. Not many people would do that."

She remained silent and still.

"I had no idea how to be a father." He studied her face, the flush blooming on her freckled cheeks. "Had no idea how to take care of them or what to do for them, and you..."

Throat tightening, he looked away and focused on a cedar tree at the end of the porch. He clenched his jaw and watched a branch dip in the breeze, dew sparkling in the morning sunlight.

"Anyway..." He withdrew an envelope from his back pocket, smoothed the slight bend in the middle, then offered it to her. "It's in here. What I wanted to say."

She looked at the envelope then slowly took it from him, her fingertips brushing his.

He flexed his hand, the warm softness of her touch still lingering on his skin. "I'd like to talk to you. To ask you a few questions about my sons if you'll allow me."

She stared down at the envelope she held for a few moments then looked up. "That's all you want? To ask questions?"

"Yes." To begin with, at least. He felt sure that was all she'd allow for now.

"I don't think..." She glanced over her shoulder then sighed. "Do you drink coffee?"

He smiled wide, hope swelling within him. "Yes."

"Then I guess you can come in for a cup." She stepped back, opened the door wider then hesitated, her voice firm. "But just one. I don't have time for more than that."

"I understand." He eased past her and entered the cabin. "Thank you."

The living room was small but cozy. A stone fireplace took center stage, a low fire crackling within, to stave off the slight morning chill, he assumed. One TV, two wooden end tables and a plush sofa and recliner in mismatched fabrics filled the rest of the room.

"Have a seat on the sofa. I just put a pot on." The clean scent of her hair—*sweet honeysuckle… or fresh apples?*—hit his senses as she walked past him and left the room. "Won't take but a sec."

Holt glanced at the large sofa then crossed the room, his right knee bumping one of the end tables, rattling a delicate Tiffany-style lamp. He caught it with one shaky hand before it toppled over and steadied it back in position, unscathed. A relieved breath escaped him.

"It's okay." She'd returned, steam rising from a cup she held toward him. "That lamp's been broken twice before." Her lips twitched and a teasing light entered her dark eyes. "We managed to piece it back together both times."

"We?" His hand stopped in midair as he reached for the cup. "You and your husband?"

"No." The word was clipped. Her tone brisk. "Have a seat and ask your questions. I did tell you I didn't have much time."

Tensing at the abrupt change in her demeanor, he accepted the cup of coffee she thrust toward him then sat, sinking into the soft cushions of the sofa. She sat in the recliner facing him and he returned her stare for a few moments, a heavy silence falling between them.

Her eyes left his twice, veering off to a point high behind his right shoulder, and her fingers picked restlessly at the seam of her jeans along her thigh.

"Are my sons doing well?" he asked. "Are they safe and happy?"

She nodded but her expression remained stern.

Oh, man. Where to begin? His name, maybe? He'd known this task would be difficult, but he hadn't anticipated that the bright, revealing light of day and the knowing look in her eyes would be so intimidating. He leaned forward, propped his elbows on his knees and sipped from the cup, flinching as the bitter brew scalded his tongue.

Her face paled. "I'm sorry. It's too hot. Or maybe I should've added cream or sug—"

"It's okay. I normally take it black anyw—"

"But I didn't expect you to show up here, you know?" Her cheeks flushed a bright pink. "Right out of thin air." She snapped her fingers. "Just like that, after seven years."

"I know I should've called, but—"

"I never thought you'd come back. No one ever comes back."

"I realize my coming here is a shock, bu—"

"What is it you really want?"

He froze and searched her expression. Her gaze had moved beyond him again, past his right shoulder. Focused intently on that same spot. "I didn't come to upset you," he said softly.

Her eyes returned to his. "Then why? Why'd you come?" Her tone hardened. "And tell me the truth. I've dealt with enough men like you to know you're withholding something."

"Men like me?" The judgmental grimness in her expression sent an unexpected ache through him. He set the coffee cup on the end table and stood, then spun away and strode around the couch, his gaze skimming the wall adorned with pictures in various styles of frames. "I'm not perfect, Jessie. Never claimed to be. But I'm not worthless."

He glanced over his shoulder at her. She sat

on the edge of the recliner, her face paling again as she met his eyes.

"Do you understand?" His voice cracked and he turned away, his neck heating. "I'm not worthless…"

Holt stilled as his eyes focused on one framed photo. A large twelve-by-eighteen picture of Jessie in the most beautiful state he'd ever seen her: damp hair plastered in disarray to her sun-flushed cheeks, framing her bright smile as she knelt among smooth rocks in the shallow end of a mountain river. She hugged two boys—twins—their wet blond heads tucked beneath her chin. One boy hugged her back, smiling as he kissed her jaw; the other boy held up a flat black stone, laughing as he showed off his proud find.

The boys' features were familiar. Painfully so.

Holt tilted his head back, taking in the dozens of photos splayed across the wall in the shape of a tree with sprawling branches, each picture filled with the same boys at every age from bath time at infancy to blowing out candles at their seventh birthday party. And all of them included Jessie with the broadest, happiest of smiles.

"You kept them," he rasped. "You kept my sons."

"They're not yours."

Jessie closed her eyes, unable to believe the words had escaped her lips. What had she been thinking, inviting him in? From the moment she saw that truck parked across the road, she'd known something was up. She always kept a careful eye on who visited Hummingbird Haven to protect the privacy and safety of the troubled women and displaced children living at her shelter, and this morning an uneasy churn in her stomach had alerted her to the fact that something wasn't quite right.

But like that night seven years ago, the same pained, vulnerable look in Holt's hazel eyes as he'd stood outside her door had tugged at her heart and prompted her to lower her defenses.

"Those are my sons." Holt lifted one arm and pointed at a recent photo of Cody and Devin that hung on the wall. "I'm a twin, myself. This could easily be a picture of me and my brother at that age. You don't think I'd recognize them?"

"I know you recognize them." Inhaling deeply, she placed the coffee cup she held on the end table and stood. "And I know how similar Cody and Devin look to you and your brother, Liam."

His eyes narrowed. "How do you know my brother? You don't even know me. All you know is that I dropped my sons off here seven years ago."

"I know your name is Holt Williams," she said. "It was on the birth certificates you packed in the diaper bags for the boys. Once I knew your name, it was easy to search for information about you. I always conduct research on the families of children who are left with me to better care for them and find the most suitable homes. Besides, you knew who I was when you came here. You knew my name, where I lived. You left two infants with me. It was only fair that I found out at least a little bit about you."

Holt frowned. "What else do you know?"

"That your father left your mother when you were eighteen to return to the rodeo circuit and that you went with him, competing as a bull rider." She eyed his muscular stature, clad in jeans, a white T-shirt and muddy boots. "Still do, from the looks of you. You won a couple championships six years ago, so there were several articles and interviews online. Most of them highlighted your career and how similar you were to your father when he'd competed at your age."

And that Holt shared his father's reputation as a fun-loving bachelor who partied hard, drank heavily, chased women and gambled on rodeo events, though that she wouldn't mention.

"There weren't many other biographical details except for one article I found," she said. "The journalist mentioned you'd been estranged from your mother and brother since you left home, but that you were a twin and he included a picture of you and your brother as kids." She glanced at the photo where he still pointed and managed a smile. "You both looked to be around the same age as Cody and Devin are in that picture. You and Liam are identical twins from what I could tell from your childhood photo."

He lowered his arm to his side, his jaw hardening. "Anything else?"

She studied his handsome features, the slight stubble lining his angular jaw, his sculpted cheekbones and thick blond hair. Every inch of his impressive stature was that of the athletic, charismatic, carefree man the journalist had described in the article. The kind who chased every moment of fun in life and dodged all the consequences, abandoning any responsibilities.

"You say you've changed," she said softly, "but according to what I read in the article, you were what? Twenty-nine, seven years ago. You weren't a boy then. You were a man. A man who chose to abandon his own flesh and blood at a stranger's door."

He grimaced and looked past her out the large window by the front door, his hazel eyes wounded.

She ducked her head. "I... I'm sorry. That was unfair and wrong of me. I'm sure you did what you thought was best for Cody and Devin at the time. You protected them by doing the responsible thing and I'm glad you brought them here. More than that. I'll always be grateful to you for bringing them to me that night."

More than he'd ever know. Her attention strayed to the photo he'd noticed on the wall where Cody and Devin smiled as they hugged her in the river. A friend had taken that picture only a week ago on the same day she'd asked the boys how they felt about her adopting them. She'd been nervous about discussing the topic with Cody and Devin. She felt sure the boys would ask why she'd waited so long. Truth was, she'd held fast to a self-imposed rule to not get too emotionally attached to any resident at Hummingbird Haven since she'd opened the shelter over a decade ago. Her goal was to help abused women start a new life and place children in loving homes with supportive families—not create a family of her own.

But Cody and Devin had stolen her heart the moment they'd settled into her arms seven years ago, and she'd been unable to part with them since. Essentially, she'd served as Cody and Devin's mother from day one and as the years passed, adoption seemed like the natural, right thing to do.

Thirty-five years old now, she'd known ever since her teens that due to ovarian cysts and subsequent surgery she'd never be able to have children of her own. But Cody and Devin had changed that. They'd made her a mother in every sense of the word save for the legal technicality, and with the boys' blessing, she'd begun the process of achieving that as well.

"You don't know me as well as you think you do." Holt's hoarse voice pulled her eyes back to him. He still stared out the window, his broad shoulders lowered. "Where are my sons now?"

"They're at school," she said.

"I want to see them."

She shook her head. "That's out of the question."

He faced her then, a piercing look in his eyes. "Why?"

"I—It's been too long. Seven years." She spread her hands. "Legally, you have thirty days after leaving them to change your mind and re-gain custody. As it stands, they're settled with me. I applied for adoption recently."

One blond brow lifted, and his smooth lips curved humorlessly. "And you feel you have the final say in whether or not I have a role in their lives?"

She pulled back her shoulders and straight-ened to her full five-foot-six inches, resentful of still having to tilt her head back to look up at his face. "Yes. It would confuse them to meet with you now. Not to mention, possibly hurt them emotionally."

He remained silent for a moment then spoke again, his lips barely moving. "Why did you ask me that question that night—what matters most to me?"

Her brow furrowed at the abrupt change in

subject. "I always ask that when someone abandons a child." She squeezed her palms together, her hands trembling at the painful memories of the various responses she'd received over the years. "I guess I hope that at some point, it'll help me understand why they chose to leave them behind." She jerked her thumb toward the front door. "Now, I appreciate your concern for Cody and Devin, but they're happily settled and it's time you left."

His gaze roved over her face and his mouth moved as though to speak but he seemed to think better of it and instead, he strode across the room and opened the door.

Pausing on the threshold, he looked back at her. "I'm sorry my returning is difficult for you, and the last thing I'd ever want to do is hurt Cody and Devin. But they *are* my sons, and I won't leave them again. My cell number is in the card I gave you and I'm staying at the Hope Springs Motel. I'd like the opportunity to explain myself and see my sons. Even if only from a distance."

Jessie clenched her teeth. "Please go. I don't understand why you think you can just waltz back into Cody and Devin's lives like this."

He did as she asked but before closing the

door behind him, he said, "Because from what I remember of you that night and knowing what it is you do here, I hoped you believed in second chances."

doesn't bind him in case. ... reminder or ... If it you don't know. I hoped you believed in second ...

CHAPTER TWO

You don't know *me as well as you think you do.*

Jessie, standing at the kitchen island in her cabin, chopped a carrot into small slices then glanced at the envelope Holt had given her six hours earlier. There it sat on the kitchen island where she'd left it this morning, unopened and unread. She'd passed it a dozen times through-out the day as she'd loaded dirty dishes into the dishwasher, swept and mopped the kitchen floor and carried loads of laundry through the kitchen to the washer and dryer. Each time she'd passed the letter, her eyes had fixated on it, Holt's pained voice whispering through her mind.

I hoped you believed in second chances.

She tightened her grip on the knife she held, grabbed a cucumber from the pile of vegetables she'd placed on the kitchen island and chopped. That was the problem—she did. She absolutely did believe in second chances, and normally, she would be welcoming and receptive to any parent who returned to her door and inquired about their child—although that had never occurred before—and she should've extended the same welcome to Holt as well.

Only, offering Holt a second chance meant so much more than it would were she to extend the opportunity to someone else. Offering Holt a second chance meant more than just disrupting Cody and Devin's lives—though that was concerning enough. It also meant jeopardizing the future she was working so hard to secure for them. A future that included the long-awaited adoption that would legalize her as their mother.

And that realization alone—that she was placing her own selfish wishes above what might be best for Cody and Devin, and to some extent, even Holt—made her feel even guiltier than she already did for turning him away so quickly. After all, hadn't her mission at Hummingbird Haven always been to unite children with families who loved them rather than keep them apart?

Her head throbbed. She dropped the knife onto the counter, rubbed her temples then paced around the kitchen island. A queasy sensation filled her stomach as she recalled Holt's expression the night he'd left Cody and Devin in her care seven years ago. She'd had no doubts that he'd been desperate, frightened and exhausted. There had been tears in his eyes when he'd placed his sons in her arms, and he'd paused more than once as he'd walked back up her driveway toward his truck, glancing back at her cabin as though he'd changed his mind. But in the end, he hadn't returned. He'd hopped back in his truck, cranked the engine and driven off into the dark summer night without a word of explanation as to why he'd abandoned his sons.

Though...

Her steps slowed. Despite that, she had to admit he'd done the responsible thing and sought help. He'd brought Cody and Devin to a shelter where he knew they'd be taken care of properly and would hopefully be placed with a loving family. Holt had done exactly what she'd begged troubled mothers to do for years for their infants: bring them to safety rather than abandon them in an irresponsible manner.

How could she blame him for doing exactly as she hoped more troubled parents would? He'd done more for his sons than her own mother had done for her.

Jessie's steps halted. Her mother—whoever she was—had wrapped her, unwashed and only hours old from what Jessie had been told years later, in a blanket and left her on the paved ground of a motel parking lot. It'd been below freezing that night and only by God's grace had someone stumbled upon her in time. That was, after all, the reason she'd established Hummingbird Haven. She never wanted any child to suffer or feel unloved, lost, or neglected.

After being abandoned, she'd lived in foster care until she'd aged out at eighteen years old, worked odd jobs for seven years and saved every penny she earned to be able to afford the property Hummingbird Haven resided on now. The property itself had been a blessing from God. Eager to move and unload the land, the previous owner—recently widowed—had reduced the purchase price substantially once she learned of Jessie's plans for the shelter and donated a hefty sum to help Jessie with the initial costs of creating the shelter. It had taken three years to finish restoring six of the eight cabins on the lot, including the one she, Cody and Devin lived in now, and two more years to get the word out properly and collect enough donations, grants and financial aid to establish her shelter permanently as a secure, reliable safe haven.

She'd spent the past ten years using funds she'd raised—and continued to solicit—to care for abandoned children, place them in good homes and help abused women establish a new, safe life for themselves. And over those years, of all the people who had abandoned children at her door, the memory of Holt's expression of despair and regret had stayed with her the most.

But feeling guilty and regretful over leaving his sons didn't necessarily make him good father material, did it?

Sighing, Jessie picked up the envelope from the kitchen island. She slid her nail under the lip of the envelope and withdrew the card it contained. Colorful flowers adorned the front of the card but there were no factory-printed words inside, only a message scrawled in rough cursive as though penned by a masculine hand. She began reading.

Jessie,
I'll say right out that I'm not good at this. I'm
not good at finding the right words to say what I

*mean, and I've never been good at trusting peo-
ple enough to share what I think or feel. To be
honest, I've never been the best at anything of
significance in life so far, except finding ways to
hold on and endure pain without complaint. But
because I've lived fast and hard, I've learned just
about everything there is to know about people
and this I know for sure.*

*There isn't anyone else like you. I've never
met anyone filled with the kind of empathy
and compassion you greeted me with the night
I brought my sons to you. And I've never met
anyone who would take in someone else's children without hesitation. I'm sure there are other
people in the world with hearts as big as yours,
but I've never met them. And I know from experience that they're hard to find.*

*Thank you for saving my sons. For finding
them a home and security for seven years. For
doing for them what I couldn't do at the time.*

*Now I'm asking for your help again. Please
help me find my sons and get them back...be-
cause they are what matter most to me. I can
answer your question now. I love my sons and
I'm ready to be the father Cody and Devin de-*

serve. The father I should've been years ago. I just need a second chance.
Sincerely,
Holt Williams

Jessie stared down at the card in her hands, blinking back tears. "Oh no. Oh no, not now. He can't be asking this of me now. Not when I'm about to become their mother." She dropped her head back and stared up at the exposed wooden beams that comprised the vaulted ceiling. "*You* can't be asking this of me. Not n—"

A horn blared outside.

"Great." Jessie wiped her eyes, stuffed the card in the waistband of her jeans and ran to the other side of the island. She swept the freshly chopped carrots and cucumbers into a large bowl and sealed the plastic lid on top. "Just great."

She was late. Holt had already disrupted the boys' carefully planned routine.

Jessie stacked another large plastic container she'd filled with pimento and cheese tea sandwiches on top of the vegetable bowl, scooped both up in her arms and race-walked outside onto the front porch just as a large multicolored van, painted with rainbows, hummingbirds and

a large yellow sun, turned onto the driveway.
Every window was open and six young faces
smiled at her from the openings, hands waving
and voices shouting in unison, "We're home,
Jessie!"

"I missed you," Jessie shouted back, struggling to hold on to the plastic containers in her
arms as she waved back with one hand.

The van rumbled past her cabin, turned left
onto a dirt road and continued through a patch
of thick forest toward the large Hummingbird
Haven community building located several feet
behind Jessie's cabin.

Clutching the food containers to her chest,
Jessie hustled down her front steps and down
the dirt path, following the van as it slowly
maneuvered its way to the community building and parked beside the log structure. The
doors opened and a young woman hopped out
of the driver's seat, then assisted the six children as they all scrambled out of the van and
walked into the community building save for
two blond-headed boys who jogged over to
Jessie, their backpacks jostling around on their
backs.

"You're late." Devin, a seven-year-old with
the shrewdness of an eighty-year-old man,

propped his fists on his hips and narrowed his eyes up at her.

Jessie nodded. "I know."

"What's wrong?"

She summoned a smile. "Not a thing. I'm just running behind is all."

His hazel eyes—the same shade as Holt's—narrowed even more on her face. "Really? You're okay?"

She smiled wider. So wide her cheeks hurt. "Really. I promise you I'm fine. There's nothing to worry about."

And there wasn't. Not really. She'd see to that. Devin had begun asking questions about his parents two years ago and she'd been as truthful as she could be without oversharing to the point of hurting him. But Devin was smart—gifted, even, if what his teachers suspected about his abilities turned out to be true. And he'd spent far more time than Cody over the past two years prodding her for information about his parents, wondering why they'd never been around and worrying about the future. She'd hoped initiating adoption proceedings would put his mind at ease. And it had, to a certain extent, but while Cody led with his heart, Devin led with his head, and easing

Devin's worries about his and Cody's future had proven to be more difficult than she'd expected.

"Hey, Jessie." Cody, flashing his ever-present smile, hugged her waist and eyed the containers she held. "Peanut butter and jelly day?"

"'Fraid not." She bent and kissed his forehead. "You had that yesterday, and two days in a row is a bit too much sugar. Today is pimento and cheese day."

Cody groaned but asked hopefully, "Did you cut the crusts off?"

"Indeed."

Devin scooted close and peeked into the clear bowl she held in her arms. "Veggies, too?" He looked up at her and licked his lips. "Cucumber? And did you bring the ranch dressing?"

Grinning—sincerely this time—Jessie kissed his forehead, too. "Yep on both counts. I put a bottle of dressing on the table earlier and have an extra bottle at our cabin if needed, so you can glop on as much as you want." She glanced at Cody. "And I made chocolate milk to go with the mini sandwiches and veggies, so you'll still get a decent dose of sugar."

"Thanks, Jessie!" Both boys spoke in unison, hugged her waist one more time then darted inside the building.

Jessie laughed. Aside from video game hour, snack time was the boys' favorite part of the day, and though they were small, they put away enough sandwiches and salad every afternoon after school to feed two horses.

"Those two are gonna eat you out of house and home one day." Zoe Price, a vivacious and eternally optimistic twenty-nine-year-old who served as Jessie's assistant manager, grinned as she strolled over.

Jessie shrugged. "They're growing boys, and goodness knows they get their fair share of exercise the way they run around this place."

"Still..." Zoe lifted the lid on one container, slipped her hand inside and stole two tea sandwiches. "I hope you have enough."

Laughing, Jessie smacked her hand. "Get your grubby paw out of there."

"Hey," she muttered around a mouthful of pimento cheese, "I'm still growing, too." She giggled and motioned outward with her arms. "Just the wrong way."

Jessie laughed and shook her head. "Girl, I wish I had your metabolism." Not to mention Zoe's energy and athleticism. Zoe loved exploring the outdoors and her muscular physique showed it. "Why do you think I've cut back on making peanut butter and jelly sandwiches? I gain five pounds just smelling those things."

"Aw, hush up." Holding a tea sandwich in one hand, Zoe took the veggie container from Jessie's overloaded arms and walked with her toward the community building. "You're gorgeous and you know it."

Jessie smiled. "Oh, now I remember why I hired you."

"Because I give it to you straight." Zoe popped her last tea sandwich into her mouth, saying around a mouthful, "The good and the bad."

That was true. In the past five years Jessie had worked with her, Zoe had always been honest to a fault. She'd never held back her opinions—especially if they differed from Jessie's—and she'd always been equally eager to compromise. Their business partnership and close friendship had laid the foundation for a thriving and welcoming safe haven for everyone.

"Which," Zoe continued, "I think I should warn you that Devin had a rough day at school today."

Jessie frowned. "What happened?"

Zoe lowered her voice as they entered the community building. "The teacher told me she asked the class to write about what they planned to do over spring break next month. They were asked to read what they wrote to the class and when Marjorie Middleton stood up and read about going camping with her dad and how great he was—"

"Let me guess." Jessie winced. Marjorie Middleton had been Devin's nemesis since kindergarten when she'd beaten him in a relay race and given him a Valentine's card. He couldn't stand that Marjorie was a faster runner than he was or her *ooey-gooey-girly stuff* as he'd put it, and Marjorie's tendency to wax poetic about her beloved father had only exacerbated their rift. "Devin had something negative to say."

"Yep," Zoe whispered as they approached the kids, who sat at one of several wooden tables laden with plates, cups, napkins and utensils. "He said dads were good for nothing and that moms do all the work anyway so who needed them? Then he refused to read what he wrote, balled up his paper and threw it in the trash."

"Oh no." Jessie set the tea sandwich container on the table and caught Devin's eye. She pointed to a seat at another table away from the other kids. Noticing the stern look on her face, he complied, blushing and ducking his head as he walked over to the table and had a seat.

"Here it is." Zoe set the salad on the table, withdrew a wrinkled piece of notebook paper from her pocket and pressed it into Jessie's hand. "I'll take care of snack time so y'all can have a talk. Go easy on him, okay?"

Jessie took the paper and nodded. Zoe had always had a soft spot for Devin.

"Now, then." Zoe clapped her hands and briskly rubbed them together. "I'm in charge of snack time while Jessie and Devin have some alone time, then we'll start on homework. Who wants to help me pour the chocolate milk?"

Tabitha, a thirteen-year-old who'd lived with her mother and younger sister at Hummingbird Haven for two months, volunteered, smiling shyly at Jessie as she passed her to join Zoe on the other side of the table. Her younger sister, Katie, sprang up and, sticking close to Tabitha's side, offered to help as well. They'd be missing their mother, Peggy Ann, by now. After escaping an abusive marriage, Peggy Ann had gotten her first job in fifteen years as a cashier at a local hardware store and wouldn't be home for another three hours.

Miles, a quiet five-year-old boy who'd arrived at Hummingbird Haven two weeks ago after being abandoned by his mother, smiled as Jessie walked by. Confused and frightened when he'd first arrived, he hadn't spoken or smiled for the first full week. He'd managed his first smile and words three days ago and seemed to be settling in but was still clearly uncomfortable. Which was to be expected.

Miles' mother, his only living relative, had packed her bags and left home early one morning with her boyfriend and didn't return. Miles, left alone in their apartment, had gone to a neighbor's house two days after his mother had left, seeking help and had eventually been placed at Hummingbird Haven. Miles struggled to trust others and, his sense of security having been shattered, feared being abandoned again.

Cody, seated next to Miles, smiled as Jessie walked by but his eyes kept veering toward Devin with a worried expression. He and Devin had been protective of each other from the very start, and he'd be worried for Devin now that he'd found himself in trouble. A pleading look of forgiveness entered Cody's eyes as though he hoped he could soften her up for Devin. She gave him a slight smile. No matter how close she'd grown to Cody and Devin over the years, they still craved reassurance on a frequent basis.

They all needed her, but Devin seemed to need her the most today.

"So…" Jessie sat in a chair opposite Devin at the otherwise empty table and spoke quietly. "I heard you had a rough day at school today."

He didn't answer, just crossed his arms on the table and lowered his chin onto the backs of his hands.

Jessie unfolded the paper Zoe had given her and narrowed her eyes, reading around the wrinkles creased into the page.

SPRING BREAK
by Devin Williams

Spring break will be great! Me and my brothur will have a real mom of our on. Jessie won't just be our fostur mom she will be our real mom. Forever. She told us so. And it's better than other kinds of moms because she choosed us. She gives us sanwitches and hugs and plays with us and takes care of us. She loves us. She loves us so much we don't need a dad and can be a family on our on. Just us three. Cody don't think so becuz he wants a dad. but I don't. Dads aren't good for nothing. I love Jessie and don't ever want a dad.

For the second time that day, Jessie blinked hard, holding back tears that gathered on her lashes.

"I didn't mean to make you cry." Devin lifted his head and looked at her. A wounded expression—startlingly the same one she'd seen on Holt's face earlier that day—appeared. "We don't need a dad, you know? Cody wants one but I don't. Not when I got you."

She folded the paper back up slowly. A deep ache spread through her chest at the pained tone of his voice. "You and Cody didn't mention this when we spoke about the adoption last week. Are you sure you don't want a dad, too, Devin? Even as a wish or for pretend, maybe? It's okay. You can tell me if you do."

He scowled and balled his fists on the table. "No. Not ever. I want you. Just you."

Laughter broke out across the room, and she glanced at the other table where Zoe did a silly dance and growled as she handed each child a tea sandwich. "Y'all better eat these up before I do. They're my favorite!"

As the kids dug into their snacks, Jessie faced Devin again. "Will you do me a favor, please?"

Devin nodded.

"Will you apologize to the teacher and Marjorie Middleton tomorrow at school for what you said in class?"

He frowned. "But—"

"Marjorie loves her dad as much as you love me and I'm sure what you said probably hurt her feelings. She deserves an apology."

"But she—"

"You wouldn't want someone to say something mean about me, would you?"

He sighed and shoved his hand through his blond hair. "No, ma'am."

"And you have a good heart." She reached out and smoothed his ruffled hair. "If you make a mistake, you want to fix it as best you can, don't you?"

He nodded. "Yes, ma'am. I'll apologize."

"Thank you." Jessie smiled. "Now, I guess you can rejoin the others. You're to eat your snack and do your homework right after."

"Yes, ma'am." He scrambled up from his chair and headed toward the other table.

"Devin?"

He stopped and faced her.

Jessie's smile wobbled. "I love you, too, you know?"

A wide grin broke out across Devin's face. He ran back, hugged her tight and whispered against her neck, "I know." Then he darted over to the children's table, sat beside Cody and dug into his pimento and cheese sandwich.

"I think we're gonna need another bottle of ranch dressing," Zoe called out as she upended and smacked an empty bottle over Devin's vegetables.

"I'll grab one from my place." Jessie stood and headed for the door. "Be back in a sec."

Once outside, she pulled Holt's card from her waistband. She held it in one hand and Devin's paper in the other, her gaze moving slowly from one to the other for a full minute. Then she tilted her head back and glared up at the clear blue sky.

"I get it," she whispered. "I hear loud and clear what You're asking of me. But I can't do it."

There were no sounds other than the pleasant chirp of birds and rustle of leaves from the slight afternoon breeze. No response—or rebuke—from heaven.

"I can't do it," she repeated, still staring at the sky. "You sent them to me, and You don't make mistakes. They're my sons now—mine. And not everyone truly deserves a second chance, do they?" She trembled, her voice strained as both the card and wrinkled paper crumpled beneath her rough grip. "I *won't* do it."

CHAPTER THREE

HOLT PRESSED HIS cell phone closer to his ear, muted the TV and sat on the edge of the bed in his room at the Hope Springs Motel.

"It's been four days," he said, dragging his hand over his stubbled jaw. "I don't know why I even unpacked. Jessie made it clear she has no intention of contacting me and I haven't heard a word from her." There'd been no messages for him at the front desk and no missed calls on his cell. "And I can't very well go back to her place after she made it clear I was no longer welcome."

"She'll call." His brother Liam's voice sounded confident across the airwaves. "I know she will."

A humorless laugh escaped Holt's lips. "And what makes you so certain of that? You've never met her, and you didn't see her face. I'm telling you she doesn't want me anywhere near Cody and Devin."

"I know she'll call," Liam stated firmly, "because this time is different. You're different. If she has only a fraction of the goodness you thought she had in her, she'll take a chance on you. You're worth taking a chance on, Holt."

He stilled, his throat closing as he watched the weatherman's mouth moving silently on the muted TV. The weatherman gestured toward a map behind him, pointing out temperatures in neighboring counties during the morning newscast. His hometown of Pine Creek was too small of a community to be recognized on the map and though it only took a four-hour drive to get there from Hope Springs, it felt as though home were a thousand miles away.

Liam's heavy sigh crossed the line. "I never told you that and I probably should've done so years ago. Then maybe we wouldn't have lost so much time."

Holt closed his eyes, a feeling of bittersweet gratitude washing over him. He hadn't expected that. He'd been estranged from his twin brother for most of his adult life—ever since their father had packed a bag and left Holt's mother to return to the rodeo circuit and hitch up with another woman… And Holt, having just turned eighteen at the time, had chosen to go with his father rather than stay at the family farm and help Liam and his mother fight foreclosure. At the time, Holt had been desperate for his father's approval and willing to sacrifice his relationship with his mother and brother for his attention. He'd followed his father's lead and severed ties with his mother and brother.

It'd taken one year for Holt to realize—and finally accept—that his father had intended to leave his entire family—not just his wife—and that Holt had become unwelcome baggage on the circuit. After embracing a new wife and new life, his father had little interest in nurturing a relationship with his son from a former marriage.

Hurt and angry, Holt had been too ashamed to return home to the mother and brother he felt he'd betrayed and had struck out on his own, touring the rodeo circuit solo rather than with his father. Success had come fast and fierce, along with the reckless excesses that were in abundance when traveling the circuit. Holt had abandoned his Christian principles and embraced his new life wholeheartedly to escape the pain of having a father who didn't love him and his guilt over abandoning his mother and brother. He'd thought he'd succeeded...until his sons had been conceived. He'd been unable to bring himself to return home and seek help from the family he'd betrayed and, as a result, had failed to support and provide for Cody and Devin.

After he'd left Cody and Devin with Jessie, the pain of abandoning his sons had been so great that touring the circuit no longer offered the comforting escape it once had. Eventually, after a lot of prayer, he'd chosen to face his fears, guilt and shame head-on and become the dependable brother, son, Christian—and hopefully, father—he should've been. To his surprise, upon his return home, his mother had accepted his apology and welcomed him with open arms and no resentment. His brother, however, hadn't been as forgiving. Though they'd begun patching things up five years ago, Holt knew Liam still needed more time before he fully trusted him again. Still, Liam had never thrown around compliments lightly and Holt doubted he'd start now.

"Thank you," Holt said. "That means a lot to me, especially knowing I still have a long way to go in proving my loyalty to you and Mom."

Liam was quiet for a moment then grunted. "You start getting all sentimental on me and I'll hang up. I mean it."

Holt chuckled. "One minute older than me and you still think that entitles you to boss me around. Put Mom on. I'm tired of talking to you, old man."

Liam laughed softly then a faint rustling crossed the line before his mom spoke.

"Jessie hasn't called?" Concern and worry flooded her tone.

"No, Mom. I was hoping that after our visit she might cool down and, well, it doesn't seem she's going to call."

"But…" He could picture her on the other end of the line, biting her lip and twirling a long strand of gray hair around her finger. "Liam says she'll call." Her tone firmed. "And if Liam says so, it's bound to happen."

Holt smiled. His mother, Gayle, had leaned hard on Liam since the day Holt and their father had left her eighteen years ago, and Liam had been the one to stay behind and revitalize the family farm that now served as a bed-and-breakfast in southern Georgia. Without Liam's dedication, hard work and willingness to remain at the family home and put his life on hold for Gayle, Pine Creek Farm would never have stayed afloat after Holt and his father had left, much less have rebounded to the thriving vacation attraction it had become. According to Gayle, whatever Liam said was the gospel truth.

"But if she doesn't call..." Gayle's confident tone faltered. "Well, we'll just have to go another route, won't we?"

Holt grimaced. "This is my responsibility. I'll see it through in whatever way is best for Cody and Devin."

"I know you don't want to involve a third party," she continued gently, "but you may have to if you want to see Cody and Devin again. I'm sure Jessie is a nice woman—must be to have taken in Cody and Devin as she did—but you deserve a chance to see your sons, too." She sighed. "When the boys were born, you and I didn't have a relationship and you didn't feel you could come to me, so I wasn't able to help you. But now I can. Darlene Fulton from church gave me the name of a good lawyer who specializes in parental rights—"

"No." Holt softened his tone. "No, thank you, Mom. But I don't want to involve lawyers unless it's absolutely necessary. I want this to be as easy for Cody and Devin as I can possibly make it."

"Yes, bu—"

"Can you hold on a sec, Mom?" Holt tilted his head at the sound of footsteps and muted voices outside the window of his motel room. Instead of continuing down the breezeway as usual, the footsteps stopped outside the door of his room.

He stood, walked to the door and looked through the peephole. Jessie and a clerk he recognized from the reception desk stood on the other side of the closed door, talking softly.

Holt lifted the phone back to his ear, his heart pounding so loud he could hear it echoing through the cell phone. "Mom? Tell Liam he was wrong. Jessie didn't call."

She had shown up at his door.

"Wha—?"

"I'm sorry, I gotta go, Mom. I'll call y'all back."

Holt ended the call, shoved his phone into the pocket of his jeans and continued staring through the peephole.

"And you're sure this is it?" Jessie asked in a low voice.

The desk clerk nodded. "Holt Williams,

room three nineteen. This is it. I can ring his room first if you'd like."

"No, thank you." She reached into her jeans pocket and withdrew what Holt suspected was a tip—or bribery—and pressed it into the desk clerk's hand. He smiled then walked away, whistling.

Jessie stared at the closed door, smoothed her hand over her bright auburn curls, raised her fist to knock—then froze. She shook her head, her long lashes fluttering over her dark brown eyes briefly, before she spun on her heel and turned away.

Holt's hand shot to the doorknob just as she spun back, her fist rising again hesitantly. He stopped, afraid to move for fear he'd startle her into bolting.

Keenly aware of the effort it must've taken for Jessie to bring herself to his door, he forced himself to remain motionless and whispered under his breath, "Come on, Jessie. Knock. Just once to meet me halfway. That's all I need."

And...she did. Her knuckles had barely tapped the door when he opened it in response. She stumbled back in surprise.

"Sorry," he said. "Didn't mean to startle

you." He motioned toward the peephole. "I saw it was you."

She nodded, her gaze roving over him from head to toe, taking in every detail. "I came too early, I guess." Her cheeks flushed. "It's only seven thirty. I'm used to getting the boys up and off to school by seven. I didn't stop to think that you might not be up yet."

He shook his head as he rubbed his stubbled cheeks and jaw. "I've been up for a while." To be honest, he'd barely slept the past three nights. "Just haven't had a chance to shave." He stepped back and opened the door wide. "Thank you for stopping by. Would you like to come in?"

She nodded again. "Yes, but…" Her eyes drifted from his face down to his chest, and her cheeks flushed a deeper shade of red. "W— would you please put on a shirt?"

He glanced down and realized—too late— that he had yet to fully dress for the day. Bare chested and shoeless was no way to greet a lady, especially one of Jessie's caliber. "Uh, yeah. Sorry. Just…" He held up a finger as he backed away. "One sec. Don't move, okay?"

He opened a dresser drawer, retrieved a T-shirt and yanked it over his head. Thrusting his fingers through his hair, he paused long enough to smooth the hem of his shirt over the waist-band of his jeans and tug clean socks on his feet before he faced her again.

She stood on the opposite side of the room. Her gaze scanned the freshly made bed, his watch and wallet laid out neatly side by side on the nightstand and the partially opened door to the small bathroom he'd showered in a half hour ago. The spicy scent of his body wash still drifted on the humid air left behind from his hot shower.

Maybe he should open the window? Suggest relocating to the lobby? Any request from her would be welcome so long as he could entice her to stay and talk.

Her chest lifted on a deep inhale, and she pressed her lips together before saying, "You're very neat." She met his eyes. "I wasn't expect-ing that."

He shoved his hands into his pockets. "What were you expecting?"

"I don't know. That's why I came." She stud-ied his expression, the wariness in hers receding slightly. "I wanted to get to know you better. Find out if you're trustworthy. It's my job to protect Cody and Devin."

Holt walked across the room, grabbed his

wallet off the nightstand and held it out. "Here. Take a look around. I have no secrets—not any-more."

Her brows rose and she stared at the brown leather wallet in his hand then took it from him, carefully avoiding his fingers. She opened it slowly, lifted each slim compartment with one pink polished nail and tugged his license free.

"You're from Pine Creek?"

He nodded. "My family owns a farm there. They run a bed-and-breakfast."

Her brow creased. "Do they know about Cody and Devin?"

"Yes. But they didn't seven years ago."

She studied his license for another moment then slid it back into the wallet and returned it to him.

"Please." Holt waved his arm toward the dresser at the front of the room. "Feel free to poke around. I've already unpacked. Everything I brought with me is either in that dresser or in the bathroom."

She frowned and fiddled with the collar of her T-shirt. Three small freckles were at the base of her throat, clustered together almost in the shape of a heart, drawing his eyes to the graceful curve to her neck.

He cleared his throat and glanced down at his socked feet. "Go ahead. I know you're looking out for my sons. No secrets, remember?"

Jessie hesitated, then did as he suggested. She pulled out each drawer of the dresser, sifted gently through his T-shirts, jeans and socks, but shut one drawer quickly when she encountered his boxers. Then she explored the bathroom, tugging back the shower curtain and eyeing the bottle of body wash and used bar of soap on the tub's ledge, and glanced at the shaving kit, toothbrush and toothpaste tube sitting on one side of the sink.

"You didn't bring much," she said softly.

"I don't need much," he said. "Just my sons." An awkward silence fell between them. He grinned, lifted his arms and teased, "I promise I don't pose a threat but if you feel the need to frisk me for weapons, please feel free to do that, too."

She smiled and her entire expression lit up, warm and affectionate. The sight made him catch his breath. "Well, I already know you're not hiding anything under that shirt." Her smile dimmed. "But you have a bit too much charm for my comfort. Do you drink?"

"Used to," he said. "Not anymore."

"Smoke?"

"Same."

"Where's their mother?"

His head jerked, the blunt question catching him off guard. A latent pain returned and flooded his chest. "Cheyenne left Cody and Devin two days after she gave birth to them. The pregnancy was unplanned, and she didn't want children." He met her eyes. "I wanted them, though. That's the reason she went through with the pregnancy."

"You…" She nibbled on her lower lip then continued. "I don't mean to pry even more, but it's necessary. You weren't married?"

"No." He released a heavy breath. "We didn't know each other well. We'd only met a few weeks before when I was in Arlington, Texas, touring the circuit. We spent a couple weeks together. Later, when I found out about the pregnancy, I proposed but she declined. She liked her life the way it was and wasn't ready for a family with a man she barely knew." He rubbed his stubbled cheeks with a shaky hand and cringed. "I led a different life back then. One I'm not proud of. And I surrounded myself with people who lived the same kind of life." Holding her gaze, he stepped closer. "You don't think I deserve another chance with Cody and Devin, do you?"

She returned his stare, sadness moving through her expression. "That's not my decision to make." She slipped her hand into her pocket and pulled out a folded piece of notebook paper. "I read your letter. It was very open and honest, and I thank you for that." She lifted the paper toward him. "This essay isn't quite as honest as your letter, but the truth is in there and I think it's only fair you know what you're up against."

He took the paper from her, opened it, and began reading.

SPRING BREAK
by Devin Williams

He turned his back to Jessie and his hands trembled harder as he read the words scribbled by a seven-year-old's hand—his son's hand. Each word sent a stabbing pain through his chest and coaxed a fresh sheen of tears to his eyes.

"He's hurt," Jessie said gently at his back. "And very angry."

"He has every right to be." Holt faced her then, searching for a small trace of forgiveness and understanding in her eyes. The kind he imagined he glimpsed the night he brought his sons to her. "Do you think some mistakes can't be mended? That sometimes there's no way to set things right again even if you want to?"

"I don't know." She looked away briefly then peered up at him. "But I won't keep secrets from you, either. I'll be as honest with you as you've been with me. I don't want you to disrupt Cody and Devin's lives again after abandoning them for so long. I don't want you in their lives, period. Especially not when I'm about to adopt them." Her shoulders slumped and she rubbed her forehead. "But that's my selfish streak talking. And who am I to judge you?" She shook her head and walked to the door. "This isn't up to me. I just follow where I'm led."

He followed in her wake, his hand lifting in appeal. "Jessie—"

"Grab your wallet." She opened the door but stopped on the threshold and glanced at him over her shoulder. "You'll need your license to get in where I'm taking you."

"Where are we going?"

"Back to the beginning," she said softly.

"Then I'll decide how—or if—we move forward from there."

Holt ignored the sting of pride at her commanding words, grabbed his wallet and clenched his jaw. "I'm willing to do whatever it takes."

Jessie eyed him again, her gaze drifting over him from the top of his head to the tips of his toes. "We'll see."

CHAPTER FOUR

HOLT KNEW JESSIE had decided to test him and he also knew he had to pass if he wanted to see his sons.

"You wanna tell me where we're headed now?" he asked, arranging his seat belt into a more comfortable position as he sat in the passenger seat of Jessie's SUV. She hadn't said a word since they left his motel room and driven off in her vehicle ten minutes earlier.

The morning sun broke fully over the horizon as Jessie drove up a steep mountain, its rays striking his eyes with bright heat. Wincing, he flipped the visor down. "I agreed to do this your way, but I'd like to prepare myself a little, at least."

Jessie stared at the road curving ahead, her eyes hidden behind sleek sunglasses. After easing past the bend and reaching the mountain's ascent, she glanced at him, the mirrored lenses of her sunglasses reflecting his image. "Did you feel prepared seven years ago when Cody and Devin were born?"

He shifted uncomfortably in his seat, hating the look of weak vulnerability appearing on his reflected expression in the lenses, but answered honestly. "No."

"Exactly. You walked away from them once and you could do it again." She faced the road again. "I think it's only fair that I have you test the waters first before I allow you to dive in."

A heavy breath escaped his lips. "A test it is, then." He pressed his palms tight against the rough denim covering his thighs and refused to rub the gnawing ache in his chest.

He could do this. No matter what she had planned. He had a lot of mistakes to make up for.

The SUV began its descent down the mountain and Holt's gut dipped with unease. He jerked his head to the side, peering down at the passing scenery.

Homes and businesses comprising the small community of Hope Springs dotted the undulating valley along the foothills of the Blue Ridge Mountains. Technically a part of the sprawling mountain town, the Hope Springs

Motel where Holt had chosen to bed down resided several miles outside the densest part of Hope Springs city limits and provided a welcome respite from the prying eyes of locals. He'd been careful to steer clear of the downtown community during his stay.

As a bull rider, Holt had led a nomadic life for years. He'd roamed the back roads of the smallest of small towns and enjoyed the bustling sights, sounds and diversions of the biggest cities, but had never grown accustomed to being treated like an untrustworthy stranger.

Having grown up in Pine Creek—a small town where everyone knew each other and their life story, or a somewhat inaccurate version of it—he'd had the fortune of others knowing him and his family well. His mother's and brother's reputations as upstanding citizens had extended to him for a time…until he'd abandoned them with his father and then later, traveling the circuit, his own Christian principles. Guilt and shame had rooted so deeply inside him that he'd become a stranger even unto himself, and he'd remained one for years.

But things were different now, he reminded himself firmly, turning away from the imposing sight of the buildings comprising Hope Springs city limits. He was no longer a stranger to himself. Instead, he'd become the good man he should've always been and was, as Liam had said, worth taking a chance on. Surely with time, even Jessie would be able to see that.

"So tell me," he said. "If I fail to impress you, how prepared are you to turn me away? To keep two boys away from a father who is eager to provide for them and truly wants what's best for them? Especially when one—or both—of them are missing a father in their lives?" He cast Jessie a sidelong glance. A muscle ticked in her delicate jaw. "Would that sit well with your conscience?"

Her slim throat moved on a hard swallow. "I don't know." She slowed the SUV and palmed the steering wheel, turning into a parking lot. "Guess this will be a test for both of us."

Holt closed his eyes briefly then forced himself to study the imposing structure in front of them. The multifloored brick building with a U.S. flag flapping in the breeze high above a blue metal roof had a familiar look to it. A large sign stood tall at the front entrance of the sprawling building in front of them: Hope Springs Hospital.

Instantly, he recalled the hospital in Arlington, Texas, where Cody and Devin had been born seven years ago. He'd memorized every inch of the building—it had haunted him over the years—and the thought of it made him stiffen.

Cheyenne had called him the night she'd gone into labor, and having supported her through prenatal visits and birthing classes, he'd been at the ready. He'd picked her up at her friend's house in Arlington where she'd stayed for the duration of her pregnancy, then driven her to the hospital and spent hours pacing the halls and lobby until receiving the good news that the C-section had been a success and that both Cheyenne and the twins were doing well. He'd been invited to the nursery to visit his sons and when he saw Cody and Devin swaddled comfortably in their cribs, sucking their tiny thumbs, he'd stood outside the nursery window, cherishing the sight of their precious faces for over an hour. Alone. Every second of that hour, he'd never felt more proud, ashamed, or terrified in his life. The conflicting emotions had been so overwhelming, he'd almost walked away the night they were born, convinced Cody and Devin would be better off without an irresponsible man like him in their lives.

"Were you present when Cheyenne had Cody and Devin?"

Holt nodded. "I still toured the circuit but stuck close to Arlington where she was living and never stayed gone long." His muscles tightened as Jessie parked in front of the hospital. "She didn't want to hold them. Never even wanted to see them." He glanced at Jessie, a strange surge of empathy for Cheyenne welling inside him. Unlike him, she, at least, had had the courage to follow her convictions. "Cheyenne knew she wouldn't be the kind of mother Cody and Devin deserved, and she didn't want to get attached to them. She'd already made her decision to relinquish her rights and give them to me. I was surprised that she agreed to go through with the pregnancy at all."

"I'm grateful."

The firmness in Jessie's tone prompted him to scrutinize her expression, but the reflective lenses shielding her eyes hid so much.

"If she hadn't gone through with it," Jessie continued, "Cody and Devin wouldn't be here now."

Holt stilled. "No. They wouldn't."

Chances were, neither would he. He'd probably still be touring the circuit, lost and alone. Desperate for another round of violence in the arena, the angry jerk and kick of a bull beneath his body breaking off another chunk of bitterness, wringing free another painful regret. He wouldn't have looked back or slowed down, and commitment would've never taken root inside him. He would've continued to wander with no purpose and no obligations, serving himself instead of others. And he would never have returned to his mother and brother.

"Cody and Devin have so much to offer." Jessie tilted her head. "Other than providing material security and the title of father, what do you have to offer them?"

The question caught him by surprise. So much so, she'd already exited the SUV and shut the door before he managed to open his mouth in a weak attempt to answer.

She rapped the hood of the SUV with her knuckles, the sun glinting off her sleek sunglasses. "Let's go."

The walk across the parking lot and into the hospital was a quiet one, neither of them speaking. Holt shoved his hands into his pockets as they boarded an elevator and traveled to the top floor of the hospital, his elbow brushing hers as they stepped to one side and allowed others to exit on previous floors.

When the doors slid open at their destination, a nurse, seated at a wide desk across from the elevator, looked up from a desktop computer and smiled.

"Jessie. Right on time, as usual." The nurse stood, brushed her blond ponytail behind her shoulder and held out her hand. "I take it this is your guest."

Jessie nodded. "Holt, this is Sharon James, head of the Hope Springs Boarder Baby Unit."

Unease coiling inside him, Holt shook her hand but remained silent, unsure of what to say and even more uncomfortable with what might lay ahead.

"Welcome to our safe haven, Mr. Williams. If I could please see your state-issued identification?" Sharon's smile remained polite and impassive when he did as she asked, but skepticism lurked in the depths of her green eyes as she studied his driver's license then returned it to him. "Thank you." She pointed to a lengthy form fastened to a clipboard. "Please fill that out. When you're finished, I'll give you the grand tour then introduce you to our newest boarders."

Holt completed the form with his personal information, signed an agreement regarding rules, policies and procedures then joined Jessie, who spoke in a low tone to Sharon, at the entrance of a wide hallway. The conversation ended with his presence.

"I'll begin with an overview of the facilities, then I'll introduce you to one of our boarders." Sharon's guarded gaze swept over him as she waved a hand and walked down the hallway. "Follow me, please. Feel free to ask questions at any time."

Holt joined her, glancing once behind him at Jessie, who stayed behind, watching him with a blank expression.

Sharon began the tour by describing the process by which they receive abandoned children. "Georgia law provides moms—" she winced and smiled apologetically "—or dads with thirty days to leave a child responsibly. At one time, our state was, I believe, second in the nation for discarded infants. The law allows for safe havens beyond solely hospitals. Fire stations, police stations and entities licensed and staffed with volunteers trained by the state, such as Jessie and Hummingbird Haven. They can also receive babies. But to avoid criminal charges, the parent must place the child in the safe care of a person when leaving them. In other words, they can't just leave the infant on a doorstep or in a chair in one of our waiting rooms unattended. The child must be left with a responsible party."

Pausing midstep, she glanced up at him. "As you did when you left your sons with Jessie. And because you did just that, I imagine you know most of what I've told you already. I suppose I should've thought of that before I gave you the full spiel."

"No, I..." He shrugged awkwardly. "I didn't know the technicalities at the time. I just knew I couldn't take care of them properly and that Hummingbird Haven was an option." Face heating, he rubbed the back of his neck. "My sons were born in Texas and I traveled for work and found reputable babysitters locally whenever I stopped in a new town. That's how I found out about Jessie." He forced a laugh. "I've always found motel desk clerks are great at knowing all the best secrets of a city. Anyway, I, uh... After my sons were born, I tried to make it work for a while but after three weeks on the road, struggling in motels, I could see it

wasn't going to. I couldn't afford a down pay-
ment on an apartment or house without working, I couldn't work without hiring a babysitter
and I couldn't save money when I had to pay
babysitters. I didn't have experience with babies, had no idea how to take care of them ef-
fectively, and at the time, I barely had enough
money in my pocket to keep a roof over our
heads."

And, he thought ruefully, he'd been too
ashamed and afraid to seek help from the
mother and brother he'd betrayed and had been
too enticed by his carefree, solo life on the circuit to take on the responsibilities of being a dad
and raising two boys on his own. All mistakes
he'd regretted ever since. Continuing with the
status quo had been easy...but the thought of
going back—of facing up to his failures—had
been too painful and overwhelming.

Sharon nodded. "That's a prominent reason
why some of our babies are left here. We've had
many single mothers who live in poverty find
themselves unable to provide for their babies or
find reliable housing. Many times, they're also
dealing with dangerous situations like home-
lessness or domestic violence, or they have no
family to lean on. They love their children and

want to protect them, so they rely on safe havens as a last resort out of desperation. That's one reason we've expanded our efforts over the past few years to include more preventative measures and provide support and resources early."

She continued down the hallway, opening the doors of two rooms, each nursery painted with bright colors, equipped with cribs and padded rocking chairs, and decorated with baby-friendly mobiles and toys. "Although we receive annual grants and financial aid from local businesses that keep us in operation, we also rely on donations and community volunteers to fund additional projects. Since Jessie joined our team and became our strongest advocate, we've been able to secure extra funds to renovate our nurseries." She smiled. "It's important for every child to feel comfortable, safe and secure while they're here. We want to nurture their minds and spirits as well as meet their physical needs for as long as they remain with us."

Holt eyed the small sheep, moon and stars dangling from a crib mobile and imagined a pudgy hand and tiny fingers, like those he remembered belonging to Cody and Devin as infants, reaching up to touch the plush figures. "How long do the babies stay?"

"Up to one year." Her smile faded. "Beyond that, we're unable to maintain ample space for new boarders. But we do our best to place each baby in a loving adoptive home as early as possible."

"And if no one adopts them?"

"We place them in a supportive foster home or safe haven licensed by the state where a foster parent will continue the work of finding an adoptive family best suited for the child."

Holt pulled his gaze away from the crib and met her eyes. "Like Jessie?"

Sharon's expression softened. "Yes. She's been a lifesaver for many children over the years." She looked at the empty crib across the room. "Literally. Without Jessie and the hard work she does at Hummingbird Haven, many more children would be lost, as well as the desperate, abused women who need her."

"I can't take all the credit."

Holt spun around and found Jessie standing behind Sharon. Her expression remained inscrutable, but the tight line of her mouth had gentled.

"I've had a ton of help," she added. "Sharon

and her team here at Hope Springs Hospital and my assistant manager, Zoe, have taken on as much—if not more—than I have. We work to build strong relationships with the community as a team and are stronger as a result. I suppose that's how the desk clerk at the Hope Springs Motel was able to direct you to Hummingbird Haven." Her head dipped briefly. "And why he was willing to lead me to your room this morning. We're a small community and don't forget strangers who wander through."

Holt stiffened.

"Well, now that you've been given the tour," Sharon said, "there's one last stop to make." She eased past Holt, farther down the hall, opened a door and swept an arm toward the inside of the room. "After you."

Holt hesitated then entered the room, the soft scent of baby powder and fabric softener settling around him. A discontented cry and shuffling sounds emerged from a crib on the other side of the room.

"Baby Ava's our newest boarder," Sharon said, walking over to the crib. "She's only been with us for two weeks but even though she's only one month old, she's an old soul and we feel like we've known her forever." A wail broke out as Sharon smiled down into the crib and she murmured soothing words before briskly walking toward the door. "I'll bring her tray and leave you to it."

Leave him to what? Holt stared at the small pink bundle wiggling and wailing in the crib, his gut hollowing.

"It's time for Ava's feeding." Jessie, standing by the door, gestured toward the rocking chair beside the crib. "Have a seat. You're her caretaker this morning."

"I'm what?" His voice caught. The weak, high-pitched tone of his words made him flinch. He looked down and flexed his hands, noting the thick calluses coating his fingers. Hands like his—big, rough and commanding on the back of a bull—had no place near an infant's delicate skin or fragile limbs. He'd never grown comfortable holding Cody and Devin during his brief time with them and had struggled with the awkwardness of it. "I...thought this was just a tour."

Brows lifting, Jessie leaned back against the doorjamb and crossed her arms. "Is that what you thought your return into Cody and Devin's lives would be? Just a tour? A hands-off spectatorship?" Her lip curled as her voice rose over the crying of the infant in the crib. "You're used to performing, right? Center stage on the circuit? All bravado and swagger? If you can't handle this, you can't handle Cody and Devin."

The rebuke in her big brown eyes pierced his skin and dove deeper into his conscience than he'd anticipated. One thing he'd learned in his short time with Jessie thus far, was that she was honest. Bluntly so. And honesty had been a rarity in his life for years.

"No," he said softly, the word lost amid the increasing wails of the baby. "That's not what I thought." He walked across the room and sat in the rocking chair. The arms were narrow and the pink pillow lining the seat thick, forcing him to squirm for a moment or two before he was able to settle into the constraints of the chair. "Okay. What do I do?"

She frowned. "What do you mean, what do you do? You fed Cody and Devin when you had them."

He cleared his throat. "Yes." He dragged his clammy palms across the rough denim covering his thighs. "But I was never very good at it." His face flamed. "I used to prop them up on pillows on the motel bed with one hand, sit in a chair by the bed and feed them with the other hand." He forced himself to look up at her. "I was afraid to hold them most of the time."

Jessie moved to speak but closed her mouth when Sharon returned, tray in hand.

"Her bottle is warm and ready to go," Sharon said, setting the tray on a small table beside the rocking chair. "Burping cloths are here, too. If you need anything else—" she pointed to a phone on the wall "—just give me a ring."

After she left, Jessie uncrossed her arms, pushed off the doorjamb and walked over to his side. "Are you right-or left-handed?"

"Right."

She picked up a soft white cloth off the tray and tossed it onto his lap. "That goes over your shoulder—your left will probably be most comfortable—but you can switch up if you need to. You'll want to settle her in the fold of your left arm and give her the bottle with your right." She hesitated, her tone gentle. "She won't bite, you know." A small grin teased her lips when he glanced up at her. "Well...she can, but it won't hurt." She smiled and tapped her fingernail against her straight teeth. "Not until she gets these, at least."

Surprisingly, a smile crept across his own lips.

He exhaled and turned his hands over, palms up. "All right. I'm ready."

She moved to the crib, bent and lifted the pink bundle into her arms. A tiny pair of feet kicked free of the pink swaddling blanket and miniature fingers flailed in the air.

"It's okay, sweetheart. Breakfast is on the way." Jessie's soothing tone drew close as she lowered the baby onto his arms. "Keep her head cradled in the crook of your elbow and lift her head slightly." She pressed a bottle into his free hand. "Go ahead and offer it. She knows what to do."

One of Jessie's long red curls tickled his cheek as she straightened. He wiggled his mouth to ease the itch and focused on the warm weight of the bundle in his arms. She was small. So small, if he closed his eyes, he'd doubt she was even there...if not for the disgruntled cries filling the small room.

Hand shaking, he moved the bottle close to the baby's thrashing head. The nipple brushed her open mouth then her lips latched on, her body stilling and cries quieting.

"There," Jessie said. "That's better."

Holt stared. The baby's eyes, wide and blue, focused on his, a slow, occasional blink of her thick lashes the only interruption of her scrutiny. Her hungry sighs and rhythmic pull on the bottle in his hand tugged at something deep in his chest. Cracked the tall walls surrounding his heart and freed a fresh, overwhelming surge of pain.

"Ava," he whispered. An innocent child as young as Cody and Devin had been years ago. An infant someone had left behind, weak and alone. Vulnerable to the whims of those surrounding her.

Ava continued studying him. Her clear gaze moved over his forehead, nose, mouth and chin, then returned to his eyes again. A questioning look entered her expression, and he could only imagine how he must appear to her: rough, imposing and unfamiliar. A stranger.

Despair surged through his veins, hollowed his gut and weakened his frame. It slinked deep into his being and began rooting itself in his body, mind and soul, conjuring up all his fears of inadequacy as a father from seven years ago to the point that he wondered if he could even trust himself or his own intentions. He could feel doubt taking hold of him now, capitalizing on his guilt and insecurity.

His hand trembled and his fingers shook

around the bottle, dislodging the nipple from Ava's mouth. Her expression contorted, intensifying with fear and distrust, and she reared away, her cries echoing sharply against the nursery walls as she refused his clumsy offers of the bottle.

Wet heat filled Holt's eyes and coated his lower lashes. "She doesn't trust me."

"And once they know who you are," Jessie said softly, "neither will Cody and Devin."

CHAPTER FIVE

JESSIE HAD LIED to Holt—and herself—and she'd never felt like a bigger heel in her life.

The drive from the Hope Springs Hospital back to the motel seemed ten times longer to her than it had when she'd first undertaken it two hours before. Jessie glanced at Holt, who sat silently in the passenger seat.

Earlier, when Ava had grown uncomfortable in his arms as he'd fed her in the nursery, he'd ducked his head, and the moment they'd settled back into the SUV, he'd turned his face away and stared intently out the passenger window, his strong shoulders slumped and big fists curled tightly around the edge of his seat. Since she'd driven out of the hospital parking lot ten minutes ago, he hadn't spoken and neither had she, but a subtle glance confirmed what she'd suspected. Afternoon sunlight, spearing through the windshield as the SUV ascended a mountain, glinted off moisture trailing down Holt's stubbled cheek and jaw.

"I'm sorry."

His left shoulder lifted, and he dipped his head to the side, subtly rubbing his wet cheek on the sleeve of his T-shirt. "For what?"

His deep voice sounded strained, and his expression of grief lent him a less intimidating, vulnerable air. It was an odd sight, seeing a big, seemingly unbreakable man like Holt crumpling with pain.

An unexpected urge unfurled inside her, beckoning her to place a comforting hand over his or sift her fingers through his thick hair in a consoling gesture.

She squirmed in her seat then readjusted her grip on the steering wheel. "I'm sorry for judging you. I said I wouldn't, and I had good intentions but..."

It'd been too easy to let her residual anger and resentment over his reappearance in Cody and Devin's lives to resurface, especially after she'd placed Ava in his strong arms. After all, Cody and Devin had been nestled there once, seven years ago, and a part of her still believed that Holt—no matter what his circumstances— had been strong enough to make it work back then if he'd truly wanted to keep his sons. Instead, he'd chosen not to commit—just like her own mother had. Either that, or he'd simply decided to leave the hard work of raising them to someone else until it became easier and more convenient for him to assume his role as father.

She winced. There she went again, judging and blaming. Something she had no right to do. Especially if her prejudice cost Cody and Devin a chance to meet and possibly form some sort of bond with their father.

"I took you to the Boarder Baby Unit because I wanted to see if you'd shy away from holding Ava," she continued quietly. "If you'd be intimidated and tempted to walk away at the first sign of discomfort. To reconnect with your sons, you'll have to set aside your own needs and comfort in favor of Cody and Devin's. There's so much potential for this to backfire. Not just on Cody and Devin—but on you as well." She bit her lip. "But worse... I wanted to make you feel guilty for leaving them."

He nodded, still staring at the road ahead. "You succeeded."

"That was wrong of me," she said quietly. "You made a responsible choice to place them in someone else's care and I had no right to judge you for it. For Cody and Devin's sake, I should be finding a way to help you right now not hinder you."

The flashing Hope Springs Motel sign emerged over the curve of the mountain. Jessie slowed the SUV and made the turn, eased the vehicle to a stop in front of Holt's room, then cut the engine.

Holt unsnapped his seat belt, thrust open the passenger door and exited.

"Holt."

He paused, one hand on the door frame, face turned away.

"Give me a name." She leaned toward him and placed her palm on the passenger seat, the warmth he'd left behind seeping into her skin. "Not family, but someone who knew you seven years ago and still knows you now. Someone who can vouch for you."

His jaw clenched and he didn't respond.

"Please." She reached for his arm, but the distance was too great, and her upturned palm hovered helplessly in the still air between them. "I'm trying to do the right thing. I'm trying to give you a chance."

He faced her then, studied her hand then her expression, his eyes finally meeting hers.

After a few moments, he withdrew his wallet from his back pocket, tore a crumpled receipt in half then held out his hand, upturned beside her own. She grabbed a pen from the glove compartment and handed it over, watching as he wrote on the small scrap of paper in his hand.

When he finished, he handed it to her wordlessly, shut the passenger door then ambled up to his motel room and went inside, closing the door behind him.

Sighing, Jessie placed the piece of paper on her thigh, grabbed her purse from the backseat, pulled out her phone and dialed the number Holt had scrawled.

It rang several times before a gruff male voice answered. "Yeah?"

Jessie narrowed her eyes, read Holt's writing, then licked her lips nervously. "Is this Ty Branton?"

Something rustled in the background. "Well, now, that depends on who this is." He sniffed, a hint of amusement creeping into his tone. "See, you called me. So you gotta gimme your name first, baby."

Tensing, Jessie rolled her eyes. This did not bode well. "This is Jessie Alden. I'm calling on Holt Williams's behalf for a recommendation of sorts. Do you have a moment to speak with me? Answer a few questions about his background?"

Silence settled across the line then more rustling. "Uh...yeah. I'm guessing this is about his boys?"

"Yes. You mind if I switch to video?" In her experience, eyes were much more expressive than tone.

Squeaks, a thud then a heavy sigh. "Sure. Go ahead."

Jessie switched the call to video chat, propped the phone on the dash and eyed the middle-aged man who appeared on the screen. Mussed brown hair standing up in tufts, strong stubbled jaw and drowsy blue eyes faced her. He was in the act of lighting a cigarette, his blunt thumb flicking a lighter as he sat on the edge of a bed.

"I apologize for disturbing you, but I need some information regarding Holt's character and it's a bit time sensitive."

"Not a problem." Cigarette lit, he drew deep from it then blew out a thick cloud of smoke. "Jessie, was it?"

She frowned but nodded.

Ty sat up straight and presented a polite, professional smile, which she suspected he reserved for rare formal occasions. "Had a late night, so today's a late start, is all."

Don't judge, Jessie, she admonished herself silently. *And keep your opinions to yourself.*

She looked down and squeezed her hands together in her lap. "Thank you for taking my call."

He shrugged. "Anything for Holt."

"How long have you known him?"

"Oh, about sixteen, seventeen years, I guess. Met him on the circuit when we were both nineteen."

"The circuit?"

"Rodeo." He smiled, a crooked—almost cocky—one this time. "Bull riding. We were both touring solo, going for broke at the time. He'd just parted ways with his dad and was competing alone. Never seen someone ride like Holt. No nerves, no fear. Just angry heat. A born performer. Night I met him, he owned that bull he rode and the arena. Crowd lit up like dynamite when he walked in." He chuckled then took another drag from his cigarette. "I was eager to learn from him, so I sought him out after, asked if he was interested in giving me a few pointers. Suggested we pool resources— I had a top-notch truck and trailer, his rusty pickup would barely crank at the time—and he took me up on it."

"How long did you two travel together?"

"Oh, years." His smile widened. "Two rascals running the road, catching winks between competitions in the cab of a truck day in and day out, you get to know someone real well. Holt partied hard, but he worked hard, too. Always pulled his weight and then some. If he said he was gonna do something, he did it. I never questioned his word. Never had a reason to. It was tough making ends meet, but we had good times. Great times, really. We were like brothers."

The nostalgic—almost boyish—gleam in Ty's eyes made Jessie smile, too. "So you knew him well."

"Inside and out." His smile fell. "Back then, at least."

His gaze strayed from hers, moving off to the side, staring into the distance as he frowned.

"And now?" Jessie asked.

Ty blinked. Refocused on her. "Now?" He shook his head as he stubbed his cigarette out in an ashtray on the bedside table. "That's the thing. We parted ways when his sons were born. He said he wanted to raise 'em different than how we were living. Then, a couple months later he turned up alone, we partnered again and picked back up where we left off. But…things weren't the same. *He* wasn't the same. He worked but didn't play. Kept to himself and wasn't easygoing like he used to be." The corner of his mouth lifted in a rueful grin. "He missed them boys. Never got over leavin' 'em. He left the circuit again a couple years later to go back home to his mom and brother and start fresh. Said he felt like God was calling him in another direction. I've never been a religious man, so I didn't really understand it. All I knew was he was taking off on me again. I didn't give him a very good send-off, you know? We've only seen each other once since then, but he kept in touch over the phone pretty regular-like. Only, it didn't sound like him anymore. Still doesn't."

Jessie waited, her heart thumping rapidly in her chest.

"What I mean is…" Ty scooted to the very edge of the bed, closer to the phone's screen. "Holt's changed so much since he left the circuit that if I ran across him now…" He spread his hands, searching for the right words. "You know? Passed him on the street? I don't think

I'd know him. Wouldn't recognize him even. That's how much he feels like a stranger to me now."

Jessie's mouth parted soundlessly. She cleared her throat and tried again. "A stranger?"

"Yeah." Ty nodded several times, mulling it over. "That's the best I can describe it." His grin returned as he gestured toward his rumpled hair and wrinkled T-shirt. "Now, I ain't much to look at right this moment, and no one in their right mind would say I'm anyone to be—" he made air quotes with his fingers "—recommending somebody for something. But honestly, Holt loves those boys something fierce. And though he and I live different kinds of lives now, he ain't never looked down on me. He checks in on me from time to time, sees if I need anything. Who he is now…well, he's the kind of man I wish I could be."

Jessie studied his expression, the wistful admiration in it warming her chest.

"Well…" He cocked his head to the side and wrinkled his nose, his boyish grin returning. "To be fair, I only wish for it Monday through Thursday. The weekends are too much fun for me to trade for that strait-laced life Holt's living nowadays."

Laughter burst from Jessie's lips. "A strait-laced life can be fun, too, Ty."

"With you?" He chuckled. "I bet."

Jessie's face flamed.

"Forgive me." He winked. "Old habits die hard. Anyways, I hate to cut short time with a gorgeous woman, but I gotta compete tonight and I need my beauty rest. Anything else you wanna know?"

She shook her head. "That's all I need. Thank you for taking my call."

He grinned. "You bet. Give Holt a shout for me."

Ty's image disappeared and a message popped up, noting he'd ended the call.

Jessie removed her cell phone from the dash, tossed it back into her purse and stared at the closed door of Holt's motel room.

Said he felt like God was calling him in another direction.

He feels like a stranger to me now.

"A stranger," she whispered.

According to Ty, Holt *had* changed over the years. And if she decided to give Holt a chance with Cody and Devin, a stranger might be exactly what Holt needed to be.

"SAY WHAT?"

Zoe sat in a rocking chair on the front porch of Jessie's cabin, a homemade bacon, egg and cheese biscuit in one hand, except for one big bite half-chewed in her open mouth, and a mug full of hot coffee in the other hand. An expression of horrified disbelief enveloped her face.

"An unpaid handym——" Voice catching on a bit of unchewed biscuit, Zoe closed her mouth long enough to fully chew and swallow, then continued. "You say you intend to hire a handyman who'll work for no pay?" Her brows rose. "I've searched for months for someone to accept the wage we can actually afford to pay and there've been no takers. Do you seriously think you're going to find someone who wants to work without being paid at all? Especially in this economy?"

Jessie rocked back in her own rocking chair and tried to adopt a neutral expression. "I've already found one." She sipped coffee from the mug she held, hiding her eyes behind the rim of the cup. "Or may have found one. He's on his way here now. He's keen on sticking around town for a while, so I thought he might agree to volunteer. I called him this morning, told him to pack his bags and come around. That I had a proposition for him. And I wanted you to meet him, take a good look at him and let me know if you approved of him staying on the property."

After her video chat with Ty yesterday afternoon, she'd driven home and gone about the regular duties of the day—laundry, cleaning cabins, yard work, cooking supper and spending time with the boys after school—but she'd been unable to think of little else but Holt.

The regrets in his eyes and tears on his face as they'd driven away from Hope Springs Hospital yesterday had stayed with her throughout the night and into the first light of morning. Holt wasn't a perfect person, but who was? And according to Ty, he had changed.

But exactly how much had he changed? And what risks would she be allowing into Cody and Devin's lives if she introduced Holt to them? Those were the worries that still irked her conscience.

Zoe's eyes widened. "Who is he?"

Jessie stared down at her coffee and watched a lone dreg float aimlessly across the brown liquid. "He's staying at the Hope Springs Motel."

A hint of suspicion crossed Zoe's expression.

"I didn't ask where he's staying. I asked who he was."

"I know." Jessie rocked her chair faster, placing one hand on the untouched bacon, egg and cheese biscuit on her lap to prevent it from sliding off. "Just thought I'd give you some context is all."

Zoe frowned, a bit of egg dangling from her lower lip as she looked from Jessie's face to the biscuit in her hand then back. "You're trying to butter me up, aren't you? That's why you made me your famous biscuits, fresh-brewed coffee and rolled out the red porch carpet when I got back from dropping the kids off at school."

Jessie took another sip of coffee to hide her smile. She was indeed guilty of all Zoe accused. "Maybe." She glanced up and met Zoe's eyes. "I need your advice."

"That's always available to you." Zoe set her half-eaten biscuit and coffee mug on the porch rail, wiped her mouth with a napkin then crossed her arms. "But you've got to be honest with me."

Jessie closed her eyes and pinched the bridge of her nose. "I know." Opening her eyes, she met Zoe's gaze again. "His name's Holt Williams."

"Holt Will…" Zoe's gaze veered away as she

mulled over the name, then her eyes, full of surprise, met Jessie's again. "Holt Williams? As in
Cody and Devin's Holt?"

"He's not Cody and Devin's," Jessie stated
firmly. "And Cody and Devin are definitely
not his."

"Oh, but they are." Zoe leaned closer and
frowned. "We are talking about the same Holt
Williams here, right? Cody and Devin's biological father?"

"Yes."

"Is this a joke?"

"No."

Zoe froze for a moment, then stood up and
began pacing. "I'm not understanding. Didn't
you just talk to the boys about adopting them?"

"Yes."

"So you've changed your mi—"

"No." Jessie shot to her feet and held up one
hand. The biscuit in her lap hit the porch floor
and broke open, scattering across the wood
planks. "I'm still going through with the adoption. There's no doubt about that."

Zoe stopped pacing and faced her. "Then,
what's going on? I don't understand why you
would—"

"Holt showed up here last week. He knocked

on the door and asked for my help in reconnecting with Cody and Devin."

"And you agreed?"

"No. Not at first. I absolutely refused." Jessie rubbed her temples where a painful throb had taken up residence. "But then Devin came home from school after getting in trouble over Marjorie Middleton's essay about her dad, and he said he didn't want a dad, but it was right there in the essay he wrote for class, and Holt gave me the card asking me to help him find Cody and Devin on the same day and that just couldn't be a coinciden—"

Zoe sighed. "Jessie, please make this make sense."

"The boys still want a father." Jessie's breath caught, the pain of saying it aloud cutting deeper than she'd expected. "You and I both know that and I… I can't ignore it." Her lower lip trembled. She raked her teeth over it and rolled her shoulders. "I'm going to adopt Cody and Devin—nothing's going to change that— but I can't ignore Cody and Devin's needs in the process. And I've done some checking on Holt and he seems to have tried to turn his life around and he's adamant about wanting to be in the boys' lives, so I thought if I introduced Holt as a handyman, a stranger, then their meeting would be less risky to the boys. I think this strategy might be an opportunity for Cody and Devin to meet Holt in a way that I can still control the situation and protect them. If I don't agree to some sort of compromise, Holt may pursue legal action and that'd be the worst thing for the boys." She waved her hands helplessly in the air. "I can't explain it, but I feel like I'm being called to do this. For whatever reason."

Zoe watched her wordlessly.

"Is it a mistake?" Jessie asked. "Please tell me if I'm doing the wrong thing."

Zoe shook her head, a humorless smile briefly appearing. "You know I have no way of knowing that." She reached out and squeezed Jessie's hand. "But if you feel this is something you need to do—if you think it's best for Cody and Devin—then you know you have my support."

Jessie nodded. "I need to do this. The way I see it, Cody and Devin will have a chance to meet and have a man in their lives for a little while, and Holt will see the amount of work, dedication and responsibility that's involved in caring for two children. By the end of his stay, he'll be satisfied with having met them and will realize they're better off with me and then he'll be on his way."

"And if the opposite happens?" Concern clouded Zoe's eyes. "If Holt decides he wants to be their father on a permanent basis? That he wants to take them away from you?"

Jessie recalled the awkward set of his arms as he'd held Ava. The sheer look of terror on his face as she'd cried. "He won't. The way I see it, this is a passing urge on Holt's part prompted by guilt. Giving him a close-up view of the work involved in raising two boys will nip that in the bud. And by not knowing who he really is, the boys will be no worse for wear when he walks away this time. Then the boys and I can start our lives together."

"Like I said, I'll support you," Zoe said. "But I have a bad feeling about this."

"That's why I want you to meet him. You're great at sizing people up—always have been. Just meet him, listen to him, and if he comes across as too shady to be allowed on the property, tell me and this is over."

Zoe smirked. "And if I think he's okay to stick around?"

Jessie shrugged. "Shake his hand or something. Just give me a sign you're comfortable with him staying in the Creek Cabin on a temporary basis and meeting the boys."

"You plan on puttin' him in the Creek Cabin?" Zoe scoffed. "Why ask for my opinion? Just show him where he'll be staying and if he doesn't hightail it out of here right then, you'll know he's in it for the long haul."

A low rumble sounded in the distance and moments later, a large truck rounded the curve and turned in to the driveway, moving slowly toward the cabin.

"Please," Jessie prompted urgently. "Please help me out."

Zoe glanced at the truck that rolled to a stop several feet from the porch. "All right," she murmured. "I still feel like someone's gonna get their heart broken. Let's just hope it's not the boys."

The driver's-side door of the truck opened, and Holt slid out, unfolding his muscular stature to its full six-foot-plus height.

"That's him?" Zoe stared as he strode across the lawn, his long strides eating up the distance between them. She glanced at Jessie then back at Holt and an expression of dismay appeared as she released a low whistle. "Mercy."

CHAPTER SIX

FOR YEARS, HOLT had ambled up to bullpens, straddled thousand-pound beasts and firmed his grip for a back-breaking ride without so much as a sweat. But approaching two stern-faced females sizing him up from above…well, that inspired terror the likes of which he'd never known.

"I, uh…" He halted at the bottom step of Jessie's cabin and eyed Jessie and a blonde woman he didn't recognize who stood by her side. Eyes narrowed and fists propped on their hips, they returned his stare. "I assume it's safe for me to join you?"

The blonde's lips twitched.

"Yes." Jessie broke rank first, gesturing toward a rustic rocking chair that faced her and the blonde on the porch. "Please have a seat. I have something I'd like to discuss with you."

He hesitated, glancing at the blonde's solemn expression once more, then climbed the porch steps and sat in the rocking chair Jessie had indicated.

After a few uncomfortable moments of silence, he drummed his fingertips on the armrests of his chair. "So...you called, I came. What's this about?"

Jessie rubbed her hands together briskly. "I have a proposition for you. A compromise of sorts that I hope you'll consider. The boys are in school right now, so it's a good time to talk."

She was nervous. Despite the firm set of her features, the soft curves of her mouth trembled, and her knuckles whitened as she clenched her hands together in front of her. In spite of it all, his tense muscles sagged with an odd mix of sympathy and relief. Her thick shell of composure had cracked just a bit, and that brief glimpse of vulnerability provoked a protective instinct he hadn't expected.

He eased back in the chair and nodded encouragingly. "Please go on. I was happy you called. As I've told you, I'm eager to see Cody and Devin so I'm willing to hear you out."

"Meet Cody and Devin." The trembling stopped and her mouth thinned into a tight line.

He frowned. "What?"

"You're eager to *meet* Cody and Devin," she repeated. "Not see them. They're no longer the infants you knew. They're seven-year-old boys with unique personalities, strengths and weaknesses, likes and dislikes, fears and—"

"Yeah." He leaned forward, propped his elbows on his knees and met her gaze head-on. "I get it. Again, that's why I'm here."

The blonde cleared her throat and scooted closer to Jessie's side. "Seems like a good time to introduce myself since no one else is going to." She leaned back against the porch rail, her blue eyes surveying him. "I'm Zoe Price, Jessie's friend and assistant manager. I help run Hummingbird Haven, take care of the kids, maintain the grounds and whatnot."

"Thanks for having me." He stood and held out his hand. "I'm Holt Williams, Cody and Devin's father. Though I'm guessing you already know that."

Zoe stared, unblinking, at him and made no move to accept his hand.

Holt sat back down. A rueful grin rose to his lips. "Not the friendliest of welcomes, but that's neither here nor there." He looked at Jessie. "Since you've been up-front with me, I feel it's only fair that I be honest with you. I've agreed to your requests so far with very few—if any—complaints." That slight tremble returned to her mouth. Ignoring it, he quelled the urge to soften his tone and continued, "But I have my limits, too, Jessie. I'm not invulnerable to insult and though I'll admit I've made mistakes—more mistakes than any one man should make in life—I'm also not willing to pay for them indefinitely."

The confident light in her eyes dimmed.

"Tell me what you have planned and I'll consider it," he said. "But please leave out the insulting recriminations, and keep in mind that cooperating with you is not the only option I have to *meeting* my sons."

Her mouth parted and her lashes fluttered rapidly, hiding her eyes as she looked at his boots.

Man, this was not how he'd expected this morning to go. Her invitation for him to visit, bag in hand, had excited him into hoping for the prospect of seeing his sons or, at the very least, having an opportunity to be close to them here at Hummingbird Haven for more than a brief encounter.

But his sons weren't even here at the moment

and already, he'd allowed his pride to goad him into sparring with her.

"Look, I'm not trying to be hard here," he said softly. "And I know you have valid doubts about me. I'm just trying to get you to compromise with me respectfully to some degree. Even with what little experience I've had with Cody and Devin, I know it's better for my—" her head shot up, her angry expression halting him midsentence "—*our*...okay? As a figure of speech, it's better for our sons if we go about this with some civility between us."

She considered this and he eased back in his chair again, rocking slowly to the distant chirps of birds and snaps of twigs under burrowing squirrels' feet.

A spring breeze whistled below the cabin's roof, swept across the porch and tugged an errant strand of bright hair across Jessie's freckled cheek. She swept it back absently then sighed and faced him again.

"Okay. I agree." She braced her hands behind her on the porch rail, similar to Zoe's pose, and dipped her head. "Civility. That'll be my goal for the duration of what I'm about to propose."

He stopped rocking. "And how long will that be?"

"For as long as either you—or I—decide is best suited for Cody and Devin." She crossed her feet at the ankles, her well-worn jeans clinging to her shapely legs. He pulled his gaze away and focused on her face as she continued, "What I'm suggesting is that you take up temporary residence here at Hummingbird Haven."

He sat up, the rocking chair dipping beneath his weight as he scooted forward.

She held up a hand. "Temporarily. And on a possibly unwelcome condition."

"Very unwelcome," Zoe murmured.

Jessie shot her a sidelong glance then returned her attention to him. "We have a few cabins on the property that need renovations or updating but we're strapped for cash at the moment, so Zoe's been unable to find anyone willing to do the work for what we'd be able to pay them. My thinking is, you want time with Cody and Devin, and we need a strong hand around the place, so it'd be a nice trade-off if you worked for us during the day and had some time to spend with the boys in the afternoons after school." She bit her lip. "We can't afford to pay you anything other than what we would've offered someone we hired, but I figure instead of money, we'd offer you room and board. Free meals, time with the boys." She motioned toward the surrounding woods and mountain range in the distance. "Whatever equipment you'd need to take advantage of what the mountains have to offer."

"There're great fishing holes all over," Zoe said, crossing her feet, too. "Lots of trails, if you like to hike. And now that it's spring, there'll be plenty of warmer nights for camping, if that's your thing. We have bonfires and s'mores with the kids on the weekends sometimes."

"It won't all be fun and games," Jessie said. "You'll be expected to work, and when I say work, I mean manual labor. Zoe and I have repaired everything our collective muscle can move so the biggest projects on the property are what's left and that's where you'd come in."

Holt nodded. "Of course. I'm used to hard work, and utilizing muscle was my career for several years."

"What about your family's farm?" Jessie asked. "Won't they need you?"

"Yeah, but I'm due for some time off and my family's very understanding when it comes to Cody and Devin."

Her brows rose and he could almost see the gears grinding in her mind. Her unspoken question: *If they were so understanding, where were they seven years ago?*

"I was estranged from my mother and brother for years, but ever since I returned home and they found out about Cody and Devin, they've been nothing but supportive." He smiled at the thought of Liam and his mom seeing Cody and Devin for the first time, knowing he'd reunited with them. "They'll be ecstatic when they hear I'm with them, and they'll be champing at the bit to meet them, too."

A soft sound emerged from Zoe's direction. She shifted from one foot to the other as Jessie pushed off the porch rail and straightened.

"That's the thing," Jessie said. "I don't think it's a good idea for you or your family to jump right in with Cody and Devin. I think it'd do more harm than good to the boys and you if they know who you are."

Holt tensed. "What do you mean if they know who I am? How else would they—"

"We won't tell them you're their father," Jessie said. "We'll tell them you're Hummingbird Haven's new temporary live-in handyman. That's all they'll need to know."

Holt's breathing quickened. His gaze flicked from Jessie to Zoe. "For now?"

Zoe looked down. Rubbed the heel of one of her tennis shoes over the toe of the other.

"For possibly forever," Jessie said, lifting her chin at him. "That depends on you."

"How so?"

"Whether, after you've spent some time caring for Cody and Devin, you decide that you're ready to fully commit to co-parenting them."

He sat still, allowing her words to sink in, then stood, stalked to the opposite end of the porch and braced his hands on the rail, bowing his head. "You're suggesting that I be introduced as a stranger? Some random man off the street?"

The word *stranger* caught in his throat, and he glanced up beneath his lashes, staring at the tops of the cypress trees against the blue sky.

"I think that's the best approach." Jessie's quiet words barely drifted to him on the breeze. "Until we're able to decide a more permanent way to proceed. That way, if you change your mind or the boys don't seem receptive to more than a casual acquaintance, then it won't be as difficult for you to disentangle yourself and move on with little consequence or pain to Cody and Devin. Or…yourself."

"A stranger," he repeated, his throat constricting. A man of no importance or significance. An untrustworthy nomad of no consequence. His mouth twisted. "It's nothing I haven't been before." Exhaling heavily, he raised his head toward the sky and closed his eyes. "I don't prefer it, but you know Cody and Devin the best and I want a chance to get to know my boys. If you say it's the right thing to do, I'm willing to give it a try."

It was quiet for a while then footsteps shuffled across the porch and Zoe's voice emerged at his back. "Welcome to Hummingbird Haven, Holt."

Slowly, he turned, eyed Zoe's outstretched hand then shook it.

This was either the smartest or dumbest idea of Jessie's life, and she was afraid she wouldn't know which until it was too late.

"Creek Cabin is where we're putting you," she said, glancing over her shoulder.

Holt, treading a couple feet behind her on the dirt trail, hitched his bulky overnight bag over his shoulder and glanced at the thick line of trees on both sides of them. "How many acres do y'all have here?"

"Twenty-six." She kicked a rock off the trail.

"We have eight cabins—six of which Zoe and I have already renovated and one of which serves as Hummingbird Haven's community cabin. All our cabins are surrounded by relatively untouched hardwood forest and have great views of the Blue Ridge Mountain range."

"Must've cost a pretty penny to secure this lot."

Jessie harrumphed. "You have no idea." The dirt trail forked off into three gravel trails, all leading in different directions. She veered left and motioned for him to follow. "We caught a break, though. The previous owner used to run this place as a summer camp for local kids but over the years, interest waned. According to her, it was hard to promote an internet-free retreat to kids who were born digital natives. So the property sat empty for over a decade. She was in her fifties when she lost her husband, who helped her keep up the place, and she had no desire to undertake a complete overhaul of the property. She decided to unload it for a reduced price, pocket the cash and relocate closer to her daughter and grandchildren in Florida. And when she learned of my plans to create a shelter, she reduced the price even more, helped us secure funding from a few local businesses that used to fund her and her husband's camp and made a hefty donation herself."

"How long had she and her husband lived here?"

"Oh, around thirty years, I think."

"It's beautiful land. Must've been hard for her to let it go."

"It was." Jessie shrugged. "But she believed in our cause and is much happier being closer to her family. She sends us a Christmas card with a donation every year."

They continued walking in silence for a while, following the winding gravel trail past thick underbrush, ducking beneath low-hanging branches along the way. Finally, they reached a small clearing littered with fallen leaves, wild vines and uneven slopes. A log cabin with a wide porch slumped on the back of the lot in front of thick woods and a deep, rocky creek whose bubbling waters filled their surroundings with a rhythmic rush.

"It's not much to look at." Jessie glanced at Holt. His guarded expression revealed very little. "But I promise you it's sound." Her step slowed as they ascended onto the front porch. "Except for the back deck that borders the creek. Several of the wood planks have rotted and I'm afraid it's not safe to venture out on it until they've been replaced."

One corner of his mouth lifted. "I suppose that's one of the instances where I come in?"

She smiled. "Yeah."

He renewed his grip on the bag slung over his shoulder and spun slowly around, surveying the property. Her eyes followed his gaze, taking in the patches of overgrown grass, scattered wildflowers and jagged rocks, as well as a fallen tree and nearby fire pit surrounded by three log benches, each one covered with twisting vines.

What were those pesky vines anyway? She scratched her arm. Poison ivy, maybe?

"The yard's gonna need some attention." He leaned to the side and craned his neck, taking in the trees towering over the cabin. "And I see another tree or two that're probably gonna hit the ground—or cabin—the next time a stiff breeze pushes through."

"Yep. That's on your to-do list, too."

He looked at her, a rueful expression crossing his handsome face. "Any chance I can get a copy of that to-do list?"

"Soon." Dodging his gaze, she opened the front door and motioned for him to follow.

"For now, I'll show you the digs and let you get your bearings."

Musty air hit her as soon as she stepped inside, clogging her throat and wrinkling her nose. Stifling a cough, she hustled over to the small window by the door and tugged. "I should've thought to open this up a couple weeks ago when it started getting warmer."

It didn't budge.

She leaned into it and yanked harder, wincing as it creaked but didn't open. "Uh, it works, I promise. It just—" she yanked again "—needs a bit of—" another yank "—elbow gr—"

Two big hands covered hers, blunt thumbs tucking under the bottom of the window, then pulled, opening the window with a *swoosh*.

"Oof!" Jessie stumbled forward and yanked Holt, who still held a firm grip on the window, with her, tumbling his brawny frame into the back of hers and smooshing her cheek against the rusty screen.

He recovered first, pushing himself upright and tugging her with him by her shoulders. "Sorry about that." His forefinger gently flicked a speck of rust from her cheek. "Just wanted to help."

Face heating, she stepped away and blew a strand of hair out of her eyes. "Yeah, well…"

She clasped her hands together, trying not to notice the way his strong, callused touch still lingered on her skin. It wasn't him, per se, she reassured herself. It was the sensation of support that stirred her attention; that was all. The security of a firm, steady presence she was unaccustomed to having around.

"I appreciate your help," she forced out gruffly. "I mean, that's one of the major benefits of having you stay here."

His brow creased. "Besides spending time with Cody and Devin, you mean?"

She rubbed her left shoulder, right where his wide palm had settled briefly. "Yes, of course."

"Because I'm trusting you, Jessie."

She stilled as the directness of his hazel eyes locked on to hers.

"Just as much as you're trusting me," he added. "Or trying to trust me." A muscle in his sculpted jaw ticked. "If you're angling for a leg up in any part of this situation, you should know it's not easy to take advantage of me… even if I am desperate to be a part of Cody and Devin's lives."

"I know." She lifted her chin. "And you

should know I'm not easy to take advantage of, either."

His tone softened as he grinned. "No. Of that, I'm certain."

Maybe it was the gentle way he said the words, or it might've been that tempting grin he sported, but either way, she relaxed, her own smile rising easily to her lips.

"Good. Because I'd hate for you to find out the hard way." She eased past him and led the way through to the kitchen. "As you can probably tell by now, this is one of our smallest cabins. There's an electric stove, a fridge and a microwave that works great." She waited as he looked around then led him down the narrow hallway. "There's one bathroom—" she opened a door to the right "—shower, toilet, sink. And the one bedroom is over here."

She opened the door on the left and gestured toward the double bed with a bare mattress and a single dresser without a mirror.

He grimaced. "You trying to run me off already?"

She leaned against the doorjamb as he walked over to the bed, dumped his bag on the mattress. "No, not at all. But the rest of our cabins are either in use, reserved to shelter new residents who will arrive soon or in the process of final renovations, so this is the best of what's available."

He crossed the room and opened the sole window in the bedroom, breathing deep as fresh air billowed in. "It'll do. Thank you."

"You're welcome. I haven't stocked supplies here yet and I wasn't exactly sure what you might need, so you'll need to run into town tonight and pick up groceries and toiletries. I'll give you money for that, of course. It's part of the room and board we'll provide."

He faced her, propped his hands on his lean hips and cocked one blond eyebrow. "You agree that we're going to work together as a true team? Honesty and trust on both sides?"

What was it his friend Ty had said? *Old habits die hard.*

It'd be easy to come clean. Tell Holt right now, this second, that she still didn't trust him. That she may never trust him. But...she had to start somewhere, for Cody and Devin's sakes.

She nodded. "Yes. I agree."

Holt smiled, flashing his perfect white teeth and mischievous charm. Two of his many attractive attributes that made a normally sensible woman, such as herself, doubt her ability to trust the tempting scoundrel. "I assume it'll be a while before the boys get home?" At her nod, he asked, "So what now?"

Jessie gritted her teeth, dragged her attention away from his handsome face and left the room. "We work."

CHAPTER SEVEN

OF ALL THE potential tasks with which Holt
imagined Jessie might entrust him, one involving an ax had never crossed his mind.

"You sure you trust me with this?" Standing
outside Creek Cabin with said ax in hand, Holt
cocked one eyebrow and eyed Jessie over a large
pile of logs. "I mean, there're no limit to the
amount of malicious damage a ne'er-do-well
stranger—" he touched one hand to his chest
"—such as myself, might do with one of these."

Jessie hefted a thick log from the pile, tossed
it toward two sturdy chopping stumps nearby,
then picked up a second ax that lay on the grass
by the log pile and grinned. A bit sarcastically,
he had to admit. "Not if I have one, too." Her
tone turned teasing as she slapped the handle of
the ax with her free hand. "I'm pretty adept at
chopping and there's no telling which of your

appendages I'd remove first. Just try something amiss and see what happens."

Ah, so there was a bit of humor hiding behind that stern expression of hers. He'd wondered after her abrupt departure earlier in the cabin whether she truly agreed with him in terms of working as a trusting team. The soft tone of her voice had changed at his mention of it, turning harder and possibly...angry.

Of course, he'd expected that. When he'd received her call yesterday asking him to pack a bag and return to Hummingbird Haven, he had prepared himself to bear the brunt of all sorts of emotions from her and possibly Cody and Devin—if she'd been willing to let him near them. So when she stalked out of the cabin before, he had unpacked his clothes from his bag and given her some breathing room.

The technique had paid off. She'd returned about a half hour later, calmer and seemingly more welcoming, and asked him to follow her outside for the first task of the day. Who knew what he was in for during his days of working with her, and a laugh or two mixed into their time together was a welcome relief.

He smiled. "Don't think I'll chance it, thank you. I think I've been around you enough now to guess what punishment I'd suffer." Glancing at the massive pile of wood in front of him, he bent, grabbed a log and tossed it next to the one Jessie had thrown. "How much of this wood are we chopping?"

"All of it." She pointed at another massive pile of logs near the edge of the clearing surrounding Creek Cabin. "And that, too. And possibly, if there's time before the boys get home, we'll start hacking up the two trees that fell near the trail as well. Given the number of cabins we have and the guests we expect to continue housing through the winter, we'll need as much firewood as we can round up between now and the end of summer. The earlier it gets chopped and stacked, the better, though. That way it'll have more time to season up properly." She reached into her back pocket and tugged out two pairs of gloves. "Here. You'll need these. Not sure they'll fit, but they're the biggest we have on hand."

Holt caught the gloves she tossed against his chest, unfolded them and tugged one on. "A bit tight, but they'll do." He put on the other glove, flexed his hands and strolled over to one of the chopping stumps. "How long until the boys get home?"

She picked up another heavy log and tossed it on the ground in front of his feet. "'Bout four hours. Zoe picks all the kids up around three and they have snack time right after in our community cabin. I figure we should be able to make it through this pile by two o'clock then we'll go to my cabin, fix the snacks and be ready to meet them when they arrive."

His heart thumped against his ribs with an onslaught of emotions—excitement, fear, nervous tension and anxiety—at the thought of seeing Cody and Devin. Focusing on the task, he grabbed a log, balanced it on a chopping stump and gripped the ax handle with both hands. "Do they like school?"

"Yeah." She tossed another log on the ground beside the chopping stumps. "Especially recess."

He chuckled, swung the ax and split the log with one strike. "That sounds about right."

"About right for what?" Joining him, Jessie placed a log on the chopping stump nearest her and glanced at the two halves of the log resting on his stump.

"About right for how Liam and I were about that age." He tossed the split halves of the log onto a patch of dirt to his left. "Liam was always more studious—more serious—than I was, but even he could put worry in Ms. Whitham's eyes when he was cut loose in the wilds of the playground for recess."

"Ms. Whitham?"

He balanced another log on the stump. "Our first-grade teacher." Laughing, he split the log in half with one swing. "She always had to keep an extra eye on us. And the good Lord help her if one of us got ahold of a jump rope."

Jessie braced her legs apart and swung, cutting about a third of the way into her log. She frowned, eyed his second split log, then swung again. It cracked another third of the way down. "What'd you two do with a jump rope?"

He tossed the split logs on the dirt, grabbed another and split it. "We liked to tie each other to the jungle gym, upside down." Chuckling, he split another log. "Sometimes, we used the seesaw. Liam liked me to lie on my back on one end, he'd tie me down, then jump on the other end and give me the ride of my life." He tossed the halves onto the dirt. "What about Cody and Devin? They ever get into mischief?"

She swung her ax, finally splitting her log. "They're not quite that rambunctious, but they certainly have their days."

He paused as she grabbed another log, eyed

his stump again then swung. The ax only made it halfway through the log. "And you? Were you mischievous when you were a kid?"

She glanced at him, surprise flickering through her expression, then returned her attention to the log in front of her. "Not really."

Hmm. That was hard to imagine, Holt thought. As headstrong and determined as she was, he'd imagined she would've been a handful at that age. "Not even a bit? You mean, you never got into trouble as a kid?"

She swung her ax again, gaining another inch into the log. "No." The ax was stuck. She propped her heel on the log and yanked with both arms, prying the ax head free. "Why? What would you expect me to have been like?"

He rubbed his jaw. Studied her long auburn ponytail flopping over her shoulder with the next swing of her ax. Eyed the cute freckles scattered across the bridge of her nose. He grinned. "I don't know. Tidy pigtails, strong right hook and an attitude."

Cheeks reddening, she batted a fly away from her glistening face and swung again. Finally, the log split in half. She grabbed another.

"What about as a teen?" he asked. "You find trouble then?"

Her mouth tightened. Eyes glued to the log on the stump, she swung the ax again. Still, she didn't answer.

"Did you grow up 'round here?" he prompted. "Your parents live nearby?"

Another swing, this time missing the log and striking the stump instead.

His grin fell. He watched as she rebalanced the log on the stump, braced her legs apart and swung again. "This isn't a competition, you know."

"Oh, I know." She dropped the ax to her side, leaning on it as the blade dug into the dirt. "I'm working on these logs while you're just jawing."

Her tone bit. The mean cut of it was so out of touch with the mission she'd dedicated herself to here at Hummingbird Haven and the compassionate way she'd greeted him that night seven years ago.

Holt studied her tight expression, and she returned his scrutiny, those dark brown eyes of hers piercing into his. But this time they were clouded with something else. Some deep-seated pain.

Yeah. There was something there. Something she hid mighty deep, if his suspicions were correct.

"I didn't mean the firewood," he said quietly. "I meant—" he gestured between them "—you and I. We're not supposed to be working against each other. We've agreed to work together. And seeing as how you know quite a bit about me, I don't see the harm in getting to know you better."

He stopped, an unfamiliar sensation unfurling in his chest. A hint of what? Want? Desire? No...*need*. A need so different from any he'd felt in the past for other women. A tender curiosity. One that had nothing to do with physical attraction, though it was impossible to deny he certainly felt that for her, too. But this was something else. Something he'd never felt before. A different kind of curiosity. One he hoped she'd acquire for him, too.

"I'd like very much to get to know you better," he said softly. To get inside her head and see the world as she saw it. Hear her thoughts and fears, wishes and dreams. To get inside her heart and...?

"You know me well enough." She snatched the ax back into the air and braced her legs. "And as your teammate," she stressed, "what I'd appreciate the most in this moment is for you to help me chop this pile of wood."

The ax flew downward under the momentum of her swinging arms, splitting the log on the stump with one strike, the cracking wood echoing against the thick woods surrounding them, abruptly ending the conversation.

Sighing, he grabbed another log, positioned it on the stump in front of him and hefted his ax back into his hands. It was probably best he focus his energy on preparing to meet with Cody and Devin this afternoon. He'd do as she asked and let it go. For now.

Four hours later Holt chopped his twelfth cucumber in Jessie's kitchen, picked up the cutting board and dumped the slices onto a large paper plate. "Surely these kids won't down all these cheese, crackers and cucumbers." His nose wrinkled. "Especially the cucumbers."

Jessie, standing beside him, reached across the kitchen island for a cucumber. Her bare arm brushed his and her soft, fresh scent whispered against his nose. "You got something against cucumbers?"

"No, but they're not my favorite kind of vegetable. If I were a kid, I'd go for the cream cheese first. Or better yet, I'd wish there was some peanut butter and jelly."

"Not as healthy," she said.

He caught himself leaning closer as she placed the cucumber on her cutting board and chopped, her movements releasing another sweetly scented breeze to his senses. Good night above, how had she managed to keep that intoxicating scent through three and a half hours of chopping wood, stacking logs and trekking dirt trails back to her cabin?

He spun away, tossed his knife into the sink and turned on the tap, shoving his wet fingers beneath the running water. A squirt of the moisturizing lavender gel soap on the counter got rid of the cucumbers seeds on his fingers and left his hands feeling clean and rejuvenated.

Man, how he wished he could say the same for the rest of him. Unlike Jessie, three and a half hours of outdoor manual labor had wrung what felt like every drop of sweat from his body, soaked his T-shirt and dampened his jeans, leaving his clothes clinging to him uncomfortably and, he suspected, emitting an unpleasant smell in his wake.

He plucked his sweaty shirt from his chest and fanned it, hoping to dissipate the odor. "I don't suppose I have enough time to run back to my cabin and take a shower?"

The steady chop of Jessie's knife continued. "Nope." Finished, she dumped the cucumber slices into a container then joined him at the sink to wash her hands. "Zoe should be pulling up any minute now with the kids and we still have to transport everything to the community cabin. Plus, I asked Peggy Ann to get permission from her supervisor to end her shift early at the hardware store and come as well."

"Peggy Ann?"

"Yeah. She and her two daughters, Tabitha and Katie, have been living here for a couple months now. I thought it'd be best if you met everyone at once and it's very important that we stick to the usual schedule. That's your first lesson," she said. "Kids—especially kids in Cody and Devin's situation—need structure."

Wonderful. His first encounter with Hummingbird Haven's guests and his sons would be overpowered by his sweat, grime and stink. Not exactly how he'd pictured the reunion.

Wincing, Holt rubbed the back of his neck. "You sure there's no time for a shower? I'd be real quick."

"Relax. I know you're nervous and I was hoping for a little downtime before everyone got here, but it just didn't work out that way."

"But I'm soaked with sweat." He fanned his shirt faster. "And I have a feeling I stink."

Hands clean, she grabbed the dish towel and dried them. "I haven't noticed anything. I mean you might." She leaned close and sniffed, her lips quirking. "Oh, well…maybe you do need a little something." She tossed the dish towel back into the dish drying rack. "How 'bout you run to your cabin and put on a little deodorant? I think that'd do the trick."

"That's the thing." He rubbed the back of his neck. "I ran out of deodorant and body wash yesterday and used up the last bit of the stuff in those little bottles they give you at the motel, so I'm out. Fresh out of everything. I'd planned on stocking back up but then you called and invited me here and now, seeing as how there's nothing in the cabin—"

"Oh." She made a face. "I wasn't certain you'd go for my proposal, so I didn't think far enough ahead."

He waved away her concern. "Not your fault. I should've grabbed something on the way here."

"Hold up." She left the kitchen and headed down a hallway. "Think I can help."

Holt returned to the sink, turned on the faucet and lowered his head, splashing water on his face and neck. Barely a birdbath, at best, but it was the best option for the moment.

"Here you go." Jessie returned, holding out a small blue deodorant container. "Just picked this up the other day in a discounted two-pack, and this is the one I haven't used yet. It's all yours until you make it to the store later this afternoon."

He shut off the faucet, wiped his face with the dish towel then took the deodorant from her and glanced at the label. Pink flowers and white daisies sent a shudder through him. "Wild-flower Delight?"

Jessie smiled. A bit too wide for his liking. "Yep."

He stared. "This is for women."

She smiled bigger. "But you know what they say, it's strong enough—"

"Nuh-uh." He held it back out to her. "Nope."

"Come on. You said you needed something, and I provided it. Give and take." She nudged his arm and winked. "Like a team, you know?"

"Seriously?" He narrowed his eyes. "You're enjoying this, aren't you?"

She shrugged. "Use it or don't use it, it's up to

you. But there aren't any other men living here, so there's no chance of finding a more manly scent." Returning to the island, she fastened the top on the large container of cucumbers as well as two others on additional containers loaded with crackers and herbed cream cheese. "You need to make up your mind soon, though, because they'll be here any minute and you're in charge of bringing the napkins, cups and sweet tea to the community cabin."

With that, she stacked the sandwich containers in her arms and headed for the door.

Holt stared at the deodorant in his hand and weighed his options. Unfortunately, there weren't many. He uncapped the deodorant, took a deep whiff, then, shaking his head, lifted his shirt and applied it liberally, hoping it'd help him seem slightly more presentable.

The screen door of Jessie's cabin squeaked, and her voice drifted back into the kitchen. "Come on. The van's pulling in the driveway."

Quickly, he shoved the deodorant in his back pocket, grabbed the cardboard box containing packs of napkins, plastic cups and two jugs of sweet tea and walked outside.

Sure enough, a large van was slowly making its way down the winding driveway toward the community cabin Jessie had pointed out to him earlier that afternoon. He hustled alongside the vehicle, falling in step beside Jessie as she waved in the direction of a chorus of voices calling down from the van's open windows.

Hi, Jessie! We're home! and *What're we eating?* quickly gave way to stunned silence at the sight of him. Then one young voice, curious with a hint of suspicion, called out, "Who's he?"

Holt glanced up and sought out the owner of the voice. A blond boy with hazel eyes and familiar features frowned back at him. Moments later a second blond boy with identical features but an excited expression shoved his face into the window's opening to stare down at him as well.

Cody and Devin. His sons.

Holt's hands trembled and his grip slipped on the box he carried. Feeling Jessie's eyes on him, he renewed his grip on the box and refocused on the path ahead.

"Remember," Jessie said below the rumble of the van's engine as it passed. "You're the new live-in handyman. Nothing more."

He glanced at her, unable to stop two firm words from escaping his lips. "For now."

She held his gaze for two steps then picked up

the pace, edged in front of him and led the way up the front stairs into the community cabin.

By the time Holt made it inside, set the cardboard box on one of the wide dining tables and unpacked its contents, Zoe opened the front door of the community cabin and ushered the kids inside.

"Come on, my young ones," Zoe called. "I heard through the grapevine that there's a special surprise in store for y'all this afternoon so please be on your best behavior."

A cacophony of kids' voices filled the entryway as they filed in, their eyes eagerly scanning the room and freezing when they encountered Holt. The voices quickly lowered to barely discernable whispers as they each took a seat at a table to the left of him and stared in his direction.

There were five children total: two girls with brown hair, one in her teens and the other looked to be a bit younger, a young boy with black hair and frightened eyes who couldn't be more than five or six and, of course, Cody and Devin.

Holt stilled, his eyes glued to the two boys who sat next to each other, staring up at him with wide, unblinking eyes. Excitement and fear bubbled up from his middle and weakened his legs.

He bit his lip. Imagine that. He'd been thrown across arenas by thousand-pound bulls hard enough to break his back on more than one occasion and he'd rolled over in the dirt, shot to his feet and walked away smiling. But one look from these two boys—*his sons*—and he lost his balance, his heart bursting with love, pride, regret, guilt, fear and anticipation. He'd never felt anything like it before.

"Hi, everyone!" A tall woman with brown hair the same shade as the two girls sitting at the table walked in, waving at the kids. She glanced at Jessie, Zoe then Holt, her next words trailing away. "Hope I'm not late…"

Jessie followed the woman's gaze to Holt and strode to his side quickly, speaking in a calm tone. "Not at all, Peggy Ann. You're right on time." She gestured toward the table where the kids were seated. "Please have a seat and get comfortable. We have an introduction to make and I'm glad everyone could be here at one time." She surveyed the crowded table before her then looked at Holt. A glimmer of uncertainty flickered through her gaze before she blinked, dashing it away. "We have a new guest that'll be staying with us temporarily."

Was it him, or did she add extra emphasis to *temporarily*?

"Holt Wil—er, *Mr. Holt* is what we ask you to refer to him as—has joined us here at Hummingbird Haven and will be serving as our handyman," she continued. "He'll be staying in Creek Cabin and will renovate that cabin as well as Hummingbird Hollow on the outskirts of the property. I hope you'll provide him a warm welcome."

Jessie and Zoe clapped their hands in welcome and nodded encouragingly at the kids. Each child slowly joined in, clapping quietly, their wide eyes still taking him in. The expressions on their faces were similar—tense and suspicious.

Tough crowd. Holt shifted nervously from one foot to the other. Perhaps he should make a concerted effort to greet them properly, too. Make himself friendly and approachable.

Clearing his throat, he walked over to one end of the table where the woman named Peggy Ann sat, bent and held out his hand. "Nice to meet y—"

The woman, fear flashing through her expression, visibly shrank back in her chair, and the two girls sitting by her side huddled closer, apprehension in their eyes.

Holt withdrew his hand immediately and stepped back. "I—I'm sorry. I didn't mean to—"

"It's okay," Zoe said, walking over to Peggy Ann's side. She reached down and squeezed the other woman's shoulder. "Everyone can take as long as they like getting to know each other, and Holt understands that the space and time needed will be different for everyone. Things will continue exactly as they have before, and you'll all still be in control of your surroundings. Holt will respect your boundaries and leave your immediate area anytime you ask him to." She looked at Holt. "Right?"

Taken aback, he nodded. "Yes." He nodded again. "Of course." He glanced at Cody and Devin, who still eyed him from afar, then looked at Peggy Ann, who still seemed disconcerted by his presence. "If you'd like me to leave while you visit with the kids, I c—"

"No." Voice shaking, Peggy Ann squeezed her hands together in her lap and smiled up at him. It was strained. "I—I'm just a little tired, is all." She looked at Jessie—almost desperately.

"We had a busy day at the hardware store today. That's why I'm a bit jumpy."

Jessie smiled gently. "There's no need to explain, Peggy Ann—ever. This is your home. You're entitled to be open with how you feel and what you want. Everyone here will respect that."

"It's a rule," Cody—or maybe it was Devin?—piped from the other end of the table.

"Absolutely." Jessie winked. "Which brings me to the invitation of the day." She looked at Holt. "Holt, would you mind if anyone would like to introduce themselves to you up close?"

His throat was dry. He swallowed hard, eyeing his sons expectantly. "No, not at all."

Jessie spread her arms. "Any takers?"

Silence fell across the room. Peggy Ann looked down, along with the two girls at her side, whom he assumed were her daughters. The youngest boy took an immediate interest in his napkin, folding it intently as though undertaking an artistic work of origami. And Cody and Devin? They continued to stare, unblinking, at him. Neither of them moved and neither of them spoke.

Holt smiled and offered an encouraging look, but it made no difference. Cody and Devin made no effort to approach him. Maybe Jessie was right. Maybe his sons were happier without a father in their lives than they could ever be with one in it. And the way things were going so far, they might only ever know him as a stranger.

Come on, Lord, he prayed silently, *please let them give me a chance.*

And right then, one of his sons stood up, walked over to Holt's side and said with surprise, "You smell like a girl!"

CHAPTER EIGHT

ALL SORTS OF scenarios had tumbled around inside Jessie's head when she imagined how a first meeting between Holt and the boys would unfold, but this moment had not been one of them.

Cody, standing beside Holt in Hummingbird Haven's community center, wrinkled his nose and looked back at his brother. "Come see, Devin. He smells just like a girl!"

Devin stood and strolled over to Cody's side. Eyeing Holt, he stuck his chin out in Holt's direction and took a whiff. "Yep." He glanced over his shoulder and frowned at Jessie with disapproval. "He smells like you. And kinda like Marjorie Middleton, too."

Jessie rolled her lips together, stifling a smile. "Boys, commenting on someone's scent is not a very polite way to greet someone."

Though she had to admit, it did tickle her funny bone for some reason.

Aw, who was she kidding? She knew exactly why. Seeing Holt—an imposing masculine tower of sinewy strength—cringe at two boys comparing his scent to that of their six-year-old female arch nemesis was just the moment she needed to set her biggest fears at ease. No way would her boys run out of her arms and blindly into those of a strange man who smelled like Marjorie Middleton.

Frowning, in a remarkably identical way as Devin, Holt looked at her, too. "Who's Marjorie Middleton?"

"Oh, just a girl from school," Zoe said, rounding the table and joining the trio. "And, boys, Mr. Holt does not smell like..." She tilted her head. Sniffed the air a time or two, a perplexed expression appearing on her face as she glanced at Jessie. "Well, he doesn't smell like Marjorie, but he does smell kinda like—"

"Wildflower Delight," Holt grumbled.

Jessie choked back a laugh. "Never mind how he smells, guys." Conscious they had an audience of young, impressionable minds, she continued, "How should you greet someone you first meet, boys?"

Cody faced Holt again, tipped his head back and stuck out his hand. "Nice to meet you, Mr. Holt. I'm Cody Williams. And this—" he pointed at Devin "—is my brother, Devin."

"Pleased to make your acquaintance," Holt said, his words trembling slightly.

The husky note in his voice and the tenderness in his smile and gaze as he looked down at Cody melted away more than just Jessie's easy smile. Her heart warmed unexpectantly at Holt's reverent approach to his sons.

Holt shook Cody's hand, his own brawny palm enveloping the little boy's small one, then he released Cody's hand somewhat reluctantly, it seemed, and held his upturned palm out to his other son. "Devin. It's an honor."

More difficult to impress than his brother, Devin walked past Holt's outstretched arm and circled his brawny frame, eyeing him from head to toe. "When'd you get here?"

Holt straightened and smiled down at Devin. "This morning." He motioned toward his sweat-stained shirt. "Started working first thing."

"What'd you work on?" Cody asked, trailing in Devin's footsteps as he continued circling Holt.

"Firewood." A slow smile lifted Holt's lips as he watched his sons stroll slowly around him with prying eyes. "I helped Jessie chop up a pile out by Creek Cabin."

"That's where you're staying tonight, right?" Devin asked.

Holt nodded.

"And tomorrow, and the next?" Cody asked.

"Yep."

Devin stared at Holt's feet. "Your boots are old."

Holt's slow grin widened. "'Cuz I use them a lot. They're broken in just right. Served me well for a lot of years."

"For doing what?" Devin glanced up, narrowed his eyes. "Repair stuff?"

Holt hesitated. "Among other things."

"What things?" Cody asked.

Holt's gaze met Jessie's and she blinked in surprise at the unspoken question in his eyes. *How much should he share? What was permitted?* Good grief, if only she knew. But the simple fact that he'd looked to her before answering was reassuringly welcome...and strangely disconcerting all at once.

She glanced at the boys then looked back at Holt and nodded.

"I've had other jobs," Holt said quietly.

"Like what?" Cody asked.

Holt's smile returned. "I used to be a professional athlete."

Cody's eyes widened as he surveyed him closer. "What kind?"

"Rodeo."

Devin cocked his head, the first hint of genuine interest sparking in his expression. "Like a cowboy?"

Holt nodded. "I rode bulls, broncs, wrestled steers a few—"

"Bulls?" Devin perked up. "Real bulls? Horns, hooves, snot and all?"

Holt laughed. "Yep. All o' that and then some."

"He's got the muscles for it," Cody told Devin, tugging at Holt's left biceps.

Jessie stepped forward. "Cody, don't do th—"

"It's okay." Holt held up his free hand, stilling her movements, then showed Cody and Devin his palm. "See that? That long, rough patch of skin? That's a callus from holding on."

A breathy sound of awe left Cody's lips. He grabbed Holt's wrist, tugged his palm closer and waved at the other kids still seated at the table. "Come look, Miles! He's a real honest-to-goodness bull rider."

Miles craned his neck for a better view but remained seated at the table with Peggy Ann and her girls.

"Just 'cuz he's got a callus doesn't mean he's a bull rider," Devin scoffed. "Besides, bull riders don't smell like girls."

Holt pursed his lips. "Actually, they do. Some bull riders are girls, and some of those girls ride better than the boys."

Devin scowled. "Nuh-uh."

"Yeah-huh." Grinning, Holt winked. "You can put your money where your mouth is, but I wouldn't recommend it. Those ladies are tough."

Devin considered this, his scowl easing. "How good were you?"

Holt grinned wider. "I held my own."

"You ever win anything?" Cody asked.

"I've won a few times."

"How many?"

"You get any trophies?"

"Break an arm?"

"Wear a cast?"

Questions continued tumbling out of the

boys' mouths, blending together and drowning out Holt's responses.

Jessie stepped in. "That's enough, you two. The snacks are ready and there are others waiting to eat." She gestured toward Miles, Peggy Ann and her daughters, who sat at the table laden with herbed cream cheese, crackers and cucumbers, their gazes darting back and forth between Holt and the boys. "Ms. Peggy Ann took time off her new job to join us, so I say we all have a seat, say the blessing and dig in."

The slew of questions stopped and the boys, grumbling, complied with her request and took their seats at the table.

Cody patted the chair next to him. "Sit here, Mr. Holt."

Jessie wove her fingers together and squeezed, watching nervously as Holt pulled out the chair Cody had referenced and prepared to sit.

He hesitated and glanced at Peggy Ann, who sat at the other end of the table. "Is this okay with you, Ms. Peggy Ann?"

Peggy Ann surveyed him once more then sat up straighter and nodded stiffly. "Of course."

It was progress. Jessie pressed her sweaty palms together and bit her lip. When Peggy Ann had arrived at Hummingbird Haven—

for the third time—two months ago, bruised and bloodied, with her daughters in tow, she'd barely lifted her head to ask Jessie if she could stay. *Just once more*, she'd said, *this time for good, I promise*.

It'd taken several weeks for the bruises to fade and another month for Peggy Ann to summon the courage to lift her head and look Jessie and Zoe in the eye. Since she'd started working at the hardware store—the only job opening at the time of Peggy Ann's job search—and working with the therapist Jessie had provided for her and her daughters, she didn't startle as easily and the low light Jessie had glimpsed in the kitchen window of Peggy Ann's cabin had stopped flickering on at odd hours of the night, Peggy Ann seemingly able to sleep through the night again.

"Thank you," Holt said, sitting beside Cody.

Zoe rubbed her hands together and smiled. "Let's say the blessing."

Fifteen minutes later the containers were empty, and a lone cracker remained amidst scattered crumbs on a serving plate, but there continued to be a never-ending supply of questions from the boys.

"Why do you do this with your arm when

you ride?" Cody asked, stretching his left arm above his head and undulating it slowly. A bit of cream cheese fell from his bottom lip onto the table. "Don't it get tired?"

"Cody," Jessie said, "please don't talk when your mouth is full."

"Sorry." He chewed then swallowed. "So don't it, Mr. Holt? Get tired, I mean."

Holt wiped his mouth with his napkin then tossed the napkin onto his empty plate. "Not particularly. Other things get tired a lot faster, and to answer your question, we use that arm to help maintain our balance. Plus, we're not allowed to touch the bull with our free hand."

"But what about when the bull kicks?" Devin asked, popping his last bite of cream cheese and cracker into his mouth. "Doesn't it throw you forward? What do you do when you're about to fall onto the bull's head? And what about the horns? Won't they stab you?"

"Okay, that's it." Jessie folded her unused napkin and placed it neatly on top of her untouched cream cheese and crackers. "That's enough discussion about bull riding. Y'all are wearing Mr. Holt out."

Cody made a face. "But, Jessie—"

"No buts." Jessie stood, grabbed her plate,

walked to the end of the table and grabbed a roll of aluminum foil from the box Holt had carried earlier. "I'm sure Mr. Holt is tired of being interrogated." She ripped off a portion of foil, folded it over her plate and glanced at Peggy Ann under her lashes. "Are you feeling okay, Peggy Ann?"

Peggy Ann, her food barely touched, pushed her chair away from the table. "I'm sorry, Jessie. I'm not very hungry this afternoon." She tried—but failed—to smile, her lips barely lifting before they fell again. "If you don't mind, I'd like to take my girls to our cabin and help them with their homework there."

Jessie dipped her head. "Of course. But let me wrap your plate first. You might get hungry later and that snack will come in handy."

After covering Peggy Ann's uneaten food with foil, Jessie walked with her and the girls to the door and waved goodbye as they walked down the front steps and strolled down the trail toward their cabin.

"...can we go, Jessie?"

A small hand tugged at the hem of her shirt, and she looked down, finding Cody by her side.

"Can I?" he repeated.

Jessie frowned. "Go where?"

"To the store with Mr. Holt later on." Cody, practically bouncing with excitement, glanced over his shoulder at Holt. "He said he has to go get supplies and stuff."

Jessie watched as Holt gathered up the dirty paper plates from the table with Zoe and tossed them into a nearby trash can. Miles disposed of his own dirty plate, cautiously following Holt to the trash can.

"No," she said. "That's not a good idea."

"Why not?" A plaintive tone entered Cody's voice. "We don't got no homework tonight and it ain't even dark yet."

"You don't *have any* homework," Jessie corrected, "and it *isn't* dark yet. And the answer's no."

"But he says he's got to get—" Cody stopped, his brow wrinkling, then continued. "He says he has to get some de-oh...de-oh-du..."

"Deodorant." Devin, walking over, stood on the other side of Jessie and smirked. "He said it's your deodorant that's making him smell like a girl and that he needs to get his own." He looked up at Jessie. "And Cody doesn't need to go anyway."

"Aw, hush it," Cody said. "You don't tell me what I can and can't do."

Devin frowned. "I can tell you whatever I feel li—"

"Okay, okay, that's enough, boys." Jessie rubbed her forehead. "Look, I get that you're excited to meet Mr. Holt, Cody, but today's his first day here and I'm sure he'd rather do his shopping by himself."

"I wouldn't mind." Holt, repacking left-over cups and paper plates into the box on the table, tapped the sides of the cardboard box and shrugged. "I'm just gonna swing by the grocery store and pick up some supplies, is all."

Jessie plucked Cody's fingers off her shirt hem. "Excuse me, boys." She walked over to Holt's side, leaned in and whispered, "Are you serious right now? You just got here. It's not a good idea for you to haul one of the boys off somewhere by yourself."

One blond brow lifted. "Why not?" he whispered back. "You afraid I'll run off with him? I'd never do that to you—or the boys. Besides, it takes what? Eight to ten minutes to get to the store and I'll only be in there for five to ten minutes. That's no more than half an hour to get there and back. You'd barely even notice."

"Oh, I'd notice. I'd notice every second Cody wasn't with me."

Holt sighed. "I didn't mean it like that. You know I didn't." He leaned closer. "But Cody's interested in me. Even you have to admit that. And isn't that the point of me being here? The reason why you invited me? To get to know the boys and for them to become acquainted with me?"

"Yes, but—"

Someone cleared their throat. Zoe poked her head in between Jessie's and Holt's. "You've got three little sets of eyes and ears intently focused on you right now, in case neither of you has noticed," she said softly.

Jessie and Holt straightened slowly and looked around. Sure enough, Cody, Devin and Miles all stood in a neat line on the opposite side of the table, each of them straining forward, their wide eyes fixed on Jessie and Holt and their heads tilted in their direction.

Jessie cleared her throat and Holt shoved his hands into his pockets.

"Look," Zoe whispered, turning her face away from the boys and smoothing her hand over her ponytail. "Maybe it's not such a bad idea." She glanced at Jessie, a small smile appearing as she said sheepishly, "After all, the purpose of you inviting Holt here is—like he said—to get to know the boys. It's a quick trip and making a big deal out of it will only make the boys think you don't trust him, which will make the boys not trust him, either."

Jessie's eyes widened. "Zoe..."

She couldn't believe this. Absolutely could not believe that Zoe would take Holt's side over hers. Especially now—on day one!

"But you..." Jessie's throat ran dry. "You're..."

Right. As always. As much as she hated to admit it, Zoe was absolutely right. A quick trip to the store wasn't a big deal. And she should be happy that Cody, at least, had taken an interest in Holt. But something about this just didn't sit right with her. Too much was happening way too fast right off the bat—disruption to their routine and Cody's immediate admiration for Holt. And what did that mean for the future she'd so carefully planned for herself and the boys? A future in which Holt hadn't figured at all?

"Okay," Jessie mumbled. "On one condition." She glared at Holt. "I'm going, too."

IN THE END, Cody, Jessie and Devin all went and that was just fine with Holt.

"Everyone comfortable?" he asked.

Jessie, seated in the passenger seat of his truck, buckled her seat belt and nodded—the very same stoic expression she'd adopted a couple hours ago in Hummingbird Haven's community cabin when she'd announced she would be accompanying him on the trip for supplies as well.

"Yes." The forced smile on her face made Holt frown. She glanced over her shoulder at the boys, who sat in the backseat of his cab. "You guys comfortable back there?"

Cody grinned. "Yep."

Devin shrugged, leaned his elbow on the windowsill and propped his chin on his hand.

Holt looked in the rearview mirror, the sight of his sons sitting in the backseat so reminiscent of the night seven years ago when he'd nestled them in their car seats and driven to Hummingbird Haven. So many years had passed. He'd let them down so badly and had missed so much. So many milestone moments of his sons' lives that he would never be able to recapture.

How had he ever imagined reconnecting as a father with Cody and Devin after just an introduction and a few meaningful interactions? Jessie had been right. The risks associated with him reentering Cody and Devin's lives were high and he had no way of mitigating those risks without Jessie's help...and trust. Something she didn't seem too keen on offering him, despite what she'd said, given her less than enthusiastic response to him having a short outing with Cody and Devin.

Excitement fizzling, he forced a smile, too. "Well. Let's have a grocery store adventure, shall we?"

Cody laughed, Devin rolled his eyes and Jessie continued staring stoically ahead. Fifteen minutes later, the three of them surrounding him in the deodorant aisle of Hope Springs Family Grocery, their demeanors remained unchanged.

Seeking to break the ice, Holt grabbed a red container of deodorant, uncapped it and held it toward Cody's nose. "Now, this," he said, "*this* is deodorant made for a man."

Cody leaned in, took a big whiff and grinned. "Smells like pine."

"Uh-huh." Smiling, Holt turned to his right and offered it to Devin. "Outdoorsy. Full of a rich, woodsy, earthy type of scent."

Devin sniffed, an expression of reluctant approval in his eyes. "It does smell better."

A disgruntled sound emerged from Jessie's

direction, but her lips twitched ever so slightly, giving Holt hope. "Are the three of you trying to say my deodorant stinks?"

Cody spread his hands. "Maybe."

Devin shook his head. "I didn't say that."

"What I'm saying," Holt clarified, "is that as delightful as the wildflowers are, I think this scent is better suited to me."

That lip twitch stretched into a full-blown smile. "You're delighted by my wildflowers?"

His neck heated. "No. I mean, I think it's nice on you."

A teasing light entered her eyes. "Really?"

He smiled—sincerely this time. That bit of humor in her tone was promising. Maybe this trip wouldn't be a complete dud. Maybe she'd give him a chance to show her that he could get along well with the boys *and* with her. "Yeah." He held her gaze. "Really."

Jessie's smile slipped, her cheeks flushing as she looked away. She headed for the exit, pausing briefly to say, "Boys, please help Mr. Holt pick out his supplies and I'll meet you at the truck."

The stiffness in her tone made Holt's stomach drop.

The drive back to Hummingbird Haven was

silent. Jessie and Devin stared out their windows as the sun slowly began to set and Cody drifted off a time or two, waking himself up with a snore as Holt parked the truck in front of Jessie's cabin.

Holt helped Cody hop out of the truck and Jessie did the same for Devin.

"All right, boys," she said. "Let's get you washed up and ready for bed."

"Jessie?" Holt leaned against the bumper of his truck and waited for her to look back at him. "You mind staying behind a minute? Have something I need to ask you."

She hesitated then nodded. "Boys, why don't you go on in, brush your teeth and get your towels ready for your baths? I'll be in soon."

They complied, trudging up the steps and onto the porch where Cody stopped to wave at Holt.

"Bye, Mr. Holt." A sleepy smile crossed Cody's face. "Thanks for taking us to the store."

Holt smiled back, an intense longing rising within him as the boys headed inside the cabin. "You're welcome."

The screen door snapped shut behind them just as dusk fell and a chorus of tree frogs and crickets rolled along the tree line at the edge of the lawn. Cool air drifted in, prompting Jessie to cross her arms over her chest and rub her shoulders.

"So?" she asked, facing him. "What is it you want to ask me?"

Holt dragged his boot across the loose dirt of the driveway, noting the space between them. "Why did you invite me to stay if you're so afraid of my being here?"

She bristled. "I'm not afraid of you."

"I think you are," he said softly. "This is day one and already, you're pushing me away. You got that arm of yours stretched out so stiff, I may never get past it."

Suspicion flashed in her eyes. "And why would you want to do that?"

"To get to know the boys." He shoved off his truck and stepped closer. "And you. I'd like to—no, I need to get to know you better. For the boys. For us."

She stepped back. "What us? I told you that—"

"You think I know you well enough already." He took another step, small rocks crunching under his boots. "But I don't. I know you're a great mom." He motioned toward the cabin where the boys were. "Anyone can see that.

And I've known you were a great woman since the day I put my sons in your arms." He moved closer. "Look… I know I'm the furthest thing from perfect, but I'm not a bad guy and I'm trying here. I'm really trying. I just need to know when—or if—you're going to start trying, too."

"Try to do what?"

"Try to let that wall of yours down, open up a little and give me a chance with my boys. And maybe…" *Maybe with you?* He stopped walking, the thought catching him off guard, a deep longing unfurling in his chest. "You're a family," he said softly. "You and the boys. The only way I can truly become a part of the boys' lives here is if you let me in. I thought that's what you were trying to do by inviting me here, but you continue to push me away at every opportuni—"

"And why shouldn't I push you away? Because you say you've changed?" Her voice broke, the dying light of the setting sun glinting across a sheen of tears in her eyes. "Because now you say you're ready to be Cody and Devin's father?"

He shook his head, an exasperated sigh bursting from his lips. "I was just hoping—"

"I had plans." Two big tears broke free, dangled precariously on her long lashes for a moment, then plunged down her cheeks. "I've been here for Cody and Devin every moment of every day since you left them with me." A fresh set of tears coursed down her red cheeks. "I just applied for adoption. I was going to make it official—be their mother in every sense of the word—and then here you come. Showing up at my door again, asking me to give them back to you. *My* sons."

Holt's throat tightened at the pained expression on her face.

"And what is it you're asking me to do?" she asked, a heavy sob racking her slender frame. "To trust that you've changed? To believe that it's okay to allow myself—and Cody and Devin—to be vulnerable to you? To put Cody and Devin at risk of being abandoned again like you abandoned them once before, like my mother abandoned me?"

He froze.

"You wanted to know more about me." She spoke softly. So softly he could barely hear. "So there it is. I didn't end up opening this shelter by chance. Years ago, hours after I was born, I was left behind like the children I offer shelter to here. Except my mother didn't hand me off to someone like you did Cody and Devin. She just left me in a parking lot like I was nothing of value. As though she didn't care if I was found alive or not. I spent my entire life in foster care. I've never had a family—not a real one. Certainly not the kind I plan to give Cody and Devin."

Eyes burning, he sucked in a strong breath. "Jessie—"

"Yes," she said. "I do think it's possible you've changed. I do think you mean well...that you truly want to be a part of Cody and Devin's lives. But I'm afraid. I'm afraid of you getting close to Cody and Devin then changing your mind, leaving them again and breaking their hearts—like my mother broke mine the night she left me. But I'm even more afraid of things going well—of you keeping true to your word and becoming the father Cody and Devin deserve, the boys taking a shine to you...and wondering where that will leave me." She folded in on herself, her head lowering, arms wrapping around her waist and tears flowing freely. "Allowing you in is scarier than you think. And it's harder than you could ever imagine."

"Jessie..." Heart clenching, he moved slowly to her side. Lifted a shaky hand and touched her arm. "Jessie."

She raised her head then, met his eyes and held his gaze, tears pooling in the corners of her trembling mouth as she studied his face. Then, slowly—so very slowly—she stepped forward and touched her forehead to his chest, her words barely discernable as she said, "I'll try. I promise I'll start trying."

Instinctively, his arms lifted, but he halted his movements, forced his hands to still in midair and hover inches from her back, afraid to intrude more than he already had. He lowered his head and breathed in the sweet scent of her hair, fighting his desperate desire to wrap her safely in his arms and hold her close, trying to be patient and give her the space she needed instead.

"I know," he whispered, allowing his lips to barely brush the top of her head. "I know."

CHAPTER NINE

GOD HAD A reason for everything. Jessie truly believed that—at least, that was what she told herself as she stood outside Creek Cabin at six o'clock the next morning.

It was dark out, the spring sun still snoozing, and only a few lavender tendrils of light unfurled along the mountain range in the distance. A lone bird chirped from the depths of a thick Cypress tree and a chilly breeze rustled through thick branches and swept across the clearing, coaxing goose bumps along Jessie's bare arms.

Jessie tugged the short sleeves of her T-shirt down a bit, shoved her hands into the pockets of her jeans and bounced in place. "Shoulda brought a jacket," she mumbled to herself as she eyed the front door of Creek Cabin.

She should've brought a lot of things and left others behind. Take her pride, for instance. She could've left that at home in favor of a light windbreaker. It would've made this endeavor a whole lot less painful. But then again, in her experience, eating crow was never a very pleasant experience under any circumstances.

And maybe that's the problem, a little voice chimed inside her head.

She made a face. Perhaps it was. Maybe her conscience had a point. Maybe apologizing to Holt for her emotional outburst last night and taking the first step to openly invite him into her and the boys' lives only seemed like an insurmountable task because the act itself proved one thing above all: she had been pushing him away as a result of her own fears and insecurities—unfairly, as he'd suggested—despite offering to help him reconnect with Cody and Devin. And she'd allowed it to all spill out in a tearful tirade last night.

A light flickered on above the tiny window of the cabin's kitchen. Holt, clad in a short-sleeved T-shirt and jeans, ambled into view and stretched one muscular arm upward to the left of the window.

He was probably rooting around in one of the cabinets for a mug. Jessie lifted her shoulders toward her ears and stamped her feet, fighting off the early-morning chill. A hot cup of coffee would be more than welcome right about now and clearly, Holt was up and about now, which left her no more excuses as to why she should delay the inevitable.

Oh, buck up, girl, that annoying voice chimed. *You promised him last night that you'd try. So apologize and…try.*

Sighing, she squared her shoulders, marched up to the front door and knocked twice.

The door opened a moment later and Holt, surprise in his eyes, surveyed her silently for a moment then stepped back and swept his arm toward the interior of the cabin. "Please, come in."

She did so, saying as she stepped across the threshold, "Thank you. I hate to bother you so early but…" She glanced around, eyes flicking nervously over the familiar features of the living room. "Um, Zoe and the boys are fixing a big breakfast at her cabin and we wanted to invite you over to eat with the boys and see them off to school this morning." She withdrew a small piece of paper from her back pocket. "And I made a list—like you mentioned yesterday— of the to-dos we need done around the property so you'll know what to expect for the next few workdays." She rubbed at a speck of ink on her thumb, left behind from the pen she used to compose the list before walking to Creek Cabin. "I also wanted to talk to you before we started work for the day, if that's okay?"

"Always."

The warm tone of his voice stilled the nervous flutters in her stomach. She refocused on his face and her gaze fixated on a lock of blond hair that had fallen over his left eye. It caught on his dark lashes, moving as he blinked. Her fingers itched to reach up and smooth it back. Maybe take a step forward and lean her cheek against his strong, warm chest as she had last night.

But that would be a mistake—one she couldn't afford. His physical attraction...well, she'd become pretty adept at fending that off, but his tenderness—the kind he'd shown her last night with his patient demeanor, soothing tone and comforting presence—that was much more difficult to ignore.

She'd dated in the past—though having dedicated most of her time to Hummingbird Haven the dates had been few—but none of the men she'd dated had stirred the intense emotions in her that Holt did. The feelings she experienced for him were an odd new mixture of tenderness, excitement…and dismay for how deeply he affected her. She was used to being in control of her surroundings and emotions, and Holt's presence evoked a vulnerability in her she hadn't expected.

He shoved his hair off his forehead, revealing an unobstructed view of the kindness in his hazel eyes. "I'm always available anytime you'd like to talk and I'd love to have breakfast with the boys." He glanced at the list then put it in his pocket and smiled. "And thank you for the to-do list. It'll help me manage my time better."

The sculpted curves of his mouth caught her attention, his soft words seeming to linger in her ears and on his parted lips as she stared.

She shook her head, stepped back and resumed surveying the living room again.

Gurgling sounds emerged from the kitchen.

"I just made a fresh pot of coffee," he said. "Would you like some while we talk?"

Grateful for the distraction, she managed a smile. "Yes, please."

He led the way into the kitchen where the aroma of freshly ground coffee beans hovered on the air. One white mug sat on the laminate countertop by the coffeemaker and after grabbing another from a cabinet beside the kitchen window, he picked up the carafe and filled each mug to an inch from the rim with coffee.

"I picked up some milk and sugar last night at the store," he said over his shoulder. "Would you like both?"

"Please."

"You like it dark or light?"

"Light and heavy on the sugar."

He smiled. "You got it."

Once he'd doctored one mug with milk and a heaping spoonful of sugar, he cradled the mug in his big hand and offered it to her.

She took it from him, trying to ignore the way his warm fingers brushed against hers, then took a sip and made a sound of appreciation. "It's perfect. Thank you."

"You're welcome." He leaned against the counter and brought his own mug to his lips, eyeing her expectantly over the rim as he sipped.

"I..." She drank another quick swig of coffee and winced as the hot liquid scorched her throat on the way down. "I'd like to apologize for my behavior last night. I should've been more receptive with Cody's request to go shopping with you, and I should've encouraged their interest in you rather than trying to discourage it. That is, after all, the reason I invited you here."

He lowered his mug, and her gaze was drawn to the strong column of his throat as he swallowed.

"A—and I'm sorry for my outburst last night," she added. "I didn't mean to dump my baggage on you like that. Especially when we already have enough to carry what with figuring out how Cody and Devin's future will look."

Brow creasing, he looked down, tapped his blunt fingertips against his mug then met her eyes again. "I'm glad you told me. I expected my return to be difficult for you, but I didn't realize just how difficult. I can't imagine how painful this must be for you."

It didn't sound like a question, but she answered him honestly anyway.

"Yeah. It's not exactly easy." She wrapped both of her palms around her mug, attempting to still the tremor running through them. "Though I don't think this situation is any easier for you, either, especially after I compared your behavior with my mother's—which I shouldn't have, by the way. You took great care to protect Cody and Devin and I shouldn't have made things so personal last night."

"But this is personal," he said quietly. "It's very personal for both of us, isn't it?"

She stared at her mug, watched two small bubbles float around the creamy brown surface of the liquid, then nodded.

"I'm glad you told me," he said. "And there's no need to apologize."

Acutely aware of his gaze, she drank another sip of coffee and cringed as heat suffused her face.

"Jessie?"

She licked her lips, the sweet taste hitting her tongue, then forced herself to meet his eyes.

"I'm in this for the long haul and have no intention of leaving my sons again. And I know how hard that is for you to believe." He set his mug on the counter and moved closer, dipping his blond head to level his gaze with hers. "But I also know—all legalities aside—that you are, always have been, and always will be, their mother. I know how much Cody and Devin love you," he continued, "and how much I..."

Breath catching, she parted her lips and inhaled, the spicy scent of his aftershave rushing in, filling her senses. His broad chest was close enough that his warmth drifted over to her, bringing to mind the remembered feel of his solid strength beneath her forehead last night, how comforting and protective his presence had felt.

She studied his expression as his eyes roved over her face. "How much you what?"

"How much I care about you as well."

Her hands tightened around her mug, the hot ceramic cup almost burning her palms as a bittersweet sensation stirred in her middle. "You c-care about me?"

"Yeah." His eyes met hers again, darkening as a slow smile lifted the corners of his mouth. "Even though you weren't aware of it, you've been a part of my life for seven years. I've admired you from afar. Thought about you every day, just as I have my sons. I've never forgotten what you did for my sons that night—or for me. And I've thanked God every day for you answering the door. For offering compassion instead of turning me away and for providing me the opportunity now to get to know my sons again. Your kindness and generosity are part of what prompted me to change, to wish I could be as good a person as you."

That bittersweet feeling vanished. She stared down at her coffee again. "Oh."

He appreciated her as a good person...but

not as a woman. Her stomach sank. Perhaps her attraction to him was one-sided. Maybe she didn't stir the same emotions in him that he evoked in her?

His hands curved around hers, his callused palms settling over the backs of her hands, coaxing her eyes back up to meet his. "I would never—ever—even think of taking Cody and Devin out of your life. No matter how we end up working this out, you will always be their mother, and you will always be entitled to that role in their lives. I hope I can at least put that fear to rest."

She held his gaze for a moment, the sincerity in his words and expression unmistakable... but not exactly what she wanted to hear. "You might not take them out of my life but you'd still consider taking them out of my home, wouldn't you?"

His earnest expression fell, and he slowly removed his hands from hers. "I won't lie to you, Jessie. There's nothing I want more than to have my sons with me again on a permanent basis. So yes. For me, the ideal outcome of this situation would be to resume my role as their father and take my sons home to my family in Pine Creek—for good."

Jessie walked to the kitchen counter, set her mug down beside Holt's and dragged a hand through her hair. "And, for me, the ideal outcome would be adopting Cody and Devin and keeping them here at Hummingbird Haven with me. Which leaves us at an impasse." She turned back to face him. "Still."

Holt turned his head and looked out the kitchen window, a pensive expression on his face. "But at least we know where we stand and it's up to us to carve a new path out of this standstill we've reached." He refocused on her, his eyes locking with hers. "I hope what I've shared with you will help you understand my intentions better."

Oh, sure. She nodded slowly, studying his thick rumpled hair, the light stubble lining his jaw and the strong curves of his brawny form. He saw her as some self-sacrificing, matronly figure of the past whose high standards and dedication to his sons had cemented an obligation in his mind to do right by her. To work with her in an honest and forthright manner for the boys' sake. *Our boys*, as he'd referenced Cody and Devin last night.

Sincerity had been ingrained in every inch of his being as he'd shared his thoughts with her, and every bit of it sounded great—exactly the type of candid, respectful approach that would be expected from a man who claimed he'd changed. So why did his every word leave her feeling deflated and...empty?

She stole one last moment, admiring the handsome features of his face, as she summoned her most professional tone, the meaning of his words that left her feeling hollow fully sinking in. "Yes," she said. "Everything you do will be done in the best interest of your sons. Solely for Cody and Devin's sake."

It HAD TO be the company but Holt had never tasted pancakes as scrumptious as the ones Cody and Devin plopped on his plate at the kitchen table in Zoe's cabin—even after Cody submerged them in two inches of syrup.

"Mmm." Holt forked another saturated hunk into his mouth, his eyes watering when 100 percent pure maple sugar coated his sensitive teeth, but he smiled anyway, the sweetness of the moment shooting straight to his heart. "These are the best pancakes I've ever had in my life."

Cody, now seated in a chair beside Holt at the table, beamed. "We made 'em special. Ms.

Zoe let me add cinnamon to the batter even though Devin didn't want it."

"You're s'posed to use cinnamon at Thanksgiving," Devin grumbled. He sat on the other side of Cody and eyed his empty plate with disdain. "That's when Jessie always uses it."

"So?" Cody pointed at Devin's empty plate. "You ate 'em all so you must've liked them."

Devin shrugged. "Yeah, I guess."

Holt ate the last bite of his pancake and patted his middle. "That was some good eating, boys." He glanced at Miles, who sat at the other end of the table, still nibbling on his last pancake. "What about you, Miles? Did you enjoy the pancakes?"

Miles glanced up, meeting Holt's eyes for a moment, then quickly looked back down and nodded.

Well, that was an improvement at least.

After his conversation with Jessie, he'd walked with her along one of the trails to Zoe's cabin. It had been a nice, but quiet, stroll as Jessie had responded to his few polite attempts at chitchat with mute nods and smiles. Eventually, he'd fallen silent, too, lulled into the same type of contemplative reflection Jessie seemed to have undertaken and had focused instead on the rays of the rising sun as they spilled slowly through the treetops and dappled the dirt trail with patches of light and shadow.

When they'd reached Zoe's cabin, Zoe, Cody and Devin had welcomed them in with big smiles and excited fanfare but Miles, whom Holt assumed lived with Zoe, had sat silently at the kitchen table, his wide eyes following each of Holt's movements. Miles had ignored Holt's greeting and hadn't spoken throughout breakfast, so Holt decided to count the nod as progress.

"I know I enjoyed them." Zoe, standing at the kitchen sink, loading dirty dishes into the dishwasher, groaned good-naturedly as she rubbed her belly. "The bacon, too. I ate enough to hibernate through the winter. But, boy, was it tasty." Wincing, she set the dirty plate she held back into the sink and picked at her teeth. "And I'll probably have a cavity by morning."

Holt laughed, stood and started stacking the dirty dishes left at the table. "I know what you mean. I take it y'all stockpile syrup somewhere on the premises?"

Zoe grinned. "Better. Our closest—well, pretty much only—neighbor, Brent Cason, makes his own. He doesn't usually sell it, but

I talked him into making a few bottles for us every year."

Jessie, sipping coffee as she stood by the kitchen table, raised her brows at Zoe. "Bribed him, you mean?"

Zoe spread her hands with an innocent expression. "All I did was make him an offer he couldn't refuse."

"Yeah…okay," Jessie said. "You best give Brent a wide berth. He's not keen on visitors."

Zoe's grin dimmed. "He's not keen on much of anything as far as I can tell."

There was something in her voice—a hint of longing and disappointment. The same despondent tone that had laced Jessie's words earlier in Holt's cabin. He recognized it immediately.

Holt glanced at Jessie, who'd turned her attention to the kitchen window, silently gazing out at the scenic beauty of the mountain range. Something had shifted between them.

She'd surprised him with her visit this morning and the small leap of eager excitement within him at the sight of her standing at his door hadn't escaped his notice. Now aware of her past, he'd grown more appreciative of her allowing him into Cody and Devin's lives. She could've so easily turned him away, but she'd decided to continue, to try to let him in even when it was painful for her.

He respected her all the more for it…and he hoped that the slight tinge of disappointment in her tone when she'd acknowledged he was here solely for the boys might have been a reflection of her softening toward him. That maybe, after allowing herself to lean on him last night, she'd begun to feel the same stirring of affection for him. Maybe she wasn't quite as unaffected by him as a man as he'd assumed. And maybe, given time, she'd grow to trust him as a man and not just as Cody and Devin's father.

He pulled his gaze away from her. That wasn't the reason he was here, he reminded himself firmly. He was here for Cody and Devin—not to explore his attraction to Jessie, no matter how honorable his intentions might be.

"Here, let me get that for you." Holt joined Zoe at the sink and started loading the dirty plates into the sink. "You and the boys worked so hard cooking breakfast, the least I can do is take care of the dirty dishes. And maybe I could return the favor and cook a meal for you, Jessie and the boys one day?"

Zoe's grin returned, complete with a look of impressed admiration. "Oh, I think I'm gonna like having you around." She glanced at Jessie as she strolled around him, nodding. "Yep. I could definitely get used to this kind of help."

Holt chuckled. Zoe's good mood and easy-going nature were infectious. "That's good to hear." He glanced at Cody, Devin and Miles, who still sat at the kitchen table, eyeing him with curiosity. "Lesson number one on being a gentleman, boys. Never leave a lady in the kitchen alone with dirty dishes. It doesn't matter who cooks. If you eat, you clean."

The trio nodded solemnly.

"Wanna give me a hand?" Holt asked.

Cody sprang to his feet and Devin followed his brother, joining Holt at the sink. Miles walked over to Zoe's side and watched from afar.

"How many lessons does it take to be a gentleman?" Cody asked, grabbing a handful of dirty forks and loading them into the dishwasher.

"As many as it takes," Holt said.

Devin picked up the dirty plate Zoe had placed in the sink. He looked up at Holt, a cautious look in his eyes. "Will you teach us some of them? Or all of them?"

Holt stared down at Devin, his blond hair,

tanned cheeks and stubborn chin so like his own when he was a boy. But the look in Devin's hazel eyes—that untrusting wariness—Holt had put that there seven years ago.

Throat closing, Holt reached out and ruffled Devin's hair gently. Then, glancing at Jessie, who watched him with the same expression, he said, "Jessie and I will teach you all of them together, if that's okay with you?"

Devin considered this, watching warily as Holt withdrew his hand and lowered it to his side. "Yeah," he said, glancing at Cody. "I guess that'd be okay."

Cody squealed. "When's lesson two?"

"Right now," Jessie said, striding over. "It's time to load up in Zoe's van, and gentlemen are sometimes early but never late. Finish up with the dishes then grab your bookbags."

Ten minutes later Holt stood at the end of the driveway with Jessie, Cody and Devin standing between them as Zoe warmed the engine of Hummingbird Haven's colorful van.

Cody hitched his bookbag higher on his back and smiled up at Holt. "When will lesson three be? This afternoon after school? Are you gonna have snack time with us again? Help us with our homework? Can we go shopping with you again?"

Holt laughed as he held up a hand. "Hold up, there. There's no need to rush through anything. And yes, I'll have snack time with y'all again after school if that's okay with Jessie?"

She smoothed her hand through Devin's hair, straightening a few strands Holt had ruffled earlier. "Of course. Mr. Holt will be pitching in all over while he's here. And his first order of business is——"

"To fix the back deck at Creek Cabin." Holt tugged the to-do list from his back pocket and scanned the tasks Jessie had written. "I'll need to pick up decking boards and I thought I'd apply some stain, if that works for you? I think a dark stain would help it blend in with the surrounding woodland better and give it a more aesthetic appeal. I could pick up supplies this morning and start on the deck this afternoon."

"Sounds good," Jessie said. "I have an account with the hardware store in town where Peggy Ann works. I'll call the manager and let him know you're coming."

"Can I help you fix the deck?" Cody asked, tugging Holt's wrist. "I can carry a deck board for you."

Holt smiled. "Thank you. I'd love the help."

Zoe, seated in the driver's seat of the van, leaned out the open window and motioned at Cody and Devin. "Come on, guys, everyone's loaded up but you and it's time to go."

"For now," Holt told Cody, "I think it's best you board the van like Zoe asked and focus on your schoolwork. Lesson number three," he said, holding up three fingers. "A gentleman is dedicated to doing his best work—no matter the task at hand."

Smiling wide, Cody skipped over, threw his arms around Holt's waist and squeezed. "I will, Mr. Holt. I promise."

Breath catching, Holt blinked against the tears pricking at the backs of his eyes and hugged Cody back, the realization of his son being in his arms for the first time in seven years overwhelming him, even though Cody's hug was meant for a stranger—not his father.

The moment ended too soon.

"Bye, Mr. Holt!" Cody had already sprung away and bolted up into the backseat of the van, following Devin, who'd already boarded.

"Bye, guys!" Jessie called, waving. "Have a great day at school."

Cody, Devin and Miles waved back from the windows of the van as Zoe drove away.

Holt frowned. "Peggy Ann's girls don't ride with Zoe to school?"

Jessie remained silent for a moment. "They usually do. But Peggy Ann decided to drive them to school herself this morning on the way to the hardware store." She fidgeted, picking at her fingernails. "I think she wanted some alone time with them. Or maybe just—"

"There's no need to explain," Holt said. "I picked up on the fact that meeting me last night must've been unexpected and possibly unwelcome for her and her daughters."

Her hand touched his forearm, her fingers laying gently against his skin. "It's not you, Holt. It's the idea of a stranger—a man—she doesn't know being so close. She just came out of an abusive relationship. She has doubts."

Holt moved, took her hand in his, cradling her graceful fingers gently as he met her eyes, the cautious uncertainty in her gaze wounding him as deeply as Devin's had. "I know," he whispered. "We all do."

CHAPTER TEN

"WHAT DO YOU mean they don't know who you are?"

Holt frowned at the recrimination in Liam's tone, palmed the steering wheel of his truck and turned, guiding the vehicle into the parking lot of Bennett & Sons Hardware. After parking, he unhooked his cell phone from the dashboard mount and sighed.

"What I mean," Holt said, "is that neither Cody nor Devin—nor any of the rest of the residents—know I'm their father. Only Jessie and her partner, Zoe, know who I am and why I'm really there."

The voice on the other end of the line was silent for a moment, then, "And you signed up for this? You got to be kidding me, Holt."

Liam was not happy.

"Look," Holt said, cutting the truck's engine.

"The reason Jessie suggested we do things this way was—"

"To take advantage of the situation—*and you*." A frustrated growl crossed the line. "Don't you see what she's doing? She's keeping you boxed in a corner right under her nose and throwing you a scrap now and then to keep you content long enough to come up with a reason to get rid of you. She has no intention of letting you close to your s—"

"Cody hugged me this morning." The words caught in Holt's throat, emotion overwhelming him again. Blinking hard, he stared out the windshield at the entrance of the hardware store, watching as an elderly couple, holding hands, strolled inside. "Granted, he didn't know he was hugging *me* instead of a stranger, but he actually hugged me. And all I could think about was how good it felt to have my son in my arms again. How I should never have let them go to begin with and how much I have to make up for."

"Holt—"

"No." Holt shifted in his seat, sitting taller. "Jessie didn't coerce me into agreeing to anything. I knew what I was getting into. I trust Jessie. She's been a great mom to my sons and more than accommodating to me, given the circumstances."

"Okay," Liam said quietly. "Am I allowed to ask what these circumstances are?"

"The shelter she runs isn't just for abandoned children," Holt said. "It's for abused women, too. From what I've witnessed and heard, Jessie's worked hard for a long time to make Hummingbird Haven a safe place for these women and children, and she has every right to protect them—even from me. I'm abiding by her wishes for now."

Liam grew quiet again. "Is there something else going on here?" His tone altered. Turned hesitant. "Something more going on between you and Jessie you wanna tell me about?"

Holt stilled, a slight smile tugging at his mouth. "You've never been one to beat around the bush, have you?"

His deep chuckle sounded in Holt's ear. "You know me well."

"As well as I hope you know me now," Holt said, his smile fading as he thought of Jessie. How loving and protective she was of his sons… and how vulnerable she was in all of this. "In the past, I never shied away from being attracted to a woman, but things are different now. What

I feel for Jessie is different. Going into this, I knew I admired her, that I was grateful to her for all she did for me and Cody and Devin, and I never expected to feel something more than that. But I do—more and more every day. Thing is, there couldn't be a worse time or place to feel what I'm feeling, and I don't want anything to jeopardize what might be my only chance to be a part of Cody and Devin's lives."

Liam was quiet for a moment then asked, "Have you spoken to her about how you're feeling?"

"No." Holt shook his head, his gut sinking at the memory of the wary look in her eyes when they'd spoken last night. "She's dealing with as much as—if not more than—I am right now and, besides, I can't even put a name yet to what I'm feeling." He shook his head again, dismissing the notion. "No. It's better to keep things as they are for now. To just focus on Cody and Devin and their future to the exclusion of everything else."

Silence lingered across the line, then Liam said, "Okay. I told you I'd support you and that's what I'll do. I'm just a call away if you need to talk. And, Holt?"

"Yeah?"

"Mom asked if she'll be able to see the boys sometime soon. And you. She misses you." His tone softened. "She knows you've changed—she has no doubts about that—but she lost so many years with you when you left with Dad that she gets a bit antsy when she doesn't see you occasionally."

Holt closed his eyes and rubbed his eyelids. "I know. I'm working on coming home and bringing the boys for a visit, but it may take a while. Just...would you please ask her to be patient and trust me?" He paused. "And you, too, Liam?"

He answered without hesitation. "You got it, brother."

Holt said goodbye and ended the call, put his cell phone in his pocket and entered the hardware store. As expected, Peggy Ann stood by a cash register behind a large counter in the center of the store.

"Good morning, Peggy Ann." Holt approached the counter slowly, stopped in front of Peggy Ann and placed his hands flat on the counter. "I spoke with Jessie this morning about needing to pick up deck boards and stain to repair the deck at Creek Cabin. She said she was going to call the manager and let him know I'd be swinging by to pick up supplies."

She smiled, though it seemed strained, and nodded. "Yes. She called and Mr. Bancroft, our manager, and one of our other employees are rounding up what you need." She hesitated, her gaze skittering away from his. "I'm sorry about the wait. I was hoping they'd have it ready to load by the time you made it here."

"It's okay," he said gently, trying his best to put her at ease in his presence. "There's no rush at all. As a matter of fact, I was hoping to take care of something else while I was in town. Would it be okay if I left and came back in about an hour or so?"

Peggy Ann's polite smile returned, her shoulders seeming to sag with relief. "Of course. If you'd like to leave your number, I could text you when everything's ready."

Holt smiled back. "That'd be great. Thank you."

She handed him a notepad and pen and as he wrote his cell number down, he felt her intense gaze on him. He slid the pad back to her.

"When you come back," she said, gesturing toward the back of the store, "just pull around to the loading dock and Mr. Bancroft will have someone load everything up for you."

"Thank you, Peggy Ann. I really appreciate it." He headed for the exit.

"Mr...er, Holt?"

He stopped, glancing over his shoulder.

Peggy Ann stared back at him. Her mouth opened and closed twice before she said, "I'd like to welcome you to Hummingbird Haven. I...uh, I don't think I told you that yesterday when we met."

Holt nodded. "That's okay," he said gently. "And thank you for that."

"I know Jessie and Zoe are grateful to have your help around the place." Some of the tension left her expression and she smiled once more before returning her attention to a stack of invoices and a laptop that sat next to the cash register.

Holt's smile grew, his chest lifting just a bit with a newfound sense of pride at the thought of being helpful. Of easing someone else's burdens. Of contributing to a valuable cause, the likes of which he'd never engaged with before.

He was still smiling as he returned to his truck, cranked the engine and drove away.

Fifteen minutes later Holt exited an elevator and walked onto the top floor of Hope Springs Hospital where he and Jessie had visited the Boarder Baby Unit days earlier.

"You're back." Surprise lit Nurse Sharon's eyes as she sat behind the welcome desk.

Holt nodded. He hadn't expected to turn off the main road into town and park in the hospital lot, but that feeling of pride he'd felt minutes earlier in the hardware store still lingered, and when he'd spotted the hospital, he'd thought of Ava, alone in her nursery crib, and he'd acted automatically, parking his truck and going inside.

"Jessie isn't with me today." He walked up to the welcome desk and smiled. "I'm running an errand in town and have some time to kill, so I thought I'd check and see if it's okay if I visit Ava on my own."

Sharon tilted her head, her gaze roving over him for a moment, then lifted her shoulders. "Well, I don't see why not. You were cleared with a background check for your original visit, and it would just take one more signature to put you on the list as an official volunteer." A perplexed expression crossed her face. "Is that what you're asking? If you can volunteer?"

"Yes, please." Holt withdrew his wallet from his back pocket and produced his license. "I have my ID, too, in case you needed it again."

Nodding, Sharon accepted his driver's license and smiled. "Thanks. I'll just grab the paperwork."

Five minutes later Holt's name had been officially added to the volunteer list. He was, as he had requested, assigned to Ava.

Sharon glanced at her watch. "It's almost time for her next feeding. Would you like to take up where you left off the other day?"

"That sounds good. Thank you."

Holt followed Sharon down the familiar hallway and into Ava's room. The room was the same as before, cheerfully decorated and peaceful. Small babbling sounds emerged from the crib.

"She's been a hungry girl the past day or two." Sharon peeked into the crib and smiled. "Haven't you, beautiful?"

Holt joined Sharon and leaned in, smiling as Ava's big blue eyes found him and widened as she studied his face. "How long does it take for a baby her age to recognize someone?"

"Oh, it depends. Babies her age tend to recognize individuals they spend a fair amount of time with. Feedings, diaper changes, cuddle sessions, they all add up over time."

He leaned closer, smiling as he returned Ava's stare. "So if I were to come every day and feed Ava at my lunch break and sit with her every evening, she'd begin to recognize me?"

Sharon didn't answer. She shifted beside him, her hand curling around the crib rail near where his own hand lay. "May I ask what motivated you to come here today? On your own, I mean. Without Jessie."

Holt straightened and faced her, hoping his sincerity showed in his expression. "I've made mistakes in my past. I assume Jessie has filled you in on some of the details of our current arrangement?"

"A bit," Sharon said softly. "But she didn't mention you'd be coming by to check on Ava. Is that why you're here? Because Jessie asked you to come?"

Holt shook his head. "No. This was my decision. I'd like to be the best version of the man I think I should be—the man I hope I already am. And I want to make a difference. I want to do some good to make up for the mistakes I've made. The kind I'll never be able to fully amend with my own sons. I don't want Ava to feel alone like my sons did. I want her to know that someone's thinking of her, that someone cares about her."

Sharon smiled, then gestured toward the rocking chair next to the crib. "Have a seat. I'll get Ava's bottle."

Holt did as she directed, glancing up at her as she reentered the room, a bottle in one hand and a metal folding chair clutched in the other.

"Bottle's warm and I brought a burping cloth," she said, placing them in his hands. "You remember how this goes?"

Nodding, Holt tossed the burping cloth over his shoulder, positioned the crook of his arm and held the bottle ready in his right hand.

Sharon lifted Ava from her crib and placed her gently in his arms. Ava squirmed, her face scrunching up, as Holt settled her into a more comfortable position within his arms.

"Hi, beautiful," he whispered, tilting the bottle and bringing the nipple close to her rosebud mouth. "You hungry?"

Eyes wide, Ava latched on hard, drawing deeply from the bottle, her hungry sighs breaking the silence in the room as Sharon sat in the folding chair opposite him.

"It seems easier this time, huh?" Sharon asked

quietly, crossing her ankles and easing back into her chair.

Holt smiled, keeping a careful grip on the bottle, and his muscles relaxed under Ava's delicate head and neck. "Yeah, a bit."

Holt stilled, a shaft of pain cutting deep into his chest as he stared down at Ava and thought of Jessie as a vulnerable infant, alone in the cold, crying as someone who should've loved and protected her walked away.

Tears pricked at the backs of his eyes. He blinked hard then stared down at baby Ava. No wonder Jessie's disdain—and distrust—for him ran so deep. He'd abandoned Cody and Devin just as Jessie's parents had abandoned her.

"What will happen to Ava?" he asked softly.

Sharon issued a sad smile. "Well, a search is being conducted for her mother but the authorities who are investigating her case haven't discovered her yet. Neither Ava's father nor any other relatives have come forward, either. If nothing changes, she'll be placed in foster care until she's either adopted or ages out at eighteen."

"But..." Holt glanced at Ava, who still pulled steadily from the bottle. "Isn't it almost a guarantee that she'll be adopted? I was under the impression that infants were usually adopted more easily than older children."

"They are," Sharon said. "But in cases like Ava's, well…the circumstances surrounding a child's abandonment will sometimes dissuade a potential adoptive parent from following through. Sometimes, there are fears—mostly unfounded—that there may be some psychological or emotional damage down the road due to the nature of the abandonment. Or there are other fears such as the mother having an alcohol or drug addiction and the effects passing on to the fetus."

I spent my entire life in foster care. I've never had a family—not a real one.

Holt stilled, pain engulfing him as he recalled Jessie's words from last night and thought of her as a child, alone, with no family. No child should ever feel as though they weren't valuable or loved.

Sharon looked at Ava, her eyes glistening. "That's why Jessie works so hard to keep Hummingbird Haven and—" she gestured toward their surroundings "—this Boarder Baby Unit an integral part of our community. She does everything she can to remove the stigma surrounding the babies we care for as well as the women she shelters on her property. She believes everyone's entitled to a fair shot and fresh start in life no matter where they began."

"Everyone?" Holt considered this, wondering if Jessie's support might extend to someone like him—a man who'd left his sons just as Jessie's mom had left her. A man who'd caused many of his own unfortunate circumstances. Then he asked, "Even someone like me?"

Ava's movements in Holt's arms had slowed. Her eyes had grown heavy, and her thick lashes lowered to her rosy cheeks as her mouth slackened, releasing the bottle.

Holt set the bottle to the side, carefully lifted Ava to his shoulder and rubbed her back gently, a brief grin crossing his lips as a small burp sounded near his ear.

Sharon smiled as she studied him, watching his hand rub slow circles over Ava's back. "Given time and opportunity? Yes. I believe so."

JESSIE, KNEELING ON the back deck of Creek Cabin, turned a pry bar over in her hands and trailed her fingers along the metal, recalling the gentle touch of Holt's hand cradling hers hours earlier as she'd shared that Peggy Ann had doubts.

We all do, he'd said, acknowledging he was aware of the struggle she'd undertaken inviting him into Cody and Devin's lives and taking a chance on trusting him. He'd been so patient and compassionate this morning, not for one moment making her feel embarrassed or uncomfortable about sharing her pain over her mother's abandonment or fears of his return into Cody and Devin's lives.

Holt had been every bit the gentleman he was teaching Cody, Devin and Miles to be.

She tapped her fingernail against the pry bar and closed her eyes as a swift spring breeze rippled through the trees and over the creek rushing alongside the deck, the *whoosh* of fresh, cool afternoon air sweeping over her.

It was silly—and surprising, really—that she'd begun fixating on Holt's voice, his words, his brief tender touches, instead of what was most important—Cody and Devin. Ever since Holt had left Hummingbird Haven and driven his truck out of the driveway and up the winding mountain road out of sight to pick up supplies for the deck repairs, she'd thought of little else but him.

Holt—and his intentions—had been on her mind as she'd called the hardware store and asked the manager to charge the supplies to her bill. She'd thought of Holt as she'd washed and dried a load of Cody and Devin's laundry, her fingers stilling on their small shirts when she'd folded them as her mind had drifted off again. And when the boys had returned from school an hour ago, hopped off the van, scarfed down their snacks and followed Holt eagerly to the Creek Cabin to begin repairs, she'd caught herself recalling his words from early that morning, the same hollow gaping in her stomach as she reminded herself why Holt had changed from the man he was and returned in the first place.

Solely for Cody and Devin's sakes.

"Lesson number four of being a gentleman." Holt, crouching next to her on the deck, motioned toward Cody, Devin and Miles, who stood by the back door of Creek Cabin. "You should always offer a helping hand to someone when they're working on a project and accept their wishes if they decline the help and prefer to complete the task on their own." His left biceps, bare below the short sleeve of his T-shirt, brushed her arm as he turned to the side to face the boys. "It'd be great if one of you offered Jessie some help with removing the rotten deck boards."

Cody's voice rang out. "But I want to help you with the joyces."

Jessie grinned, the mistake a welcome distraction from Holt's presence. "You mean joists," she said, scooting an inch away from Holt, just enough to evade the brush of his smooth muscle against her upper arm. She looked up at Cody. "You want to help Mr. Holt repair the joists."

"It's called sistering," Devin said, lifting his chin at Holt. "Isn't that what you said?"

Holt nodded, a gleam of pride lighting his eyes. "That's exactly right, Devin." He tilted his head and whispered to Jessie, "He has a good head on his shoulders, yeah?"

Jessie nodded. "He's very advanced for his age. Gifted, they think. Cody is much more extroverted and very inquisitive."

"Sistering?" Cody repeated, scrunching his nose as his eyes widened. "Hey. You got a sister, Mr. Holt?"

Holt laughed. "No, I don't."

"What about a brother?" Cody asked.

"I've got one of those," Holt said.

"Is he younger or older than you?" Cody asked.

"Older."

"How much older?"

Holt grinned. "One minute."

"One minute?" Cody tilted his head and frowned then... "Wait!" Excitement shined in his eyes. "You got a twin? Like me and Devin?"

Jessie looked at Holt, his gaze meeting hers. He shifted his weight from one foot to the other as she slowly shook her head, then returned his attention to Cody.

"Yeah." His gaze settled on Devin, who stared back at him. "I have a twin brother."

"A twin?" Devin repeated.

Oh no. Jessie set the pry bar down and eased back on her haunches. She could almost hear the wheels turning in Devin's advanced young mind.

Devin frowned. "He has blond hair, too?"

"Yes," Holt said.

Devin's eyes narrowed. "You look the same? Identical, like me and Cody?"

Holt nodded.

"Devin." Jessie scrambled to her feet and jogged to Devin's side, carefully sidestepping two rotten deck boards. "I could really use your help. How about you and I grab a plastic bag from the kitchen?" She glanced at Holt. "I assume there are still a couple in one of the kitchen drawers?" At Holt's nod, she placed her hands on Devin's shoulders and steered him through the back door of the cabin. "And you can sit with me while I remove the rotten deck boards and you can collect the old nails and screws for me. That way none of them will end up on the deck for someone's bare feet to step on in the summer."

Devin's frown deepened but he complied, allowing her to lead him through the cabin and into the kitchen.

"Now," she said as she opened a drawer by the sink, "where do I remember seeing those plastic bags?"

"Jessie?"

She closed the drawer and opened another. "Hmm?"

"He has a twin."

No bags here, either. She shoved the drawer shut, walked across the kitchen and opened another, turning her back to Devin. "Yep, he does."

"And he has blond hair."

She sifted through another drawer.

"Like me and Cod—"

"Found one!" Jessie snatched up a clear plastic bag, spun back to Devin and waved it high in the air. "This will work perfectly. All you need to do is drop the nails and screws in the bag when I hand them to you and make sure none of them end up on the deck."

Devin, silent, continued staring at her.

Jessie sighed. "Yes." She braced her hands behind her on the kitchen counter. "Mr. Holt has blond hair and is a twin. Like you and Cody."

She waited for what she knew would come next: Devin's piercing questions regarding Holt's identity, and any possible relation to him and Cody. How in the world was she going to answer him?

But Devin, thankfully, didn't pursue it. Instead, he walked across the kitchen, took the plastic bag from her and headed for the back exit of the cabin.

Jessie followed a few steps behind and lingered in the doorway as Devin carefully walked over to where she'd worked previously, sat down and watched Holt explain to Cody and Miles which tools to hand him as he worked to repair joists on the opposite side of the deck.

Devin didn't speak; he simply studied Holt, watching his face, studying his movements, his thoughtful expression deepening as he stared.

"I'll need to put some scaffolding in place before we can start." Holt stood from his kneeling position in front of the boys and propped his hands on his hips. "It'll take a while to get this done, boys. I can definitely use your help, but you sure you want to sacrifice your free time in the afternoons working on this?"

Cody beamed. "Yes!"

Miles looked at Cody and Jessie, then tilted his head back and looked at Holt, saying quietly, "Yes, please."

Slowly, Holt knelt again and held out his hand. "Thank you, Miles," he said. "Offering your help is truly a gentlemanly thing to do."

Miles blushed, his lips tipping up at the corners, and shook Holt's hand. "You're welcome."

A slow smile spread across Jessie's face as Miles drew his shoulders back and lifted his chin, the brief attention from Holt seeming to bolster his confidence. It was amazing, really, how such a small bit of personal attention from this big, impressive man could warm Miles's heart…and her own as well.

She stiffened, her fingertips touching the base of her throat.

"…in town. Jessie?" Holt was facing her now, concern creasing his brow, as the boys pilfered through a toolbox resting on the deck nearby.

"Did you hear me? I said I'm going to work on the deck during the day and in the afternoons with the boys, but I was wondering if it's okay if I spend my lunch break in town? And the evenings, too? After the boys and I finish up for the day?"

"O-of course." She forced a smile, trying— and failing—to still the questions popping up in her own mind. "Your free time is your own. You're welcome to do with it what you'd like."

But where would he spend all that time? And with whom?

CHAPTER ELEVEN

Two weeks later Holt sat on his backside in dirt, laughing as Cody, Miles and Devin struggled to yank a vine from one of the thick legs of the wooden benches surrounding the fire pit outside Creek Cabin.

"It might help if y'all pulled in the same direction," he said, leaning back onto his hands. "You know, line your hands up on the vine, decide which direction to pull then give it the ol' heave-ho."

Devin, who'd served as the leader on this particular project for the past ten minutes, released the vine and stepped back. "All right," he said, pointing at Miles first, then Cody. "Miles, you take the bottom hold because you're the strongest."

"No, he's not," Cody said. "I'm strong, too."

Devin heaved out a heavy breath. "I'm not

saying you're not strong, Cody. I'm just saying Miles is the strongest out of all of us."

A wide smile appeared on Miles's face and his chest puffed out just a bit with pride, prompting a deeper chuckle from Holt.

Miles assumed the position Devin directed and after Miles had wrapped his small hands around the lowest part of the vine, Cody moved in next, grabbed the vine just above Miles's hands and waited for Devin to join them.

"Now, when I give the signal," Holt said, "I want all of you to yank as hard as you can, okay?"

The trio shouted *yes, sir* almost in unison and once Devin fastened his hands securely around the vine and braced his legs, Holt gave the command.

"Pull!"

In unison, the boys yanked hard on the tightly coiled vine, pulling backward in one direction. It gave way, snapping at the base, unraveled almost instantly from the bench's leg and sprang free, leaving the boys stumbling backward onto their backsides in a heap. Legs and arms entwined, the boys laughed and rolled apart, tears of laughter mixing with dirt as they scrambled to their feet.

Cody, breathing hard, brushed the dirt off his palms, jogged over and grabbed Holt's hand. "That was the last one, Mr. Holt. Come try out the bench with me."

Holt shoved to his feet and let Cody lead him over to the bench, then sat on the smooth wooden seat.

Cody plopped down beside him and dragged the back of his hand across his sweaty forehead. "Whew! That was the toughest one, Mr. Holt."

He laughed again. It had been. For the past two hours, he and the boys had spent their Saturday morning clearing deadfall and dead leaves—the last of winter's debris—from the small clearing beside Creek Cabin. They'd tackled the wooden benches next, unwinding, twisting and pulling tangled clumps of vines from all three benches, and clearing broken tree limbs from the fire circle itself, exposing a large span of dirt circled by large stones of various colors.

The boys had worked hard during what should've been their free time this morning just as they had every afternoon after school for the past two weeks. With their help, he and Jessie had managed to replace all of the rotten deck boards on Creek Cabin's back deck and give it a beautiful dark stain. They'd also swept off the porch and cleaned the accompanying Adirondack chairs as well as spruced up the landscaping by trimming the hedges surrounding the cabin and planting tiny blue petunia plants along the front porch. And now the fire pit was ready, save for wiping the winter mold and grime from the benches.

"They were all tough." Devin stood, held out a hand and helped Miles to his feet. "We might not have gotten that one loose if Miles hadn't helped us."

Miles, grinning, skipped over to the bench and sat on the other side of Cody. "Wouldn't none of us got it down without Mr. Holt."

"Thank you, Miles," Holt said. "You're turning out to be a true gentleman in every way."

And it was true. As they'd worked over the past couple of weeks, Miles had gained a bit more confidence each day, every task lifting his head a bit more and putting a proud look in his eyes. He'd grown more comfortable in Holt's presence, asking to help with each task almost as eagerly as Cody.

"And me, too?" Cody asked. "I'm turning out to be a gentleman, too, ain't I?"

Holt smiled wide and ruffled Cody's hair,

saying softly, "Yes, you are. You're a gentleman in every way."

And he couldn't be prouder. Cody and Devin, both, had not only worked hard and followed direction well but had grown as comfortable with him as Miles had—Cody even more so.

It felt so good to have his sons in his life again, though... Holt's smile slipped. He wished it were on a permanent basis and that Cody and Devin knew who he really was and what he wanted to be to them. He couldn't imagine how wonderful it'd feel to hear them call him Dad. Right now, even the thought itself felt foreign, but with hard work, dedication and careful consideration of everyone's feelings, he truly thought it could become a reality. And despite his best efforts to the contrary, he couldn't help but feel resentful of having to keep his identity secret.

Two small hands nudged his knees apart as Devin pushed his way in between Holt's legs and leaned close to his face.

Holt stilled as Devin's eyes, the same shade of hazel as his own, perused his face. "What is it, Devin?"

Devin's gaze returned to Holt's then strayed

again, moving in tandem with his hand to Holt's hair where it stilled. "Can I?"

Unsure what he wanted but equally unwilling to refuse any request as Devin rarely made them, Holt nodded.

Devin slowly sifted his fingers through the strands of Holt's hair. Devin's hand lowered, his fingertips tracing Holt's brow, straight nose then chin, his thumb and forefinger settling on either side of his jaw. His hand settled there, Devin's gaze moving slowly between Holt's face and Cody's as they sat beside each other on the bench, his nails lightly scratching the stubble lining Holt's jaw as he stared.

Holt's mouth parted on a small breath. Ever since their conversation about him having a twin brother, Devin had been especially observant, watching his every move, scrutinizing his features and examining Cody's compared to his. Devin was smart, just as Jessie had said, and Holt was worried Devin had picked up more than he and Jessie gave the boy credit for.

"What is it, Devin?" he asked softly.

Fingers stilling, Devin met Holt's eyes again then backed away from him, frowning.

"I see y'all managed to conquer that monster vine." Twigs snapped underfoot as Jessie strolled across the clearing and joined them at the fire pit. She held a pack of scrubbing sponges in one hand and a bucket of soapy water in the other. "I brought some supplies to clean the benches with and once we take care of that, I think we can knock off for the day."

She halted abruptly by the fire pit, glancing between Holt and Devin.

"Everything okay?" she asked.

Breaking eye contact with Devin, Holt stood and nodded. "I can't take credit for the monster vine." He managed to smile as Devin walked around the fire pit and sat on the opposite bench, apparently deep in thought. "The boys took care of that on their own."

"Miles was the strongest," Cody finally admitted, springing off the bench and grabbing Holt's hand. "Wasn't he, Mr. Holt?"

Holt squeezed Cody's hand in his, the act having become familiar—automatic, even—over their days spent together. "Yeah, I'd say so, though all of you are plenty strong."

"But not as strong as you." Cody bounced in place with excitement, shaking Holt's hand up and down. "You can lift the big deck boards by yourself, ride the bulls and wrestle—"

"All right, already." Jessie laughed. "We all

know how strong Mr. Holt is. Goodness knows he sure has spruced up Creek Cabin in record time."

The compliment warmed Holt's cheeks—and heart. Throughout their time together over the past couple of weeks, Jessie had slowly begun giving him the lead more and more when it came to the renovation tasks. As soon as the overhaul of Creek Cabin's deck had been completed without a hitch, she'd turned the to-do list completely over to him along with free rein as to what they tackled next each day. And she hadn't sat on the sidelines, either. She'd worked just as hard—if not harder—as he and the boys had, tackling each laborious task with gusto then, once the sun set, returning to her daily tasks for the shelter inside the cabin.

Each night Holt returned from visiting Ava, he'd noticed the lights on in her cabin and sometimes had been able to see her silhouette in the window as he'd driven by, sometimes sweeping or mopping, washing dishes, folding laundry. Once, he'd even spotted her chopping more firewood by Hummingbird Haven's community cabin. She'd looked up when the truck's headlights had flooded over her and waved Holt off when he'd offered to stop and help.

One thing he'd learned for sure about Jessie was that she felt the most comfortable when she was in control. But now, as he studied the dark shadows that had formed under her eyes, he realized that need for control—at least while he was present at Hummingbird Haven—had begun wearing her down. She put everyone before herself and never stopped to pamper herself.

An almost overwhelming urge waved over him to cradle her in his arms, hold her close and protect her. Jessie deserved a break. More than that. She deserved to be catered to, to be considered and cared for in a way that left her feeling valued...treasured even.

"Don't I owe you a dinner?"

Jessie, amid passing scrubbing sponges out to the boys, stopped and glanced at him. "What do you mean?"

Holt smiled. "I mean, you and Zoe have taken over preparing the afternoon snacks for the past couple of weeks and barely let me help."

"That's because you were busy out here," she said. "We didn't want to disturb you when you were making such good progress."

Holt held up a hand. "I know, and it wasn't an accusation, just an observation. Plus, Zoe and the boys cooked a great breakfast for me the first morning I woke up here, and Peggy Ann and her daughters have had to step in and help out with cooking dinners on the nights you've stayed late to help me out here. So I figure the least I—and the boys—could do would be to cook dinner for all of you."

Jessie considered this, tilting her head and smiling. "Hmm. I think that might go over well. What night were you thinking?"

"Oh, I figure it'll take..." Holt glanced around. "Maybe two or three more days to finish getting Creek Cabin spic-and-span, inside as well as out, and I'd need a couple more days to plan the menu and pick up food and decorations. So maybe next Sunday after we all get back from church?"

Jessie made a confused face. "Decorations?"

Holt smiled. "You know it. This will be a celebratory dinner for the completion of Creek Cabin renovations and you, Zoe, Peggy Ann and her daughters will be the guests of honor."

"Oh, I see." She grinned. "I think Zoe would like that." She laughed. "Very much!"

"What're you going to cook?" Cody asked, tugging Holt's hand again.

Holt raised a brow. "Don't you mean what're we going to cook?"

"Is this another gentleman lesson?" Cody asked.

"Yep." Holt propped his fists on his hips and thrust his chest out. "Every gentleman should know his way around a grill." He eyed Jessie as she laughed louder. "Is there a grill at Hummingbird Haven?"

Jessie's laughter trailed away and she wiped her eyes, smiling. "We have one, though I wasn't aware operating a grill was meant solely for men."

Holt dipped his head, producing a sly smile. "Forgive me. I meant operating the grill will be a job for the gentlemen during this celebration. All the ladies will be expected to do is sit back, relax, enjoy a good meal and let the gentlemen cater to them. I promise you you'll enjoy every moment."

Jessie smiled, her gaze lowering to his smile. Her cheeks flushed a pretty pink then darkened almost the same shade as her auburn hair before she shook her head and resumed passing out the scrubbing sponges to the boys. "If you say so."

Holt smiled wider. Her words didn't offer much encouragement, but that pretty blush did.

JESSIE HADN'T BEEN sure what to expect at Holt's celebratory dinner but surprisingly, she was enjoying herself.

"Now, I know Katie and Tabitha want their hamburgers with extra cheese," Holt said as he stood at the grill on the back deck of Creek Cabin, "but how would you like your steak cooked, Peggy Ann?"

Peggy Ann, seated on one side of a large folding table set with a bright pink tablecloth and pink paper plates, smiled. "Medium-well, please."

Holt lifted the spatula he held in the air. "Medium-well it is, then. Gentlemen, since the food's about ready, would you please offer the ladies a beverage?"

Cody, Miles and Devin, all clad in baggy aprons and oversize chef hats, marched across the deck, carrying pitchers of soda, tea or water, and stood in front of the table.

"What would you pur-fur, ma'am?" Cody asked, tilting up his chin and beaming.

Katie and Tabitha, seated on either side of Peggy Ann, covered their smiles and giggled, before they each burst out with an answer: "Soda!"

"Tea!"

Jessie grinned. Holt and the boys had worked hard putting this dinner together and it showed. The pink tablecloth and chef uniforms were the tip of the iceberg. Glass vases shined in the Sunday afternoon sunlight and bright pink-and-white rhododendron blooms spilled elegantly over the rims and trailed onto the table. Pink plastic cups, pink paper plates and white plastic silverware comprised the place settings and—though this was a touch of God's hand rather than Holt's—a chorus of birdsong drifted across the creek below them on a warm spring breeze.

It was a perfect afternoon for an outdoor celebratory dinner and more fun than Jessie had expected.

"Jessie." Holt's tone held a hint of warning. A lock of blond hair escaped his chef's cap and flopped endearingly over his forehead as he waved his spatula toward the table. "You're not sitting down and relaxing."

Jessie laughed then saluted. "Yes, sir."

She walked over to the table and sat beside Zoe, opposite Peggy Ann and her daughters.

Zoe elbowed her side. "Can you believe this? Chef's hats and all?" She whistled low. "Mercy. He's pulled out all the stops. Only thing missing is candlelight." She grinned. "He gave that a try, too, from what Cody told me when we arrived. Said Holt lit two candles several times but the wind kept blowing them out."

Jessie cast a subtle glance at Peggy Ann as she chatted on the other side of the table with her daughters and smiled. "It's a nice gesture," she whispered in Zoe's ear. "Peggy Ann's been working a lot of hours lately and she and the girls haven't had an afternoon together like this in ages."

Zoe leaned closer, her whisper tickling Jessie's ear. "I don't think Holt did all of this solely for Peggy Ann's benefit."

Jessie batted Zoe's teasing face away and rolled her eyes. "For the boys, then. Holt knew they deserved a special day."

"And you," Zoe murmured, lifting her napkin and spreading it across her lap. "He knew you deserved a break, too."

Her cheeks heating, Jessie waved her hand in front of her face as though batting away a pesky gnat, hoping the extra breeze would cool her overheated skin and hide her expression. Deep down, she knew this day had been for Peggy Ann and the kids, but it was tempting to think that Holt might have thought of her as well. That maybe, just maybe, she crossed his mind once in a while because she still thought of him—much more than she expected and definitely much more than she'd like to admit.

Every day at lunchtime and every night when the day's work was done, she'd watch him climb into his truck, crank the engine and drive off without a word as to where he was going or what he was doing. She'd sit at the window and watch as he returned over an hour later each time, watching as he drove slowly up the driveway, completely disappointed in herself for the prickle of irrational jealousy as to where he was spending his time—or more to the point, with whom.

She'd seen firsthand over the past few weeks how much of a gentleman he was, but like his friend Ty had said, *Old habits die hard*. How many of Holt's old habits had he actually left behind?

Somehow, over the past few weeks, the attraction she'd felt for Holt had begun blossoming into something more. Every gallant gesture, kind word and tender demeanor he displayed touched her heart more and more, deepening her feelings for him. She'd finally begun to admit—at least to herself—that she wanted to believe he'd fully reformed, not just for Cody and Devin's sakes, but for her own.

"Dinner is served," Holt's deep voice boomed proudly.

Two hours later all but one quarter of a hamburger had been eaten, every drop of soda, tea and water had been consumed and the sun hung low in the late-afternoon sky.

Cody, seated beside Zoe at the table, slumped back in his chair and rubbed his belly as he groaned. "I stuffed my gut."

Devin, eyes heavy and seated beside Cody, lowered his chin onto his folded arms. "Me, too." A yawn overtook him. "And I'm kinda tired."

Zoe wiped her mouth and tossed her napkin on the table. "I think it's time little boys took a bath and got in bed."

Cody and Devin sprang upright in their chairs and shouted, "Nuh-uh!"

Zoe laughed. "Yeah-huh!" She stood, pushed her chair in and squeezed each boy's shoulders. Miles was last and she kissed the top of his head, making him giggle. "Come on, you three. How 'bout you come back to my cabin and once y'all have had your baths, we'll watch a movie until it's time for bed?"

Jessie stood, too, and smiled. "You sure you want to take that on, Zoe? Even tired, my boys can—" She clamped her mouth shut and glanced at Holt, the sadness moving through his expression making her cringe. Oh, boy. The last thing she wanted to do was offend him—especially after he'd gone to so much trouble to be kind. "Cody and Devin can be a handful even when they're run-down," she amended, offering a tentative smile.

Holt dipped his head but didn't smile as he watched the boys take off their chef's hats and aprons, then gather their paper plates, plastic cups and silverware and toss them in the trash can Holt had set out earlier.

"I don't mind." Zoe grinned. "Besides, Miles and I like having company, don't we, dude?"

Miles nodded and hugged Zoe's waist as Cody and Devin hustled over and hugged Jessie.

"Don't forget to wash behind your ears." Jessie tugged their earlobes and kissed their cheeks. "And don't give Zoe a hard time, okay? I'll be by to get you when it gets close to bedtime."

"Yes, ma'am." Cody kissed her back then slipped out of her arms, jogged over to Holt and threw himself against Holt's middle. "You wanna come watch a movie with us, Mr. Holt?"

Holt glanced at his watch and grimaced. "I'd love to, but I have somewhere to be tonight. Maybe another time?"

Jessie stiffened, wondering for the umpteenth time where he went when he left every day.

"Sure thing." Cody looked up, his arms around Holt's waist and chin resting against Holt's flat abs. "Thanks for the party. I had a great time."

Holt's smile returned as he looked down at Cody and ruffled his blond hair, a fond act Jessie had noticed Holt do often. She looked away, the sight of Cody hugging Holt with innocent abandon flooding her with bittersweet emotion.

Devin walked hesitantly toward Holt and smiled up at him but didn't offer a hug. Instead, he waved. "It was fun, Mr. Holt. Thank you."

Holt's smile faded. "You're welcome, Devin."

"We had a wonderful time as well," Peggy Ann said, leaving her seat and motioning for her daughters to follow. "Thank you for the dinner, Holt. It's been ages since the girls and I shared an afternoon like this together and we've never had a man cook for—" Blinking rapidly, she waved a hand in the air and smiled. "This was so considerate of you and just what we needed."

Jessie watched, surprised, as Peggy Ann offered her hand to Holt.

He accepted the handshake, returning it gently and said softly, "It was a pleasure, Peggy Ann, and if ever you and the girls need anything, please don't hesitate. I'm hoping we can be friends."

Peggy Ann nodded. "Me, too."

Visions blurring with tears of her own, Jessie turned away and started stacking dirty plates and cups and tossing them into the trash. Moments later Peggy Ann and the girls left, their footsteps and happy chatter fading away.

"Jessie?"

Her hands stilled in the middle of folding the pink tablecloth and she faced Holt again. He stood in the same spot, a somber look in his eyes.

"I think Devin is beginning to realize who I am."

She blew out a heavy breath and sank back against the table. "I guessed that was coming. Ever since you told him you were a twin, he's been thinking and wondering. But—"

"But what?" Holt moved closer, the expression on his face more intense. "Don't you think it's time we tell them? Has anything I've done—anything at all—over the past several weeks helped you see that I'm a different man than I was?"

She closed her eyes, the pain in his voice sending a wave of guilt through her. "Yes. Everything you've done has been considerate and magnanimous and kind but—"

"Then no more *buts*." He shook his head. "Devin will realize it soon enough. Last weekend when we were cleaning the fire pit, he looked at me strangely. Touched my face and seemed to be comparing my features to Cody's. He's a smart boy—"

"I know." Jessie opened her eyes, wanting to give in, wanting to comply with his request and follow through with what she'd hoped might not occur. "I just can't bring myself to shatter Cody and Devin's trust in you. You're getting along so well with them that it may break their hearts to know that—that you…"

"Abandoned them?"

Her chin trembled. She rolled her lips together tightly and tried to steel herself against an onslaught of pain.

"I'm not that man anymore. I'm not the same man you met seven years ago."

She wanted to believe him. She wanted to believe so badly but—

"You're never going to truly trust me, are you?" Holt moved closer. His warm knuckles touched her chin, tilting her face up to his. "No matter what I do, you'll never trust the man I am now because of the man I once was."

The gentle touch of his hand beneath her chin and the pleading look in his eyes coaxed tears to her eyes. She blinked up at him, struggling to speak, but her throat was so tight with emotion, she could only open and close her mouth silently.

He stared down at her a moment more, then his touch left her skin and he walked away, each of his long strides widening the distance between them.

HALF AN HOUR later Jessie stood in the hallway of Hope Springs Hospital, staring into Ava's nursery, her heartbeat pounding in her ears.

"This is who you've been seeing during your lunch break and evenings?" Jessie whispered, a flutter of affection stealing her breath.

Holt stood by Ava's crib, Ava cradled snugly in his brawny arms, her wide eyes blinking up at him, her mouth curved in a smile as she babbled happily. Surprised, he looked at Jessie, studied her expression for a moment then frowned. "Who did you think I was seeing?"

Heat scorched her face, from the hairline on her forehead all the way down the back of her neck. Oh, gosh. She'd never felt more embarrassed—or nosy—in her life, but earlier, after watching Holt walk away, she hadn't been able to quell her curiosity...or that nagging bit of jealousy that wouldn't let her rest. So she'd followed him and now she felt like a complete idiot.

"I...well, I just thought—"

"You thought things that may have been true seven years ago, but wouldn't be true now," he said quietly. A small grin curved his lips despite the wounded look in his eyes. "Though I have to say, I'm flattered you cared enough to check up on me." He tilted his head toward the rocking chair beside the crib. "Please, have a seat."

She bit her lip but did as he asked, then folded her hands together in her lap. Her fingers shook and she squeezed them together to still their nervous tremble.

"Here." Holt moved closer, bent and placed Ava in her arms. "Talk to her. She loves a good conversation in the evening."

Jessie cradled Ava in her arms and smiled down at her through a sheen of tears. "Hello, beautiful," she whispered.

Ava stared up at her, eyes wide, still smiling around another bout of babbles.

"I've been thinking about her a lot since we first came here," Holt said, kneeling on one knee beside her. He cupped Ava's downy head, his big thumb smoothing gently across her soft cheek. "I couldn't help thinking about her alone here, in her crib, without someone holding her, telling her they cared about her."

Jessie sniffed, her throat tightening to the point of pain. "Holt..."

"I understand," he whispered. His hand left Ava and lifted to Jessie's cheek instead, his big palm settling against her skin, his thumb brushing over her trembling mouth. "It's hard for me to accept, but I understand why you have trouble trusting me."

She blinked hard but a lone tear escaped, falling from her lower lashes and settling in the corner of her mouth.

His thumb touched the corner of her mouth, moving the tear to his fingertip. "I never knew how hard it must've been for you accepting Cody and Devin that night seven years ago.

How many painful memories I brought to your door with my actions, and how much you must've resented me for it."

She slid one hand out from under Ava and took his hand in hers, squeezing. "I don't resent you being here and I'm no longer afraid of letting you in anymore. I just need more time before we tell them."

"How much time?"

"I don't know," she whispered. "And I don't know how to explain. It's just that... I'm still worried."

Pain flickered through Holt's expression. "About what?"

About the future. About her feelings for him, which grew stronger every day.

Over the past month Holt had slipped beneath her defenses as easily as he had Cody and Devin's. In the beginning, she'd expected Holt to fumble through her to-do list and falter in reconnecting with his sons. Instead, he'd met every challenge she'd thrown his way, exceeded her expectations by going out of his way to be respectful of Peggy Ann and her girls and had shown genuine affection and dedication for Cody and Devin. And he had been just as considerate of her own concerns and wishes.

Holt had proven himself to be a good man who deserved an opportunity to become the devoted father his sons deserved.

But Zoe had been right on day one. There was no way to move forward without someone's heart breaking. And what worried Jessie the most was that she knew she would never be able to bring herself to break Holt's. Which meant her future with Cody and Devin would no longer be the same as she'd once pictured it.

"I'm worried about what comes next," she whispered.

He shook his head slowly, confusion in his eyes as he leaned closer. "You have nothing to worry about. Whatever happens, I've told you that you'll always be Cody and Devin's mother. We'll work this out. We're in this together."

Oh, how she wanted that. More than he knew.

"I'd like to take my sons home," he said softly. "Just for a visit so my mother and brother can meet them. And I'd like you to come with us, so I can show you what I have to offer them. To prove to you that I mean to be the best father possible. We don't have to tell them who I am yet. It'll just be a little trip—a vacation of sorts—when the boys are out of school. Will you let me do that, Jessie? I promise I won't let you down."

She brought his palm to her mouth and kissed the center of it softly, watching his eyes darken as her lips touched his skin.

"Okay," she whispered. "I trust you."

CHAPTER TWELVE

THREE WEEKS LATER Jessie peered out the passenger window of Holt's truck, barely able to take her eyes off the sprawling green landscape lined with white fencing. The sun's afternoon rays poured golden warmth across acres of lush grass, colorful wildflowers and blooming southern magnolia trees, their bountiful creamy blooms along the white fence lending an elegant air to the grounds.

"Are we there yet?" Cody piped for the trillionth time from the backseat of the cab.

Holt, seated in the driver's seat, chuckled. "Yes, we're here." His smile widened as he navigated the truck up a long, winding paved drive toward a white, two-story house with a wraparound porch and immaculate landscaping. "Finally."

Holt's voice held a heavy dose of dispelled impatience, which Jessie understood.

After their visit to the Boarder Baby Unit three weeks ago, she and Holt had decided to take the boys to Pine Creek Farm over spring break. Until then, he'd continued working his way through the to-do list she'd given him, had added a few tasks of his own and had kept to his usual schedule of working at the shelter during the school day, spending every afternoon with Cody, Devin and Miles, and visiting Ava during his lunch and in the evening. Up to this point, the only change in routine had been that Jessie began accompanying Holt on his visits to Ava and they'd taken turns feeding her, changing her diaper and making her laugh.

Well, that hadn't been the only change.

Jessie glanced at Holt under her lashes, noting the excitement in his expression. The time she'd spent with Ava had not only strengthened her bond with the baby but also with Holt. She'd grown comfortable riding in the passenger seat of his truck, sharing funny anecdotes about the boys when they were little, catching Holt up on all their likes and dislikes and academic mishaps and successes thus far. And, in the midst of it all, they'd found themselves laughing at each other's jokes, sharing a Big Mouth cup of soda they'd pick up from a local gas station after a long day

of work on the way to see Ava. And every evening, before Holt retired to Creek Cabin for
the night, he took her to the door of her cabin,
hugged the boys good-night and stood outside
on the front porch until he heard the lock on
the door click shut. Then he'd climb back into
his truck and drive off to his cabin alone.

More often than not, Jessie would walk from
window to window in her cabin, watching the
red taillights of his truck until they faded out
of view among the dark trees.

She'd fallen for him. She could admit it
now—at least to herself—which complicated
matters all the more.

Now they'd finally arrived at Holt's family
farm and from the look on Holt's face, it was
clear this introduction—despite not revealing
the full truth to Cody and Devin—would be a
massive step forward in Holt's mind.

"Ah, there's my mom," Holt said. "Sitting on
the porch already."

Jessie tore her gaze from the lush rolling
green hills of the pasture and focused on the
older woman sitting in a rocking chair on the
porch. She sprang to her feet as soon as she noticed the truck and ran down the steps to the

driveway, calling to someone over her shoulder as she went.

"That's your mom?" Devin echoed, craning his neck for a better view. "What's her name?"

"Gayle." Holt smiled and glanced in the rearview mirror at Devin, before parking the truck. "I mean, Mrs. Gayle."

He exited the truck, opened the back door of the cab and started helping the boys out of the backseat.

"You're home!" Holt's mom, a lovely woman with long gray hair, met Holt at the front of the truck and enveloped him in a big bear hug. "Oh, how I've missed you. Every day seemed like a month!"

Holt hugged her back and kissed her cheek, the tenderness in his expression unmistakable.

A wistful smile lifted Jessie's mouth. What did that feel like? Coming home to a biological parent you knew? One who raised you from birth and loved you—unconditionally in most cases? And how would it feel to have a home to return to? A place where your most cherished memories resided around every corner? A place that resided in your heart no matter where you traveled, where those who loved you waited eagerly for you to return?

She'd wondered often over the years. Each time she'd helped place a child in a loving adoptive home, she'd looked on as a child she'd loved was united with a new family in a new home and wondered what that child's life would look like years from then. How that child would feel years down the road as an adult, coming home from their travels, embracing their new parents.

Holt, smiling, eased out of his mother's embrace, bent his head and kissed her cheek again. "I missed you, too, Mom."

Jessie's smile faded. It'd feel just like that, she supposed. Like the reverent tenderness in Holt's relieved smile and the admiring adoration in Gayle's loving gaze. Togetherness, support and protection. Strength in numbers. Something Cody and Devin would benefit strongly from.

"So you're Holt's mom." Cody had strolled around to the front of the truck, stood beside Holt and shaded his eyes from the strong afternoon sun.

Gayle, an eager light in her eyes, lifted her arms and stepped forward then stopped abruptly. She glanced at Holt, who shook his head, then lowered her arms and refocused on Cody. Her chin trembled.

"Yes," she said, her tone gentle. "I'm Mrs.

Gayle and I'm so glad you've come to visit."
She held out her hand. "May I shake your hand,
please?"

Cody grinned. "Sure." He slid his small palm
into hers and she immediately covered their
entwined hands with her free one as though
cradling his palm. "A gentleman always shakes
hands when they meet a new person." He
glanced up at Holt. "That's lesson number
seven, right?"

"Eight." Devin, his hands shoved deep in his
pockets, strolled to the front of the truck and
stood beside Cody.

Gayle, her chin still trembling, slowly released Cody's hand and reached for Devin's.
"You must be Devin. I'm so glad to finally
meet you."

Devin hesitated, turned his head and rose up
on his toes, his eyes meeting Jessie's where she
still sat in the passenger seat of the truck. There
was a question in his gaze, a silent request for
permission.

Smiling, Jessie nodded.

Devin faced Gayle again, removed his hand
from his pocket and shook her hand. "It's nice
to meet you, Mrs. Gayle."

The passenger door of the truck opened and

Jessie, startled, looked up as a man, identical to Holt, looked back at her, one of his muscular arms propped on the open door of the truck and the other hanging freely by his side.

"You gonna join us?" A polite smile crossed his lips, but his eyes remained guarded. "We won't bite, I promise."

Liam, Jessie presumed. She dipped her head in acknowledgment and got out of the truck, briefly accepting the helping hand he offered as she lowered her feet to the paved driveway.

"I'm L—"

"Liam. Holt's brother." Jessie studied his features. "You look exactly alike."

He grinned. "He's fortunate to have my looks."

Holt raised an eyebrow. "Your looks? You took after me."

Liam laughed harder then embraced Holt, slapping his back heartily before releasing him. "Good to have you back, brother."

Holt tipped his chin. "You missed me that much?"

"At five in the morning when it's time to muck the stalls?" Liam nodded. "Oh, yeah. And by the way, now that you're back, that'll be your job starting tomorrow, seeing as how I've lined up a trail ride for you and your guests." He spun around, eyed Cody and Devin, who stared at him with curious eyes, then lowered to his haunches, bringing his eyes to the level of theirs. "How 'bout that, boys?" His tone softened as he studied their faces. "You two interested in riding a horse tomorrow and seeing the lay of the land around these parts?"

Devin nodded slowly, seemingly almost mesmerized by Liam's presence. He moved close to Liam, staring up at his face, and smiled. "You're Mr. Holt's brother."

"Yeah," he said. "I'm Liam." He lifted his hand toward Devin then stilled, asking softly, "Mind if I take a look at you?"

Devin shook his head and lifted his chin, almost in invitation.

Smile widening, Liam brushed Devin's blond bangs back with gentle fingers then held his chin between his thumb and forefinger, turning Devin's head one way then the other.

"Yeah." Liam's tone was thick with emotion, and he seemed to catch himself, releasing Devin's chin and easing back on his haunches. "You'll do, kid." He stood and cleared his throat. "You stash your bags in the back, Holt?"

At his nod, he sauntered toward the back of the truck. "I'll start moving those in."

Devin followed Liam, his steps falling inches behind the older man's. "Can I help, Mr. Liam?"

Liam stopped. "Well, let's see." He reached out and squeezed Devin's upper arms. "Those are impressive muscles you got there. I can definitely use your help."

"And mine, too?" Cody asked, jogging over to join Liam and Devin.

Liam grinned and tapped Cody's chin with his knuckle. "I'd love your help. Now, let's get to hauling."

"Jessie."

Pulling her attention away from the boys' excited faces, she turned and found Gayle standing beside her, tears brimming along her lower lashes. She wrapped her arms around Jessie, embracing her closely.

"Thank you for letting Holt bring them home," Gayle said, her words a soft whisper against Jessie's ear. "I can't tell you how much this means to all of us." She pulled back and tucked a strand of hair behind Jessie's ear, her voice shaking with emotion as she met Jessie's eyes. "And thank you so much for being there for Cody and Devin. From what Holt has told us, the boys couldn't have had a better mother."

Gayle hugged her again, holding her so tight, Jessie could feel her heartbeat against her chest.

Eyes burning, Jessie sank into the embrace, a sweet tenderness enveloping her entire being, all the way to the tips of her toes.

"Okay, Mom." Holt's voice sounded near Jessie's ear as he tugged Gayle's arms away from Jessie. "Let's not smother her right off the bat, all right?"

Gayle laughed and wiped tears from her cheeks as she hugged Holt again. "I'm just so happy to have you back. And the boys…" Her voice caught. "It's like a dream come true." She released Holt and shook her head. "Y'all must be famished after the long ride here." She hustled off, heading for the front steps as she said over her shoulder, "Come on in! I've got dinner hot and ready. There's fried chicken, mashed potatoes, sweet potatoes, green beans seasoned with ham hock, broccoli casserole, baked mac and cheese, apple pie, corn on the cob…"

Holt blew out a breath as Gayle entered the house still rattling off the list of Southern delicacies she'd prepared. "Hope you're hungry." He looked down at Jessie. "The way

Mom cooks there's probably enough in there to feed fifty people and send 'em home with two days' worth of leftovers." He held out his hand. "Shall we?"

The boyish grin on his face sent a delicious thrill of excitement through her. Strangely, feeling years younger—as though the future stretched far ahead, brighter than ever—she slid her hand into his and nodded.

DINNER TURNED OUT to be exactly all that Holt predicted and Jessie had enjoyed every moment.

Gayle had covered every inch of the large dining room table on the first floor of the main house with beautiful dishes stuffed to the brim with mouthwatering casseroles, seasoned vegetables, dinner rolls and desserts of every kind. The tantalizing aroma filled the entire first floor of the house and filled the senses as fully as the food did their hungry bellies.

"Gracious, Mom." Holt, seated between Jessie and Cody, eased back in his chair and rubbed his flat midsection. "That was delicious, but I think I gained ten pounds in one meal."

Liam chuckled. "Get used to it. She's been cooking all week—ever since you called to say you were coming home—so you'll be eating like this at every meal."

"I hope I made enough for the whole week." Gayle, seated opposite Jessie, leaned across the table and patted Holt's hand. "Y'all are staying for the entire week, right? That's what you said on the phone?"

Holt nodded. "Cody and Devin are out of school this entire week for spring break."

Gayle's expression brightened. "Then maybe you can stay a bit longer? Over the weekend, too?"

Jessie looked down, removed her napkin from her lap, folded it neatly, then placed it on the table beside her plate.

"Mom." Holt's low voice held a note of caution. "Let's not get ahead of ourselves, okay?" He pushed his chair back, stood and glanced out the wide picture window framing the front lawn. "Dusk is settling. It's 'bout time to go round up the horses and get 'em settled for the night." He smiled at Cody and Devin, who had grown heavy-eyed as they lounged in their seats with full bellies. "But first, I think it's time we take these two upstairs and get 'em ready for bed. Whatcha think, Jessie?"

Heart warming at the sight of the boys'

sleepy—but happy—faces, she stood, too. "I think that's a good idea."

The boys grumbled as Holt and Jessie led them upstairs but were too tired from the long day of travel and a good meal to put up much resistance.

"Here's where you guys will sleep," Holt said, opening a door to the left of the stairs on the landing.

Inside, there were two twin beds made up neatly with blue sheets and a white lightweight quilt. A nightstand sat between the beds and long white curtains graced ceiling-to-floor windows on the wall facing the front yard. Liam had placed the boys' overnight bags on the ends of the beds.

Holt pointed at the windows. "Good thing about this room is Jessie won't have to set an alarm for you. Those curtains are transparent, and the sun'll pour right there in the morning and tug your eyes open." He smiled. "Good thing, too, because Liam and I are taking y'all on a trail ride."

Cody clapped his hands. "Will we get to ride a horse of our own?"

Holt nodded but held up a hand. "But you'll have to wear a helmet and follow our directions to the letter—and I mean, to the letter. It's always better to be safe than sorry."

Devin smiled. "Another lesson."

"Yeah." Holt kneeled on the soft beige carpet and spread open his arms. "Can I have a hug before I head out to round up the horses? I won't be back until you're in bed and won't see you again 'til morning."

Cody dashed across the room and threw himself into Holt's arms, hugging his neck and kissing his cheek. Devin moved more slowly but complied, walking over, hugging Holt briefly and murmuring, "Good night, Mr. Holt."

Holt's exuberant expression fell slightly but he smiled and stood, his tone warm. "Good night, Devin. Sleep well."

"Boys, please get your pajamas and toothbrushes out of your bags," Jessie said as she and Holt eased out onto the landing. "I'll be back in a few minutes to help you start your baths." She shut the door behind her and looked expectantly at Holt. "Which room should I stay in?"

Holt led her across the landing to a room opposite the boys'. "Here," he said, nudging open the door.

A queen bed sat center stage, decorated with fluffy pillows and a brightly colored hand-woven quilt. It was positioned opposite the same type of ceiling-to-floor windows as those in the boys' room, offering an unimpeded view of the exquisite grounds below.

Everything she'd seen at Pine Creek Farm so far was elegant and refined but, at the same time, warm and welcoming. Exactly what she'd always imagined a beautiful home should be and the guest quarters, located near the main house, that Gayle rented to overnight visitors, lent an even more picturesque appeal to the grounds.

The thought of Cody and Devin here on a permanent basis, waking up to such splendor, under a roof with so much love, care and attention from a father, grandmother and uncle... well, it made her lone presence and small cabin at Hummingbird Haven pale in comparison.

"This is beautiful, Holt," she said, struggling to smile as she blinked back tears. "Thank you."

Holt's fingertip touched her chin and tilted up her face. His eyes peered down at her, roving over her expression, and his thumb traced the slight wobble in her lower lip.

"Jessie..." His chest rose on a deep inhale, and he moved closer, his palms cupping her cheeks. His expression changed, the happy light in his eyes deepening into warm affection. "I—"

He bit his lip and halted his words, his gaze straying to her mouth.

Jessie studied his expression, her eyes tracing the handsome curves of his face, her face tilting up as though in invitation.

"I'm grateful we met when we did and not before," he whispered. "Because the man I was then wouldn't have treated you the way you deserve." He hesitated, then bent his head, his lips barely brushing her cheek as he whispered, "Good night, Jessie," then turned and walked away.

Jessie went inside the room, shut the door and leaned back against it. She stood that way for several minutes, her palm pressed against her cheek, covering the fading warmth his lips had left behind.

What would it be like to be loved by Holt? To be by his side, treasured, supported and protected? To be welcomed by his family with open arms as more than just an acquaintance... but as a part of Holt's family instead?

She closed her eyes and envisioned it, allowing herself to cherish the brief glimpse of a life she'd always imagined but feared would always be out of reach. A life she found herself longing for more than ever. One that included Holt appreciating her as more than just a good person. A life in which Holt admired her as a woman... and loved her as well.

CHAPTER THIRTEEN

SOMETHING WAS MISSING.

"We've got everything, right?" Holt asked, checking his saddlebag one last time. "I feel like we're forgetting something."

Liam, standing nearby, patted his mare's neck and shook his head. "Nope. We planned everything carefully, down to the time it'll take to traverse the trail and back with one break at the creek." He glanced over his shoulder where Jessie and Gayle fussed over Cody and Devin, checking the straps of their riding helmets, making sure they were fully fastened. "No. We're good."

But he wasn't. Holt frowned, taking in his surroundings. The grounds of Pine Creek Farm looked exactly the same as they always had—lush green hills and valleys, clean white fences, immaculate stables, well-maintained guest quarters and a beautiful main house. But something felt off—he rubbed his chest, his blood pulsing beneath his palm—in here. Right where his heart should be.

He'd felt it the moment he'd driven his truck up the long driveway yesterday afternoon. His childhood home looked as welcoming as always and his mom—even Liam, in his own way— had been overjoyed to see him and the boys. Gayle's home cooking had tasted just as delectable as always last night, and the horses had returned under his and Liam's leads to the stables last night peacefully, settling in their cozy stalls for the night.

But the bed Holt had slept in for the past few years had seemed less comfortable, and the sounds outside his window less familiar. He'd tossed and turned for the better part of last night, barely sleeping. When he opened his eyes with the first soft rays of morning sunlight, he'd still felt as though he was in unfamiliar surroundings. A place that looked exactly the same on the outside but began to feel oddly alien to him on the inside.

Even now, standing outside the stables on a beautiful spring morning with clear skies and warm breezes, he still felt out of place somehow.

"Something's missing," he said again, wondering if verbalizing the sensation might dispel the unwelcome emotion.

"I told you, nothing's missing." Liam stopped adjusting the saddle on his horse and walked over, concerned. "Are you okay?"

Holt met his eyes, exactly the same shade as his own, the comforting sensation he usually felt when facing his brother not as strong as in the past. "No," he said. "I don't think I am."

Liam frowned and squeezed his upper arm. "Look, if you're not up to a trail ride today, I don't mind taking Jessie and the boys out on my own—"

"No." The word burst from his lips more sharply than he'd intended.

Nodding slowly, Liam stepped back. "All right." He gestured toward the boys and headed toward them. "We best get the boys settled on their horses if we're gonna make it back in time for the lunch Mom's planned."

"Liam?"

He stopped and glanced back.

Holt summoned a smile. "Thanks for arranging the trail ride today. I think the boys will love it."

Liam shrugged. "Not a problem." He grinned. "Those boys are perfect, Holt."

He nodded, his smile fading as Liam walked over to the boys and double-checked their helmets. Cody and Devin were perfect and having them here at his childhood home should feel perfect, too. But it didn't.

"Come on, slow poke," Cody called out, his hands cupped around his mouth. "Mr. Liam said you're slower than a snail in JELL-O."

Holt laughed, grabbed his horse's reins and walked his mare over. "Well, let's see if we can pick up the pace a bit."

Thirty minutes later they were all saddled up, their horses strolling across the peaceful grounds of Pine Creek Farm in single file.

"And to your left here," Liam said from the head of the line as he pointed at an expansive stretch of green grass, "you'll see one of the pastures where we turn the horses out from time to time."

"How many horses do you have in all?" Devin, riding a gray Welsh pony, followed Liam next in line.

"Twenty-two at the moment," Liam answered, smiling over his shoulder at Devin. "And I'm hoping to snag a pretty quarter mare next week."

"But there ain't one prettier than mine,"

Cody, third in line, piped. He patted the neck of his chestnut Welsh pony. "Peanut's the best horse in the world."

Jessie, riding behind Cody and in front of Holt, straightened in her saddle. "Cody, please sit up straight and keep both hands on the reins and saddle horn like Mr. Holt and Mr. Liam taught you."

Holt smiled. "Oh, he's all right, Jessie. He listened and practiced well and Peanut's as calm and gentle as they come. Besides, I'm keeping a close eye on him and if we moved any slower we'd be going backward."

Jessie glanced back at him, that auburn hair of hers trailing below her helmet and almost sparkling in the sunlight as she laughed. "I'm rather fond of the slow pace, thank you very much. Any faster and I'm afraid I'd topple off."

"Yeah." Holt grinned. "I hate to say it, but I kinda noticed that."

Her eyes narrowed at him over her shoulder. "Are you trying to say I'm not a natural with horses?"

Holt burst out laughing. "No, ma'am. I wouldn't say that. I'd like to make it back to the house in one piece."

They continued on, Liam leading the horses

along a flat trail that circled the property at a slow, relaxed pace. The grounds were tranquil but busy, the first large group of guests having recently arrived for their spring visit. The visitors milled about the serene grounds, taking in the sights as they strolled across the fields or rode horses along the trails, taking advantage of the cool breezes before the heat of summer sizzled in.

Halfway to the end of the trail, they reached a large pond Liam had stocked with fish. Tall willow trees framed the grassy banks of the sparkling pond, creating a picturesque view.

"Break time," Liam called out, slowing the horses to a stop. "We're gonna hop off and let the horses rest here for a while. Boys, stay put and Holt and I will help you down."

Cody and Devin did as Liam directed. As soon as Holt and Liam lowered them to the ground and helped them remove their helmets, Cody was eager to move.

"Can we go check out the pond?" he asked, already straying in that direction.

Holt glanced at Jessie as she stood beside her mare and removed her helmet. Her cheeks had flushed a pretty pink during the ride and the sunlight had coaxed a couple freckles out along the bridge of her nose.

He smiled. "You mind if I take the boys down to the pond for a few minutes?"

She dragged her hand through the shiny length of her hair and blew out a heavy breath. "Not at all, though I'm going to hang back here and rest a bit." She leaned forward, stretching her hamstrings. "My legs feel like they've been wrapped around a barrel."

Holt laughed. "Yep. That sounds about right. We'll be back soon." He motioned toward the pond. "Follow me, boys. I'll show you where Liam and I used to fish when we were your age."

He led the way down the grassy incline, below the low-hanging branches of the weeping willow trees, to the sandy bank of the pond.

"Right here." Holt walked over to a set of large roots that protruded from the ground and stretched deep into the murky depths of the pond water. He smacked his hand on the knotted roots and grinned. "Right here is where Liam and I snagged a couple bass so big they almost yanked us into the water."

Cody's eyes widened. "Really? That big?"

Holt held up his hands and spread them a good two feet beyond the bass's actual length. "Huge, I tell you. Massive."

Devin smirked. "No bass is that big."

Holt grinned. "Is that so?"

Devin shrugged then walked to the edge of the bank and tapped the surface of the water with the toe of his tennis shoe. "What kind of fish you got in here?"

Holt rubbed his chin. "Oh, bass, bluegill, threadfin shad and catfish. But it's the bass that put up the biggest fight."

Devin considered this as he eyed the rippling water. "Could we go fishing while we're here?"

"Of course," Holt said. "I'd be happy to take you tomorrow morning, if you'd like?"

"Yay!" Cody shouted, thrusting his arms in the air.

Devin's reaction was much more subtle. "Sure." He looked up and an honest-to-goodness smile appeared. "That'd be cool."

Holt shoved his hands into his pockets to keep from hauling Devin close and smothering him in a bear hug, the empty feeling he'd felt all morning fading just a tad. *Progress*, he thought. *Definitely progress.*

JESSIE TILTED HER head back and drained the last drop of water from the plastic bottle she held. "Oh, boy, that's good."

"Want another?" Liam, standing nearby, reached into his saddlebag.

"Yes, please."

He withdrew an unopened bottle of water and handed it to her.

"Thank you." Jessie unscrewed the cap, brought the bottle to her mouth and tilted it back, closing her eyes as the cool water cascaded down her throat. "Whew." She screwed the cap back on. "I needed that."

Liam retrieved another bottle of water and partook of it himself, tilting the plastic bottle in the direction of the pond as he swallowed. "I imagined Holt's showing the boys our fishing hole. They're probably gonna want to fish themselves once they hear a few of his tall tales from us fishing back in the day."

She followed his gaze to where Holt crouched on the ground near a weeping willow tree, plucking another handful of stones from the ground and passing them to the boys. "Holt's a good man." She blushed as she felt Liam's gaze settle on her profile. "I didn't know him seven years ago when he...well, when he left Cody and Devin with me, so I have no idea who he was then."

"Except for your first impression of him."

She stared as Holt laughed at something Cody said. "Yes."

"And what was that?" he asked. "Your first impression?"

Her cheeks heated. "I thought he was a guy who liked to have fun, had too much fun and then walked away from the consequences." She looked up and met Liam's gaze head-on. "But it wasn't easy for him to walk away from Cody and Devin and I can say with absolute certainty that he never wanted to."

Holding her gaze, Liam nodded slowly. "Do you know why he walked away despite not wanting to?"

She shook her head.

"He knew he needed to change," Liam said quietly. "He'd taken a wrong turn years earlier, landed on the wrong path and forgot who he was. My dad abandoned me and my mom years ago. Holt and I were teenagers at the time. Young, impressionable. Holt chose to go with him. We didn't hear from him for years and we didn't know about the boys. He was too ashamed to tell us and too guilty for leaving us to come home."

He gestured toward the land around them. Green and pristine. "All this." He shook his head. "It was rotting right where it lay. After our dad and Holt left, the place slowly fell apart. Even the air tasted sour when it hit my tongue. That was bitterness," he said softly. "I resented Holt for years after he left. He walked away as though Mom and I meant nothing to him."

He met her eyes again. "But he came back."

"Yes," she whispered, that bittersweet sensation returning, spearing through her chest. "Yes, he did."

"He's worked so hard to turn his life around," Liam said. "He spent years here, rebuilding the guest houses, sprucing up the land and helping me turn this place around. We sweated, bled and laughed together. Worked every day, sunup to sundown. And eventually, I knew I had my brother back. He's the good man you say he is. He's a better man now than any I've ever met in my lifetime. Cody and Devin—they've changed him for good and the only thing he wants in life now is to be a good father to them. To give them what he should have years ago. Security, love and family." His gaze intensified, a pleading look entering his eyes. "Please don't take those boys away from him. Not now. Not after he's worked so hard and changed so much. It would break his heart if he lost his sons again. He'll give them a good life here."

Jessie turned away, the image of Holt and the boys blurring as she stared at them, and whispered, "I know."

CODY, MOUTH FULL of foamy toothpaste, spit in the sink then smiled up at Jessie. "They got bluegills, bass, catfish and thread salad."

Devin, having finished brushing his teeth, wiped his mouth with a hand towel. "Thread-fin shad," he said. "That's what Mr. Liam said they're called."

Cody brushed his teeth and waved a hand in the air. "Woo clares? S'long as you clan hook 'em."

Jessie hid a smile and shook her head. "Cody, please don't speak when your mouth is full."

He frowned up at her. "Blut we ain't eatin'."

"Doesn't matter." Jessie grabbed a hand towel and wiped blue foam from his chin. "If your mouth is full, you shouldn't babble around it. Now, rinse your mouth and meet us in your room. It's getting late and you both need your rest."

"'Cuz we're going fishing!" Cody spit in the

sink again, grinned then turned on the tap and shoved his face in the flow of water.

Smiling, Jessie sighed and steered Devin out of the bathroom. "Come on, dude. From the look of his toothpaste face, your brother's going to be a while."

They walked across the landing of Pine Creek Farm's main house and into the room Holt had designated as Cody and Devin's for the duration of their visit.

"What time are we going fishing tomorrow?" Devin asked as he hopped into his twin bed.

"Oh, pretty early, I think." Jessie lifted the covers, waiting as Devin scrambled under them, then covered him up to his chin. "Fish wake up at the crack of dawn and start biting early."

At least, that was what she'd heard. She wasn't a big fisherman herself, but she'd enjoyed it the few times she'd been over the years, and she hoped Cody and Devin would enjoy it tomorrow morning. Holt was definitely excited.

After the trail ride earlier that afternoon, Liam had led them back to the main house for lunch—another round of belly-stuffing delicacies Gayle had prepared special just for them. After everyone pitched in to clean the dishes,

Holt and Liam had taken the boys outside for a game of football, which had transitioned into a tour of the guest houses, stables and gardens surrounding the main house.

Regardless of how Liam had described Pine Creek Farm as it had been in the past, the property was certainly beautiful now, and Jessie had trailed behind along the tour of the grounds, admiring every new sight and sound, the boys' excited laughter reminding her time and time again how wonderful a home like this could be for them.

"Jessie?"

She sat on the edge of the bed and brushed Devin's blond bangs out of his eyes. The boys' hair was getting shaggy. It'd be time to cut it soon. "Hmm?"

"Will you be mad if I tell you something?"

Jessie smiled but the heavy tone in his voice made her stomach churn. "I'd like to say no but I won't know until you tell me. How about you give it a shot anyway?"

"But…" His fingers toyed with the quilt that lay beneath his chin. "What if it makes you sad?"

Her smile slipped but she recouped, keeping it firmly in place. "I'll tell you something I want you to remember. You can always be honest with me, no matter what, okay?"

He nodded but remained silent, his eyes roving over her expression, then he whispered quietly—so quietly she had to lean down to hear. "Me and Cody like it here."

He'll give them a good life here.

Her breath caught in her throat. The sentiment Liam had voiced was expected, the same as Devin's. She'd noticed the boys reveling in the beautiful countryside and attention of Holt's extended family over the past days just as she had but facing the thought head-on—the realization that Holt had so much more to offer them than she did—broke her heart all the same.

Maintaining her smile, she covered his hands with hers and struggled to keep the sadness out of her voice. "I'm glad to hear that."

"We like Mr. Holt, Mr. Liam and Mrs. Gayle," he said quietly. "We like the beds, and the horses and the food."

"I think you should tell Mrs. Gayle that. It would warm her heart to know you and Cody love her cooking."

"Could me and Cody come back here again?" he asked.

Her lungs stilled painfully. "I think we could arrange that."

"How long could we stay?"

She hesitated, her throat tightening. "How long would you want to stay?"

He looked down at their hands, his brow creasing, but didn't answer. "Is this what it's like for the others? The ones who get adopted and leave Hummingbird Haven? Do they go to places like this? Places that have a dad, a grandma and an uncle?"

"Yes," she whispered, her heart breaking just a bit more. "Some of them do."

Avoiding her eyes, he asked softly, "Can I ask you one more question?"

"Ask away."

"Who is Mr. Holt?"

Jessie froze, knowing the moment was inevitable given Devin's intellect and curiosity but not ready for what would surely follow once he knew the truth. "What do you mean?"

His eyes returned to hers, a shrewdness that always surprised her shining brightly in his gaze. "Is Mr. Holt my real dad?"

Her mouth opened then closed as she searched for the right words—any words that might help explain their current circumstances. But really, there was only one word that needed to be said. She just wasn't the right person to say it.

Jessie leaned down and kissed Devin's forehead, committing the soft scent of his hair and feel of his small hands between hers to memory, holding on to each moment she had with him and wondering how many she might lose with him and Cody in the future if Pine Creek Farm became their permanent home. "I think you should ask him that first thing tomorrow."

CHAPTER FOURTEEN

HOLT LOADED TWO fishing poles into the bed of his truck and shut the tailgate. "I think that'll do it."

Liam, reaching into the bed of the truck and checking that everything was secure, nodded. "I'd say so. Mom packed at least a dozen pimento sandwiches in the cooler and two dozen bottles of water. I'd say you're set for two days at the pond, at least."

Holt laughed. "She can't stand to see anyone go hungry. You sure you don't want to come with us? We could have a good old-fashioned competition like we used to."

Liam smiled. "Nah, I'll let y'all have it today. There's a lot I need to catch up on around here. The boys will have a blast. You couldn't have picked a better morning for fishing. Bet they'll be biting up a storm at the pond."

Holt tilted his head back and inhaled. Fresh

morning air rushed in, filling his lungs and lifting his spirit. He closed his eyes and lingered in the moment, the scent of honeysuckle surrounding him. He was about to take his sons fishing—and not just anywhere, but he was taking them fishing at the pond of his childhood home.

The thought should've been exhilarating. Should've rushed over him in an intense wave of gratitude. But the unsettled feeling from yesterday still lingered within him, creating a hollow in his heart, which should be otherwise full if not overflowing.

Despite the success of the visit home thus far, he couldn't help but think something wasn't quite right.

"Good morning."

At the sound of Jessie's voice, he smiled and opened his eyes. There she was, walking across the front lawn with Cody and Devin on either side of her, holding their hands, her auburn hair cascading over her shoulders. Morning sunlight peeked over the hilly horizon at their backs, casting a rosy glow over them as they made their way across the grassy lawn. For some reason, the sight soothed his soul.

"Morning," Holt called back, waving. "Hope I'm not dragging y'all out of the bed too early."

Jessie shook her head as they drew close. "The boys were so excited they barely slept last night."

Releasing her hands, Cody and Devin ran across the short distance separating them from Holt and proceeded to climb onto the tailgate of the truck.

"What kind of fishing poles you got, Mr. Holt?" Cody asked, grabbing one and inspecting the clear fishing line.

"The user-friendly kind." Holt steadied Cody with a hand on his waist as the boy bent way over into the bed of the truck and lifted a blue fishing pole out of the bunch. "You see that right there?" Holt asked, pointing at the round red-and-white cork attached to the line. "That's your cork."

Cody wrinkled his nose. "Cork?"

"Yep." Holt tapped the wrinkles in his nose. "Some people call them bobbers or floats. When a fish chomps down on your bait and pulls, that little guy goes under water and that lets you know it's time to yank on that rod and reel a fish in."

Cody bounced with excitement. "I want to use this one! Can I?"

Holt laughed. "Yep. It's all yours. But for now——" he removed the fishing rod from Cody's hands and returned it to the truck bed "——it needs to stay back here until we reach the pond."

Placing one hand on Holt's wrist, Cody jumped from the truck and ran toward the passenger door. "Then let's go! I'm ready to fish!"

Smiling, Holt looked at Devin, who was still surveying the contents of the truck bed, his expression somewhat somber for a fishing trip. "How 'bout you, Devin? What type of fish are you itching to reel in from the pond?"

Devin fiddled with the handle of a tackle box for another moment then ducked his head and climbed down off the truck bed. "A bass, I guess."

Holt watched him walk around the truck toward the driver's side, his arms hanging by his sides. "You all right this morning, Devin?"

He glanced back and shrugged. "Yeah. Just tired, I guess."

That was two *guesses* so far. Holt frowned. Maybe Devin would perk up a bit once they reached the pond.

"He had a long night," Jessie said, walking over to Holt's side. "There's something he'd like to talk to you about this morning, if you don't mind."

The expression on her face was so similar to Devin's he was hesitant to proceed until whatever situation this was could be resolved. "Should we go back to the house?" he asked. "We could talk there and—"

"No." Jessie bit her lip as she glanced in Liam's direction, the two of them exchanging a look, then met Holt's eyes. "It's a beautiful morning. We'll take them to the pond and we can talk there."

Unease crept up his spine, but he nodded. "Okay. If you think that's best, that's what we'll do."

ONE HOUR LATER the sun was up, the fish were biting and Holt was having a fantastic time.

"I think I see a nibble, Cody." Holt, seated on the bank of the pond between Cody and Devin, leaned over and whispered in Cody's direction again. "Have a look at your cork."

Cody scooted a couple inches forward across the sandy dirt, his eyes fixated on the red-and-white cork in the distance. "You sure?" he whispered back. "I didn't notice noth—"

Devin gasped. "Right there." He reached across Holt and pointed toward Cody's cork, bouncing his legs when the cork bobbed deeper below the water. "There it goes again, Cody."

"I see it!" Cody sprang to his feet and jerked his fishing pole upright, squealing when it pulled tight against him. "I got him! I got him!" He bounced up and down, his fishing rod almost falling from his hands. "Do you see I got him, Mr. Holt?"

Laughing, Holt placed his fishing pole on the ground, sprang to his feet and wrapped his arms around Cody's, covering Cody's small hands with his around the pole. "You got 'em, kid. But you won't have him long if you don't keep a firm hold on this pole."

"Pull him!" Devin shouted as he jumped to his feet, grabbed Cody's fishing pole and started yanking, too. "Pull him in, Cody!"

A giggle burst from Cody's lips, and he yanked harder, his small frame jerking violently against Holt's chest. "We're gonna get him, Jessie! You watch. We're gonna get him!"

A familiar laugh rang out and Holt glanced to his right. There Jessie sat as she had for the past hour, leaning back against a massive knot of roots protruding from the ground, her long, jean-clad legs stretched out in front of her. Now, instead of her flushed face tilting in the direction of the sun as it spilled across the pond, she watched the three of them wrestle a stubborn fish in deep water.

She laughed again and Holt stilled, a sense of déjà vu washing over him. He'd seen that look before on her face—that same bright smile and beautiful expression on her sun-flushed face.

He smiled as her gaze found his, their eyes meeting. Ah, the picture! The large framed portrait on the wall of her cabin, depicting her in a mountain river with the boys, all smiles. The one he'd noticed on the very first day he'd returned to her door, seeking her help in finding Cody and Devin.

Happiness. Pure and whole.

But a moment later that look was gone. Once she noticed him watching her, her smile slowly faded to a fraction of what it had been and the excited light in her eyes died. She glanced at him and the boys then looked down, her hands fidgeting nervously in her lap.

Holt frowned.

"Got it!" Cody heaved hard on his fishing

pole and the line sprang free of the water, a large bass flopping through the air, its shiny scales flashing in the sunlight as Cody and Devin toppled backward, slamming into Holt's gut and knocking all three of them to the ground.

Winded, Holt closed his eyes, his smile growing wider as Cody and Devin, still piled on top of him, wriggled around, trying to get to their feet and grab hold of the bass.

"Easy, boys, easy." Jessie's sweet voice sounded above him, and the boys' extra weight rolled off him, freeing him to breathe deeply. "Holt?"

He opened his eyes and there she was, standing over him now, her long hair cascading down around her face as she stared down at him with a concerned expression.

She frowned. "Are you okay?"

He nodded just a bit, looking up at her, then at the boys tussling on the bank with the bass, wanting to hold on to the moment just a little longer. "Yeah. I'm good."

"You're great!" Cody's little body hurled back onto Holt's middle, stealing his breath. "Best fisherman ever!"

Laughing, Holt flexed his abs and pulled himself to a seated position. "Hey, easy there. Let me catch my breath."

"But look!" Cody shoved his fishing line in front of Holt's face, the bass wriggling on the end of the hook. "Look at how big he is! We could have him for dinner!"

Holt smiled. "We sure could."

"You're kinda good at this, aren't you?" Devin asked, smiling. "You catch a lot of fish when you were our age?"

Holt wrapped one arm around Cody, who still beamed at his catch and shrugged. "I caught my fair share. Liam was always right behind me, though. A lot of the biggest fish I caught, I wouldn't have snagged without his help." His chest warmed as he glanced from Devin to Cody then back. "Kind of like what you two did just now. You worked together and that made all the difference."

Devin looked at Cody, who lifted his floppy fish in the air, then he met Holt's eyes again, that somber look Holt had noticed on his face earlier that morning returning. "Can I ask you something, Mr. Holt?"

Holt nodded. "Of course. You can ask me anything."

Cody, still wriggling happily against Holt's side, suddenly froze. His eyes fixated on Holt's face, wide with expectation.

"Here," Jessie said softly as she bent between Holt and the boys and took Cody's fish and fishing rod from him. "I'll put the fish on ice in the cooler."

"Jessie?" Devin called as she walked toward the truck. "Will you stay?"

A hesitant expression crossed her face, an anxious look in her eyes as she bit her lip. "Do you want me to?"

Devin nodded. "Yes, ma'am."

"Okay," she said quietly. "Give me just a moment."

Holt frowned, his heart aching at her discomfort, wondering what had unsettled her. He studied Devin's face, but the boy lowered his head and picked at a bit of grass between his shoelaces, hiding his expression.

Jessie returned shortly and eased onto the ground a couple feet away from Holt and the boys. She nodded encouragingly at Devin, but her mouth shook slightly. "Go ahead, Devin."

Devin looked up then, his gaze roving Holt's face as he asked, "Are you our dad?"

Holt's heart kicked against his ribs, stealing his breath. He glanced at Jessie and she seemed unsurprised, as though she'd been expecting

Devin's question, but there were shadows of sadness in her eyes and her lips still trembled.

Holt supposed he should've seen this coming, too, but he'd imagined it all playing out differently. That he and Jessie would sit down and discuss the situation again, she would tell him when she was ready to inform the boys of his identity and they'd break the news to Cody and Devin gently...together.

Instead, Cody and Devin had taken the lead, put him on the spot and left him floundering for words. And Jessie seemed as though she felt all alone, sitting on the outside and looking in when instead, she held a place in his heart right alongside the boys.

He studied his sons' faces for a moment, the hope in both of their eyes giving him courage. "Yes," he whispered. "I'm your dad."

Devin and Cody fell silent, their wide gazes moving from Holt's face to Jessie's then each other's.

Finally, Cody sighed. "Devin thought you were. He said you have a twin like us and hair like us and eyes like us and—"

Devin scowled, his chin trembling. "But why did you leave us? Didn't you want us?"

It was like a gut punch, sucking all the air

out of Holt's lungs. Eyes burning, he shook his head and scooted forward across the dirt, sitting as close as he possibly could to both of them, struggling to steady the waver in his voice. "I wanted you both very much." His throat tightened. "Very, very much."

Two big tears rolled down Devin's cheeks as he stared back at Holt, his voice breaking on his next words. "But you never came to see us. You never called. Never came to our birthday parties, never took us anywhere. You didn't do any of the things the other dads do for their kids."

Holt dipped his head, wet heat coursing down his cheeks. "I know. I should've stayed with you both. I should've made better choices. I should've been braver. Stronger."

Cody, tears running down his cheeks, dragged the back of his hand across his face and swallowed hard. "But you're brave now, aren't you? You're strong enough for us now?"

His hands shook. Holt held them out, palms up, one on each leg, keeping them steady. "Yes. I've spent a lot of time changing, becoming the father you both deserve, and I came back for you. I came back because I missed you. Because I want to be a part of your lives. And I want the chance to be your dad, if you'll have me. Because I love you."

"No, you don't." Devin's hands balled into fists as he stared at Holt's face, picking apart his expression. "Y-you can't. If you loved us, you wouldn't have left us."

"Devin." Jessie's soft voice sounded by Holt's side. She reached out and covered one of Devin's hands with her own. "Holt left you because he thought it was what was best for you at the time. He gave you to me because he knew I would take good care of you and Cody. He loved you enough to ask someone to do what he wasn't able to at the time."

Holt, choking back a sob, nodded. "I know how hard this must be for you both to believe, but I love you both more than you'll ever know."

Cody threw himself against Holt's chest, clutched the front of Holt's T-shirt and pressed his face to Holt's neck, sobs bursting from his lips as he whispered, "It's okay. I'm not mad at you," he said. "I love you, too."

Devin stared at Holt, tears coursing down his cheeks.

"I'm here now, Devin," Holt said, hugging Cody close. "Whenever you need me, I'll be here for you and I'll wait as long as it takes for you to trust me."

Devin dragged the back of his hands over his cheeks and looked at Jessie then back at Holt. "But...but you're not leaving again?"

Holt, his throat tight with emotion, shook his head.

A fresh set of tears coursed down Devin's cheeks. "You promise?"

"I promise," Holt said, holding out his hand.

Devin stared at it for a moment then looked at Jessie again, a question in his eyes.

Jessie nodded. "It's okay to give him a chance if you'd like to," she whispered.

At her reassurance, Devin threw himself against Holt, wrapping his arms around Holt's neck and pressing himself as close to Holt's chest as possible. They cried together, Holt closing his eyes and hugging them tightly, their tears and heartbeats mingling with his own as he silently thanked God for giving him this moment. This chance. This reality.

His chest felt fit to burst and it was hard to believe this much happiness could swell inside it, could consume his entire being so intensely without his body breaking.

Joy billowed through him in waves, and he

opened his eyes and mouth to look at Jessie and call out to her, to share this moment, to thank her for giving him a chance, for seeing the man he was even when he harbored his own doubts.

But she'd slipped silently away, her slender figure walking slowly across the field on the other side of the pond, the sun bright at her back.

CHAPTER FIFTEEN

THREE DAYS LATER, the last day of his visit home, Holt stood in the dark on the front porch of Pine Creek Farm's main house, sipping a bitter cup of coffee and staring toward the horizon.

"Couldn't sleep?" The screen door creaked as Liam walked out onto the porch and joined Holt at the railing, a steaming cup of coffee cradled in his hands, too.

Holt shook his head. "No."

Although that was nothing new. It'd been three days since he'd revealed his identity to Cody and Devin at Pine Creek's fishing hole and every night since, he'd tossed and turned, stared up at the ceiling of his bedroom, waiting for the sun to rise so he could show Cody, Devin and Jessie around the farm and put in a decent day's work. Anything to slow the thoughts tumbling in his mind and help him close his eyes at night. Only, nothing had worked.

After his conversation with Cody and Devin by the fishing hole, he and the boys spent the rest of the afternoon together, fishing, talking and laughing. Holt's heart had never felt so full...until they'd returned to the house and he'd caught a glimpse of the pained expression on Jessie's face. Rather than bringing them closer together, revealing his identity to Cody and Devin had seemed to cause Jessie to withdraw.

And later that evening, when Jessie had shared with him that she would step back for the next few days and give him and the boys space to acquaint themselves with each other better alone, his high spirits had deflated at the thought of enjoying time with Cody and Devin without her as well. He knew she was supporting his relationship with his sons and giving them time alone together, but it had only taken one subsequent fishing trip with the boys without her for him to realize how much he missed her being there with them. How much they'd begun to feel like a family. And how much he wanted to formally make them one.

Only, it wasn't the right time to tell her. Not until he'd spoken with his mom and Liam.

"It's four forty-five in the morning," Liam

murmured before taking another sip of coffee. "You gonna stand out here 'til the sun rises?"

Holt nodded. "Probably." He glanced over at Liam. "And you're one to talk. What're you doing up?"

He shrugged, his lips twitching. "Pangs of twin sympathy, I suppose. And that French roast aroma found its way into my left nostril and woke me right up."

Holt laughed.

They stood there silently for several minutes, sipping their coffee and peering into the dark, then Liam said, "Listen, you haven't had enough sleep to work today. Take the day off. Spend it here at the house with Jessie and the boys. Eat a big lunch and take a long afternoon nap before y'all hit the road later."

Holt shook his head. "I can't."

Liam fell silent and faced forward, staring out into the darkness. "And why not?"

Holt closed his eyes. Because he'd made a decision. One he was afraid might break Liam's and his mother's hearts. Though that wouldn't reverse the decision he'd made. At some point during the dark, endless hours he'd spent staring at the ceiling last night, he'd come to a realization. One that changed everything.

"Do you know," he asked Liam softly, "that ever since I came back home, I've felt as though something was missing? As though something wasn't right?"

Liam shifted beside him, and Holt could feel the weight of his gaze on him.

"I couldn't put my finger on it," Holt continued. "I couldn't figure out what was bothering me so much. And then, as soon as Cody and Devin were in my arms by the pond the other day and I looked up and saw Jessie walking away, I knew exactly what it was."

Liam remained silent.

Holt stared ahead into the darkness, peering into the distance, trying to find the horizon. "Pine Creek doesn't feel like home to me anymore." He glanced at Liam hesitantly, unsure of how he'd respond. "I don't want to offend you or Mom, but I want to be honest with you."

"I know." Liam sipped his coffee again then asked, "Where *do* you feel at home?"

An image of Creek Cabin rose to Holt's mind. He could almost smell the fresh wood on the back deck and charcoal smoldering in the grill. He could hear Cody, Devin and Miles' cheerful chatter during snack time in the community cabin. Feel the warm spring breeze on his face and see Jessie's auburn hair swinging softly along her back as she led the way along a dirt trail winding through a thick line of trees. And he could still feel baby Ava's slight weight in his arms, see her wide eyes and bright smile and hear her cheerful babble.

"Hummingbird Haven," he whispered. "With Jessie, Cody and Devin, and with Ava nearby or in my arms. That's where I feel most at home."

Confusion filled Liam's eyes. "Who's Ava?"

Holt smiled. "A baby girl with the biggest blue eyes I've ever seen who helped me reacquaint myself with the man I really am." He looked at Liam, an earnest tone entering his voice. "I didn't end up on Jessie's doorstep with Cody and Devin by accident seven years ago. I was led there by word of mouth and something more." He touched his chest, his palm covering the spot where his heartbeat pulsed against his skin. "I felt it here. Something called to me, led me to Jessie back then. I felt it again when I returned to her cabin a couple months ago. When I knocked on her door, summoning up the courage to ask her to help me find Cody and Devin."

Holt stopped and looked out across the

grounds again, the corners of his mouth tipping up as a faint glow peeked just a smidge over the horizon. "And I feel it again now— ever since I arrived here. I feel a pull to take a different path. To be something more. To make a difference in others' lives." He looked at Liam and smiled, the proud gleam in his brother's eyes urging him to continue. "I'm being called to a new purpose. The same one as Jessie. I've never felt more valuable or worthy as I did when I worked with her and the residents at Hummingbird Haven these past weeks. When I helped Ava feel safe in my arms and helped Peggy Ann smile. When I helped Miles find his confidence—enough so, that he was willing to try new things and discover he was stronger than he ever knew."

Liam smiled. "Sounds like you've already made up your mind about what you want to do."

"I have. And I hope it's what Jessie wants, too. I want her, Cody and Devin to be in my life every day." Holt winced. "But I don't want to disappoint you or Mom. You both waited so long for me to come back and as soon as business is thriving and things are going well, here

I am wanting to leave again…and take my sons with me."

The porch door creaked again, and a feminine voice asked softly, "Do you love her?"

Holt spun around, surprised to see his mother standing there in her fuzzy bathrobe and slippers, a tremulous smile on her face.

"Are you doing this for you and not just for the boys?" she asked.

"Yes," he whispered. "I love Jessie as much as I love my sons. I've never forgotten her over the years, and I can't imagine my life without her now."

Gayle lifted her chin and nodded. "Then your home is with her."

Holt walked across the porch to her side and took her hands in his. "I don't want to leave you like D—"

"Oh, I'll have none of that." Gayle waved away his words with one hand then pulled him close for a tight hug. "You're nothing like your father, Holt," she whispered in his ear. "You're a good, strong, loyal man who will be an excellent dad. And I'm so glad you've found your way." She released him and stepped back, cupping his cheek with one hand. "You don't need my permission to begin a new life with Jessie

290

and the boys at Hummingbird Haven," she said softly, "but you have my blessing."

Smiling so hard his cheeks hurt, Holt hugged her tight then hugged Liam and slapped his back for good measure. He took off down the front porch steps and across the lawn, tugging his cell phone from his back pocket and lifting his face toward the first tendrils of morning sunlight as they reached just above the horizon and brightened the sky to a spectacular blend of pink, lavender and gold.

"What are you doing?" Liam called from the front porch.

"Gotta make a call." Holt kept walking and smiling as he dialed then brought the phone to his ear and waited for a familiar voice to answer.

"Hope Springs Hospital. This is Sharon James. How may I assist you?"

JESSIE, SEATED AT a table in Hummingbird Haven's community cabin, poked at the salad on her plate twice then laid her fork down.

"Lettuce is good for you, Jessie. Zoe says it's roughage and helps clean out your system."

She looked across the table at Miles, who studied her closely, his plate empty, and smiled as Zoe, sitting beside him, tsked her tongue.

"I know I said that, Miles," Zoe said, "but it's not exactly the best topic to bring up at the table."

Jessie laughed. "It's okay. You're absolutely right, Miles, and normally, I'd eat this salad right up. I'm just not feeling well today. That's all."

Miles perked up. "Then can I have your salad? The rest is already gone and I'm still hungry."

Jessie glanced at the large salad bowl she'd placed on the table an hour earlier and it was indeed empty...as should be expected.

Spring break at Hummingbird Haven had always been a busy, energetic time for everyone what with the kids out of school for the week with tons of free time and wonderful weather. And after returning from Pine Creek yesterday, she'd filled the last day of vacation with extra loads of laundry, meal preps and coordinating outdoor activities. Only, something was missing. Three somethings, to be precise.

"Have at it." Jessie nudged her salad plate across the table to Miles, watching as he dug into it with gusto.

She looked to her left down the table where Peggy Ann's daughters, Tabitha and Katie, played a round of Crazy Eights, their tenth competition, Jessie guessed, and chatted about different techniques of braiding hair. Glancing to her right, she noticed Zoe staring back at her, a question in her eyes.

"Please don't look at me like that," Jessie said quietly, casting a quick glance at Miles, who continued munching happily on her salad.

Zoe blinked, striving valiantly for a bewildered expression. "What do you mean? What look?"

Jessie pointed at her face. "That look. The one you make when you're covering up the other look I don't like."

Zoe frowned. "Which one is that?"

"The pity one." Sighing, Jessie rubbed her forehead. "The one you've given me way too often the past twenty-four hours when you think I won't notice."

Zoe slumped back in her seat, disappointment in her eyes. "Really? I thought I was hiding it better than that and I assure you, I've been trying very hard."

And she had been. Ever since Jessie had returned home, told Zoe the boys knew Holt was their father then expressed her fears over what the future may hold, Zoe had worked extremely hard to simultaneously cheer her up and keep an inconspicuous but concerned eye on her. Zoe was a good friend—the best, really—and Jessie loved her all the more for her attempts to ease her concerns.

Unfortunately, the kind of worries she carried weren't easily assuaged. She was glad Cody and Devin knew Holt was their father, and even happier they'd begun showing a greater interest in him the last three days at Pine Creek Farm—an interest that had only continued to grow since their return to Hummingbird Haven. Even now, they were out with Holt again, either hiking mountain trails or fishing in one of the creeks behind the cabins.

She was glad they were spending time together, but it was an odd, unwelcome feeling to sit in an empty cabin without the boys. A feeling she wasn't sure she would ever get used to but would have to at some point now that she and Holt would be sharing custody of the boys.

Jessie stood and headed for the door.

Zoe called after her. "Where are you going?"

She paused in the doorway and summoned a small smile. "I still have more cleaning to do. Would you mind watching the kids while I work on it?"

Zoe smiled back but concern still lingered in her eyes. "Not at all. I'm taking them on a hike down a new trail later anyway. We'll be passing by your cabin. I'll stop by on the way and if you feel up to it, you're welcome to join us."

"I'll think about it," Jessie said.

And she would…think about it, that was. Because she knew that in the end, she wouldn't go. It was just too hard to be around the kids more than she needed to right now. Their very presence reminded her of Cody and Devin's absence…as well as Holt's, and that soon, Holt would probably approach her with the request to take Cody and Devin home with him to Pine Creek Farm. She would agree because it was the right thing to do and all three of them would be missing from her daily life more often than not.

She walked to her cabin and swept the kitchen floor and polished the hardwood floors in the living room. She dusted the lamps and changed the sheets on her bed then returned to the kitchen and stood by the island idly for a few minutes, rubbing her middle right where a hollowness had settled ever since Holt and the boys had left early that morning.

Staying busy didn't ease it but standing still didn't seem to help, either.

Shaking her head, she lifted her chin and forced a smile instead. "They're happy," she reminded herself. "I should be happy because they're happy and that's exactly what I'm going to be."

She meant it, every word. But she didn't quite feel it as she looked around at the empty cabin.

A knock sounded at the front door and she crossed the room and opened it. "I'm sorry, Zoe. I'm not feeling like a hike tod—"

Her words trailed away, her voice failing her as she saw the man standing on the other side of the door.

"Holt." She stared at him, her gaze lingering on the tender look in his eyes, the strong curve of his jaw, the bright smile curling his lips and...*the pink bundle in his strong arms?* "You— you have another one?"

His smile widened as he looked down at her, a chuckle rumbling through his wide chest.

"I—I mean..." Heat burned up her neck and suffused her cheeks. "Of course I know you didn't have another baby. I just meant you brought another one to me." She shoved her hair away from her hot face. "Is—is that Ava?"

He removed one big hand from beneath the pink bundle and drew back the blanket, revealing the baby's face. Ava's big blue eyes met hers and the baby smiled, kicking her legs and waving her tiny fists in the air with gleeful recognition.

"She's missed us both while we were away this week," Holt said. "So I thought we'd stop by and visit on the way to my cabin."

"Your cabin?" Jessie shook her head. "What do you mean, your cabin? I thought you and the boys—"

"The boys and I had a long talk this morning," he said softly. "I shared a few of my plans with them and they liked the sound of them." He turned to the side and spoke over his shoulder. "You can come on up now, boys."

Footsteps scrambled up the front steps as Holt shifted to the side, revealing Cody and Devin dashing toward her, huge smiles on both their faces. They barreled into her, throwing their arms around her waist and pressing their cheeks to her middle.

"We're gonna have a sister, Jessie!" Devin shouted.

"And Dad's gonna work on one of the cabins

so we can all stay in the same house together," Cody said, bouncing against her.

Jessie, hugging them close and kissing their blond heads, stilled and looked up at Holt in surprise. "Holt, what're they talking about?"

"Boys." Holt waited as Cody and Devin released her and looked up at him. "Do you remember how I showed you how to hold Ava on your lap earlier?"

Devin nodded, a solemn look in his eyes. "Always support her head."

Holt smiled. "That's right. Why don't you have a seat on the couch over there and hold her for a minute while I talk to your mom?"

Jessie's mouth parted, her breath pausing as Cody and Devin smiled up at her then skipped over to the couch and sat down beside each other, keeping still as Holt lowered Ava carefully onto Devin's lap, then waiting patiently as he took care to make a safe little nest of pillows to ensure she was safe and secure in Devin's arms.

"Stay right there and don't move 'til we come back, okay?" Holt asked.

Devin and Cody answered in unison. "Yes, sir."

Beaming with pride, Holt cupped his hand

under Jessie's elbow and tugged her out onto the porch. "There's something I want to ask you."

Jessie gripped his forearms and stared up at him, almost unable to believe he stood in front of her. "What's going on, Holt? A cabin for all of us to stay in together?"

A slow smile lifted his tempting lips. "Well, that depends."

Her pounding heart slowed a bit. "On what?"

"On how long it takes me to renovate Hummingbird Hollow and add an extra room suitable for a nursery."

Her pulse picked up again. "A-a nursery?"

His smile widened. "Yeah. Ava's going to need her own room when she gets older. We can't expect her to share with Cody and Devin."

Feeling dumb, but unable to do anything other than repeat his sentences, she dipped her head and asked, "Ava? And Cody and Devin?"

"And it'll depend on your answer." He lifted his hand and cradled her cheek, his thumb smoothing across her temple as he spoke. "I love you, Jessie." He stepped closer, his thighs brushing hers. "I want to marry you. I want to hold you in my arms every night and kiss you every morning. I want to raise our sons—and daughter—together. To give them—and whoever else God sends us—the same loving home and family that I've found here with you."

She smiled, unable to stop the tears flowing down her cheeks. "Y-you love me?"

He nodded, certainty in his gaze. "And I'm hoping you love me, too. I no longer have any doubts—not about who I am or my ability to be a good father, and certainly not about my love for you. I have faith in us, and I know you have faith in me. And the two of us, together—our love and our new family—would be the best haven my sons could ever have." He lowered his head, his eyes searching hers. "Please say yes," he whispered. "Say you'll marry me. Say you lo—"

She did better. She showed him.

She rose up to her tiptoes and her lips met his, her palms cupping his face as she kissed him, breathing him in, savoring the feel of his mouth against hers, his strong arms around her, his chest vibrating gently against hers on a low groan.

Lifting his head, he drew in a ragged breath, his eyes darkening as he smiled wide and looked down at her. "I'll take that as a yes," he whispered.

Jessie smiled back. "Yes. I love you." She

traced the curve of his cheek lovingly. "And I'd be honored to be your wife."

He lowered his head and kissed her once more, slowly and tenderly, then took her hand and led her inside the cabin where Cody, Devin, Ava…and a future full of love awaited them.

A Country Christmas
Lisa Carter

MILLS & BOON

Lisa Carter and her family make their home in North Carolina. In addition to her Love Inspired novels, she writes romantic suspense. When she isn't writing, Lisa enjoys travelling to romantic locales, teaching writing workshops and researching her next exotic adventure. She has strong opinions on barbecue and ACC basketball. She loves to hear from readers. Connect with Lisa at lisacarterauthor.com.

Visit the Author Profile page
at millsandboon.com.au for more titles.

Know therefore that the Lord thy God, he is
God, the faithful God, which keepeth covenant
and mercy with them that love him and keep his
commandments to a thousand generations.
—*Deuteronomy* 7:9

DEDICATION

For those who went above and beyond to stand in the gap for me as a child, thank you.

CHAPTER ONE

FAMILIES WERE COMPLICATED. She was running late. In a nutshell, the story of her life.

Buffeted by a brisk November wind, Kelsey Summerfield hurried down the sidewalk. Outside the Mason Jar Café, she reached for the door. A man's calloused fingertips brushed against her hand. Sparks electrified her nerve endings.

"I'm sor—" Her lip curled. "Oh, it's you."

Clay's hazel eyes narrowed. "Oh, it's you."

Last week, she'd driven over from Asheville to meet her widowed grandfather's new friend, cattle-ranch matriarch Dorothy McKendry. She'd also met Dorothy's grandson, Clay. She and the cowboy had taken a mutual dislike to each other.

She tucked a strand of hair behind her ear. "Grampy is expecting me for lunch."

Kelsey liked tall men, but not overly tall men.

From her five foot four perspective, at six two Clay McKendry was definitely overly tall.

"I'm meeting Nana Dot for lunch." He reached for the door again. As did she.

Their hands touched, setting off another round of electricity. Like a scalded cat, she snatched her hand away. "I can open my own doors, thank you very much," she hissed.

She rubbed her still-tingling palm down the side of her charcoal trousers. The static electricity in the air must be off the charts today. He bowed up, crossing his arms over a massively impressive chest. Not that she was impressed. She disliked barrel-chested men.

"Opening a door for a woman is about being a gentleman." He smirked. "Your constitutional rights are in no danger from me, I assure you."

"Let me assure you—"

"While this exchange between you two has been highly entertaining and *extremely* informative—" an angular, faintly terrifying woman with ice-blue eyes and a short iron-gray cap of hair, GeorgeAnne Allen's thin lips flattened "—you're blocking the entrance to the café. The Double Name Club is waiting for me."

Did Clay's tanned, chiseled features pale a trifle?

The seventysomething ladies of the Double Name Club—more notoriously known as the Truelove Matchmakers—took the town motto Truelove, North Carolina: Where True Love Awaits a little too seriously. Her father had sent her to Truelove to prevent Grampy from falling into their clutches.

Married, divorced or spinster, *Miss* was a title of respect bestowed on any elder Southern lady. No-nonsense GeorgeAnne was the bossy one—although when it came to the Double Name Club, that was splitting hairs.

Clay yanked open the door and made a sweeping motion. "Allow me, Miss GeorgeAnne."

Lips pursed in what for GeorgeAnne passed as a smile, the uncontested leader of the matchmaker pack marched into the diner. She headed straight for the Double Name Club's favorite table under the community bulletin board. Her compatriots in matchmaking mischief—Erma-Jean Hicks, IdaLee Moore, Martha Alice Breckenridge and CoraFaye Dolan—waved her over.

Kelsey took a whiff of the tantalizing aromas of coffee, fresh-baked pastry and apple galette. Southern comfort food meets Parisian bistro. She couldn't imagine how a hick town in the Blue Ridge Mountains had managed to score such an upscale foodie establishment. Of course, it was Truelove's only eating establishment. Not exactly what she was used to in Asheville. But then, what was?

Her dad promised if she kept an eye on Grampy, he had a position for her in the family corporation. She merely had to prove herself.

Clay squeezed into the jam-packed entryway. "That was a close one."

From his beige Carhartt jacket, she caught subtle tones of leather, clean-smelling soap and a latent hint of aftershave. Her heart sped up a notch. Immediately, she squashed the vaguely happy feeling. She didn't do pleasant with Clay.

He shuddered. "GeorgeAnne called us *you two*."

Kelsey batted her eyes. "Isn't that an Irish rock band?"

He pinched the bridge of his nose. "This isn't funny, Keltz."

A warm sensation like melted butter passed through her with lightning speed. So fast she wasn't sure she hadn't dreamed it. Her family didn't do nicknames.

She arched an eyebrow. "I'm not afraid of a bunch of old ladies sticking their powdered noses where they don't belong."

"You ought to be afraid. Very afraid," he growled in her ear.

Smelling of sweet cinnamon, his breath blew a tendril of hair against her earlobe. Another not *un*pleasant sensation. Heat crept up the collar of her sweater.

"No one plays chicken with a matchmaker and emerges unscathed. Ask my friend Sam Gibson what happened to him several Christmases ago, if you don't believe me." Removing his Stetson, Clay held the hat over his heart. "Those women have made it their personal mission to help everyone find their happily-ever-after. Whether we want them to or not."

"This town needs a collective backbone." She flicked her hair over her shoulder. "Maybe it takes someone like me to tell them to mind their own business."

"I just saved us from a long, embarrassing and possibly matrimonial entanglement."

She edged around him. "Get over yourself, McKendry."

Owner and chef Kara MacKenzie handed her a menu. "Your grandparents are waiting for you."

"They're together." He grimaced. "In the booth next to the matchmakers."

"Might as well embrace the inevitable." She elbowed him in the ribs. "There could be a Christmas wedding in your future."

He rubbed his side. "I'm not interested in settling down. I'm enjoying the field."

"This is Truelove." She made an expansive gesture. "What field?"

Waggling her fingers at him, a brunette swung around on one of the red vinyl stools lining the counter. "How ya been, Clay?" A well-dressed, cool blonde, almost as tall as him, strode past them on her way to the exit. "Hey, Clay."

"You were saying something about a field?" He shot Kelsey a look. "I'm may be the last unattached man standing in Truelove."

What she wouldn't give to wipe the self-satisfied smile off his stupid, cowboy face.

Some women loved cowboys. There was no accounting for taste. Most women probably found him ruggedly handsome and winsomely appealing.

He had the whole square-jaw, straight-nose, firm-lipped, strong-white-even-teeth thing going for him. He didn't look bad in jeans, either. But she wasn't most women. And she wasn't remotely, in this lifetime, on this planet interested in him.

"Last man standing, huh?" She followed him to the booth. "There's probably a reason for that. And not the one you imagine."

Dorothy McKendry smiled at them. "Hi, kids." Behind the wire-framed glasses, her hazel eyes had the same gold flecks as her grandson.

"Glad you could join us." Silver hair glinting under the fluorescent lighting, her grandfather motioned across the table. "Leave Clay the outside spot, honeybun. He'll need room for his long legs."

"Yeah, Keltz." He broadened his chest. "My *long* legs take up a lot of room."

She threw herself onto the bench. "Your over-size ego takes up a lot of room."

Clay sat down. "As a matter of fact, I—"

"Will you two stop fussing?" Dorothy laid her hand atop her grandson's. "We have big news."

Grampy put his arm around Dorothy's shoulders. "We're getting married."

Kelsey stared at her grandfather. This couldn't be happening. Her father would not be pleased. Not pleased at all.

CLAY FELT ABOUT as stunned as Kelsey looked. "What do you mean you're getting married?"

A beginning-to-be irritated expression flitted across Nana Dot's wrinkled features. "I feel sure *getting married* is fairly self-explanatory."

Beside him, Kelsey continued to open and close her mouth like a guppy drowning on air.

He fell onto the seat. "You only met in April."

Nana squeezed Howard's hand. "When you know, you know."

Kelsey's grandfather grinned. "We fell in love."

Nana Dot nodded. "The chemistry was just there."

Howard winked. "Lots of endorphins popping."

Making a choking sound, Kelsey got a deer-in-the-headlights look.

Clay leaned forward. "But at your age—"

Kelsey kicked him under the table.

Scowling, he rubbed his leg. "What I mean is, Mr. Howard, you're eighty-seven. And Nana Dot is eighty."

Mr. Howard kissed his grandmother's hand. "My child bride."

Hand to her chest, Kelsey started that hyperventilating thing again.

Nana Dot wagged her finger. "We're old

enough to know what we're doing. After my dear friend, IdaLee, found happiness with her long-lost beau, Charles, we were inspired."

Clay threw a glance at the matchmaker table, uncharacteristically quiet. He should have known this outlandish notion had been match-maker-engineered.

Howard's gaze clouded. "Kelsey, what're you thinking?"

"I think…" her mouth trembled "this is a little sudden."

Thank you, Keltz. Way to come through.

Howard lifted his chin. "At our age, we understand how short life is, and how truly precious it is to find someone special to share it with."

Clay found it difficult to swallow around the sudden boulder in his throat.

"Joan and I were married for fifty-nine years. Dorothy and her husband were married for thirty-five. We know what real love feels like." Howard opened his hands. "We want to enjoy the rest of the years God gives us as fully as possible."

Nana turned to Clay. "Last weekend at Apple Valley Orchard, Howard dropped to one knee and proposed."

"An artificial knee, mind you." Howard's eyes—the same cornflower blue as Kelsey's—twinkled. A lifetime of smile lines fanned out from the corners. "Both knees are metal, but they worked just fine, didn't they, Polka Dot?"

Kelsey gave them a slow nod. "Why can't y'all remain friends?"

Nana patted Kelsey's hand. "We considered that."

Howard shared a smile with his bride-to-be. "But we decided the platonic thing wasn't going to work for us."

Cheeks as scarlet as her winter coat, Kelsey sputtered. Clay wanted to clamp his hands over his ears. But it was too late to unhear that.

Kelsey pulled herself together. "When were you thinking of getting married, Grampy? In the spring?"

"The first weekend in December."

His jaw dropped. "That's less than a month away."

Nana scooted out of the bench. "Exactly." Howard edged out behind her.

Clay unfolded from the booth.

Kelsey scrambled out, too. "What about lunch?"

"Stay and enjoy lunch on us." With a serene

smile, Nana Dot touched his cheek. "If you'll excuse us, we have wedding details to work through."

"Including putting in a call to our children." Howard stuck out his hand to Clay. "I appreciate you not making us feel like a bunch of senile, old geezers."

Clay shook his hand.

Kelsey's eyes appeared suspiciously bright. "If there's anything I can do to help, please don't hesitate to ask."

He jammed his hands in his jean pockets. "Me, too, Nana."

"I want a small wedding." A calculating look flickered across his grandmother's face. "But I might take you up on that offer." With a quick wave, the elderly couple bid them farewell.

He dropped onto the bench vacated by the geriatric sweethearts. "I didn't see that coming."

She climbed into the bench across from him. "Me, either."

"You didn't sit on my hat, did you?"

She picked his hat off the seat and handed it to him. Groaning, she buried her face in her hands. "My dad is going to kill me."

"What are we going to do about them?"

"There's not much we can do. Except for

the major damage control I'll have to do with Dad." She gazed at him through her fingers and a curtain of hair. "Not a phone call I'm looking forward to taking." She smoothed the hair out of her face.

If he ran his hand through the dark brown waves of her hair, would it feel as silky against his fingertips as it looked?

Had he lost what was left of his mind? He'd met black bears more friendly than Kelsey Summerfield. He must still be in shock over Nana Dot.

The majority of the Double Name Club filed out of the restaurant seconds after the lovebirds. Not born yesterday, he figured the timing of their exit wasn't a coincidence. The double-named cronies were probably already strategizing how to further ruin his life. After the heartache with his former fiancée, they'd left him alone. Until now.

This close to Christmas, he didn't relish being caught in their matchmaking cross hairs. The holiday only prompted them to bring out the big guns of matrimonial mayhem. *Thanks, but no thanks, Double Name Club.*

And if they were considering pairing him and Mr. Howard's snobby granddaughter? The idea was beyond ridiculous. He disliked short women. Also, she wore haughty like a second skin. Then there was her face...

Okay, so maybe he didn't dislike her face. She wasn't exactly hard on the eyes. But that mouth of hers... He inhaled sharply. Best not to go there, either.

Her blue-eyed gaze swung to him. "What?"

"Nothing."

His Aunt Trudy, a fiftysomething, hip-swinging peroxide blonde who'd worked at the Jar as long as he could remember, approached them. "Y'all gonna place an order or carp at each other all day?"

Kelsey slumped. "I've lost my appetite."

"I'll take the French special thingy I can't pronounce, a glass of water and a slice of apple galette, Aunt Trudy."

Removing a pen from behind her ear, his aunt wrote down his order. "Anything for you, Miss Summerfield?"

"Water, please." She fiddled with the sugar packets in the dispenser. "Maybe Clay will let me have a taste of his pie."

He folded his arms. "Get your own."

Aunt Trudy rapped him over the head with the order pad.

He rubbed the top of his head. "What was that for?"

"Get used to sharing, Clay." Trudy threw him an amused glance. "By Christmas, you two will be kissing kin."

What was with this *you two* business? But the image she conjured in his mind—of Kelsey's lips—lingered long after Aunt Trudy headed to the kitchen.

He got a sinking feeling that, like it or not, this Christmas was going to be one he'd never forget.

UNDER DURESS, CLAY shared the apple galette with Kelsey. After lunch, they parted. She stuck around the Jar for a mocha latte caffeine kick start. She'd just stepped onto the sidewalk outside the diner when a silver GMC pickup barreled up Main Street.

With a screech of brakes, Clay pulled to a stop next to the curb. The passenger window scrolled down. "Get in."

She planted her hands on her hips. "I wouldn't get in a hurry with you, McKendry, much less a vehicle."

Leaning across the cab, he flung open the

door. "Nana's taken your grandfather to the hospital."

Kelsey gasped. "What's wrong with him?"

"She didn't give specifics." His face, which usually only did scowling when he looked at her, softened. "I told Nana we'd meet them at the hospital."

This couldn't be happening. Not again. When she'd lost her mother, her emotionally distant father had abandoned her for work. A year ago, Granna had died. What would she do if she lost Grampy?

She scrambled into the truck. *Dear God, please let him be okay.*

"What happened?" She fumbled for the seat belt, but her hand shook so badly she couldn't lock it in place. "I–I can't..."

"Take a breath, Keltz."

Leaning over, Clay pulled the strap taut. Worried as he was about Nana and Mr. Howard, he couldn't help appreciating the fruity notes of perfume wafting off her. She looked delicious, and she smelled even better.

But this wasn't the time nor the place to be noticing such things about a person he didn't like. With a click, he secured her seat belt. Put–

ting the truck in gear, he steered down Main. The pickup rattled over the bridge.

"This isn't the way to Asheville."

He blew past the Welcome sign and headed toward the corkscrew road that wound over the mountain ridge. "The closest emergency room is at the county seat."

"But they don't have the same state-of-the-art equipment as the hospital in Asheville." She jabbed her finger at him. "What kind of stupid town doesn't have an urgent care?"

He clenched his jaw tight. "The kind of town that will do anything for one of its own."

Kelsey Summerfield was exactly like his erstwhile fiancée. Last year, Angela had dumped him for the bright lights of the state capital. The litany of Angela's frequent complaints against Truelove echoed in his head. He loved Truelove, the mountains and the ranch. He never wanted to live anywhere else.

She sighed. "I do carp at you. I'm sorry."

His eyes cut to her. Maybe she wasn't exactly like his former fiancée. Angela only received apologies, never gave them.

"I appreciate you taking me to Grampy."

Angela hadn't done gratitude, either. Perhaps

Kelsey wasn't the spoiled, overprivileged rich girl he believed her to be.

"When Granna passed…" Not meeting his gaze, she fiddled with the hem of her ivory sweater. "If I was to lose Grampy, too…" She stared out the window at the evergreen hillsides of spruce and fir.

An altogether new feeling stirred inside his chest. How much of her in-your-face bravado was a defense mechanism? Not unlike the pains he'd taken since the Angela debacle to steer clear of women and keep emotional attachments at a minimum.

He swallowed. "I'm sorry, too."

"I have trust issues." Her lovely lips—which again, he had no reason to be noticing—quivered. "I can be a bit of a control freak."

"No way." He threw a grin at her. "Not you."

"Amazing," she said with a laugh, "but true."

She had a nice laugh.

After Angela's betrayal, he'd self-isolated at the ranch to lick his wounds. His life became a never-ending cycle of cows, Nana Dot and occasional outings with a few buddies from high school. In truth, he was often lonely for something he didn't know how to define.

He pulled into the parking lot outside the

emergency department. "Hang on a sec." He came around the hood to the passenger side. He yanked open the door and offered her his hand. "It's a jump for a vertically challenged person like yourself."

She tilted her head. "You just called me *short*, didn't you?" Her hand was soft and warm in his. "But thank you."

In the chilly winter air, their breath fogged. She let go of his hand. He immediately missed the touch of her fingers.

At the entrance, the glass doors slid open. He removed his hat. They approached the lady at the reception desk.

"We're looking for our grandparents." He could practically feel the worry radiating off Kelsey. "Dorothy McKendry and—"

Kelsey leaned over the desk as the woman typed in the name. "And Howard Summerfield."

The lady scanned the monitor. "Howard Summerfield was taken into triage about thirty minutes ago. He's being assessed by an ER physician. I'll notify the duty nurse to let Mrs. McKendry know you're waiting here in Reception. Once your grandfather is stabilized, the doctor will give you an update."

Finding a quiet corner, they sat down. Kelsey's phone rang. She declined the call.

He balanced his hat on his knee. "Do you need to get that?"

"It's my father." Her eyebrows bunched. "No need to alarm him until I find out what's happened to Grampy."

His eyes cut to her, and his heart ticked up a notch. What was it about Kelsey Summerfield that got under his skin?

To keep her from agonizing over her grandfather, he decided to keep her talking. "Favorite pizza topping?"

"Pineapple." Her mouth curved. "And you?"

"Canadian bacon."

She sighed. "Did you know my Granna died in her sleep?"

His gaze flitted to her.

She laced her hands together in her lap. "Granna hadn't been sick. We went to bed, and the next morning she was gone." She bit her lip. "I've tried to be there for him since Granna died. But he won't need me now."

Clay frowned. "Mr. Howard will always want you in his life."

"It won't be like before, though."

"Change is hard." He drew in a deep breath. "But they seem to make each other happy."

She gave him a wobbly smile. "All that matters to me is my grandfather's happiness."

Perhaps he and Kelsey weren't as different as he'd supposed.

"I'm not real good with words, Keltz." He rubbed the back of his neck. "But what a sweet gift from God. As one love story ends, another one begins."

Something inscrutable flickered in her vivid blue eyes.

The triage doors swung open. Accompanied by a sixtyish woman in a white lab coat, his grandmother emerged. Hat in hand, he rushed forward to embrace his grandmother. "What's going on, Nana?"

"We'd run to the jewelers to pick out wedding rings. Coming out of the shop, Howard dropped his keys, and that's when it happened." His grandmother introduced them to the attending physician.

"Is it a stroke?" Kelsey asked in a near whisper. "Or a heart attack?"

Tucked against his side, he could feel her shaking like a beech tree in a winter gale.

Dr. Redmayne adjusted the stethoscope

hanging around her neck. "When he bent to retrieve his car keys, something tweaked in his lower back. I've given him a relaxant for the muscle spasms."

"Grampy has thrown out his back?"

The doctor nodded.

Her shoulders lowered. "That's happened before."

"Painful, but not life-threatening." The doctor tucked her hands in her coat pockets. "He'll be off his feet for two or three weeks, but I'm sending him home with a prescription to reduce the inflammation."

"The doctor says he'll need regularly applied ice-pack treatments." Nana folded her arms across her cardigan. "I'm taking Howard to the ranch so I can provide him with round-the-clock care."

An orderly wheeled Howard out to them.

Kelsey dashed forward. "Grampy!"

"Hello, honeybun."

She wrapped her arms around him.

He winced. "Gently, if you please. The old man's had a bit of an afternoon."

Dr. Redmayne touched his shoulder. "As long as he follows doctor's orders, he'll return to his normal activities within no time." The doctor reminded him to schedule a follow-up appointment and excused herself. An orderly wheeled him out to the sidewalk.

Mr. Howard winked at Clay's grandmother. "Got to be in tip-top shape for a honeymoon cruise with my new bride."

Kelsey wagged her finger. "All the more reason why I need to get you to Asheville where you can receive the best possible care."

"I'm going with Dot." Her grandfather lifted his chin. "However, Dorothy and I have a great favor to ask you, Kelsey." He took hold of Nana Dot's hand. "I want Dorothy to have the wedding of her dreams, but my injury places us further behind the wedding eight ball. Would you consider putting this wedding together for us?"

Kelsey's mouth rounded. "I'd be honored, but I've never planned a wedding before."

"You're so good with details, honeybun. Spare no expense. Put the charges on my credit card."

Clay stiffened. "I've got money put aside."

Nana shook her head. "It's taken years to save the money to increase the herd."

He widened his stance. "McKendrys pay for their own weddings."

Nana Dot pursed her lips. "I won't let you

jeopardize your future by refusing Howard's generous offer."

He folded his arms across his coat. "A wedding is the responsibility of the bride's family."

"The clock is ticking, Clayton. We're on a deadline here." Nana threw Howard an affectionate glance. "We want to make that cruise."

He clenched his jaw and said no more. But this conversation wasn't over by a long shot.

"A Christmas wedding." Making *Ls* with her thumbs, Kelsey held her hands midair, framing her vision. "The glitz. The glam. I'm thinking possibly neon uplighting."

He scowled. "Nana said she wanted a small wedding."

"Orchids." Kelsey gave her grandfather a huge smile. "Remember the Schively wedding? The acrobats in the plastic bubble? How fabulous would it be if we recreated that, but in a giant snow globe." She clapped her hands together.

Seriously?

Howard beamed at his granddaughter. "Keep those big ideas coming, honeybun."

Clay scrubbed his face with his hand. "Nana?"

His grandmother's eyes darted from Howard to Kelsey. "Truelove's church will soon be decked out for Advent. Poinsettias are Christmasy."

Mr. Howard threw his bride-to-be an apologetic look. "I'm sure Kelsey can come up with something grander that befits our special day."

Kelsey clasped her hands under her chin. "I promise you a wedding no one will ever forget."

No way was he turning Kelsey and her over-the-top ideas loose on his nana's wedding day.

He thrust out his chin. "I'll help Kelsey plan the wedding."

Nana's shoulders visibly relaxed. "That would be such a relief to have you on board, dear heart."

Howard's forehead creased.

Nana touched her fingers to her mouth. "I mean, there's so much work to be done in such a short time." She tilted her head at her groom. "How wonderful it would be for both our grandchildren to work on this project together."

Clay leaned against the wall. "We'll be co-planners."

Kelsey frowned. "You have a cattle ranch to run."

He broadened his shoulders. "Winter is our slower time."

"While this is so incredibly generous of you, Clay..." She moistened her bottom lip. "And sweet of you to offer…" The crinkle in her nose belied the sincerity of her words. "Your assistance is completely unnecessary." She gave him a bright, totally fake smile. "I'd hate to waste your valuable time."

"I don't consider giving my nana and your grandfather their special day a waste of my time."

Spots of red peppered her cheeks. "I don't need your help."

"Actually, you do." He glared back. "And you're going to have my help whether you want it or not." He threw her a lopsided smile. "For the next few weeks, consider us joined at the hip."

"You are impossible," she growled.

"Thank you." He smirked. "I try."

He vowed to do everything in his power to prevent Kelsey Summerfield from turning Nana Dot's wedding into a circus.

CHAPTER TWO

CLAY RETRIEVED HOWARD'S car from the parking deck for Nana Dot to drive back to True-love.

Grampy was obviously in a great deal of physical discomfort. With some maneuvering, Clay helped him lie flat in the back seat. In the truck, Kelsey and Clay followed behind Nana Dot over the winding mountain road toward the McKendry ranch.

She laced her hands together. "About you being a co-planner for the wedding."

He gripped the steering wheel. "Now is not the best time to hash this out."

Veering off the secondary road, he steered the truck through the crossbars of the Bar None Ranch. Split-rail fencing lined the long, graveled drive. Trees edged the perimeter of the pastureland.

Her first impression of the McKendry home

was that it was exactly that—a home. A wrap-around porch encircled the two-story, white Queen Anne Victorian.

She took a deep breath of the clean, crisp mountain air. The ranch house reminded her of the homes along Asheville's Montford Avenue in the historic district. Like something out of an American fairy tale, the house sat on a knoll with three-hundred-and-sixty-degree views of the rolling Blue Ridge horizon.

He parked beside her grandfather's sedan. She caught a glimpse of a picturesque red barn, a corral, and other outbuildings. In a distant field, cattle grazed.

Miss Dot headed to the kitchen to prepare an ice pack. With Kelsey on one side and Clay on the other, they helped her grandfather shuffle along to the guest bedroom. They eased him onto the mattress. But she still believed his camping out at the McKendry's was a mistake. Stubborn was a well-known Summerfield trait. She could do stubborn, too.

"What about your clothes and toiletries, Grampy?"

"I made a few calls. The condo manager is going to let Dorothy's neighbor, Jack Dolan, inside my place to pack a few of my things and bring them to the ranch."

"But I could've—"

Clay's grandmother bustled in with an ice pack in her hand. She fussed about for a few moments, situating the pack, fluffing a pillow, drawing a blanket. Kelsey stepped out of her way.

"No need to bother, Kelsey." Grampy threw Dorothy a brilliant smile. "My bride will take good care of me, won't you, sweetheart?"

She fingered the strap of her purse. "It wouldn't be a bother, Grampy."

The condo at the ski resort was west of True-love, nearer to Tennessee. Decades ago, he'd been one of the first commercial real-estate developers to see the potential for skiing in the North Carolina mountains. Unable to bear the memories of the Asheville home he'd shared with Granna, last spring Grampy had fled there to the family's vacation home.

"It's nearly dusk." He glanced out the window overlooking the ridge of mountains. "You should start for home." He closed his eyes.

Clay's grandmother became brisk. "Howard needs to rest."

Feeling dismissed, she bit her lip against the

treacherous sting of tears. Might as well get used to it. From now on, this was obviously how it was going to be. Subdued, she followed Clay to his truck.

She'd left her car parked outside the Mason Jar. Lunch seemed a lifetime ago. A tense silence reigned between her and Clay on the way down the mountain into town.

Keeping to her side of the pickup, she darted a quick glance at his clamped jaw. He drummed his fingers on the wheel. Her gaze returned to the scenery flashing by the window.

The glorious autumn splendor, for which the Blue Ridge was famous, had passed. The trees stood bare, the branches stark against a gunmetal sky. Brown leaves littered the roadside. Only the evergreen firs and cedars dotting the landscape relieved the bleakness of the cold November afternoon. Winter was upon them. She shivered.

Brows constricting, he reached for the dial on the instrument console. "I can turn up the heat."

"No, thank you. I'm fine."

Once the sun descended behind the ridge, darkness fell swiftly this time of year. She wasn't used to driving the steep mountain roads outside the city.

His forehead creased. "Will you be all right returning to Asheville tonight?"

She had the ridiculous urge to smooth the line away. Someone ought to tell him scowling would ruin his cowboy good looks. But not her. She didn't like cowboys.

"You could stay over at the ranch," he added.

"No." She flinched. That had come out harsher than she intended. "I should get back to my apartment. I'll be fine."

"So you keep saying." A muscle jumped in that well-chiseled jaw of his. "Sorry the ranch isn't the five-star accommodation you're used to."

Kelsey scowled at him. "That wasn't what I meant." But he was determined to cast her as a rich-girl snob. Seeing Grampy with Miss Dot was hard. Tired and more than a little blue, she wasn't up to returning to the ranch.

"As a young woman, Nana Dot trained as a nurse." He strangled the wheel. "Your grandfather will be in good hands."

She gave him a nice view of her back. They passed the Welcome to Truelove sign. "*Where true love awaits*," she muttered to the windowpane.

The truck rattled over the bridge into town. The river swirled below. As tumultuous as her fragmented emotions.

"Seems to have worked for Nana Dot and Mr. Howard."

Kelsey sniffed. "Hasn't it just."

"That's it."

He jerked the wheel and pulled into the vacant parking lot of the bank. She threw him a startled glance.

"You and I need to get a few things straight, City Girl." He turned in the seat. "First off, you can lose the bad attitude."

Kelsey bristled. "I do not have—"

"Second, we don't like each other, and we never will. I get that."

For a split second, something akin to disappointment pricked her heart, but she rallied. "Listen, Clayton..."

He grimaced as she'd known he would. He didn't like to be called by his full name. However, it was just too fun to resist pushing his buttons.

"If you're done throwing your debutante tantrum..."

Her eyes widened. "I am not throwing—"

"Were you or were you not a debutante?"

She glowered. "That is beside the point."

He folded his arms across his chest. "It is precisely the point."

She hated herself for noticing the play of muscle under his shirt.

"We're from two different worlds. And never the two should meet, except they did when Nana Dot and your grandfather fell in love." His shoulders hunched. "But we both love our grandparents and want the best for them. Right?"

She sighed. "Right."

He dropped his arms. "We're never likely to be friends, but I propose we put aside our differences for their sakes."

Again, there was that flicker of something. Regret? In different circumstances, she suspected Clay McKendry would have made a great friend.

She nodded, slowly. "A truce?"

"A cessation of hostilities for the duration. We need to give them wedding memories they can cherish." He jutted his jaw. "But tell me now before we go any further down this road of enforced association if this is something you can get on board with or not."

He made it sound like spending time with

her was a prison sentence. Good to know up front how he really felt about her. *Fine. Be that way.* Never let it be said, though, she'd done anything less than her best for Grampy's sake.

She stuck out her hand. "We have a deal."

For a second, he stared at her hand. Was he recalling the spark of electricity between them earlier? Her cheeks flamed. Her heartbeat sounded alarmingly loud.

Taking her hand, his palm felt strong, warm and calloused from hard work against her own. Disappointment rose at the loss of camaraderie they'd shared at the hospital. But it was clear how he viewed her—a frivolous creature who'd never done an honest day's work in her life. She was used to being underestimated by her father. She'd show Clay McKendry. She'd show them all.

He turned his hand over, his palm up. "Let me see your phone."

"What?"

"I'll put in my number." Avoiding her gaze, his voice went gruff. "Text me when you get to Asheville. I want to make sure you make it home safely."

She blinked at him. Just when she'd been

working up a head of steam, he went all cow-boy-gentleman on her.

"Over the next few weeks, we'll need to be in close contact." His features went ruddy. "I mean—"

She suspected underneath his cowboy tough-ness there lay a streak of sweetness he didn't like to reveal. And just like that, the atmosphere be-tween them became less frosty.

"Close contact." She laughed. "Got it."

"We'll need to stay in touch to plan the wed-ding," he growled.

She handed him her cell. "Of course."

He typed in his number and gave it back to her. "What's first on your wedding to-do list?"

"I'll research area venues and, if there's any openings, pay them a visit."

He nodded. "I want to go with you to check them out."

She opened her mouth to argue but decided not to waste her breath.

Putting the truck into gear, he eased out of the parking lot and continued down Main Street. After business hours, the café was shut-tered. Downtown, such as it was, was largely deserted. Everyone had gone home to enjoy the evening with their families. Her spirits sank

lower. She had only cheese and crackers waiting to welcome her at the apartment. To borrow a bit of cowboy slang, *Yippee*.

He steered into an empty slot next to her
blue Subaru.

"I'll let you know what I discover." She
reached for the door. "At this late date, there
may not be any facilities available for the weekend of the wedding."

"Where there's a will, there's a way. If there's
a way, I have full faith Kelsey Summerfield will
find it."

"Thanks for the endorsement." Her lips
quirked. "I think." She slipped out of the truck.

"Keltz?"

At the friendly shortening of her name, an
inexplicable relief flooded her senses.

"You won't forget to text me?" He leaned
across the seat as far as his seat belt allowed. "I'll
worry if you don't."

Something squeezed inside her rib cage. No
one had bothered to worry about her since
Granna died. "I won't forget." She tucked a
strand of hair behind her ear. "I promise."

"Good." Frowning, he turned his face toward
the closed café. "Better get on the road now."

He made no move to leave until she backed

out of the space. Someone had raised him right. She'd seen no evidence of his parents at the Bar None. What was the story there? The cowboy was proving more intriguing than she'd imagined.

It was dark when she pulled into her apartment complex, but despite the events of the day she felt considerably lighter than when she'd left the ranch. She ran up the flight of stairs and let herself inside the apartment. Shrugging off her coat, she texted Clay.

A second later, a squiggling line of dots appeared. Had he been watching for her text?

Let's talk tomorrow.

Kicking off her shoes, she smiled and typed. **Will do.**

Good night, City Girl.

Her heart did a little zing. **Good night, Cowboy.** She hit Send.

The doorbell rang. Such was her buoyancy, she didn't stop to look through the peephole but flung open the door.

"Why haven't you answered my calls?" Her father glared. "You and I, young lady, need to have a long, overdue chat." Boyd Howard Summerfield III strode past her into the apartment.

Her happy feelings sank faster than the ship that hit the iceberg.

SHE CHOKED OFF a sigh. "Dad?"

His beige wool overcoat fanned out behind him. Not one to stand on ceremony—or an invitation—he marched over to her couch and sat down. "I was in a meeting when your brother texted me your grandfather had gotten engaged." He perched on the edge of the cushion. "When my father couldn't reach me, he contacted Andrew and left it to him to break the news of his impending nuptials. When's the date?"

"The first weekend in December," she whispered.

Her father leaned forward with his elbows on his knees. His mouth twisted. "Why am I the last to hear this news?"

Because he couldn't be bothered to check his phone or email unless it involved business? She sank into an adjacent armchair.

Her father's eyes—the same color she'd inherited from Grampy—became an icy blue. "I sent you to that one-stop hick town to avoid this very situation."

She bit her lip.

"You had one job." He stabbed his fingers through his beginning-to-gray dark hair. "How is it once again you've managed to fail me?"

Since the moment of her birth, she'd never been anything but a disappointment to him. Her stomach tightened. She could kiss any prospective position in the family business good-bye.

"As for my dear old dad," her father huffed, "has he gone senile?"

Kelsey stiffened. It was one thing to castigate her many shortcomings, but it was quite another to attack Grampy. "For the first time since Granna died, he's actually happy. He's in love with Dorothy, and she loves him."

"She's a gold digger." Her father sneered. "That ranch is barely breaking even. Maybe she thinks in marrying a Summerfield, she'll put the ranch in the black for the first time in years."

Kelsey's eyes widened. "You did a background check on the McKendrys?"

He arched his eyebrow. "Did you doubt that I would? After you met this Dorothy person last week, the first thing I did was contact a private investigator."

"Grampy would be mortified if he knew what you've done."

"Don't be naïve." Her father's gaze snapped to hers. "He did the same thing when your mother and I became engaged. Where do you think I acquired my business acumen from, if not from the old barracuda himself? Nothing personal. Merely good business practice."

The man her father described in no way resembled the grandfather she'd known and loved her entire life.

"Dorothy is not a gold digger." Kelsey straightened. "The McKendrys aren't like that."

"Humans are like that, Kelsey."

When had he become so cynical? But she knew. After the slow, inch-by-inch death of her mother.

"Granna would want Grampy to be happy."

Her father stood abruptly. "My mother's barely been dead a year. Has he no respect for her memory?" Her dad paced the length of the sofa. "But what would someone your age know about loss?" He sat down again.

Kelsey knew plenty about loss. She'd lost Granna and her mom just as much as her dad had. But she could never say such a thing to him. He'd never understand.

Might as well tell him the rest, though.

Taking a breath, she told him about the pulled muscle and Grampy's insistence on staying at the ranch. "He's asked me to plan the wedding." She opened her hands. "Please don't ruin his happiness, Dad. This is the most alive I've seen him in months."

Her father's eyes narrowed. "You don't think there's any changing his mind, then?"

"I don't." She gripped the armrests. "I'm sorry."

"Don't be sorry. Fix this, Kelsey."

She frowned. "I'm not sure—"

"The Summerfields have a reputation to maintain." Her father lifted his chin. "Can I trust you to put together an event that will do us proud?"

"Of course."

His eyes bored into hers. "Pull this off, and you'll have earned a permanent position in the family company." He rose. "I'll expect regular progress reports."

This was her chance to prove herself and earn

his respect. Perhaps his affection, too. Or was that too much to hope for?

Heart racing, she walked him to the door. "I promise you a spectacular wedding no one will ever forget."

CHAPTER THREE

CLAY DIDN'T GET much sleep that night. Wide awake before sunrise, he arose earlier than usual and headed out for morning chores. His breath puffed in the frosty air. It was the perfect time to make repairs and get ready for the late-winter calving season.

Under the electric lights in the barn, he spent an hour working on the tractor. Later, his stomach growling, he made his way across the barnyard to the kitchen.

Nana Dot handed him a steaming cup of coffee.

He warmed his hands around the mug. "Thanks." He nudged his chin toward the hallway. "How's the patient this morning?"

"Not an early riser." Nana handed him a plate of hotcakes. "Unless it's tee time."

He dug into the food. It wasn't many mornings he beat his grandmother out of bed. The lovebirds would have to adjust their routines to each other.

Clay placed his plate in the dishwasher.

"You're not the only early riser, though." Nana scrolled through her cell phone. "Howard's granddaughter isn't one to let any grass grow under her feet. She's texted me four times already this morning."

He glanced at the clock. "What about?"

"What else?" His grandmother heaved a sigh. "The wedding of the century."

He chuckled. "She can be a lot."

Nana threw him a contrite look. "I shouldn't complain. She's handling details I would never have thought to consider."

"But four texts? All before seven?"

"She's a go-getter." Nana raised her eyebrows. "She's definitely got the bit between her teeth. She's put together something she calls a wedding storyboard. And there's a checklist."

"Nana, if this is too much—"

"She means well. She's just very..." Nana's mouth worked "...enthusiastic."

He slipped his arms into his coat. "This is your wedding, not hers. I won't let her steamroll you."

"Last text included a questionnaire. Favorite colors. Favorite foods. Food I dislike. Colors I dislike." Nana tilted her head. "You get the picture."

He was getting the picture, all right. Kelsey Summerfield was nothing if not intense. And exhausting. "Should I have a word with her?"

Nana shook her head. "She wants Howard and I to send the names and addresses on our guest list."

"I'll be out in the barn if you need my help with Mr. Howard."

Standing on the back porch, he filled his lungs with the apple-crisp mountain air and then got to work shoveling out the pens.

He couldn't imagine his grandmother living anywhere but the ranch. Howard would soon become a permanent fixture at the Bar None. The ranch had been Clay's home his entire life, but after the wedding, where did that leave him? Sharing the farmhouse with the octogenarian newlyweds?

Clay better get a social life of his own, or he'd find himself third-wheeling forever.

His cell vibrated. Removing his work gloves, he fished it out of his pocket. He couldn't help but smile when he saw the caller. When she wasn't completely driving him insane, Kelsey made him laugh. "What's up?"

"If you're too busy doing ranch stuff . . ."

He stuffed his gloves in his pocket. "I'm not too busy."

"What're you doing?"

He leaned on the handle of the shovel. "Cleaning cow stalls."

There was a beat of silence. "What does that involve?"

He bit back a smile. "A shovel and a wheel-barrow."

"Does this involve cow excrement?"

Always such a hoot talking to Kelsey Summerfield. "Yes, it does."

"Gross."

He pictured Kelsey crinkling her cute little nose. "What're you doing so early on this bright November morning?"

"I found several possible venues worth checking out. But since you're busy, I'll visit them."

"Nice try, Keltz, but I'm not doing anything that can't be done another time. Where are they located?"

"One is in Asheville."

He frowned. "I was hoping for something nearer Truelove."

"The second is closer. Out in the country."

Resting the shovel against the gate, he propped himself against the wall. "That sounds promising."

"I think so."

Why did he get the feeling she wasn't telling him everything? "What's the game plan?"

"I have an appointment to view the one in Asheville at ten o'clock this morning and the second one around eleven thirty. Do you want to meet me at the first location?"

He swiped his forehead with his forearm. "How about I pick you up and we ride over there together?"

"Great. I'll text you my address. How soon can you be here?"

He straightened. "I need to shower, but give me an hour and a half, and I'll be there."

"With bells on."

His brow scrunched. "What?"

"Christmas wedding bells. 'tis the season, Cowboy."

He returned to the house for a quick shower. Because they were probably going to some glitzy places, he put on an almost-new pair of Wranglers he usually only wore to church. And took the time to iron a shirt.

When he came out of his room, Nana was fixing a breakfast tray for Mr. Howard. "Don't you look fresh as the first snowfall on the ridge."

Clay smiled. "Don't want uptown Asheville to think we're a bunch of hicks." He told his grandmother about the day's mission.

"Howard and I composed our guest list while you were in the barn. I've emailed it to you and Kelsey."

Clay carried the tray down the hall for her. He stuck his head inside the guest bedroom and bid Mr. Howard good morning. He handed off the tray. "Don't know when I'll be back, but I'll see you when I see you."

"Have fun. Try not to argue." Nana leaned closer for his ears only. "And don't let her get carried away."

After double-checking his GPS, he pulled into her apartment complex without any trouble. He hurried up the three flights of stairs and rang the doorbell. Trouble answered the door.

"Hi, Cowboy." Kelsey beamed at him. "I'm ready if you are."

Trouble with a capital *T*.

Gulping, he took in the early morning vision that was Kelsey Summerfield. She wore a winter-white sweater that looked like soft cashmere and skinny jeans tucked into a pair of knee-high black boots. Wow.

He jammed his hands into his pockets. "I was born ready, City Girl."

She slipped on a wool coat the same bright blue color as an April sky over the ranch and ducked her head through the strap of a cross-body soft leather purse. He did a quick scan of her apartment. Chic and stylish—just as he would've supposed in this swanky high-rent district in downtown Asheville—but the white, modern decor seemed surprisingly comfortable, too.

At the truck, she gave him the address of the first venue.

She motioned down the block toward a parked, red double-decker bus turned coffee shop. "I belong to a monthly book club that meets there. Outdoor seating only, so this time of year we relocate to nearby Woolworth's for coffee and pie." Her eyes sparkled. "What's the last book you read?"

He steered the truck toward the River Arts District. "There's not much time to read at the ranch. If I get still, I tend to fall asleep."

"Maybe you haven't come across the right story yet."

He looked at her. "Maybe I haven't." He looked away. "Tell me about the book you're reading this month."

The story revolved around a man and a woman on the run after she witnessed a drug-cartel execution. While bullets flew, romance blossomed. Kelsey had reached the climatic, all-hope-is-lost part when he turned into the parking lot of a former textile mill, closed for nearly a hundred years.

He pushed back the brim of his hat. "Is this the right place?"

"It is." She gave him a smile. "Repurposed as an event venue. My brother, Andrew, got married in a place like this about a decade ago."

He hadn't known she had a brother. "A decade ago? That would have made you either a very old flower girl or a very young bridesmaid."

She laughed. "I'll have you know I was the best junior bridesmaid there ever was."

Outside the steel-fronted entrance, he stared at the brick building. "I don't know about this."

She cocked her head. "Give it a chance."

The venue director ushered them into the large open space with vaulted ceilings and steel beams.

"Did I understand from our phone conversation you are a Summerfield?" the woman purred.

He stiffened.

Kelsey's smile faltered. "I am." She inserted her hand into the crook of his arm. "This is Clay McKendry."

Country and proud of it, he broadened his shoulders.

"Historic. Industrial." In stilettos, dramatic makeup and a sleek, high-powered business suit, the platinum-blonde paused beside one of the cathedral windows overlooking the French Broad, the same river that flowed past True-love. "Urban chic."

As the director showed them around, Kelsey fired questions at her. He peered over her shoulder at the checklist on her phone.

"Every love story is different." The director rested her perfectly manicured hand on the exposed brick wall. "And so are we."

The venue felt cold and sterile.

At the end of the tour, the woman led them to the entrance. "The beginning of your forever starts here."

"Oh. The venue is not for us." Kelsey's eyes cut to him. "We're not together. I mean, obviously we are together." Her hand waggled back and forth between the two of them. "Here. Today. But we're not together-together, as in like, getting married."

"Ain't that the truth," he muttered.

She glowered at him. "We're here on behalf of family members."

He jammed his hat on his head and pulled her toward the door. "We'll give you a call if we're interested." He hustled her out.

"What did you think about the venue?"

He lifted his hat, ran his hand over his head and clamped the Stetson back on again. "It doesn't seem like Nana's kind of place." He sighed. "I'm sorry."

"No, you're right."

He did a double take. "Come again?"

"I wasn't feeling the Nana vibe, either."

"Where to next?"

"Prepare to be amazed, Cowboy."

He had an idea every day with Kelsey would feel pretty amazing.

The property lay between Asheville and Truelove. During the drive, he had only to insert a topic into the conversation, wait for the coin to drop and let her go. He enjoyed her animation and enthusiasm for life. Her hands in constant motion, she leaped from one quirky subject to the next. Possessing wide-ranging tastes, she touted favorite emojis—

"You have a favorite emoji?" He shook himself. "Of course you'd have a favorite emoji."

Pistachios were her favorite nut.

He rolled his eyes. "Why does it not surprise me you have a favorite nut?"

She ignored him. "This will probably gross you out, but my favorite sushi restaurant is—"

"I like sushi."

"Wait." Her mouth dropped. "What?"

"And you had me pegged as a strictly meat-and-potatoes kind of guy. Although, I never refuse a good steak."

"Way to wow, Cowboy." Her eyes shone. "I had no idea behind the swagger and rakishly dimpled chin, you had such hidden depths."

An unexpected, quicksilver warmth shot through him. "I'm a deep kind of guy." He fingered his rakishly dimpled chin.

Turned out they liked the same local North Carolina band. He wouldn't have seen that coming. Kelsey Summerfield liked contemporary indie folk music.

She settled against the seat. "I've been doing most of the talking."

"Well, when you're good at something—

Ow!" He rubbed his side where she'd elbowed him, but it was worth it to push her buttons.

"Can I ask you a personal question?" She bit her bottom lip, and his heart accelerated.

She snapped her fingers in his face. "Are you listening to me?"

He wrested his attention off her mouth. "Yes, ma'am."

She chewed her lip again, and his heart did a nosedive. *Stop with the lip-nibbling.* It was playing havoc with his equilibrium. *For the love of Christmas, Keltz...*

He'd missed her question. "Say it again, please."

She gave him an exasperated look. "There were lots of photos at the ranch house, but I got the impression you and Miss Dot lived there alone. I wondered..."

"You wondered what?"

She fingered the strap of her purse. "About your parents."

He one-handed the wheel. "What about 'em?"

"They're still alive, right?"

He nodded. "Very much so, thankfully."

"But they don't live at the ranch?" She waved her hand. "Forget I asked. None of my business. If anyone understands complicated families, it's me."

From the remarks she'd made yesterday, her father sounded like a real piece of work.

"My dad grew up on the ranch and helped Nana run it after my grandfather died. The ranch was never my dad's passion."

"But ranching is yours?"

"When I finished school, I took over as operations manager, and my parents retired to the coast, where my mom was born. They visit for the holidays, and I visit them during the summer. I'm happy they're happy. They love living within sight and sound of the ocean."

"But not you?"

He shrugged. "The mountains call me, not the sea. What's your passion?"

"I'm not sure yet. Mountains surround Asheville, too. I love the combination of eclectic energy and historic ambience there." She stared at the passing scenery. "For a foodie like me, it's a culinary hot spot."

He veered onto a long, asphalt drive. "Truelove has its own small-town charms."

"If you say so." A *V* formed in the delicate space between her brows. "You were okay with taking over the ranch, right?"

"I can't imagine wanting to do anything else."

"Good." She glanced away. "There's nothing worse than having your future mapped out for you."

Was she speaking from personal experience? "What is it you do when you're not trying to be the boss of everything?"

She snorted. "I call it *utilizing leadership skills*."

"Whatever," he grunted. "Or perhaps Summerfields don't have to work for a living like the rest of us."

"My father is the most hardworking person I know. Too hardworking." She glared at him. "My brother and I were expected to earn our places in the family firm. Since Grampy retired, my dad is the president and chief executive officer. Andrew is now the chief financial officer. My sister-in-law, Nicola, serves as general counsel."

"What is your role in the family biz?"

"To be determined." She fidgeted. "I have a business degree. I organize the yearly golf tournament that the company sponsors and various publicity launches." Her mouth turned downward. "My father has high standards for his children. I'm still working on proving to him I deserve a permanent role in the corporation."

Her father's standards sounded impossible to meet. Not that it was any of his business.

The road wound around the mountain like stripes on a candy cane before emerging from the trees into a grassy meadow with an honest-to-goodness—

His eyes widened. "A castle?"

The gray stone castle, with a turreted tower and moat, overlooked the valley below. He pulled into a graveled parking lot. "What is a castle doing in western North Carolina? Is this for real?" He cut the engine.

"Surprise!" Throwing open the door, she hopped out. "Totally real. A hundred years ago, an eccentric railroad baron dismantled a medieval castle in the Scottish Highlands and rebuilt it stone by stone here in the Blue Ridge. Isn't it awesome?"

They climbed a series of terraced steps. At the top, they ambled across the open drawbridge toward the stout iron-studded oak door.

Clay scrubbed the stubble on his jaw. "It's something, all right."

Her cell dinged. She read the incoming message. "The manager is on a business call. The door is open, and he says for us to look around. He'll be with us shortly."

Clay lifted the iron latch and pushed the heavy door open with his shoulder. The hinges creaked. His eyebrows arched. "Very atmospheric."

She marched inside. "Welcome to Castle Doone."

"Doom is right," he muttered.

He eyed the shiny armor-clad, life-size medieval knight standing guard at the foot of the stairs that led to the minstrel gallery. The Great Hall was crisscrossed with gigantic oak beams from which heraldic banners hung.

"I love it." Arms outstretched, she did a slow, three-hundred-and-sixty-degree turn. "Don't you love it?"

He didn't love it.

"Seems like something out of a horror movie with a dash of romance novel thrown in for good measure."

She propped her hands on her hips. "It's romantic. Like something out of a fairy tale."

He took off his hat. "I don't mean to keep raining on your wedding-princess fantasies, but this doesn't seem like the cozy, homestyle wedding Nana is going for, either."

"When the king and queen are in love, a castle becomes a home."

He folded his arms. "You're an expert on being in love, I suppose?"

She pursed her lips. "I didn't say that."

"Have you ever been in love?"

She flushed. "I don't see how that has anything to do with—"

"Answer the question." He wasn't sure why he'd thrown down that gauntlet, but a sudden, desperate need to know burned a hole in his belly. "Have you ever been in love?"

"Not yet. What about you? Have you ever been in love?"

"Yes. No. Maybe." He scoured his face with his hand. "At least, at the time I believed I was."

"Whoever she was, she hurt you." Kelsey's voice softened. "I'm sorry."

Unable to bear the sympathy in her gaze, he faced the armor-plated knight. "No big deal."

"It must've been a big deal for you to have lost your faith in happily-ever-afters."

"Angela and I…" He shrugged, striving for a nonchalance he didn't feel. "We were too different. It would've never worked. Better we found out before it was too late."

Kelsey nodded. "If it's meant to be, it will be."

He crimped the brim of his hat. "I guess you

adhere to the old adage that everything works out for the best in the end."

"Absolutely." She waved her hands. "If it isn't the ending you hoped for, then it's not the end."

He cut his eyes at her. "My philosophy is closer to *It may not be the party you hoped for, but while you're there you might as well dance.*"

"You're referring to the *playing the field* thing you mentioned yesterday?"

"Why not?" He threw her a crooked grin, which usually drove the females wild but on her appeared to have little effect.

She cocked her head. "How exactly is that working out for you, Clayton, other than in the obvious short term?"

His grin faded.

"Grampy and Miss Dot inspire me. At their age, finding love again." She sighed. "Here's hoping I won't have to wait till I'm in my eighties to be swept off my feet by love, though."

He couldn't imagine why some city dude hadn't swept her off her feet already. The men in Asheville must be a dim bunch.

"Before you completely nix the idea, let me show you what I put together on the storyboard for this place." She rummaged through the voluminous leather purse and took out a large sketch pad. "Imagine if we used this end of the Hall for the ceremony. Think swags of evergreen on the beams. Dozens of candles." She thrust the pad at him.

Kelsey strode toward the other end of the Great Hall. "We could set up high-backed chairs with the bride and groom at the head of a horseshoe-shaped table, presiding over a sumptuous medieval feast."

Sketchbook in hand, he joined her.

Kelsey seized his arm. "And madrigals. Oh, Clay." Her voice rose in concert with her imagination. "Imagine madrigal singers crooning Christmas carols."

"Only word I understood was *horseshoe*."

"Think of the possibilities. Bagpipes. Who doesn't love a bagpipe?"

Clay could think of several people.

Her hands created an imaginary viewfinder again. "I'm seeing a blue-and-green tartan."

Clay folded his arms against his chest. "I'm not wearing a kilt, Kelsey. Absolutely not. Get it out of your head. Not happening."

"Have you no cultural pride?" She threw open her hands. "For the love of haggis, you're a McKendry."

"I do not love haggis, and I'm a McKendry

from the highlands of North Carolina, not the Highlands of Scotland." He scowled. "I'm not wearing a dress."

She clung to his arm. "It's not a dress."

"You can stop batting those big blue eyes at me, Keltz."

She fluttered her lashes. "You'd absolutely rock a kilt, Clay. You'd be even more irresistibly handsome."

Kelsey believed him handsome?

Nonetheless, he hardened his resolve. "I'm not wearing a kilt. Not for you. Not for Nana. Not for love nor money."

"Fine. Be that way, Mr. Fun Killer." Letting go of his arm, she gave him a small push. "Clay McKendry, where dreams go to die."

He laughed. She laughed, too. A burly man with a long white beard emerged from the nether regions of the castle keep.

After a few logistical questions, she shook her head. "I'm afraid the site won't work for our wedding party."

Given her previous enthusiasm, Clay stared at her perplexed.

"Have you checked out the guest list?"

Clay shook his head.

"Between the bride and groom and older

friends like the matchmakers, while absolutely dreamy, the castle won't work for them." She motioned. "Too many stairs from the parking lot. Not accessible."

She thanked the manager for his time, and they exited.

"I would've never thought about that." He took hold of her elbow as they negotiated their way down the stone steps to the truck. "You are good at this. Your granddad was right to put you in charge of this shindig."

"Thank you." She sagged against the truck. "But this means we're down to only one option."

"You were thinking to secure a venue today?"

"What choice do I have? We're already playing catch-up. Everything else was booked months ago. I can't fail Grampy or my dad again."

He looked at her sharply. "What's this got to do with your father?"

"Dad wants to be kept in the loop about Grampy's nuptials." She gave him a wobbly smile. "I texted him this morning about the castle and the mill. If this last option doesn't work out…"

He reached for her hand, surprising himself

as much as her. "What happened to *if it's not the ending you hoped for, it's not the end*?"

"I hate that you are using my own words against me," she growled.

"We're only thirty minutes from True-love. Let's have lunch at the Jar and refuel." He squeezed her hand. "Everything will look brighter after we put some grub in our bellies."

"I feel certain Kara would object to calling her gourmet cuisine *grub*, but I take your point." She laced her fingers in his. "I didn't think I needed a co-planner, but turns out I do. Thanks for not leaving me to muddle through this alone." Her voice hitched. "And for being a friend."

At the catch in her voice, his heart did a funny sort of twang. Opening the truck door, she climbed inside. Yet as he made his way around to slip behind the wheel, it wasn't food he had on his mind.

But rather a happy/not-happy feeling—that Kelsey Summerfield saw him as her friend.

CHAPTER FOUR

"For such a small person, you sure put away the food." Clay cocked his head. He signaled his Aunt Trudy for the bill.

Looming professional or personal disaster tended to have that effect on Kelsey. After this latest failure, Dad would never give her another chance to show what she could do.

Sidling over, Trudy laid the bill on the table. Kelsey reached for it, but he intercepted it first.

"I pay my own way, Clayton."

His eyes narrowed. "I've got this."

Trudy's gaze ping-ponged between them. Behind the cutout window to the kitchen, a bell dinged. "You know the drill. Pay at the register when you're done wrangling." She moved to pick up another order.

"Whatever floats your horse, Ginger." Kelsey fluttered her hand. "Next time's on me."

He gritted his teeth. "I'm not a ginger."

She snorted. "There's none so blind than those who refuse to look into a mirror, Gingersnaps."

"I have brown hair." He ran a hand over his head. "With red-ish highlights."

"To-may-to. To-mah-to." She shrugged. "Still red."

"You are impossible."

She smirked. "I try."

His mouth twitched. "You succeed." He glanced around the always-crowded diner. "Listen, I just got a text from Allen's Hardware. A part I ordered has come in. Since we're in town, would you mind if I went over there to get it before we head to the next venue?"

She put down her coffee mug. "No problem."

"Why don't you sit tight here and finish your latte?" He grabbed hold of the edge of the table. "Won't take me but a few minutes. I'll be right back." Clapping his hat on his head, he hauled himself out of the booth.

After paying, he exited the diner. Peering through the picture window overlooking the town square, her eyes followed the broad set of his shoulders until he crossed Main and disappeared around the corner.

She lifted her gaze to the distant horizon.

Wave upon wave of undulating blue-green ridges enfolded the charming town like the worn but comforting arms of a beloved grandmother. The mountains defined the citizens of Truelove. As did the gushing river that wound around the town like a horseshoe.

"Mind if I join you for a minute?"

Jolting, she put a hand to her throat.

"I didn't mean to startle you."

The seventysomething woman's bright blue eyes twinkled behind the wire-framed glasses. Eons ago, she and Kelsey's grandmother, Joan, had been roommates at nearby Ashmont College.

Kelsey gestured toward the seat Clay had vacated.

Martha Alice Breckenridge threw her a small smile. "Quite the view, isn't it?"

Hoping she referred to the oak trees lining the perimeter of the village green, Kelsey lifted her chin. "Truelove is a lovely little town."

The elegant, older woman touched her perfectly coiffed silver white hair. "Our cowboys aren't too bad, either."

Kelsey went crimson.

Martha Alice patted her hand. "I'm teasing." Then she spoiled the effect by chuckling a tad wickedly.

"I have an appointment at Hair Raisers soon, but I've found a photo album from my school days with your grandmother you might like to see." Granna's lifelong best friend gave her the gentlest of smiles. "I miss her, too. Everyday."

Kelsey's mouth trembled. "I'd love to see the pictures sometime, Miss Marth'Alice."

She abbreviated the matchmaker's name the same way Granna had.

"I'm happy for Dorothy and Howard." Martha Alice reached across the table and took Kelsey's hand. "I think Joan would be, too."

Tears pricked her eyes. Martha Alice wasn't wrong. That was exactly what Granna would have wanted for the man who'd been the love of her life.

Martha Alice squeezed her hand. "Howard's been adrift since Joan left us. Once you've had time to grapple through your naturally mixed emotions, I think you'll find, as I have over the years, that our greatest joy lies in seeing the happiness of those we love most."

"I'm trying, Miss Marth'Alice."

Martha Alice made a vague motion in the general direction of the vacant Double Name

Club's favorite table. "I also hear you've taken on the planning of the nuptials."

"A month's notice isn't much time, but I'm giving it everything I've got." She gave Granna's friend a quick rundown on the morning's disappointing results.

"What you've got is plenty." Martha Alice nodded. "But the long commute to oversee the details is going to eat up valuable time and energy. What would you think about staying with me until the wedding?"

Truelove offered neither a hotel, bed-and-breakfast or any other rentable accommodations. "I couldn't impose on you like that, Miss Marth'Alice."

"You'd be doing me a favor." Martha Alice waved a wrinkled, blue-veined hand. "Since my granddaughter Kate married her own cowboy and moved to Jack's ranch this summer, the house feels much too empty for me to rattle around in alone, especially as we approach the holidays. What do you say?"

"I'd love to take you up on your offer." She took a breath. Already the wedding felt less overwhelming and more doable. "Thank you."

Martha Alice nudged her chin at the window. "I think your cowboy is on his way to claim you."

"Clay is not my cowboy."

"Whatever you say, sweetie. I must be off." Martha Alice inched out of the booth. "I didn't see your car out front."

"Clayton picked me up this morning at my apartment." She used her best prim schoolmarm voice, but the effect seemed wasted on Martha Alice, who laughed.

"Perfect. You can retrieve your things and drive your car back to Truelove. I'll see you tomorrow at home."

Since Granna died, home had become an elusive concept for Kelsey. She flicked a glance at the tall, muscular figure of the cowboy making his way down the sidewalk. Something pinged in her heart. He really was quite heart-stopping to look at. She got out of the booth. Too bad he was so annoying and a cowboy to boot.

Kelsey and Martha Alice walked out to the sidewalk.

The older woman gave her a hug. "If there's anything I can do to help with the planning, please don't hesitate to ask. Dorothy has a lot of friends in Truelove who'd love to chip in. That's one of the things I love most about this town. Everyone truly looks after their neighbors."

If she was referring to the Double Name Club... Kelsey pursed her lips. Their so-called help she could do without.

Clay walked up to them. She and Martha Alice said goodbye. The older woman strolled toward her car, only to stop for a chat with her garden buddy and fellow matchmaker, Erma-Jean Hicks.

He offered his arm. "Ready for our next adventure?"

She could practically feel ErmaJean eyeballing them.

Kelsey whacked his bicep. "Have you lost what little mind you possess?"

Forehead creasing, he rubbed his arm. "What was that for?"

"They are everywhere." She looked left then right. "Watching. Plotting. Conniving."

He craned his head in both directions. "Who?"

She smacked his arm again. "Can you be any more obvious?" she hissed.

He chuckled. "Does this involve the Irish rock band?"

"Very funny." She grimaced. "I'm talking

about giving a totally wrong impression. The *you two* thingy."

"A matchmaker behind every bush?" Crossing his arms across his coat, he rocked onto his heels. "Good to know I've made a believer out of you. Give 'em an inch and they'll take a matrimonial mile."

"Cowboy and City Girl?" She made an exaggerated shudder. "It doesn't bear contemplating."

"My feelings exactly. Marriage—a fate worse than death."

Did he mean marriage in general or more specifically marriage to her? She experienced a surge of extreme dislike for a woman she'd never met. That Angela person had done a real number on his heart and his head. Ruining him for anyone else. Including her?

She sucked in a quick breath. Where had that come from?

Opening the truck door, he offered his hand. When he smiled at her, it was all she could do not to swoon. Clay McKendry was the whole package. A gentleman and easy on the eyes, too.

The more time she spent with the cowboy, the less outlandish the idea of a relationship beyond friendship appeared.

We're just friends. But to her chagrin, the possibility of something more had taken root in her heart. Suddenly, friendship with Clay had lost some of its charm.

THE THIRD VENUE OPTION, a wedding destination resort, was on the other side of Truelove. At a higher elevation, a dusting of snow covered the ground. She told him about her upcoming relocation to Martha Alice's house.

Clay rapped his thumb against the steering wheel. "Favorite joke?"

"I have the perfect joke for November." She perked. "April showers bring May flowers. What do May flowers bring?"

He shrugged. "I don't know. What?"

"Pilgrims."

He groaned.

"Get it? *Mayflower*?" She nudged him. "Pilgrims?"

"I got it." He rolled his eyes. "Sounds like a kid joke."

She grinned. "I get my best jokes from my five-year-old niece, Eloise."

"I didn't know you had a niece."

She glanced at the passing scenery. "Andrew and Nicola are super busy, and I don't get to see her nearly as much as I'd like. But we have our special traditions, just the two of us."

"Like what?"

"Every February fourteenth, we have a standing sleepover at my apartment while Andrew and Nicola go to dinner. We call it Galentine's."

He chuckled.

"Grampy told me your sister has kids."

"My nephew, Peter, is also five. My niece is three going on forty-three." He flicked his eyes at her. "She has the same *leadership* skills as you."

"I like her already."

At the sign for the resort, he turned off the main road. "How did you hear about this place?"

"One of my suite mates in college was married here a few years ago. You might know her. She grew up in Truelove, but her family moved to Asheville after she graduated high school."

"Her father an attorney?"

She smiled. "He specializes in real estate. He and my dad do a lot of business together."

He cut a glance at Kelsey. "Her wedding was quite the shindig."

She turned in the seat. "I don't remember seeing you. Were you there, too?"

He shook his head. "My friend, Sam, attended. He told me about it."

"Sam... I remember him. He's very handsome, isn't he?"

Clay stiffened. "If you like the blond, blue-eyed jock type, I guess."

"No need to get a bur up your saddle. Merely making an observation. To each his own." She fluttered her lashes at him. "Some women prefer gingers."

"I am not a—" *Wait.* Did *some women* include her?

The truck crested the hill. Below them, the majestic, white-columned historic inn nestled in the sweep of a snow-covered valley.

Her eyes shone. "It's like something out of a winter wonderland, isn't it?"

The resort's clientele weren't exactly the sort of people the McKendrys rubbed shoulders with, but the place was spectacular. His stomach tanked. No way could he afford to put on a wedding here. Something of his feelings must have shown on his face or—scary thought—Kelsey knew him better than he supposed.

Releasing her seat belt, she slid across the seat and laced her fingers through his. "My father's company sponsors a golf tournament here every spring. The resort's bottom line owes us big time. I promise there'll be a deep discount."

"It would have to be a huge discount, and even then…" It meant a lot to him she respected his need to pay for Nana's wedding.

She squeezed his hand. "I can be very persuasive."

For inexplicable reasons, his gaze drifted to her mouth. "Don't I know it," he rasped. His heart sped up. She tilted her face to him. He leaned forward. Her lips parted.

His insides somersaulted. What was happening here? This would not do. Not do at all.

Clay thrust open the door. "We should get going," he grunted.

Jumping out of the cab, he hurried around to the passenger side. She gave him a curious look, but she didn't comment on what almost happened in the truck.

What *had* almost happened in the truck? Nothing, thanks to his quick sense of self-preservation. Had he so quickly forgotten the painful lessons he'd learned courtesy of Angela? *Fool me once…*

They followed the sidewalk to the imposing front entrance. He darted glances at her, but Kelsey kept her features averted. Was she upset with him? For a host of reasons, he and the city girl were not a good idea. Good thing he'd pulled the plug. But if so, why was his stomach in a knot all of a sudden?

Inside the lobby, an ornate chandelier glittered above their heads. He yanked his hat off his head and clutched it over the place his heart used to reside before Angela.

Expensive oriental carpets lay scattered around the white marble floor. Clustered on the formal, silk-covered chairs and sofas, guests conversed in low voices.

The sinking feeling deepened. "Why did I let you talk me into coming here?" This was going to be humiliating.

But he suspected there were few people on earth who could withstand the human dynamo known as Kelsey Summerfield when she got the bull by the horns.

"If the price was affordable, can you see Miss Dot liking it enough to get married here?"

"Who wouldn't like it?" He raked his hand over his head. "My grandmother has worked her fingers to the bone her entire life. It's not a matter of whether she would like it or not—she deserves pampering. But no way can I spring for this, Keltz." He felt his cheeks burn. "The

McKendrys are not in the same financial league as the Summerfields, and I won't let your family foot the bill."

"Will you trust me to negotiate the best price?" She looked at him. "A price within your means?"

He pinched the bridge between his brows. "How do you know what I can afford?"

She didn't say anything.

"Nana?" He growled. "She told you what's in my herd fund, didn't she?"

"Trust me." She twined her hand in his. "I've got this. And you."

She tugged him toward the registration desk.

A middle-aged woman in a navy-blue suit keyed in their names. "You have an appointment with our events director, I see." She picked up a phone. "I'll let Mr. Randleman know you've arrived."

Kelsey adjusted the strap of her purse on her shoulder. "Thank you."

A scarecrow of a man in an expensive coat and tie soon joined them.

Beaming like the events coordinator was her nearest and dearest long-lost friend, Kelsey introduced him to Clay. Mr. Randleman led them across a richly carpeted hallway to his office.

He gestured for them to take a seat in a pair of dark leather chairs and then settled himself behind a massive mahogany desk.

She gave Mr. Randleman the lowdown on the wedding they were putting together for their grandparents. Then she went into business mode. "Over the years, my father has brought a lot of money into the resort's coffers."

Looking down his long, sharp nose, Randleman gave her an oily smile. "It's been a profitable and rewarding partnership on both sides of the table."

"All true." She placed her hands on the armrests. "I'm looking for the resort to offer me a substantial incentive to host my dear grandfather's wedding here." Her gaze bored into his. She didn't blink.

Mr. Randleman shifted his weight. The chair squeaked. "Less than four weeks to put together an occasion of this nature is rather last-minute, Miss Summerfield."

Uncrossing her legs, she planted her feet firmly on the carpet. "Your administrative assistant assured me the date was open. I trust you've had time to peruse the details I emailed this morning.

"I have."

She arched her eyebrow. "I feel sure your impeccable staff can handle the small, intimate wedding we're proposing. Give me a figure, Mr. Randleman."

Clay had never glimpsed this side of her before—serious, driven. He was impressed. More than impressed.

Reaching for a piece of ivory stationery embossed with the resort's logo, Randleman scribbled a number. He slid it over the desk to her.

Clay swallowed past the boulder clogging his throat. Sweat broke out on his brow.

She scanned it and shoved it back. "Try again." She threw him a smile as sharp as a barracuda's teeth. "Unless you're no longer interested in doing business with the Summerfields."

"There's no need to be hasty." Randleman held up both palms. "I'm sure we can work something out to our mutual satisfaction." He jotted down another number and handed it to her.

Her features betrayed neither elation nor disapproval. "I assume this figure is all-inclusive. The rehearsal dinner? Catering for the wedding reception, including place settings and linens?"

Randleman removed a monogrammed white

handkerchief from his coat pocket and mopped his forehead. "If that is what you wish..."

"It is." She leaned forward. "I think the terms will suit us fine. I'd like to sign the contract before we leave the premises."

"Of course."

Giving the man a dazzling smile, she rose. Not sure what had just happened, Clay rose as well.

She extended her hand across the desk. "As always, such a pleasure doing business with you, Mr. Randleman. My father will be pleased."

Randleman shook her hand. "I'll have my assistant prepare the documents."

"While we wait, I'd like to take Mr. McKendry around the property to show him my vision for the wedding weekend."

Randleman ushered them out. "I'll make sure the paperwork is ready when you return."

What astronomical sum had she committed him to? Clay hardly noticed where she led him. They'd exited the main building and ventured onto a cobblestone terrace behind the inn.

"We'll hold the rehearsal dinner here." She let go of his arm. "Imagine twinkle lights strung around the perimeter." She gestured to the enormous stone fireplace. "A roaring fire.

Linen-clad round tables. Gas heaters to keep the guests warm under the blue-velvet sky glittering with stars."

He had to give it to her. Kelsey Summerfield could probably sell ice to polar bears.

This would bankrupt the Bar None.

"Wouldn't it be fabulous if there was snow the weekend of the wedding like now?" She pulled him down the stone steps toward a paved path that curved around a bend of trees. "Let's pray for that."

It was getting late in the day. Once the sun disappeared behind the ridge, darkness fell fast. Already the lavender shadows cast by the inn lengthened across the snow-covered vale.

He followed her along the path through a snow-daubed glade of evergreens lit by strings of fairy lights. The tangy scent of pine permeated the air. The small, stone chapel lay around the bend. Lights glowed through the stained-glass windows, spilling colorful reflections on the snow.

"Isn't it lovely?" She clasped her hands underneath her chin. "So romantic."

His gaze darted to her. "Very lovely." He wasn't thinking of the chapel.

But the setting *was* very picturesque. And in present company, extremely romantic.

A smile curving her lips, she tucked a dark tendril of hair behind her ear. His heart did that funny rat-a-tat-tat thing it did when he thought about her hair. And when she looked at him like she was looking at him right now with those shining big blue eyes of hers...

He could always take out a second mortgage on the ranch. Sell his truck.

"Don't you want to ask how much you're in for this wedding?"

Actually, no, but he supposed he had to face reality sometime. He squeezed his eyes shut. "Let me have it."

She named a figure.

His eyes shot open. "That can't be right, Keltz."

"I assure you it is."

Was she telling him the real price?

He made a grab for her hand. "Let me see that paper." His breath fogged in the chilly air.

She handed it to him with a flourish. "I told you to let me handle Randleman."

The number she'd quoted had been entirely accurate. He wouldn't have to mortgage the ranch. Or sell his truck. The cost would deplete his herd fund but give it a year—or two—and he'd be able to replenish it.

"It's called the art of negotiation."

"You were impressive." He toed the ground with his boot. "But I don't like to take advantage—"

"Advantage?" She hooted. "Shall I tell you how much commission Randleman makes every year off the golf tournament alone, not to mention the quarterly corporate weekends we throw his way?"

The sum she named made him weak in the knees. So much money. Her seeming lack of regard for it made his head swim. In terms of social aspirations, Angela had been a wannabe, but Kelsey was the real deal.

Which drove home their utter incompatibility in regard to social standing. And like a dose of ice water in the face, eradicating any ideas of anything between them beyond friendship.

She took him inside the small chapel with the red carpeted aisle running between two sections of wooden pews. Later, they returned to the main inn for him to sign the contract. There were lots of other details that according to Kelsey needed ironing out, but twilight would be fast upon them. He still needed to take her back to Asheville and return to True-love. She made an appointment to talk further with Felicity, their own personal wedding coordinator at the resort, to discuss rehearsal-dinner and reception-food options.

On the road, he strangled the wheel, consumed by the insurmountable differences between them.

She didn't notice his silence. "Now that we have a venue, I can order the invitations. I'll have to expedite the printing and send them through the mail ASAP." She kept up a running monologue about color schemes and something she called *tablescapes*.

With three weeks, four days and countless hours of enforced proximity until D-Day ahead of him, he'd have to be extra vigilant in guarding his affections when it came to the bubbly and effervescent Kelsey Summerfield.

They were polar opposites. Like night and day. Rather forcibly, he reminded himself of his post-Angela policy toward women. *Keep it light and at arm's length.*

He stole a side-look at her. Totally in her element, she gave him a happy smile. His gut clenched. Beguiling, that's what she was. Simply beguiling. His shoulders slumped.

Arm's length might prove easier said than done.

CHAPTER FIVE

CLAY HAD ACTED preoccupied on the ride to Asheville, but ever the gentleman he insisted on escorting her to the door of her apartment.

Wishing to prolong their time together for reasons she preferred not to examine, Kelsey reached for her cell. "Stay for dinner. We should nail down the information for the invitations. I can order take-out sushi."

He looked over the railing toward the parking lot below. "No, thanks."

Tired of wedding planning? Or of her company?

She leaned against the door. "I could order a pizza instead."

He hunched his shoulders. "Can't stay. Sorry."

Okay... Tired of her.

He stuffed his hands in his jean pockets. "Got to get back. Early morning. Chores tomorrow."

Clay McKendry wasn't the most talkative

person she'd ever known, but this evening he'd taken *stoic* and *taciturn* to a whole different level. Like he had to pay for every word he let pass between his lips. Her gaze flickered to his mouth. She flushed, recalling the split second at the resort when she'd thought for a crazy, impossible moment he meant to kiss her.

Obviously, in light of his current awkward behavior, a stress-induced hallucination on her part.

She straightened. "Right. Thanks for helping me sort out the venues today."

He took a step back. "No problem." He cut his eyes again toward his truck. Anxious to be away? "Good night."

Kelsey went inside. What was up with him? And people said women were moody?

Shaking her head, she ordered the sushi, anyway. While she waited for the delivery, she sent a quick text to her father, updating him that a venue had been secured.

Dancing dots appeared.

She curled up on the sofa, pulled a pillow cushion to her chest and laid the cell on top.

Mill or castle?

A warm feeling filled her. An unexpected

blessing from Grampy's wedding. How wonderful was it that she and her dad were talking. Communicating more than they ever had before. He was finally showing an interest in one of her projects.

Neither, she typed. Much better.

A few seconds later, more squiggly dots. Where?

Before she could respond, the doorbell rang. She lay aside the phone and retrieved her order. After eating, she packed a suitcase for her stay with Martha Alice. That night, she dreamed of castles, cowboys and Christmas.

The next morning, she ran around Asheville, gathering invitation samples and meeting with a couple of prospective DJs Felicity had recommended.

She made an effort to keep Clay in the loop, texting him about what she discovered. But his replies left a great deal to be desired. Monosyllabic words like *Fine* or *Good* finally devolved to thumbs-up emojis.

It was midafternoon before she headed to Truelove. He said he wanted to be her co-planner. He said winter was his slower time. What was his deal?

After an early dinner at Martha Alice's, she

looked through the long-ago photos of Granna and her best friend at nearby Ashmont. They laughed at the bygone hairstyles and fashion choices of the postwar era.

She made a note on her cell to set up an appointment for Dorothy with the wedding boutique in Asheville. She also realized she'd neglected to answer her father's text about the venue. She picked up her phone.

"What flowers does Dorothy want in her bouquet?"

Kelsey laid aside her cell. "She told me to use my own judgment. One more thing on my to-do list."

"You're a natural at this. I am so impressed at your level of organization." Martha Alice set down her teacup. "You could do this professionally."

"Thank you. But let's hold off on the praise until after I get on the other side of the nuptials. This is my first foray into planning a wedding, but I've been a bridesmaid in a gazillion weddings." She shook her head. "Always the bridesmaid, never the bride."

"Think how prepared you'll be when your turn comes." Martha Alice's blue eyes twinkled.

"Which, based on the attentiveness of a certain Truelove cowboy, may come sooner than later."

"It's not like that… We're not like that." She blushed. "Dad says the sensible thing is to establish my career before focusing on matters of the heart."

"The heart almost never does the sensible thing, though, does it?" She arched an eyebrow. "From what your grandmother Joan told me regarding your father's whirlwind courtship of your mother, he didn't exactly follow his own advice. They eloped."

She hadn't known that about her parents. It was hard to imagine her buttoned-up, unemotional father throwing caution and sensibility to the wind for love.

"I'm going for a winter-wonderland theme." Best to get Martha Alice off Kelsey's nonexistent, never-going-to-happen romance with Clay McKendry. "What flowers would you recommend?"

An avid gardener, Martha Alice mentioned a specific rose with velvety crimson petals.

Kelsey pulled up a photo on her phone. "I love it."

"Particularly stunning when paired with white roses." Martha Alice smiled over her teacup. "All-white weddings are elegant, but I do love a pop of color."

"I want to finish off Miss Dot's bouquet with a silver-edged, royal-blue velvet ribbon I found on the internet."

Martha Alice also had some fabulous ideas regarding Christmas tablescapes and wedding decor. Over the next few days, she ticked more items off her list. Felicity at the resort had proven incredibly helpful. They hit it off, and Kelsey began to consider her a friend.

She talked with her grandfather at least once a day. To her relief, he sounded stronger and in great spirits, especially when they discussed the impending wedding.

Dorothy had put him onto a set of daily stretching exercises to strengthen his back muscles. Kelsey would have loved to spend more time with him, but she wasn't entirely sure what the frequency or protocol should be for visiting the ranch.

Being with Martha Alice was like having Granna back. She suspected the older woman enjoyed their time together as much as Kelsey did. It was wonderful to have someone to bounce ideas off. Earlier in the week, she'd believed she was reaching a similar kind of comfortable rapport with Clay, but he'd gone radio-silent.

She lay awake at night worrying she'd unknowingly offended him.

Although always kind and polite, Dorothy wasn't her family. The ranch wasn't her home. They hadn't acquired the drop-in-anytime level of familiarity. Kelsey wondered if they ever would.

She did her best to keep Clay's grandmother apprised of every step in the planning process. Yet there were important details on the checklist that required the immediate and personal okay of the bride and groom. And she was more than a little peeved at Clay.

The next day, she called Dorothy to see if it was okay to stop by the ranch to finalize the couple's music selections for the reception. When she arrived at the Bar None, Clay's truck was parked outside the barn, but he was nowhere in sight.

Grampy was in a chipper mood. No longer confined to bed, he had progressed to sitting in a leather recliner in the living room. Kelsey sat down on the couch. With Dorothy in the flanking recliner, they went over the list of songs.

"These are great." Kelsey smiled. Classic, golden oldies from the most romantic era of American music. "I'll forward the list to the DJ."

"Something else you should be aware of." Dorothy stuck out her chin as if expecting an argument. "I've decided to ask the pastor of my church in Truelove to marry us."

"Reverend Bryant offered to do our premarital counseling." Grampy snorted. "I was married longer the first time than he's been alive."

"Nevertheless," Dorothy's voice held a touch of frost. "I've learned from experience that whether a couple is eighteen or eighty, there are topics that should be thoroughly discussed to eliminate later misunderstandings."

Kelsey glanced between them.

"Whatever you think best, dear." Grampy shrugged, but he didn't look as if he totally agreed.

His marriage to Granna had been idyllic, or so it had seemed to Kelsey. But maybe Dorothy's first marriage hadn't been as carefree. Not that it was any of her business.

She laid her cell on the cushion. "If you give me his contact information, I'll coordinate wedding details with him directly."

Dorothy removed a business card from a side table. She handed it across to Kelsey. On the table, Kelsey spotted a stiff, black hat brush. Like for a Stetson? An uneasy suspicion needled at her gut. Had Grampy's new favorite seat actually been Clay's seat first?

She felt a pang of sympathy for the irksome cowboy, dispossessed from his favorite chair. The familiar routine of his normal life had been as upended as her own by the sudden engagement. Larger than life, Grampy could be a bit much. And unthinkingly presumptuous. How was Clay coping? Was he okay?

Not that he'd appreciate any concern from her. His absence had made that abundantly clear.

She pulled up the to-do list on her phone. "What about the wedding party?"

Grampy shifted in his—Clay's—chair. "I'll ask your dad to be my best man."

She smiled. "I'm sure he'll be pleased." She told them about his unexpected interest in the wedding planning, leaving out the background check.

Dorothy folded her hands in her lap. "I've asked my son, Gary, Clay's father, to walk me down the aisle." Her gaze flicked to her groom.

"Clay will stand up as one of Howard's grooms-men along with your brother, Andrew."

Grampy cleared his throat. "Dorothy's great-granddaughter is too young to be a flower girl. We want to ask Eloise."

"Oh, Grampy." Kelsey pressed the cell phone to her chest. "She'll be thrilled."

"My great-grandson, Peter, is old enough to be ring bearer. I've asked my daughter, Trudy, to be my matron of honor." Dorothy frowned. "Although since she's divorced, I'm not sure if the proper designation should be *matron* or *maid*."

"Dorothy's granddaughter, Rebecca, Clay's sister, will also stand up with her." Grampy gave Kelsey a big smile. "In addition to your planning duties, I think you should be a brides-maid, too."

Grampy's idea? Or Miss Dot's? It would have been better if Dorothy had asked Kelsey herself. But with his characteristic exuberance, maybe Grampy had simply beat his bride to the punch. The older woman's placid gaze gave nothing away.

Had Miss Dot felt pressured by Grampy into issuing the invitation?

"Thank you, Miss Dot," she murmured.

"It would be an honor to be one of your bridesmaids."

Grampy nodded, clearly pleased. Miss Dot's thin lips creased into a small smile.

An eternal optimist, Kelsey put aside her doubts. The wedding had the makings of a real family celebration. Home and family—the two things she had longed for her entire life. This union would bring together two very different families into one brand-new harmonious whole.

"There's still one crucial item that needs to be taken care of right away."

Dorothy tilted her head. "What's that?"

"Shopping for the wedding dress." Wedding planning was turning out to be fun. Who knew she'd enjoy it so much? "There's a shop with an enormous selection near Asheville."

Miss Dot's eyes narrowed. "It doesn't require an enormous budget, does it?"

"They have a dress for every budget," Kelsey reassured her. "Thousands—and I mean that literally—to choose from. We're sure to find a dress you'll fall in love with."

Grampy chuckled. "Too late for that." He laid his hand atop the table between them.

"She's already fallen in love with me, haven't you, Polka Dot?"

Her eyes crinkling into a smile, Dorothy placed her hand in his. "Absolutely."

"I hate to rush this, but your dress and what the bridesmaids wear is one of the more time-sensitive items, in case we need to make alterations."

Dorothy nodded. "Best make the trip before the weather turns."

"Why don't we ask Trudy to come with us?"

Dorothy's lined cheeks lifted. "Trudy would love that."

They made plans to travel to Asheville the next day. Hesitant to leave Grampy unattended for so long, Dorothy called the ranch next door to ask CoraFaye Dolan if she could drop in to make sure he got his lunch. CoraFaye promised to keep Kelsey's grandfather company in her absence.

"I don't need a babysitter," he said, fuming.

Dorothy got off the phone. "There's nothing like Truelove when it comes to good neighbors."

Kelsey felt a pang of envy at the community camaraderie. She didn't know any of her neighbors in Asheville, and she'd lived in her apartment for three years. One of the bigger drawbacks to city life.

In Truelove, where the sidewalks rolled up at the end of the business day, night life consisted only of the stars. But throw a cowboy into that mix… Suddenly, night life in Truelove held an appeal all its own.

Flustered, she perused her checklist. "Speaking of wedding attire, Grampy already owns a perfectly suitable tuxedo. I'll get Dad and Andrew to stop by the men's formalwear shop where Grampy bought his so the tuxes will match."

Despite her determination not to ask about Clay, every few minutes she couldn't help her attention from straying out the window toward the barn.

"I'll have the shop coordinate with a sister store in Boone where Dorothy's great-grandson lives, and another store near Clay's father at the coast so they can be sized. Once the bridesmaid dresses are chosen, the bridal boutique will do the same for your granddaughter, Miss Dot."

Her eyes drifted toward the window again.

This time, Dorothy caught her. "Perhaps Clay should accompany us tomorrow so he can get measured for his tux."

A telltale flush heated her cheeks.

"I'm not sure where my grandson has taken himself." Dorothy smiled. "Clay usually comes in for a hot cup of coffee about this time every afternoon. Would you do me a favor, Kelsey?"

She sat forward on the edge of the leather sofa. "Sure."

Dorothy rose. "Would you take a thermos out to Clay for me? He must be extremely busy not to have come inside for his usual break."

Or hoping to avoid Kelsey. Unable to think of a good excuse to refuse his grandmother's request, she found herself, thermos in hand, tromping across the barnyard in search of the elusive cowboy.

He wasn't in the barn. She followed the thunk of an ax to an area behind one of the sheds. The slanted rays of the sun glinted off the coppery tints in his supposed brown hair. He'd shed his coat and hat, which hung from a nearby fence post. In shirtsleeves rolled to his elbows, he raised the ax over his head. He brought it down with a loud smack onto an upright piece of wood, cleaving the log in half.

Maybe sensing someone had come up behind him, his shoulder blades tensed.

"It's me," she rasped. "Kelsey."

Gripping the ax casually in one hand, he turned.

Unsure of her welcome, she bit off the smile that rose on her lips.

He frowned. "I didn't expect to see you. Here. Today."

Cringing at the idea he might think her one of those silly Truelove women who chased after him, she thrust the thermos at him. Somehow without realizing it, either she'd taken several paces toward him or he'd moved closer to her. But regardless, the thermos made hard contact with the equally hard muscles in his abdomen.

He grunted.

"Sorry." About to beat a hasty retreat, his free hand closed over hers, pinning her and the thermos in place.

"What's this?"

His gravelly voice triggered swirling loop-de-loops in her belly. Her breathing suddenly sounded extraordinarily loud to her own ears. "Coffee. Miss Dot. You."

She threw him her most charming smile, hoping to draw him out. A smile she'd learned at Granna's knee. Honed to perfection during a long-ago debutante season. A smile she put on for her father's business associates.

However, the rugged, chiseled planes of his face didn't alter. She got nothing from him. Zilch. Nada. No more teasing. No more giving as good as he got.

Yanking her hand free, she took an enormous backstep. "Don't want to hold you up from your...your...." she gestured at the ax "...lumberjack thingy."

Just before she spun on her heel, she thought she saw his lips twitch. "Bye." She waggled her fingers over her shoulder.

A wall had gone up between them, and she wasn't sure why.

"No, wait." She whirled around to face him. "I also wanted to say I'm sorry."

He blinked. "Excuse me?"

She opened her hands. "I know I can be too much. That's why Dad sent me to live with Grampy in the first place after Mom died." She was babbling. Something she did when she was nervous. "Whatever I said or did that offended you, I'm sorry."

He dropped the ax on the ground at his feet. "Your father did what?"

She clapped her hand over her mouth. She hadn't meant to let that part slip out. She'd never actually said that aloud to another human being in her life. Not even Granna. Mortified, she did an about-face.

"Keltz—"

She'd made an absolute fool of herself. Wishing the earth would swallow her whole, she dashed toward her car.

HIS LONGER LEGS ate up the distance between them. "Wait. Please." At the corner of the barn, he caught hold of her coat.

"You have nothing to be sorry about. Kelsey. Would you look at me?"

Her eyes darted from her boots to his face.

"I apologize for leaving you to deal with the wedding by yourself. I should've been there for you."

"You're busy with the ranch." She fretted the ends of her fringed scarf. "I can handle the wedding planning."

Somehow he'd known even before she'd called out or he turned around, she was near. It was like he had a sort of extrasensory awareness when it came to her. "I'm not that busy."

Kelsey motioned at the ax, lying in the dirt. "The lumberjack thing…"

"I was cutting cedar fence stays."

"Do the fences at the Bar None have a tendency to wander, Clay?"

He told himself not to laugh. "Fence stays reinforce a fence between the posts." He leaned one shoulder against the shed wall. "So the fence wire doesn't sag or gap." She smelled good, but then she always smelled good to him. Something flowery that sent his pulse pounding.

"I've worn panty hose that did that." Her expression remained deadpan. "So annoying."

He laughed outright. For the love of Christmas, he'd missed her. He'd missed her wacky humor and this thing—whatever it was, the thing he was afraid to give a name to—that resonated between them.

"I'll have to take your word for it in regards to hosiery." He raked his hand through his hair. "But it's also annoying in ranching when the cattle escape through the gaps, and I have to round them up again."

She looked at him with those beautiful, expressive eyes of hers. "I thought maybe if…" she bit her lip, and he believed his knees might buckle "…if wedding planning doesn't interest you—"

"I adore wedding planning."

She cut him a look. "Or if having to keep company with me isn't to your liking—"

"Keeping company with you is the best part of wedding planning."

Her mouth curved, but the smile quickly faded. "Then, I don't understand the silent treatment."

Clay's heart clenched. His self-imposed isolation had hurt her feelings. The last thing on earth he ever wanted to do. He blew out a breath. "It isn't you. This is my issue."

"Is there anything I can do to help?"

He shook his head. "Just something I need to work through on my own." The arm's-length strategy wasn't turning out like he'd planned. If anything, it had only made him think about her more, while denying himself the pleasure of her company.

Clay shuffled his boots. "What did you mean about your father?"

"It's not important."

She would have fled again if he'd not snagged her arm.

"If it's important to you, it's important to me."

She leveled a stare at him that made him squirm. "Why?"

Fence wire wasn't the only thing that needed mending today.

He scoured his face with his hand. "Because I care about you. Because we're friends."

"Is that what we are, Clay?"

Her gaze locked onto his. His heart jackhammered. He had to remind himself to breathe. When she gazed at him like that, he had a hard time recalling his own name, much less thinking.

"Keltz," he whispered.

Unable to resist the impulse, he wound his index finger around a tendril of dark hair that dangled against her neck. Her hair was soft and silky, just as he'd supposed.

Something gentled in her face. She gave him a genuine smile. Not like the flirtatious, armor-plated, hostess-with-the-mostest smile she turned on at will for people like Randleman at the resort.

"After my mother died, my father was unable to tolerate my presence for long stretches of time. He chose to bury himself in the firm. I lived with Granna and Grampy until I graduated."

Something that felt like an actual physical pain lanced his heart. He'd treated her exactly

like that cold-hearted excuse for a father of hers.
A man Clay in no way wished to resemble.

"I didn't know that about your relationship
with your father."

She laughed. The sound was utterly devoid
of mirth. "We don't really have a relationship."
She sighed. "Hence my overzealous enthusiasm
to impress him with Grampy's wedding."

He couldn't begin to imagine what Kelsey
could have done—what any child of Clay's
could ever do—to cause Clay to turn his back
on them. How old had she been when her father had exiled her from his home and affections? Clay had lots of questions, but now was
not the time to probe further.

"Thank you for trusting me with that." Did
Nana know what had happened to fracture
Kelsey's family? He didn't want to ask Howard. It was Kelsey's story to tell. He wanted her
to tell him if and when she chose. "I'm sorry."

"So am I."

Kelsey shrugged as if it wasn't a big deal. But
it was a very big deal. He and his dad lived at
opposite ends of the state, yet he couldn't en-
vision that kind of estrangement existing between them. He could tell from her discomfort

that she was done talking about the emotional minefield of her father–daughter relationship.

"Tell me about what's happening on the wedding front."

She threw him a grateful smile and plunged into an elaborate narrative—waving hands and all—about the latest Everest-size hurdles she'd overcome for the Big Day.

"… Miss Dot, your Aunt Trudy and I will head to Asheville tomorrow to buy your grandmother's wedding dress. This close to the actual date, it will have to be something on the rack."

"How about I come along as your personal chauffeur?" He retrieved the ax. "If you're interested, that is."

She smiled. "I'm interested."

For the love of mistletoe, him, too. What was he so afraid of? For the duration of the next few weeks, why not just enjoy each other?

After the wedding, she'd return to her real life in Asheville. He'd return to the comforting, normal ranch routine he cherished. But for the first time, the prospect of a Truelove future without her in it didn't seem half so appealing.

CHAPTER SIX

THE NEXT MORNING at breakfast, Kelsey sat at the kitchen table overlooking Martha Alice's garden. Clay was picking her up, along with Miss Dot, soon. His Aunt Trudy, recently promoted to Mason Jar manager, had been unable to join them due to an unforeseen staffing issue, but Kelsey had promised to video everything and get her input on finalizing the bridesmaid dresses.

Kelsey slathered Martha Alice's fig jam on a slice of toast and took a bite.

"Such an exciting day." Martha Alice filled her tea mug with hot water from the electric kettle on the counter. "Last summer, Kate and I had a wonderful time picking out her dress to renew her vows with Jack. Y'all will have such fun."

Kelsey was disappointed the lively, speak-her-mind Trudy wasn't coming. "I hope so."

Ideally, wedding-dress shopping was a

mother–daughter endeavor. She took another bite of toast. A sudden thought struck her. With Granna gone, who would shop with her following Kelsey's yet-to-be-determined future engagement? Frowning, she swallowed.

Without Trudy's buffering presence, Kelsey was afraid the trip would get awkward.

"Miss Dot and I don't know each other well..." How could she say this without it sounding like an indictment? "Her tastes and interests are different from mine or Granna's. We don't have much in common."

"Except the most important thing of all—your love for Howard." Her grandmother's best friend set down the mug. "Dorothy is a wonderful woman. She will never be Joan, and she shouldn't have to be anybody but herself."

"I know," Kelsey said in a small voice. "But Grampy always loved Granna's style, and Miss Dot prefers simpler things."

Martha Alice took her hand. "You need to ask yourself who you are planning this wedding for. Are you truly striving to serve Dorothy's wishes or your own?"

Kelsey's bottom lip wobbled. She was trying to please her father, who'd adored his mother. She was being completely unfair to Dorothy.

"Simple doesn't have to mean *lesser*." Martha Alice gestured at the window. "Take the garden, for instance. I love the spring with its profusion of bulbs and the aroma of my roses, but next best of the seasons in my garden I love is winter."

Kelsey flicked a glance out the window. "Why?" She bent her head. "Sorry."

Martha Alice smiled. "You just need to train your eyes better to see what's there versus what's not. It's a matter of perspective."

"I don't understand."

"Take a look again, but this time notice how the evergreen hollies provide a soothing visual structure that ties together the entire enterprise. Note the sharp contrast of the red berries against the framework of green. Oh, look." Martha Alice pointed. "A cardinal just landed on one of the branches. Another joy of winter. During the rest of the year, you can't always see the birds. But with everything stripped away, you can better appreciate the joys of the unexpected."

She'd already experienced joy during the planning of this very unexpected wedding. In the person of Clay McKendry. And even better than the position she hoped to earn in the firm, she and her father were finally communicating.

"Then, there are the trees."

Kelsey followed Martha Alice's gaze out the window.

"Stripped of their leaf finery, there is a stark beauty to the trees, their bare branches lifted to the sky." Martha Alice took a sip of tea. "Simple has a beauty all its own."

The older woman was right. This wedding was Dorothy's day. Not Granna's nor Kelsey's.

She needed to get her priorities straight. It was time to let go of the vision in her head about what Granna would have done. This wasn't about pleasing her father but about celebrating the love Grampy shared with the new woman in his life.

"Thank you, Miss Marth'Alice." She squeezed the older woman's hand. "For the master class in design and for everything else, too."

"You're welcome." At the sound of a vehicle in the driveway, Martha Alice turned her head. "I believe your chariot has arrived. Go have a fantastic day."

Granna wouldn't have been proud of how she'd too often run roughshod over Dorothy's wishes. She sent Clay a quick text to let him know she was on her way out.

Donning her coat, she prayed for God to help

her change her attitude toward her soon-to-be new grandmother. And to listen, really listen, to Dorothy's desires.

Kelsey grabbed her purse and left the house. She hoped it wasn't too late to repair her mistakes with Grampy's new bride.

In an attempt to show interest in their world, during the long drive to Asheville, she asked a lot of questions about the cattle business. At one point, Clay's gaze flicked to hers in the rearview mirror. He smiled at her as if he understood what she was trying to do and appreciated her efforts.

He dropped them off at the curb in front of the bridal boutique. "I'm headed to the men's formalwear shop down the block."

She helped Dorothy out of the truck. "Our appointment is for ninety minutes."

"No rush." He looked across the seat through the open window. "I may get a coffee from the double-decker you told me about. You ladies have a fabulous time."

She threw open her hands. "What could be more fun than wedding-dress shopping?"

Frowning, Dorothy pursed her lips. He drove away.

"This looks like a fancy place." His grandmother cast a critical look at the storefront. "I'm not a fancy person."

Kelsey put on a bright, encouraging face. "I'm sure we can find something you like."

"I'm more a casual jeans sort of gal." Dorothy clutched the strap of her purse. "Not much need for folderol on the ranch."

"Why don't we look to see if they have anything that interests you? If not, we'll look somewhere else."

"I don't know why I let you talk me into coming here." Dorothy jutted her jaw. "I hate shopping."

Shopping was one of Kelsey's favorite recreational activities. She and Granna had spent hours shopping together, enjoying each other's company. But Dorothy was not Granna. She had different interests. Kelsey scrambled for a way to save the day.

"I can cancel the appointment with the bridal specialist if there is somewhere else you'd rather shop."

Dorothy harrumphed. "We might as well go in." She motioned toward the Tiffany-blue painted door. "Since we're here." Her hand shook.

Was Miss Dot nervous?

"Everyone is nice here, I promise. But say the word, and I'll have Clay come get us."

A middle-aged sales associate greeted them. The lady, Cynthia, introduced herself to Dorothy. "Is this your granddaughter?"

"No." Dorothy held the strap of her purse on her shoulder. "My family couldn't make it."

Cynthia's smile never wavered, but her gaze flitted to Kelsey before she led them over to a sitting area with a French provincial love seat and wing chairs. On the walls hung elaborate gilded mirrors. With visible reluctance, Dorothy sank onto the cerulean silk settee. Kelsey settled beside her.

"How may I be of assistance today?"

Dorothy held her purse tightly in her lap. "I need to find a wedding dress." Her mouth tightened. "Silly, isn't it? A wedding dress for an old woman like me."

Cynthia leaned forward. "Not silly at all. Every woman should feel special on her wedding day, and we want to do everything we can to make that dream come true." She laid a comforting hand on Dorothy's. "If I might ask a few questions, to get a feel for the style of your wedding… Where, when…?"

"December third." Dorothy remained rigid.

"As for the rest...ask her. She's in charge of everything."

Kelsey gave the sales associate a rundown on the details thus far—the winter-wonderland theme, color palette and the name of the resort.

"We've worked with many brides there." Cynthia made a few notes on an iPad. "Do you have any photos of wedding-dress styles you're interested in, Mrs. McKendry?"

"I don't want a long dress. Too easy to trip on the hem. Don't need to break a hip." Dorothy fidgeted. "I want knee-length and not tight. Howard and I intend to dance."

"We have a wonderful selection of party dresses." Cynthia smiled. "In keeping with the theme, we could start by looking at something glittery and fun."

Kelsey nodded. "That would look wonderful with your lovely silver hair, Miss Dot."

Dorothy touched a gnarled hand to her hair. "You think my hair is lovely?"

Maybe Kelsey wasn't the only one unsure of herself. "Absolutely."

"I'll pull some gowns for you to preview." Cynthia surged to her feet. "Perhaps you'd care to join me, Miss Summerfield?"

She wanted to do right by Miss Dot's wishes,

but the problem was prying those preferences out of the older woman. "I'll be there in a minute."

Cynthia disappeared into the back.

She cleared her throat. "When you were a young girl, did you ever dream about the day you'd become a bride?"

Dorothy ran her hand down her slacks. "Clay's grandfather and I were high-school sweethearts. I wanted a church wedding, but Willard was drafted into the army. We eloped to South Carolina a few days before he shipped out to Vietnam. Clay's father, Gary, was born while he was overseas."

"That must've been hard, Miss Dot. To be pregnant and alone."

"It was." Dorothy's eyes became hooded. "But harder still was when Willard came home from the war. He was not the same boy I married."

Kelsey wasn't sure how to respond. She sensed now was the time to listen, though. Really listen.

"He was a difficult man." Dorothy fiddled with a stray thread on her slacks. "He had mood swings. I took over the running of the ranch. Willard was not a good father. He and Gary had a difficult relationship. It's no wonder Gary hated ranching."

"Whereas Clay always loved it?"

A whisper of a smile drifted across her lips. "As a little boy, he took to it right away. Kind of like I did when I came to the Bar None as a young bride." Her mouth drooped. "But as soon as he could get away from the ranch and his father, Gary did. Trudy, too."

"You've made a beautiful home for your family on the ranch."

Dorothy looked at her. "Unlike Howard and Joan, I did not have a fairy-tale marriage. Howard and I are so different." Her chin wobbled.

Kelsey grasped her hand. "Do you love my grandfather, Miss Dot?"

Dorothy's eyes watered. "I do."

"Then, we'll find a dress you love, which positively knocks his socks off."

"At my age, I'm not interested in a white dress, although that's fine for some." The older woman ran a finger under her eyeglasses. "To answer your question—as a young girl, I always imagined myself in lace."

Giving her a smile, Kelsey rose. "Let's see what Cynthia and I can find."

Heading for the area behind the dressing

rooms, she met Cynthia coming out with an armload full of gowns.

"What do you think?"

Kelsey gave them the once-over. They were exactly the kind of dresses that fit perfectly with her wedding design. The sort of gowns Granna herself would have chosen and worn. Sparkling with sequins. Glittering with rhinestones. But not Dorothy's style.

She put her finger on her chin. "Do you have any silver dresses in lace?"

Cynthia cocked her head. "I might have the perfect thing for your grandmother."

"Dorothy's not—" Adjusting her attitude, Kelsey closed her mouth.

Soon after, Cynthia settled Dorothy into a dressing room. Kelsey waited outside while Cynthia assisted Dorothy into one of the gowns she'd pulled. Moments later, Dorothy emerged in her stocking feet. Kelsey's breath caught.

With a matching silver lace jacket, the lacy sheath dress was sleeveless. The knee-length hem was scalloped, matching the scalloped lace trim on the jacket. The ensemble was comfortable and elegant.

She clasped her hands together. "Oh, Miss Dot. You look beautiful."

Cynthia led the older woman to a low dais, surrounded on three sides by mirrors. Dorothy plucked at the three-quarter-length sleeve. "You don't think I look too froufrou?"

"You look gorgeous." She smiled at the older woman's reflection in the mirror. "It shows off how slender and willowy you are. I've always wanted to be willowy. But at my height? Not happening."

Dorothy turned this way and that, getting a glimpse from every angle. "It does look right nice on me. I feel like a fairy-tale princess."

Kelsey and Cynthia exchanged a smile.

"It only needs one more thing to be perfect."

Cynthia stepped forward. "What's that, Mrs. McKendry?"

"Shoes." Dorothy smiled. "I want some of those Cinderella slippers. The more shimmery, the better."

For safety and comfort, Cynthia showed Dorothy several options that included a low block heel. Dorothy chose a glittery, closed-toe shoe with a large rhinestone-bow embellishment.

"Don't I look fancy." Dorothy admired herself in the mirror. "Maybe fancy isn't as bad as I believed it would be." She turned around. "What should I put in my hair? What about a hat?"

Ultimately, Dorothy chose a silver mesh fascinator with small feathers, chiffon ribbon and birdcage veiling. She clipped it onto the side of her head and stood back to admire the effect.

"Very vintage," Cynthia cooed.

"I'm more antique than vintage." Dorothy laughed. "Kelsey, what do you think?"

She smiled. "It's the perfect touch. Glamorous, sassy and trendy."

"I've had the *sassy* part down for years." Dorothy fluttered her hand. "Never been called *glamorous* or *trendy* before, though."

The bell over the door at the entrance jangled.

"Am I too late?" Trudy swept in. "Oh, Mama. Don't you look a treat!"

Dorothy held her hand out to her daughter. "I thought you had to work."

"Crisis averted, and I drove here fast as the law allowed." Trudy stepped onto the dais and gave her a hug. "I wouldn't miss this for the world."

"I'm glad you're here, honey." Dorothy reached for Kelsey to join them. "But Kelsey and Cindy have taken good care of me."

Cynthia winked at Kelsey.

"I'm gonna take a load off my feet and sit down. Trudy, you girls sort out the bridesmaid dresses. Kelsey wants something blue."

Cynthia's assistant, a younger girl in training, whisked Dorothy to the sitting area. With Cynthia in tow, Trudy headed toward the storeroom. Kelsey felt a frisson of concern.

Trudy's fashion style tended toward what Granna would have kindly referred to as *vibrantly eclectic*. Kelsey reminded herself to stop being such a control freak. She let Trudy enjoy sifting through the inventory.

And braced to wear whatever Trudy selected without complaint.

With several garments in her arms, Cynthia returned to the dressing area first. Trudy sashayed from behind the curtain and held up the gaudiest dress Kelsey had ever beheld in her life. "What do you think of this one?" She grinned. "You wanted blue, right?"

Kelsey flinched before she caught herself.

Aka Vegas showgirl, the orange–and–blue bedazzled gown glimmered under the lighting of the crystal chandelier. And then there was the white feather boa that apparently completed the ensemble.

"I-I…" Kelsey gulped. "It's very…very eye-catching."

Trudy burst out laughing. "If you could see your face… I was just funnin' you." She handed the dress to the assistant. "Cindy has the real dresses I picked out. See what you think."

Clay's aunt had chosen a velvet gown in a rich shade of blue with violet undertones. Each of the five dresses was a slight variation on the others. They were glorious.

"I'm partial to the one with the halter top." Trudy held the dress against her body. "Shows off those sculpted arms I've got from lifting trays all day." She curled her bicep. "I'll let my niece, Rebecca, pick one from among these three. But for you? This one has your name on it."

Cynthia held the hanger out to Kelsey.

"Try it on," Trudy urged. "I'll put on mine, and we'll give Mama a fashion show."

Inside the dressing room, Kelsey changed into the floor-length gown and surveyed the effect in the long gilt mirror. With a sweeping train and sheer beaded short sleeves, the dress had a V-neckline, exposing her shoulders. *Wow.* Trudy had somehow managed to completely capture the vibe Kelsey was aiming for with the wedding.

Would Clay like her in it? She flushed, annoyed with herself. What did it matter if he liked her in it or not? She liked herself in it. As long as Miss Dot was happy, she was happy.

"So…what do you think?" Trudy called through the curtain.

"You did good." She ran her hand across the butter-soft velvet of the bodice. "Real good."

"Cindy's found to-die-for shoes," Trudy hollered.

She choked back a laugh.

"Can I come in? I've got an idea for your hair." Trudy bustled in. "I'm thinking French twist for my own do. So classic." Somehow, she quickly wrangled Kelsey's long tresses into a rough facsimile of a bun. She placed a pearl comb set in silver at the base of the chignon. "Imagine what I could do with proper tools."

They stood back to examine themselves.

"I love it," she whispered.

Trudy gave Kelsey a small squeeze. "What's not to love?"

CHAPTER SEVEN

As Clay pushed into the bridal boutique, a bell jangled overhead. Ninety minutes had stretched into two hours, but he didn't mind. After being fitted for his suit, he'd stopped by the double-decker for coffee. Nana had texted him to come to the shop. She wanted to show him her dress.

Hat in hand, he stood at the entrance, feeling out of place amidst the frippery. A college-age girl ushered him into a sitting area. Nana rose.

A lump settled in his throat. "Well, look at you."

Nana Dot threw him a small smile. "You like?"

"Simply spectacular." He made a whirling motion with his finger. "Give it a turn. Let me get a gander at the whole package."

With an uncharacteristic girlish giggle, she did a slow three-sixty. He kissed her cheek. She had enjoyed herself. *Thank you, Keltz.*

"Have a seat." She patted the cushion beside her on the love seat. "Trudy made it here after all." She touched the totally feminine, frothy concoction perched on the side of her head. "Kelsey is a wonder. The girl has incredible taste. Guess how I know."

"The hat."

"Nope."

Clay chuckled. "The dress?"

Nana shook her head.

"The shoes."

"Wrong." Nana threw him a pert grin. "She has incredible taste because she likes you. And you like her, too."

"Nana," he sputtered.

"Don't bother denying it." She wagged her finger. "I know it's true 'cause y'all have all the signs."

"Signs of what?"

"Don't be coy, Clayton." His grandmother's eyebrow arched. "It doesn't become a cowboy."

"Nana," he grunted.

"I've seen the way you light up every time she walks in a room. The long glances between you. You only have eyes for each other."

"How can you say that?" He stared at her.

"We're like oil and water. Night and day. We argue all the time."

"Spark to kindling." She snapped her fingers. "Match to dynamite."

"Combustible substances shouldn't mix."

"You're fooling no one with your little differences of opinion. It's clear as the nose on your face you two amuse each other no end."

He winced at the *you two*.

She gave him a look. "I'm not the only one who's noticed."

"Please tell me the matchmakers aren't involved," he moaned.

"What you call *combustion*, GeorgeAnne and I call *chemistry*."

Groaning, he dropped his head into his hands.

Trudy stepped into the sitting area. "Howdy, nephew. What do you think? Mama?"

Clay stood.

Holding his chin between his thumb and forefinger, he frowned. "I'm afraid I can't allow you to appear in public in this getup."

Trudy's eyes widened. "What's wrong with the dress?"

"Nothing, except you're so gorgeous you'll take the focus off the bride."

His grandmother laughed.

Trudy gave him a peck on the cheek. "This is why you're my favorite nephew."

"I'm your only nephew."

"Doesn't make it any less true." She motioned him and Nana back to the love seat. "Kelsey?" she called. "Your turn. Come out here."

Nana leaned close. "Better not let this one get away. There's not many like Kelsey Summerfield."

She stepped through the curtain. His heart almost stopped from the sheer loveliness of her.

"Oh, Clay." Blushing, her eyes met his, darted away and found his gaze again. "I didn't expect to see you here."

The elegant dress was almost the exact color of her eyes. The neckline exposed her creamy shoulders. He'd never seen her hair off her neck. He liked her hair up.

His gaze traveled to the vein pulsing at the hollow of her neck. If she was this magnificent in blue, what would she look like in white as a bride? Something turned over in his chest. Their eyes locked.

For a split second it was as if everything and everyone else in the universe ceased to exist.

His aunt snapped her fingers in front of his face. "Earth to Clay."

Clay jolted, suddenly aware she'd probably been trying to get his attention for some time. "What?" He shifted.

"I said, how do you think Kelsey looks in her gown?"

Cheeks burning, he turned the hat in his hands. Caught off guard, no way could he say what actually rose to his mind—stunning, mind-blowing, world-shattering. "It's nice."

Kelsey's smile dropped. His aunt made a disgusted noise in the back of her throat. Nana shook her head.

"I'll change." Turning on her stiletto heel, Kelsey dashed behind the curtain.

Trudy rushed after her. "Men," she said and sniffed.

Nana's look of reproach left him squirming. "I should change out of my wedding duds, too. Then settle up with the shop."

When the ladies rejoined him, Kelsey gave him the cold shoulder. He twisted his hat in his hands.

The shop lady tallied their purchases. Shoes. Hats. The younger girl boxed up the items. He counted two dress boxes.

"Keltz?"

Ignoring him, she gave the wall behind the register her undivided attention.

"You're buying the dress, aren't you?"

"What do you care?" She gritted her teeth. "I didn't think you liked me in that dress." She crossed her arms.

"I love you in that dress."

Her eyes flitted to his.

"You took my breath." He put his hat over his heart. "The sight of you robbed me of words. Say you're buying it."

She propped her hands on her hips. "Just so we're clear, *if* I buy it, it will be because it works with the wedding theme and because I like it."

"Of course." One of these days, he was going to lose the war waging within himself and kiss her. He dropped his gaze to her mouth. Most probably sooner, not later. "You'd never buy a dress just because in it I think you're the most gorgeous woman I've ever seen."

"Absolutely not." Her mouth curved. "But it's nice to hear you say you like it."

The dress wasn't all he liked. All of a sudden, he wasn't ready for the day to end.

"How about we send Nana Dot back to Truelove with Aunt Trudy?"

Kelsey gave him a look out of the corner of her eye. "Why, pray tell, would we do that?"

"Spend the day with me, City Girl. Show me your town. Besides," he shuffled his feet, "I've got a hankering for sushi."

"Okay." She smiled. "Since there isn't any sushi in Truelove."

No, there wasn't. And after the wedding was over, there'd be no Kelsey either.

The smart thing to do would be to stick to his arm's-length policy. But when it came to Kelsey Summerfield, he'd already proven smart wasn't his fallback. It wasn't like they were going to fall in love or anything stupid like that.

Night and day. Fire and ice. Spark to kindling...

His grandmother made arrangements for Clay's sister, Rebecca, to visit the shop in a few days. The lady at the register handed the packages to Trudy. "This has been one of the most enjoyable appointments I've ever done."

Nana hugged Kelsey. "It has been fun, hasn't it?"

Trudy thrust a box at him. "You think this is fun, wait till I kick up my heels at the reception."

He walked them to Trudy's car. When he

announced their intention to stay in Asheville a bit longer, Nana gave him a knowing smirk.

The next few hours passed in a blur of laughter. They ate lunch at the iconic Woolworth's Soda Fountain. Kelsey gave him a walking tour of Asheville's famed Pack Square and the architecturally rich Art Deco downtown. They drove to the River Arts warehouse district. They strolled around converted studios where a range of artisans performed glassblowing, threw pottery and demonstrated wood carving.

Sometime during the walking tour, Kelsey's hand found her way into his. At a lower elevation, Asheville didn't get the snow the Blue Ridge Highlands and Truelove experienced. But it was windy and chilly as befitted a mountain day in November.

Or that was the excuse he gave himself for holding her hand. No day, however, was too chilly in his opinion for ice cream. She took him to her favorite ice cream parlor.

They talked about their childhoods. He was struck as much by what she didn't say as what she did when she talked about that time in her life. They discussed their respective university experiences. No surprise their schools were college rivals.

He broadened his shoulders. "Betcha didn't figure this guy for an agribusiness grad."

"Way to go, Cowboy." She play punched his bicep. "You're smarter than you look."

Later, she told him about what Nana had revealed about his grandfather, Willard.

"He died before I was born." Clay blew out a breath of air. "Nana loved him as much as he allowed her to, but when he died I think it was a relief for her."

Her face grew pensive. "How did it affect your dad?" Was she thinking of her father?

"My dad had no real example for being a husband or father. But he gave it everything he had and then some. He made sure Rebecca and I never suffered for what he himself had lacked."

"That's admirable."

Clay nodded. "He'd tell you he was only able to do it because of my mom's faith in him and his faith in God."

"Your parents sound remarkable."

He smiled. "I've been blessed, but every family has its struggles."

"What about your Aunt Trudy?"

His smile faded. "Nana would say Aunt Trudy went looking for love in all the wrong places. She was hurt badly by her jerk of an ex-husband. She's been single a long time now. I think she keeps it light with men friends for fear of getting hurt again."

"Is that how you feel since Angela—"

"What about you?" His ex-fiancée wasn't a topic he wanted to discuss. Hunching over the table at the ice cream parlor, he stuffed his hands in his coat pockets. "Will you bring a plus-one to the wedding?"

She shrugged. "I hadn't planned on it. I dated a guy during college. He was in a fraternity. We were quite the couple in those days."

Clay experienced a sharp, and hitherto un-realized, antipathy for frat boys.

"I think Grampy would've liked it to be-come serious."

"But it didn't?" he rasped. "Why not?"

"I wasn't in love with him." She tilted her head. "I'm sorry Angela hurt you."

Up until this conversation, he hadn't been thinking about Angela. He couldn't remem-ber the last time he'd thought of Angela at all. Upon further recollection, perhaps not since City Girl blew into Truelove.

She got to her feet. "Shall we get sushi be-fore the line gets long?"

"You just had ice cream, Summerfield."

She cocked her head. "So you're not hungry?"

He rose. "I can always eat, darlin'."

By the time they finished eating and left the Thai restaurant, darkness had fallen.

Kelsey tugged on his arm. "What would you say about making a small detour before we head to Truelove?"

"Sure. What do you have in mind?"

"There's the Winter Lights display at the arboretum. I could show you where I got some of my ideas for the wedding."

He shook his head. "Does that brain of yours ever take a vacation from wedding planning?"

"Can't afford to take a vacation." She grinned at him. "Not until after this winter extravaganza—"

"Also known as Nana's wedding," he interjected.

She smiled. "Not until Nana Dot's *winter wedding extravaganza* reaches its happily-ever-after conclusion. Actually, I sort of like organizing the details. Apparently, one of the few things I am good at."

He frowned. "That can't be true. Who told you that?"

"Which time?"

"Keltz..."

"No, it's okay. He was right."

Something told Clay she meant her father.

Kelsey linked her arm through his. "I wasn't cut out for law school."

His brow creased. "You went to law school?"

"I attended only a semester before I decided it wasn't for me, much to Dad's disappointment." She hugged his arm. "But I'm really enjoying the wedding prep. Maybe by accident, I've stumbled onto a new career."

At the arboretum, they joined the other couples and families strolling through the gardens, enjoying the light show. She pointed out the uplighting on the birch trees. He got a better understanding of her plan. Which wasn't as over-the-top as he'd feared.

Nana's wedding in Kelsey's capable hands was shaping up to be a truly magical winter wonderland. As for his heart?

He watched the play of colors flash across her face. By the time this wedding was over and done, he wasn't sure just what shape his heart would be in.

It was only later, much later, as he lay in bed thinking about their day together, he realized he'd called her *darlin'*.

CHAPTER EIGHT

CLAY DROVE HER home to Truelove.

When had she started thinking about Truelove as home? She'd spent the entire day showing him the only town she'd ever called home.

It was late when they arrived back. It had been the most wonderful of days, but she was glad Martha Alice hadn't waited up. She wasn't ready for questions about her hard-to-define, non-you-two relationship with a certain Truelove cowboy. Clay walked her to the door. She thought—hoped—he might end the evening with a kiss, but he didn't. Probably just as well.

Tumbling into bed, she remembered she hadn't updated her father in a few days. She sent him a brief text about the successful shopping expedition and the info to get his tuxedo fitted. Almost as an afterthought, she mentioned she'd booked a venue.

Immediately, squiggly dots erupted. **Where?**

She smiled. It was wonderful Dad was taking such a keen interest in this project. She replied, typing in the name of the resort.

Yawning, she shut off her phone. Surely her impossible-to-impress father would be pleased with her efforts.

Over the next week, she went to the ranch several times. Clay put her to work shoveling cow stalls. She didn't mind. She just enjoyed spending time with him at the ranch. They also fell into the habit of going to lunch at the Jar. A working lunch.

Wedding plans were at the forefront of their conversations but not all they talked about.

They were sharing a piece of chocolate chess pie when a shadow fell over the booth. Forks poised over the plate, they looked up. GeorgeAnne Allen loomed over them.

Kelsey pasted on an insincere smile. "Is there anything I can do for you, Miss GeorgeAnne?"

"I'm here to help you." The older woman pointed a bony finger at them. "I hear you two," she said, and Clay blanched, "are in charge of planning Dot and Howard's pending nuptials. It's a big undertaking. The Double Name Club wants to volunteer our services."

Clay studied the salt and pepper shakers with apparent fascination.

"While that is so thoughtful of you, Miss GeorgeAnne—" determinedly positive, she marshaled social niceties around her like a Teflon shield "—we have everything completely under control."

GeorgeAnne's ice-blue eyes narrowed. "The McKendrys are one of the founding families of Truelove. We feel it's important to utilize as much of our local talent as possible. Like Kara, who's ventured into catering."

"Kara's food is excellent, but the resort has in-house caterers." She lifted her chin. "They have everything completely under control."

GeorgeAnne gave her a curt nod. "I have other helpful suggestions."

She gritted her teeth. *Nosy, interfering busybody...* Kelsey folded her arms.

GeorgeAnne widened her stance. "Callie Jackson of Apple Valley Orchard is a photogra—"

"The resort has a photographer on staff."

GeorgeAnne arched a look at her, which probably quailed lesser individuals. Kelsey was not a lesser individual. "Coach Lovett's daughter makes the most beautiful cakes."

"The resort has everything completely—"

"Clay?" GeorgeAnne's thin lips pressed together. "Have you got anything to say for yourself?"

"Yes, Clay." Kelsey skewered him with her eyes. "Is there something you wanted to say?"

His gaze pinged between them. "No, ma'am."

GeorgeAnne sniffed. "If you two decide you need our help, you know where to find us."

At *you two*, Clay's leg underneath the table jiggled.

She bestowed on the older woman a variation of Granna's most gracious smile. "Thank you for your input, Miss GeorgeAnne. I will certainly keep your *suggestions* in mind. You have a good day, now."

The matchmaker exited the Jar with an angry jangling of the bell over the door.

Clay collapsed against the red vinyl seat. "Have you lost your mind?"

She blew out a breath. "I will not be bullied by the likes of GeorgeAnne Allen."

He shook his head. "For the love of Christmas, what were you thinking? Don't poke the bear."

She stabbed the pie with her fork. "You don't

have to run faster than the bear, Clay. You just have to run faster than the guy next to you."

"Which would be me." He glared. "When they have me lassoed and hitched by spring, I'll have you to thank."

She laughed. "Lassoed and hitched?"

He pointed his fork at her. "Maddie Lovett makes the best cakes on earth. She freelances bakery and dessert items for the Jar. You're eating one of her pies right now."

"It's fabulous, but the resort already—"

"Has everything under control. Got it." He shook his head. "Way to put a target on both our backs, City Girl."

The next day, Clay's friend, Sam Gibson, and his wife, Lila, joined them for lunch. They remembered Kelsey from the wedding of their mutual friend at the resort.

Lila had the loveliest curly red hair. She was a renowned landscape artist at Ashmont College. Bubbly and energetic, she also ran a visual-arts program for underserved children in the mountains. Her face glowed when she talked about Emma Cate, Sam's seven-year-old niece whom they'd adopted. Kelsey looked forward to meeting her.

Although, once Grampy was married, she

wasn't sure how often she'd have the chance to
visit Truelove. Her life would be firmly fixed
in Asheville and her new position within the
Summerfield company. Her gaze drifted to Clay
talking football with Sam.

The idea of returning to the city didn't thrill
her as much as she would have supposed. Nor
the potential job within her father's company
she'd dreamed of. She'd always wanted a seat
at the Summerfield table. But now maybe not.

Perhaps the dream wasn't really about sitting
at the Summerfield table but more about sitting
at her father's table. She was beginning to believe she wasn't suited for the cutthroat commercial real-estate market. But what else was
she good at?

Weddings?

Clay left to install a new wood stove in the
calving barn so the winter-born calves would
have a warm place to gain strength before heading into the corrals. Kelsey suppressed a small
sigh. She'd see him tomorrow, but she missed
him already.

Lila inched out of the booth. "You got it
bad, girl."

"I absolutely do not!"

Sam reached for the check on the table. "My ole buddy looks to have it pretty bad, too."

Her pulse quickened. Did Clay really look at her that way?

Sam insisted on paying for Kelsey's lunch. She and Lila ambled onto the sidewalk to wait for him.

Lila smiled at her. "How are you finding Truelove? Different from what you're used to, I imagine."

"It's a slower pace, for sure." With the leaves completely off the trees, she spotted an intriguing glint of metal high atop one of the mountain peaks overlooking the small hamlet. "But I'm beginning to think slower might suit me."

Her gaze traced the rounded outline of the gleaming roof, and she pointed. "Would you happen to know what that is up there?"

Lila peered into the distance. "That's probably the old Birchfield place on Laurel Mountain Road. In its heyday, it was quite the showplace, I understand. Of course, the Birchfields are long gone. Timber barons."

"Who lives there now?"

Lila shrugged. "Maybe nobody. I don't know. At one point, a historic preservation group had it restored and sold it to the college, but it was never utilized to its full potential. I think the upkeep became too much."

Sam came out of the Jar. They said goodbye. At loose ends, she wasn't sure what to do this afternoon.

But, her curiosity piqued, her gaze drifted toward the glimmering mansion overlooking the town. Why not see it for herself? Adventure beckoned.

She plugged *Birchfield* on Laurel Mountain Road into her cell. Following the GPS, she drove over the bridge and out of town. She continued past the steepled white-clapboard church she'd attended last Sunday with Martha Alice.

The road climbed, winding upward. Towering evergreen mountain laurel hugged both sides of the road. A quarter of a mile off the road, she came upon two enormous stone pillars, inscribed with *Birchfield*. This was the place.

She parked to the side of a curving drive that disappeared into the trees. She took the partially open scrolled-iron gate as an invitation. On foot, she followed the driveway another quarter of a mile. Trudging along, she was glad she'd worn the low-heel knee boots instead of her fashionably painful ones. Her breath puffed in the crisp coldness of the late-November afternoon.

A sane person would think twice before trespassing on private property. A caretaker might run her off with a shotgun. Or there could be guard dogs.

That stopped her in her tracks.

Her heart pounded in her chest. Ahead, the tree line widened. Despite her reservations, something drove her on. At the top of the incline, she emerged into a clearing.

She gasped.

The house—*what a house!*—perched on a knoll. Like an English country manor, the sprawling three-story mansion sparkled like an exquisite jewel. Taking out her phone, she snapped a picture. Unable to resist, she stood on the porch, hands framing her eyes, peering through the glass panels surrounding the massive oak door to see what she could of the interior.

What she glimpsed was impressive. Beyond the door lay an enormous foyer from which the east and west wings of the house branched off. The grand staircase was breathtaking.

She followed a stone path around the house, peeking into as many windows as she could.

She did a complete circuit of the house. French doors opened onto a series of stone terraces.

Kelsey explored the grounds. Low stone walls enclosed overgrown, once-spectacular gardens. At the bottom of the slope she found a stone gazebo on a level piece of ground. A perfect spot for a wedding. With that grand staircase and the large open spaces inside the house for gatherings, the entire estate was a wedding-venue dream. Tons of natural light.

A kernel of an idea popped into her brain.

Climbing back to the top terrace, she was struck by the panoramic grandeur of the mountain horizon. Far below, she spied the glinting silver of the river. Beyond the small hamlet, dappled fields and orchards rounded out the patchwork kingdom of tiny Truelove.

From the slanting light of the sun through the trees, she became aware the afternoon was nearly gone. The estate was isolated. No one knew where she was. If something was to happen…

She rounded the corner of the house to find a silver BMW parked in the circle drive. Was someone inside the house? Friend or foe?

Questioning the dubious wisdom of several

recent-life choices, she was slinking past the car when a voice called from the porch.

"Who are you, and what do you think you're doing here?"

She froze. Shotgun and canine scenarios floated across her brain. Her pulse quickened. Gulping, she pivoted.

A trim, well-appointed blonde woman in her late forties stood on the steps. Dressed in a skirt and suit coat, she wore the kind of high-heeled dressy boots Kelsey would've bought. If she wasn't about to go to jail or get shot or have dogs set upon her.

The woman's carefully made-up face went from a frown to a smile. "I recognize you from the Jar. You're Kelsey Summerfield, staying with Miss Marth'Alice." Bridging the distance between them, she extended her hand. "I'm Mary Sue Ingersoll, the listing agent for this property."

Her heart slowed to a more natural rhythm. She'd seen the realtor's face plastered on a highway billboard between Truelove and Asheville. Mary Sue Ingersoll ran a real-estate agency, the only one in Truelove.

She shook the woman's hand. "I shouldn't

have wandered in, but the gate was open, and I couldn't resist."

"It's something, isn't it? Built in 1925 as the mountain getaway for the prominent Birchfield family."

Kelsey studied the house. "It's magnificent. Imagine the parties and the people who probably once strolled this lawn." She flung out her hand. "Chinese lanterns. Fringed dresses. Pinstriped suits."

Mary Sue chuckled. "Very *Gatsby*. Several presidents, including Hoover, dined here over the years. It's said a silent-film actress also lived here for a while. While the Birchfields managed to survive the stock-market crash, they couldn't outwit time. Ten years ago, the last of them died without heirs. It's been lovingly restored by a local heritage society and includes most of the original furnishings."

"It's an architectural treasure."

"Three acres. Seventy-five hundred square feet." Mary Sue tilted her head. "Lots of possibilities. Your family develops commercial properties. Care to make an offer?"

"Don't I wish." She sighed. "My father develops property, not me. Million-dollar view. Million-dollar price tag."

Mary Sue coughed gently into her hand. "Try again. But round up a mil."

She cast one last, longing look at the house. "So much potential but well out of my reach."

Mary Sue handed her a business card. "It doesn't hurt to dream."

The image of a certain cowboy flitted across her mind, and her heart skipped a beat.

AT THE MASON JAR, Clay only half listened as Kelsey went over—for the umpteenth time—her to-do list. His mind ought to be focused on Nana's wedding or at least his current winter project of leveling the dirt in the corral in advance of the winter birthing season.

But despite daily admonishments to get it together, he spent most nights counting the hours until he saw Kelsey again. Pretty pathetic for a cowboy who'd renounced romantic entanglements.

He was entangled all right. He stirred cream into his coffee. Kelsey Summerfield drank more coffee than anyone he'd ever known. Must be where she got her energy from. Judging from her bright eyes and the sparkling smile she flashed his way, nothing appeared to keep her up at night, including him.

"... Per the seating charts I've created—"

"For the love of Christmas, Keltz, take a breath."

"Boring you, am I, Clayton?"

"You are the least boring person I know." Clanging the spoon against the white porcelain mug, he frowned. "But could we talk about anything other than wedding stuff?"

She closed her laptop. Her elaborate, step-by-step, day-of plans might not have been out of place at the invasion of Normandy. "What would you like to talk about?"

"I'm always up for talking about food."

She rolled her eyes. "Is food all you ever think about?"

As a matter of fact, food wasn't all he thought about. Spending time with Kelsey dominated most of his thoughts.

"I don't know where you put the food."

He shrugged. "It's my long legs. They're hollow."

Their gazes locked. His lips twitched.

She burst out laughing. "You are so ridiculous, McKendry."

He grinned. He'd made it his personal mission to make her laugh every day. His phone beeped with an incoming text.

"Nana says the jeweler has finished sizing their wedding rings. Asks if one of us could pick 'em up for her. Save her a trip to town."

Kelsey grabbed hold of the edge of the table. "Will do."

"Hold on to your stilettos there, City Girl." He replied to the text. "Makes more sense for me to take them to the ranch." He glanced up. "No reason we both can't go to the store, though." No reason he should turn down spending more time with her.

She smiled. "Great." She took hold of the table again as if to slingshot her way out of the booth.

"But—" he checked the time "—the jewelry-store owner goes home for lunch and doesn't reopen the store again until one o'clock each day. We've got a few minutes."

"You know this how?"

"Everybody in Truelove knows this. Exact same schedule for decades."

She smiled. "Small-town charm at its finest."

He loved his hometown, but he was beginning to appreciate the advantages only the city offered. Namely, the vivacious brunette sitting across from him. "Real tree or fake?"

Kelsey's mouth curved. "I prefer real."

"Me, too. There may be hope for you yet." He planted his elbows on the table. "I'm learning not to be surprised by anything that concerns you."

"Smart man. Christmas dinner or dessert?"

He cocked his head. "What do you think?"

"Both."

He chuckled. "Nailed it in one."

"Where do you see yourself in five years, Cowboy?"

"The Bar None. McKendrys have ranched that land since the Civil War. It's a legacy I don't take lightly." He cut his gaze out the window overlooking the square. "This'll probably sound lame, but it comes down to faith, family and home for me."

"Sounds pretty wonderful to me."

His eyes flitted to hers. "There you go surprising me again. What dreams are you dreaming?"

"A couple of weeks ago, I believed I had my future mapped out, but now?" She sighed. "I'm not sure where I belong or if the thing I wanted most is the right path for me." She grabbed her phone. "Let me show you what I found yesterday." She held it out for him to view the pictures she'd taken. "Birchfield. Have you ever been there?"

"I don't think so."

"A fabulous place for a wedding venue. Don't you think?"

He took the phone from her and enlarged one of the photos. "What are you thinking?"

"I've had the craziest idea ever... There aren't any event venues close to Truelove. Imagine the jobs something like this could bring and the boost to the local economy."

He continued to scroll through her pictures.

"Am I crazy? Tell me I'm crazy to even contemplate an enterprise of this magnitude."

"You're crazy." He handed back her cell. "But you've taken like a horse to a sugar cube with this whole wedding thing. You have experience planning events for your father."

"True." Shaking her head, she leaned back. "But the financial investment alone..."

"If anyone could make it happen, Keltz, it's you."

She looked at him. "I've decided to hire Maddie Lovett here in Truelove to do the wedding cake."

He smiled. "Thanks for giving her a chance. You won't be disappointed with the results."

He glanced at his watch. "Let's go pick out—I mean pick up the rings." Flushing, he got out of the booth.

Outside the jewelry store, she became entranced with the twinkling, miniature village of Truelove displayed in the front window. She oohed and aahed, locating the Mason Jar first and then Martha Alice's neighborhood.

The things that delighted Kelsey Summerfield never failed to amaze him.

Grinning, he dragged her inside the store.

While the jeweler disappeared into the storeroom to retrieve the wedding rings, he noticed Kelsey had wandered over to a section featuring antique estate jewelry.

"I had you figured for a thoroughly modern, all-about-the-bling sort of gal."

His assumption was based entirely on the fact she was a Summerfield. However, he'd never seen her wear much jewelry, other than a watch and various pairs of earrings. Nothing too over-the-top. Maybe she saved the expensive stuff for special occasions when she got glammed up.

Kelsey's gaze trailed along the glass case. "I like old things." She nudged him with her shoulder. "It's why I hang out with you."

She made him sound ancient. "Three years' difference is hardly worth mentioning."

The jeweler returned with the wedding bands, boxed and bagged. When Clay turned around again, once more her attention had become ensnared by the estate jewelry case.

He rejoined her. "Why old things, Keltz?"

She winked. "Because you're funny and a ginger and—"

"Ha. Ha. Ha."

"I admire the workmanship and the artistry." She shrugged. "I like to imagine the happy stories each piece could tell."

He wrinkled his brow. "Not every story has a happy ending."

"In my dreams, they do."

He set the bag on top of the case. "Which one speaks happily-ever-after to you?"

Fluttering her hands, she backed away. "This is silly. We should go." She tugged at his arm.

"Show me, Kelsey. I'd like to know."

Bending over the case, she pointed.

He signaled the jeweler. "Could she try on one of the pieces in here?"

Unlocking the case, the jeweler plucked out the understated sapphire ring. Two smaller diamonds rode sidesaddle. The fretwork was intricate and classy. It was so her.

The jeweler handed it to her. "A lovely little ring from the 1920s. Very Art Deco."

She slipped the ring on her finger. A perfect fit. "I love Art Deco." She moved her hand this way and that, catching the light, setting the sparkle free.

He took hold of her hand to admire the effect. They smiled at each other. He felt a gust of cold air. Someone entered the shop. He turned.

Framed in the doorway, like a gargoyle gone wrong, GeorgeAnne Allen smirked. "What are you two up to now?" She eyeballed them. "The cowboy finally takes a wife."

He dropped Kelsey's hand. Simultaneously, they backed away from each other. Her cheeks scarlet, Kelsey tore the ring off her finger and thrust it at the jeweler.

"It's not what it looks like," he stammered.

GeorgeAnne gloated. "Of course it isn't."

Kelsey waved her hand, now minus the vintage ring. "We were just picking up Grampy and Dorothy's wedding bands."

"Sure you were."

He seized the bag and held it up as evidence. Kelsey edged around the older woman.

"Marth'Alice is probably wondering where I am. Bye." *Sorry,* she mouthed to him from behind GeorgeAnne's back. Fleeing, she slipped out the door. Leaving him to slay the dragon alone.

"We weren't..." He gulped. "We aren't..."

GeorgeAnne gave him a supercilious smile. "Your secret is safe with me."

He understood what that meant all too well. He beat a hasty retreat. Outside on the sidewalk, he sucked in a lungful of air.

She'd have his grandmother on speed dial within seconds. ErmaJean, IdaLee and Martha Alice would be next on her call list. By the time rumors about another, imminent engagement finished making the rounds, the Truelove grapevine would have them roped and steered into wedded bliss by the New Year.

Yet despite his worst nightmare come true, being the other half of a *you two* with Kelsey might not be as bad as he'd feared. Heading to his truck, he hummed "It Came upon the Midnight Clear."

Since he'd met Kelsey, his life had become a lot more interesting. And fun.

CHAPTER NINE

ON TUESDAY, KELSEY drove Dorothy to the bridal boutique in Asheville. Cynthia greeted them like long-lost friends. They were meeting Miss Dot's granddaughter, Rebecca, so she could be fitted for her bridesmaid dress. Kelsey was nervous about meeting Clay's sister, but the young mother of two couldn't have been friendlier.

Kelsey saw the resemblance between Clay and his sister. Including the supposedly not-red color of their hair.

"I love my children dearly." On the dais in her gown, Rebecca did a slow twirl in front of the mirror. "But I can't tell you how much I appreciated the long, *quiet* drive from Boone to Asheville by myself." Her husband, a forest ranger, had taken a half day off to keep the kids.

The alterations were minor. Her dress on a hanger, Rebecca was soon ready to depart for her two-hour trek home. She hugged her grandmother. "Next time I see you, Nana, it will be at your wedding."

Nearly lunchtime, Kelsey took Clay's grandmother to one of her and Granna's favorite tearooms. "The chicken salad is the best I've ever eaten."

"That's what I'll order." Dorothy scanned the cozy, English chintz decor. "Such a lovely spot. I've never been here before, but of course it's not often I get into Asheville."

Kelsey poured the older woman a cup of steaming Earl Grey.

Dorothy stirred a lump of sugar in her teacup. "I hope you'll join us for Thanksgiving, Kelsey."

Her brother would be visiting his wife's family, and as was his habit, her father would spend the entire holiday working at the office. With Grampy at the Bar None, this year she'd figured she'd be alone. Martha Alice had invited her to the Breckenridge-Dolan family gathering, but this was the first Thanksgiving since Jack and Kate had married. She didn't want to intrude.

Incredibly touched, she folded her hands under her chin. "I'd love to join you and your family for Thanksgiving, Miss Dot. What can I bring?"

"Just yourself. It'll be the usual turkey and fixins' with pumpkin pie." Dorothy waved her blue-veined hand. "Everyone has their particular favorites."

"Isn't there something I could contribute?"

"No need to trouble yourself." Dorothy shrugged. "I'll take care of everything."

Dropping her gaze to the linen tablecloth, she nodded. "Oh. Okay. Thank you. It's very kind of you to include me in your family celebration." She traced her finger around the rim of the cup. Always the outsider looking in...

"On second thought."

She looked across the table at Clay's grandmother.

"I'd be nutty to refuse an offer to help with the cooking. So much to do." Dorothy lifted the teacup to her lips. "What dish means Thanksgiving to you?"

Kelsey perked. "Sweet potatoes."

"Sweet potatoes are a definite must." Dorothy smiled. "I do the traditional sweet potato casserole, but why don't we change it up this year? Do you have something in mind you'd like to bring?"

"I have the perfect recipe. Always a big hit. One of Grampy's favorites."

"That settles it, then." Dorothy took a sip of her tea. "I'm sure it will be wonderful. How- ard won't be the only one glad to see you on Thanksgiving at the Bar None." She gave Kelsey a knowing look. "I'm thinking in par- ticular of a certain cowboy."

Kelsey blushed. Of late, her thoughts were filled with a certain cowboy. The more time she spent with Clay, the less irritating she found him.

His relaxed outlook on life was growing on her. He made her laugh. With him, she felt like she could be herself. And she also felt safe. Since Granna's death, she'd wondered if she'd ever feel truly secure again.

Later, after dropping Dorothy at the ranch, she helped Martha Alice put together several items for her Thanksgiving dinner. Covering the cranberry chutney with plastic wrap, she told the older woman about Dorothy's invita- tion and her own contribution to the feast.

"I always loved that recipe." Martha Alice's eyes shone. "I'm happy you'll be with your grandfather over the holiday. Dorothy is a fantastic cook. Not fancy like Joan's gourmet cuisine but satisfying, good food."

Kelsey put the chutney in the refrigerator. "I've had my reservations about this wedding, but for the first time, I feel so hopeful." She let the refrigerator door swing shut behind her. "Like it's a chance for a brand-new start for us." She placed the apples needing to be peeled and quartered in a row on the countertop. "Like maybe there's a place for me."

"Oh, sweetie." Setting down the rolling pin, Martha Alice dusted the flour off her hands and came around the island. She hugged Kelsey. "It has hurt my heart to see how you've struggled since Joan left us, but she would be so proud of the wonderful, generous young woman you've become. She'd want you to find someone to love and care for you, too."

Hands on her hips, Kelsey shook her head. "I'm sure I have no idea to whom you refer."

Martha Alice pursed her lips. "I'm equally sure you do."

"How about we get Grampy hitched before the Double Name Club starts on me?"

Martha Alice smirked. "I think that could be arranged."

Kelsey rolled her eyes. Once a matchmaker, always a matchmaker...

Early Wednesday morning, she stopped by the large grocery chain on the highway to purchase a few items she needed for Granna's signature Thanksgiving recipe. The store was filled with last-minute Thanksgiving shoppers. Holiday music played on the intercom.

Humming under her breath, she went through self-checkout to avoid the line. In the parking lot, the wind coming off the mountain gusted the brown leaves which had fallen to the ground around her car. She'd only just slid behind the wheel when her phone buzzed.

She clicked on. "Hi, Cowboy."

Clay's low, gravelly chuckle ignited butterflies inside her rib cage. "Hey yourself, Keltz."

She smiled into the phone.

"I hear you're coming to the ranch for Thanksgiving tomorrow."

Holding the phone to her ear with her shoulder, she pulled the seat belt taut and secured it. "I'm looking forward to coming to the ranch."

"I'm looking forward to seeing you," he rasped.

Good thing she was already sitting or else her knees might have buckled.

Kelsey heard the smile in his voice. She told him about Granna's recipe.

"Sweet potato rounds with ricotta cheese sounds to die for." His voice rumbled. "I happen to be an excellent food taster, if you're in the market for one."

Kelsey fished her keys out of her purse. "Granna's rule—taste testers have to help prepare the food."

"I'll have you know, Miss Summerfield, I am also an excellent sous-chef."

She inserted the key into the ignition. "Modest, too."

"One of my many admirable qualities, yes." He chuckled. "But I do know my way around the kitchen. Trained by the best. Thank you, Nana Dot. Are you headed to Marth'Alice's to put it together now?"

"Granna's recipe doesn't need to be prepared until the day of. By then, Marth'Alice's kitchen will be in full Thanksgiving mode. I'll go over to Grampy's condo tomorrow morning to make it so I won't be in her way."

"That's actually the real reason I called you. To see if I could pick you up so we could ride to the ranch together."

"I'd love to, but Grampy's condo would make it a farther commute for you."

"For me, it's a win-win. First dibs on the food and the added bonus of your company."

Her heart skipped a beat. He enjoyed being with her? "I don't want to be a bother."

"Stop doing that," he grunted.

Kelsey frowned into the phone. "Doing what?"

"You aren't a bother, Keltz. You're an amazing person. You're funny—"

"Funny like *ha ha*? Or funny *strange*?"

"Kelsey Summerfield," he groaned, "learn to take a compliment."

She bit back a sigh. Such a charmer. No wonder the women of Truelove went wild for him. "Thank you."

"Is that a *yes* then for sous-chef and escort?"

"A definite yes, but be prepared to work, McKendry."

"It's a date, then. I mean—"

A date… The butterflies in her chest did loop-de-loops.

"What time should I arrive?"

"Is nine too early?"

Clay snorted. "By nine o'clock, darlin', this cowboy's done a half day's work and then some."

Her heart palpitated at the drawled out *darlin'*.

"See you tomorrow."

Her heart took flight. The holidays really were the most wonderful time of the year. She sang Christmas carols at the top of her lungs all the way to Truelove.

Thanksgiving morning in Truelove dawned bright, clear and cold. At the condo, she turned the holiday music on the stereo system up full blast and toed out of her calf boots. She set the oven to preheat. When the doorbell buzzed, she was doing the cha-cha-cha in the middle of the kitchen. She glanced at the clock on the wall: 8:59.

Kelsey loved a man who was early. *Whoa*. She stutter-stepped mid cha-cha-cha. Based on their short acquaintance, loved seemed a bit much. But what about *liked extremely*?

The doorbell buzzed again. She could definitely do *liked extremely* with Clay. Picking up the beat, she two-stepped her way to the entrance and flung open the door.

"Don't want to lose my place in the song," she shouted above the music. Grabbing his arm, she yanked him inside. "Dance with me, partner."

NEVER A DULL moment with Kelsey Summerfield. Keeping time in her bare feet, she threw him an outrageous grin. "We've got to practice for the wedding reception and show the old folks how it's done."

He had a feeling Mr. Howard and Nana Dot (who could do a swing dance with the best of them) would more likely show them how it was done. Setting an autumnal bouquet in a chair, he jumped into the beat with Kelsey.

Placing his hand softly on her shoulder, they joined their free hands and were off. Quick-quick, slow, slow. Quick-quick, slow, slow. They danced an imaginary line around the perimeter of the living-room furniture. Following his lead, she did a series of twirls. By the time the song ended, they were both laughing hard.

"Whew!" Gasping for breath, she fell onto the couch. "That was fun."

He fanned his face with his hat. Kelsey was fun.

She pointed her chin at the flowers lying abandoned on the armchair. "For me?"

He handed her the bouquet. "Happy Thanksgiving."

She unfolded from the sofa and buried her face in the blossoms. "They're beautiful. Thank you, Clay."

He got his first good look at her, and the

bottom dropped out of his stomach. She was beautiful. Her sparkling blue eyes. The waves of dark cascading hair. Her feet were bare. Her toenails were painted to match her dress.

She smoothed a hand over the short lacy dress, which was the color of cranberries. "Do I look okay? Miss Dot said casual."

This was Kelsey's version of casual?

"You look great." She did. So great.

She smiled. "Thank you."

The next song playing on the condo's stereo system was slower. One of the old crooners from Nana Dot's generation. Something about home and Christmas.

Her eyes glistened. "I love that song," she whispered.

Clay swallowed past the lump in his throat. "Me, too."

Their gazes locked. For a moment, time tipped sideways. They shared a long look.

With a quivery sigh, she broke eye contact. "I'll put the flowers in a vase." On her way to the kitchen, she lowered the music volume. Slightly.

He stuffed his hands into his jean pockets. "Put me to work."

She set him in front of a cutting board to

slice sweet potatoes into rounds one-quarter-inch thick. On the other side of the island, she whipped an herbed ricotta spread. "After you've sliced everything, massage the rounds with the avocado oil and seasoning."

"Let's keep Thanksgiving G-rated, Summerfield."

She rolled her eyes. "You are so ridiculous." She bustled over to show him how to prep the rounds. Soon, they transferred the sweet potato slices to a baking sheet and into the oven.

"While we wait to flip the rounds to bake on the other side, let's clean up." She handed him a dish towel. "I'll wash. You dry."

Another tune floated over the sound system. Hands in the soapy water, she warbled along to "O Christmas Tree." They stood shoulder to shoulder at the sink.

"I hadn't realized you're one of *those* people."

She stopped singing. "What people?"

He smirked. "The kind who insist on jump-starting Christmas. What ever happened to giving thanks on Thanksgiving?"

She flicked a soap bubble at him. "I happen to be very *thankful* for Christmas."

"I didn't know you liked to cook." He slung

the towel over his shoulder. "You look at home in the kitchen."

She fluttered her lashes at him. "There's probably a lot you don't know about me, Cowboy."

His heart ratcheted. But oh, how he'd like to learn.

"Granna taught me everything I know. The kitchen was our special place together."

She checked the baking sheet in the oven. Following her instructions, he removed the pan and flipped the rounds to the other side. On a lower rack, she placed another tray of walnuts to roast. Finishing the dishes, she belted out "Hark! The Herald Angels Sing."

He grinned. "Didn't realize you were so *musical*, either."

She butted him with her hip. "Don't hate, Cowboy. Appreciate."

"I appreciate plenty. It's good to see you happy."

She leaned against the cool, smooth quartz of the countertop. "The sweet potato rounds were our thing at Thanksgiving. Making them today makes Granna feel close." She looked at him. "Thanks for adding a new memory to an old one."

"Thanks for inviting me."

Somehow the distance between them had lessened. If he leaned just a little, if she lifted her face just a tad… His heart jackhammered.

Her blue eyes widened. Moistening her bottom lip, she stared up at him. Did she want him to kiss her?

Clay put his hand to her waist. "Keltz…"

A vein in the tiny hollow of her throat pulsed. "Cowboy," she whispered. Standing on tiptoe, she lifted her face. Her lips parted. He lowered his head.

The oven timer dinged. They jolted apart. The moment broken, she rushed past him to check the sweet potatoes. Over the next few minutes, she barked out directions. She was good at giving orders.

Dotting the rounds with a dollop of herbed ricotta, he swallowed a smile. Somehow, he didn't mind her bossiness as much as he would have a week ago. The rounds returned to the oven for a few minutes. Then they topped the rounds with walnuts and cranberries.

She drizzled honey over each one with a final flourish. "Ta-da!"

"Mmm…" His belly growled. "These look good. Feel free to cook for me anytime."

Slipping on a denim jacket, she laughed, not taking him seriously. "Such a flirt."

But he was serious. As a heart attack. He put his hand over his chest. The way his heart was feeling this morning, perhaps he ought to consult a cardiologist. Or maybe it was simply the Kelsey effect.

She transferred the rounds to a white platter.

"Hang on, Summerfield." He moved toward her. "Haven't I earned the right to a taste test?"

Kelsey's mouth quirked. "A taste test? That's what you want?"

For a second, his eyes drifted to her mouth before he caught her gaze. Their almost–kiss minutes earlier passed between them like a lightning bolt.

"Just one." She wagged her finger at him. "Save the rest for later."

"You talking about sweet potatoes?" He cocked his head. "Or something else?"

Smiling, she shook her head. "Whichever you prefer, Clayton."

He no longer minded as much when she used his given name.

"Now who's the flirt?" Laughing, he reached for the round. "Sweet potato first... It's called an appetizer for a reason. I'll save the other for later." He popped the warm round into his mouth.

"Promises, promises," she teased.

He chewed and swallowed. "Way to wow. Totally lives up to the hype."

She sashayed toward the couch. "So will a kiss."

He hooked his thumb in his belt loop. "Promises, promises."

She slipped into a pair of worn leather calf boots.

"Get a look at you, City Girl."

She did a slow twirl. "I'm embracing my inner cowgirl. What do you think?"

He sighed. "I think we better get on the road, or we're going to be late for Thanksgiving."

They entertained each other all the way to the ranch. Favorite Christmas carol. Favorite contemporary Christmas song. Fruitcake versus Christmas cake.

She sniffed. "You're a fruitcake."

"Takes one to know one." Veering off the secondary road, he drove under the crossbars of the Bar None. He pulled the truck up to the farmhouse. "Doesn't look like the parents are here yet."

"Your parents are coming?"

He cut the engine. "Dad wouldn't miss Turkey Day at Nana Dot's. They'll stay the entire weekend. Now you'll get to meet them before the wedding."

"Unlike my family."

He looked at her, but she avoided his eyes. Even though his dad had retired from ranch life to the beach, his family remained close. He'd given up trying to understand Kelsey's family dynamics.

Clay carried the sweet potato tray into the house. Nana Dot met them at the door. She offered him her cheek for a quick kiss.

Nana Dot took the platter. "Something smells scrumptious. Howard's resting in the living room."

Kelsey frowned. "Is he all right?"

"Not his usual chipper self." Nana Dot arched her eyebrow. "He's feeling out of sorts, but your lovely face will cheer him."

"Thanksgiving is his favorite holiday." Kelsey removed her jacket. "I hope he's not coming down with something."

Clay took off his coat. "Maybe he didn't sleep well."

His grandmother touched the lace on Kelsey's sleeve. "What a beautiful dress."

"Not too much?" Kelsey gave her a hesitant smile. "I considered jeans, but I thought if I paired the dress with the jacket and my boots…"

"It's perfect. You look a right picture." Nana Dot pushed her glasses up the bridge of her nose. "Doesn't she, Clay?"

"Yes, ma'am." He threw Kelsey a smile. "That she does."

It amazed him how she doubted herself sometimes. One thing he'd discovered about Kelsey over the last week—behind her super-confident competence lay a roiling mass of insecurities.

They followed his grandmother into the living room. In the recliner, Mr. Howard fiddled with the television remote.

Kelsey gave him a hug. "Happy Thanksgiving, Grampy."

Grunting, he patted her arm and returned to his investigation of the Thanksgiving Day football lineup. Clay cut his eyes at the older man. Not having a good day. Whatever ailed Mr. Howard, Nana Dot's cooking would soon set him right.

His stomach rumbled again. Cinnamon,

cloves and other delicious aromas wafted through the house. Thinking of Nana Dot's pumpkin pie, his mouth watered.

Kelsey stepped forward. "How can I help you, Miss Dot?"

"I've got everything under control. Waiting on the turkey to come out of the oven. Clay's dad will carve it when he arrives. That's his Thanksgiving Day job. But I'd love your help to set the table."

"Counting Trudy, you're expecting seven for dinner?"

"*Dinner* sounds so fancy." Nana Dot gave her a side hug. "Around here on Thanksgiving, we do *lunch*. But actually, there'll be ten of us."

She looked at Clay. "Ten?" He shrugged.

Nana Dot patted Mr. Howard's shoulder. "An unexpected and delightful surprise."

Clay sat on the sofa. "Already did my Thanksgiving Day job."

Kelsey batted her lashes. "And what job would that be, Cowboy?"

He leaned his elbows on his knees. "I cracked the nuts for the pecan pie."

"You're a—"

"Go ahead and say it." He grinned. "You know you want to."

Sniffing, she clamped her lips shut.

Chuckling, Nana Dot set the platter on the coffee table. "Howard, Kelsey brought an appetizer. Would it be okay, Kelsey dear, if we don't wait for the others? I can't wait to try one."

"Of course." She smiled. "I hope you like it."

"I've been up since the crack of dawn, and I'm starving. So ingenious of you to think of bringing something to snack on until lunch." Nana Dot peeled off the aluminum. "If it tastes as good as it—"

"Sweet potato rounds!" With a roar, Grampy brought the recliner upright and thumped his feet down on the carpet. "What on earth possessed you to bring that here?"

Kelsey shrank back a step.

"What are you trying to prove?" He shook his finger in her face. "Why must you always rub Dorothy's nose in it? Try to show her up."

"I-I wasn't." Kelsey's voice wobbled. "I didn't mean… It's just this is my favorite—your favorite…" She opened her hands. "I-I only wanted to share something special with…"

"Howard." Clay's grandmother put a hand on his shoulder. "Calm down. Kelsey didn't—"

"Did your father put you up to this?" Glaring at his granddaughter, Howard Summerfield turned toward Nana Dot. "She's trying to sabotage our happiness. I won't stand for it, I tell you. I won't."

Clay's jaw dropped. He'd never seen this side of Howard Summerfield. And after what Kelsey had let slip about her dad... Suddenly, he saw more than a passing resemblance between father and son.

His gaze swung to his grandmother. She appeared as shocked by the change in her usually congenial fiancé as Clay felt.

Nana Dot propped her hands on her bony hips. "You're overreacting, Howard. Kelsey wasn't—"

"Why must you spoil everything, Kelsey?" Howard fumed. "Why must you ruin Thanksgiving?"

"That's enough, Mr. Summerfield." Rising, Clay inserted himself between Kelsey and her grandfather. He clenched his hands at his side, trying hard not to disrespect the older gentleman. "I will not allow you to speak to Kelsey that way."

Her face stricken, Kelsey's eyes were huge. "I'm s-sorry." Tears cascaded down her cheeks. Sobbing, she bolted out the door.

CHAPTER TEN

BLINDED BY TEARS and vaguely aware of raised voices, Kelsey stumbled out the door. Leaving chaos in her wake, she fled the farmhouse.

Moments later, she found herself pressed against a split-rail fence staring aimlessly at the evergreen forest beyond the pasture.

Since the shopping expedition, she and Dorothy had reached a good place with each other. Had she been trying to, as Grampy claimed, show up Miss Dot in comparison to Granna? Kelsey searched her heart for unconscious motivations. But she'd only meant to share something special to her. She had no idea Grampy would react that way. In all her twenty-six years, he'd never so much as raised his voice to her.

Kelsey choked back a sob. She might not be guilty of everything he accused her of, but perhaps the fault lay in not thinking it through.

She'd not only angered her grandfather but hurt Dorothy, too. Thanksgiving, which had started out so right, was a disaster.

She was a disaster. She swiped away the tears on her cheeks. Fat lot of good crying had ever done her. It hadn't kept her mother from dying. It had only made her father run from her. It wouldn't fix this fiasco.

What was she going to do now? She couldn't return to the house. Maybe if she left, the McKendry holiday wouldn't be a complete debacle.

But having left her phone on the coffee table, she couldn't call for a rideshare or taxi. Not that Truelove had either service. Who could she call to pick her up at the road? Martha Alice's grandson, Jack, would come and get her. But it was Thanksgiving. She'd only wreck their plans.

She was so tired of being a burden. Of never belonging anywhere.

Her only recourse was to walk to Truelove. Not a great option, considering the heels on her boots. Truelove was miles away. Separated from the Bar None by several treacherous mountain roads. But at the moment, she didn't care what happened to her. She just wanted away.

"Kelsey."

She stiffened. Lost in misery, she hadn't heard Clay come out of the house. A wave of crimson flooded up her neck. He must think her the most horrible, insensitive person he'd ever met. Or the dumbest.

"Keltz?"

His little nickname stabbed like a knife in her heart. She squeezed her eyelids shut. "I-I'm okay." She flailed her arm behind her back. "Go inside with your family. I never meant—"

Clay caught hold of her arm. "What he said isn't true. That's not who you are. Would you look at me, darlin'?"

She shook her head. "I-I can't."

"It's cold out here, Keltz. The denim jacket is cute, but not enough for November in True-love."

She let her shoulders rise and fall. "I'm okay with suffering for fashion."

"That's the spirit."

She heard the smile in his voice.

"But I'm not okay with you shaking like a leaf."

He opened his coat, and she found herself enfolded by his arms. The scents of hay, leather and something masculine, something totally him, engulfed her senses.

Clay was warm. And wonderful. And kind.

"Your grandfather had no right to say those things."

She was faintly amazed at the anger in his voice. No one had ever defended her before. Not any of the men in her life, anyway.

His arms tightened around her. "It wasn't true. I saw how you were this morning."

To be known and understood... To be accepted and cherished... A pinprick of tears stung her eyelids.

What would it be like to be loved by someone as fierce and loyal as Clay McKendry? Not that she'd ever know, of course. He'd proven himself a rare friend, but good men like him fell for sweet, uncomplicated women. Like the brunette who worked at the pharmacy.

Kelsey was a complete mess. The longer she stayed in his life, the bigger the risk she'd mess him up, too. But for just a moment... Just a few moments... She leaned her head against his chest and enjoyed the comfort of his arms.

Letting out a sigh, her breath fogged in the crisp, chill air. "I do ruin everything," she whispered.

Clay rested his stubbly chin on her head. "I don't believe that."

"I killed my mother. That's why my family is so messed up. Dad couldn't stand to look at me, and my brother Andrew couldn't stand to be near me."

"Kelsey," he growled, "you did not kill your mother."

"But I did." She turned in his arms. "After Andrew was born, my mother was diagnosed with an autoimmune disease. It made it harder for her to conceive, which is why there's a decade between Andrew and me. The doctors and Dad tried to dissuade her, but she was determined to have another child."

Clay lifted her chin with his finger. "She wanted you, Kelsey."

"Dad didn't." Her gaze caught his. "After I was born, she was never the same physically. It was the beginning of a decline that ended with her death when I was seven. Dad has never gotten over her loss. He buried himself in the company. Andrew made his own life. Granna and Grampy took me in to raise."

He pressed his forehead to hers. "No wonder losing your grandmother has been so hard for you. You must feel now you've lost your grandfather, too."

She pulled back a tad. "Today proves that I have."

He shook his head. "Something is going on with Mr. Howard, but I don't think it has anything to do with you. Come inside with me."

"I won't go where I'm not wanted."

He scowled. "I want you here."

"But Miss Dot—"

"Nana Dot knows your intentions were good."

She took a shuddery breath. "Could I borrow the keys to your truck? I can get it returned tonight."

"Please, Kelsey. Stay." He pulled her against him. "You haven't met my parents yet."

She rested her cheek against the soft flannel of his green-checked shirt. Through the fabric, she could feel the strong thumping of his heart. "Clay…" Of their own volition, her arms went around his waist.

"If you leave, I'm leaving, too." His voice roughened. "I won't have you spending Thanksgiving alone."

An impossible choice. Either she stayed where she wasn't welcome, or she ruined the holiday for Clay. She'd spent a lifetime being unwanted, what was one more day if it meant salvaging Thanksgiving for him?

"Okay," she mumbled into his shirt. "I'll stay."

He drew back to examine her face. She immediately missed the warmth of him. "Really?"

She nodded.

"If he—" Jaw clenched, Clay jabbed his thumb at the house "—says anything else negative to you, I'll drive you to Asheville myself, and we'll make our own Thanksgiving."

She patted his chest. "My cowboy hero. It'll be fine."

He reached for her hand. She laced her fingers through his. Hand in hand, they strolled to the house. Dorothy met them on the porch.

"Oh, Miss Dot." Kelsey gulped. "I am so sorry."

Smelling of cinnamon spice, Dorothy's thin arms went around her. "You have nothing to be sorry about. Howard was in a mood. I told him in no uncertain terms he was out of line."

It did not escape Kelsey's attention Clay hadn't let go of her hand. Nor, apparently, his grandmother's, either. The older woman's questioning gaze cut between them. She patted

Kelsey's shoulder and then laid a gentle hand upon Clay's cheek.

Dorothy turned to the door. "Howard and I had a long talk. I don't think he'll give you anymore grief."

Kelsey took a deep breath. Squaring her shoulders, she allowed Clay to tug her inside. A quick scan revealed the sweet potato tray still lying on the coffee table next to her phone. Her grandfather slumped in the recliner. "Kelsey, could we talk?"

Clay gripped her hand.

The gesture did not go unnoticed. Something brief as to be almost nonexistent flickered in the older man's eyes. Grampy cleared his throat. "Alone."

Clay frowned.

She untangled her fingers from his. "It's okay."

"Are you sure?" he rasped.

She was anything but sure. However, hard situations were better faced straightaway. She'd learned that much the day of Granna's funeral. She nodded.

"Clay," Dorothy called from the kitchen, "would you take the turkey out of the oven for me?"

With a final look at her, Clay headed for the kitchen. Leaving Kelsey alone with her grandfather. Until today, a man she'd believed would never let her down. But that's what people did. They left, or they died. One way or the other, they always let her down.

Except Clay.

Her grandfather shuffled out of the recliner and to his feet. "I should've never said those things to you." His voice broke. "I'm sorry. Please forgive me."

"I'm the one who needs to ask forgiveness." She knotted her fingers together. "I didn't think. I—"

"You have nothing to apologize for." Grampy shook his head. "I'm a foolish old man."

She came around the coffee table. "No, you're not. I should never have—"

"I woke up thinking about your Granna this morning." His faded blue eyes moistened. "I miss her so much."

Kelsey touched his arm. "Me, too."

His Adam's apple bobbed. "I have so much more than I ever dreamed possible to be thankful for this year." His gaze darted toward the kitchen. "I felt guilty thinking about Joan when Dorothy and I are about to be married."

"Oh, Grampy."

He sighed. "With Joan's sweet potato rounds, which I love, staring me in the face, the guilt just rose up. I took out my anger at myself on you." He squeezed her hand. "I hope I haven't ruined things between us. You've been the joy of my life."

A lump rose in her throat. "You haven't ruined anything. I love you, Grampy." She hugged him.

"I love you, too, honeybun."

"Could I give you a quick piece of advice?" She bit her lip. "Though, it's not like I have a ton of experience with marriage."

He chuckled. "Exactly none, but go ahead. Say what you've got to say."

"I only wanted to remind you that you and Granna were married for nearly sixty years. You spent so many Thanksgivings together. Don't you think it's normal to miss someone you shared a lifetime with? And still perfectly okay to look forward to a new beginning with someone else?"

He gave her a faint smile. "Dorothy said the same thing."

Kelsey heaved a sigh of relief. "I'm glad you talked it over with her."

"Polka Dot and I are on track again. No worries. I plan to offer an apology to Clay, too." He reached for a sweet potato round and took a bite. "Delicious. Just like your Granna's."

Yet despite his assurances, a small worry niggled at her. Was Grampy getting cold feet? Granna had only been dead a year. Was he truly ready to get married again? In rushing forward with the wedding, was he glossing over his doubts?

She wanted what was best for him and Miss Dot. The prospect of keeping her grandfather to herself no longer held the allure it might have several weeks ago. She'd seen how happy Dorothy made him.

Kelsey had only just joined Clay and his grandmother in the kitchen when his parents arrived. She stayed where she was, setting the silverware around the dining-room table. Clay went to greet his parents.

Ushering her son and daughter-in-law into the house, Dorothy introduced them to Grampy. Kelsey peeked around the half-wall partition. From the way he fiddled with the buttons on the charcoal sweater vest, she could tell he was nervous. Like her, he'd overdressed for a McKendry Thanksgiving.

He'd worn his usual version of dressed-down casual—a starched white shirt and pressed gray wool pants straight from the dry cleaners. And the crowning touch? To Grampy's mind, the penultimate token to casualness, a sweater vest.

"Kelsey, stop for a minute." Arms folded and booted ankles crossed, Clay leaned against the wall. "Come meet my parents."

Heart inexplicably pounding, she bit the inside of her cheek. Why did this feel like such a huge deal? She felt a surge of sympathy for Grampy.

"Keltz." He held out his hand. "I promise they're much nicer than me."

"A low bar there, Cowboy."

"You'll like my mother." He threw her a crooked grin, setting her knees aquiver. "Mom will love you for your efforts to keep me humble."

"A thankless job, but somebody's gotta do it."

They headed for the living room. She'd never known such an astonishing amount of comfort could be communicated through the simple touch of his hand against the small of her back. He introduced her to his parents.

Clay had inherited his height from his father, Gary. Perhaps one day also his father's slightly receding hairline? She swallowed her smile. Either way, Clay McKendry would still possess the power to wow. Her, at least.

Grampy shoved the platter of sweet potato rounds at Clay's father. "Try these. A Summerfield Thanksgiving tradition. Kelsey made them."

"Don't mind if I do." Gary helped himself. "Yum. Great job, Kelsey."

Smiling, Clay's eyes caught hers. She nudged him with her shoulder. "You're right. They are nicer than you," she rasped.

His mother hooted. Kelsey went scarlet. Her and her big—

Susan McKendry slipped her arm around Kelsey. "I think we're going to be friends. Has my son told you about the time in high school when he—"

"Not fair to gang up, Mom."

Steering Kelsey toward the kitchen, his mother fluttered her hand at him. "Keep your dad and Mr. Howard company, baby boy. Kelsey and I are going to have a chat."

"Don't embarrass me, Mom."

Susan winked at Kelsey. He'd gotten his sense of humor from his mother. Kelsey threw him a marginally wicked smile. Kind of fun to turn the tables on him. He was right, although she'd never tell him so. She liked his down-to-earth parents.

A few minutes later, his Aunt Trudy arrived with a green bean casserole. She added another layer of good-natured fun to the gathering. Dorothy called Gary to his turkey-carving duties. Kelsey finished setting the table. Clay had a hard time standing idle. Dorothy put him in charge of making sure the biscuits didn't burn. As Susan removed the biscuits from the oven, a flurry of knocks sounded at the front door.

"Let Kelsey answer the door!" Dorothy hollered.

She jerked. Susan nearly dropped the pan of biscuits.

"Me?" Kelsey pointed to herself. "Shouldn't Clay or—"

"I'll put the food on the table." Dorothy shooed her toward the living room. "You welcome the rest of our guests."

Who is it? she mouthed at Clay.

Eyebrows raised, he shrugged.

She passed Grampy, engrossed in the Thanksgiving Day parade on television. He was of the generation that it would never occur to him to help in the kitchen. He brought home the bacon. It had been up to Granna to fry it up in the pan. Kelsey's grandmother had waited on him hand and foot. For the sake of future marital harmony, she prayed Miss Dot was of like mind.

Kelsey yanked open the door. Whatever she believed she might find on the doorstep, she'd never in a million years have guessed it would be her brother and his family.

Five-year-old Eloise threw her arms around her. "Aunt Kelsey!"

"Andrew? Nicola?" Eloise's exuberance almost knocked her off her feet. She caught hold of the doorframe. "What are you doing here?"

Eloise let go of her. "We're here to eat turkey and see the horses."

"And?" Kelsey's London-born sister-in-law prompted.

Eloise's brow creased. "Oh, yeah." Her face lit. "Meet Grampy's new family."

Kelsey glanced over her shoulder to find the McKendrys standing in the foyer behind her. "These are your surprise guests, Miss Dot?"

Dorothy came forward. "I can't tell you how pleased I am to finally meet Howard's grandson." Propping her hands on her knees, she bent toward Kelsey's niece. "You must be Eloise. I've heard so much about you."

Grampy gave Andrew a big hug and performed the introductions.

Kelsey looked at her brother. "Aren't you supposed to be in Tucson with Nicola's family?"

"Nicola's parents came down with the flu." With the tip of his finger, Andrew pushed his black framed glasses higher on the bridge of his nose. "We thought it would be nice to spend Thanksgiving in North Carolina for a change."

His wife, tall and elegant, gave Kelsey a hug. "Andrew called Dorothy. And we sort of invited ourselves."

Dorothy waved her hand. "You did nothing of the kind. I'm so pleased we can be together on Thanksgiving Day."

Eloise begged to see the horses, but Clay promised her a tour after lunch. Gary sat at the head of the table. Dorothy sat at the other end with Grampy on one side. The rest of them filled in the other seats. Eloise insisted on sitting beside Kelsey, warming her heart. Clay pulled the chair next to Kelsey.

Gary said a short grace, and everyone dug in. Platters of turkey were passed around. Trays of ham. The gravy boat. There was a great deal of laughter and joy. Clay was incredibly good with Eloise. Who knew he'd be such a natural with kids? Like females of all ages, it didn't take her niece long to succumb to his effortless charm.

She couldn't stop gazing in wonder around the table. How had this happened? When was the last time her family had gathered for a happy occasion?

He touched her hand under the table. "You okay?" His breath fluttered a stray tendril of hair against her neck.

She was better than okay. Amidst the clatter of cutlery and animated chatter, this was what a real family was supposed to be like. Something, she realized with an acute clarity, she wanted very much for herself. She cut her eyes at Clay.

Kelsey wasn't above admitting to a growing fondness for pickup trucks.

"Why are you smiling?"

"No reason." She smiled again. "Just happy."

He squeezed her hand under the table. "I'm glad." He caught her gaze and held it.

Gary cleared his throat. "Earth to Clay. Kelsey? Would one of you pass the butter?"

Looking away, she discovered all eyes glued on them. She blushed. How long had Clay's father been trying to get their attention? Grampy

hid a grin behind his napkin. Dorothy exchanged a meaningful look with Nicola.

Giving her a lopsided grin that made her toes
curl in her boots, Clay passed the butter dish.
"Sure, Dad."

The earlier hope she'd tried to communicate
with Martha Alice returned.

She wasn't losing Grampy. She was gaining a
new family. Her heart ratcheted a notch. Maybe
a cowboy, too.

CHAPTER ELEVEN

AFTER LUNCH, HIS parents and Aunt Trudy insisted on cleaning up the dishes. They sent Nana Dot into the living room to keep Mr. Howard company. Clay gave the Summerfields the Bar None grand tour. It was fun seeing the ranch through Eloise's contagious excitement.

He turned three of the horses into the paddock. In her black patent leather shoes, Eloise climbed onto the fence rail and hung over the gate. Kelsey and Nicola stood on each side to make sure she didn't pitch headfirst into the corral.

Comparing ranch life with the corporate life, Clay and Kelsey's brother ambled along the fence line. Kelsey's family was both less and more than he'd expected. Obviously, Summerfield casual attire standards were very different from McKendrys.

Wearing a hunter green sweater with leather

elbow patches and tassel-fringed loafers that probably cost as much as a month's worth of gasoline for the tractor, Andrew was the epitome of success. Andrew's wife, glamorous Nicola, with her fancy British accent added to the image of sophistication. But like Kelsey, Andrew and his family were genuine, kind and unpretentious.

"I admire what concerned citizens have done to revitalize Truelove's downtown." Andrew pushed his slightly hipster, dark-framed eyeglasses farther along his nose. "Grampy told me about it. Too many of the small Appalachian towns are dying."

Clay scuffed his boot in the dirt. "There aren't many good-paying jobs. People leave for the city. There's also the lack of access to health care and broadband in the rural areas."

Andrew nodded. "I'd like to see other communities flourish again like Truelove."

"I wouldn't exactly call Truelove flourishing, not yet, but there's a whole lot more hope out there than you would've found even five years ago.

"That's what excites me." Andrew's eyes gleamed. "Being part of the solution."

Clay cocked his head. "How so?"

"The Summerfields have done a lot to develop western North Carolina. I'd like to add an additional legacy to the company Grampy started—by providing resources and opportunities to revitalize small towns in the region."

"Is your father on board with this project?"

Andrew frowned. "I'm working on him. It's a passion of mine and Grampy's. It's time the Summerfields gave back to the people and the state who've given us so much." He jutted his jaw. "If I have to, I'm prepared to start my own nonprofit to make it happen."

"You'd leave Summerfield, Inc.?"

"Nicola would, too." Andrew crossed his arms. "For the sake of my relationship with Dad, I hope it won't come to that."

Clay couldn't ignore this opportunity to make her brother aware of the deep pain Kelsey carried. "This is absolutely none of my business, but did you know Kelsey blames herself for your mother's death? Do you have any idea how isolated and alone she's felt since your grandmother died last year?" He made an effort to not raise his voice, but every time he recalled Kelsey's forlorn face that morning, he wanted to rip somebody apart for hurting her.

Andrew shook his head. "I've never blamed her for what happened."

Clay folded his arms. "And your father?"

Andrew ran his hand over his dark hair. "My mother's death made him a bitter man. Unfortunately, Kelsey took the brunt of his inability to face his loss. I was seventeen when Mom died." His eyes shone with remembered pain. "There was a huge age gap between us, but that's no excuse. I was dealing with my own grief, but I should've been there for her." He blinked rapidly. "And caught up with the business and family, I've done it to her again after Granna died, haven't I?" He gulped. "I'm sorry."

"You should talk to Kelsey."

Andrew gave him a slight smile. "I still remember the day Mom brought her home from the hospital. I was excited. She was such a little thing."

"Still is," Clay grunted.

"I've always been so happy she became part of our family."

"You should tell her that. It would mean a lot."

"I will."

They'd looped around to the ladies. Kelsey had found a length of rope with which she endeavored to lasso a fence post, much to Eloise's delight.

She waved. "Look at me."

"Harnessing that inner cowgirl?" Clay called.

She grinned at him. "Don't you know it."

Andrew laughed. "My sister is something, isn't she?"

She was something, all right.

Kelsey handed him the rope. "Show us what you got, Cowboy."

He threw the lasso, hitting the target the first time.

Eloise applauded.

Kelsey smiled. "Show-off."

He reeled in the rope. "Practice makes perfect."

She climbed onto the fence beside her niece. "Hear the noise the cows are making, Eloise?"

"I hear them, Aunt Kelsey." Eloise held onto the top rail. "Why?"

"The noise they're making, dear niece…" Kelsey dropped her voice, and Eloise leaned closer "…is what we call *lowing*, like in the Christmas carol."

Eloise's forehead scrunched. Andrew chuckled.

Clay shoved his hands in his pockets. "Come again?"

"'Away in a Manger'!" Eloise shrieked. "'The cattle are lowing'," she sang.

"'—the baby awakes'..." Kelsey warbled.

Holding onto the top-most rail, they sang the rest of the carol to the cows.

Nicola returned to the house, but Eloise wanted to help feed the herd.

Clay gave her fancy dress and patent leather shoes a skeptical look.

Andrew shrugged. "She's only little once. Let her enjoy herself." Opting to take a stroll around the ranch, he asked Kelsey to walk with him. Surprised but pleased, Kelsey joined him.

With the old ranch truck already loaded with hay and a protein supplement, Clay and Eloise headed out to deliver the feed. The ruts in the frozen ground jostled Eloise, perched beside him on the seat inside the truck cab.

"I don't see any cows, Clay. Will they know where to find us?"

"Look over there." He pointed over the rise to a cluster of cattle making their way toward them. "Just like kids and ice cream trucks, the cows hear this old contraption and come to us."

Eloise appeared to be having the time of her life, patent leather shoes and all. These Summerfield women. Apparently, it didn't take much to delight them.

On the return trek to the barn, he spotted Andrew and Kelsey on the porch. Her eyes looked puffy and red-rimmed. Clay stiffened. But then Andrew hugged her hard. Her brother's eyes didn't look too dry, either.

Later inside the farmhouse, Nana put her arm around Eloise. "While I've got such good helpers here, let's decorate the Christmas tree."

Kelsey cut her eyes around the living room. "What Christmas tree?"

"The one I bought from Luke Morgan's Christmas tree farm and hauled over here last night." Clay smirked. "My other big Thanksgiving job. And here you thought I was only good for cracking nuts."

"You are a nut, Clay," Eloise piped up.

"Eloise!" Nicola scolded.

"Truth," his mother declared.

Kelsey elbowed him. "Out of the mouths of babes."

Everyone laughed, including him.

"Yep." He elbowed Kelsey back. "When it comes to cowboy-bashing, the Summerfields are fitting right in."

She smiled. "Show me where to find the ornament boxes, Gingersnaps."

He opted to ignore the aspersion regarding

his hair, choosing instead to believe she meant it as an endearment. Eloise wanted to go with them so he led them to the attic where the boxes were stacked under the eaves. One by one, he toted them to the second floor. Eloise dogged his every step, chatting about her favorite nuts—Clay and cashews.

Kelsey laughed so hard she had tears in her eyes.

The silvery star tree-topper clutched in her arms, Eloise scampered downstairs.

He shook his head. "Why does it come as no surprise to me your niece has a favorite nut, too?"

"Sorry to be such a bad influence." She didn't look sorry at all.

He heaved a mock sigh. "Don't I know it."

She fluttered her lashes. "Does that mean you're finding me irresistible?"

"That's one word for it."

Grabbing a box of red ribbons, she followed Eloise downstairs.

Clay and Andrew set the tree up in the living room. His parents strung the lights. Kelsey, Eloise and Nicola placed the ornaments on the evergreen boughs. Sipping coffee, Nana and Mr. Howard sat on the sofa, enjoying the Christmas activity. Like a vivacious Christmas butterfly, Kelsey flitted around, having as much fun as her niece. He enjoyed watching them together. She would make a great mother one day.

He blinked away a vision of a little boy or girl running around the barnyard in cowboy boots with not-red hair and cornflower-blue eyes.

Andrew and Nicola offered to take Mr. Howard to the condo to gather more clothes for his extended stay at the ranch. Clay and Andrew tucked him into the back seat of the SUV next to Eloise.

Howard rolled down the window. "I'll be back before you can miss me."

Nana gave him a quick peck on the forehead. "I already miss you."

"Thanks for the heads-up about my little sister." Andrew's gaze drifted to Kelsey hugging Nicola goodbye. "We had a good talk."

He and Andrew shook hands. "I'm glad." There was a lightness to Kelsey that hadn't been there before.

Nicola hugged his grandmother. "Thank you for what has been the most wonderful of Thanksgivings, Miss Dot."

Kelsey came around the car toward her

brother. "Grampy's pain is better, and he'll enjoy the drive, but—"

"I'll pack what he needs, and he can stay in the car with Eloise." Andrew smiled. "Stop worrying. We'll take care of him and bring him back to the ranch later tonight."

"Next time we see you, Aunt Kelsey," Eloise called from the back seat, "I'm going to be a flower girl."

Kelsey grinned. "The best flower girl ever."

She and Andrew hugged. Her brother got behind the wheel.

Nana waved them off. "The outing will be good for Howard." She, Clay and Kelsey watched them drive away. "Cooped up in the house the last few weeks, he's getting stir-crazy."

Kelsey's grandfather had caught him alone earlier and offered his apologies for his over-reaction. But the display of emotion had set Clay thinking. It ought to have set Nana Dot thinking, too.

They walked into the house.

"It's been so wonderful being with everyone today." Kelsey hugged Nana Dot. "But I should probably return to Marth'Alice's. Clay?"

"Let me get my hat."

His grandmother fluttered her hand. "No need to rush away. Stay for leftovers."

"I appreciate the invitation, but I'm sure you could use some downtime." Kelsey grabbed her purse and phone. "Good news, Clay. You get Friday off. But Saturday afternoon, it's back to wedding planning."

He made a growling noise.

"You'll enjoy Saturday's excursion." She batted her eyes at him. "We're taking Grampy and Miss Dot to meet Maddie Lovett, the baker you recommended, to discuss wedding-cake options."

He smiled. She'd listened to him, valued his opinion and taken his suggestion. Her gesture of goodwill did not go unappreciated. "Will this involve taste testing?"

Kelsey slung her purse strap over her shoulder. "It does. Flavors, fillings and icing."

He stuck his thumbs in the belt loops of his jeans. "I can handle cake."

"I figured as much." She smirked. "Totally in your wheelhouse."

They smiled at each other.

"It'll be fun." She nodded. "Something to look forward to."

He liked to give Kelsey a hard time about

wedding planning, but any time spent with her was something he looked forward to.

"I think I'll have a lie-down before supper." Nana Dot said her goodbyes. "See you Saturday."

On the ride to Truelove, Kelsey held the flowers he'd given her in her lap for safekeeping. She'd brought them to the ranch with her. The temperature had dropped throughout the day. The forecast called for an extended cold period over the next few weeks with the possibility of snow.

He glanced out the window at the distant mountain horizon. Like icing on a cake, the higher elevations already held a layer of snow. "You may get your wish for a wintry wedding."

"Woo-hoo!" She bounced in the seat. "What are you most thankful for, Clay?"

His lips quirked at the sudden change in topic. "Family. The ranch. Food. A good horse. What about you?"

"Family. The wedding. Turkey. A great Black Friday sale."

He rolled his eyes. Smiling, she snuggled against his side.

"There is one more thing I'm thankful for this year."

She looked at him. "What's that?"

"You."

Her face softened. "That may be the nicest thing anyone has ever said to me. Thank you, Clay." She lay her cheek against the sleeve of his coat. "Right back at you."

Clay's heart kicked up a notch. She wasn't like anyone he'd ever known. He had trouble recalling why he'd been so uptight about spending time with her. Whatever it was with her felt good and right and...inevitable?

The notion didn't fill him with the terror such an idea would have inspired within him a few weeks ago.

At Martha Alice's, he steered into the empty driveway. "Looks like the Dolans have gone home." He reached for the key in the ignition.

"No need to walk me to the door." Kelsey lay her hand atop his, igniting sparks along his nerve endings. "Whoops. Must be a lot of static electricity in the air today."

"Electricity." For real. "My mother would have my head if I didn't walk a lady to the door."

Her mouth twitched. "All right, then. In the interests of keeping your head attached to your shoulders."

Clay held the flowers while she scooted out. On the porch, he handed the bouquet to her.

"Thank you for sharing your family with me." Her voice went a shade husky. "I'll see you Saturday at the Jar for the taste testing."

Staring at her lips, his brow creased. Taste testing? Oh. Yeah. Cake. Right.

Rising on her tiptoes, she brushed her mouth across his cheek. "Until then."

His heart thudded. Waggling her fingers at him, she slipped inside the house.

Returning to the ranch, the memory of her lips lingered. His hand touched the spot on his cheek. It was no longer a matter of if but when he kissed her.

Something to look forward to, indeed.

At the Bar None, he hummed a Christmas song under his breath. Hearing noises from the barn, he found Aunt Trudy and his parents putting final touches on the Mason Jar Café float for Saturday's Christmas parade.

His dad tacked a length of gold metallic float sheeting to the sides of the trailer. "I like that girl, son."

Deliberately misunderstanding him, Clay grabbed a hammer. "Eloise is very sweet."

His mom threw a tissue-paper snowball at

him. He ducked. "Your father means Kelsey. I like her, too. And I love where that relationship seems to be heading."

"We're just friends."

"You keep telling yourself that, nephew." Hand on her hip, his Aunt Trudy cackled. "Whatever helps you sleep at night."

Grinning, he left them to it and took the opportunity to check on his grandmother, napping in her room.

Careful of creaking boards in the old farmhouse, he peeked around the doorframe. Her head resting on the pillow, his grandmother lay stretched out on top of the bedspread with her eyes closed. A handmade blue-and-white crocheted afghan covered her.

Easing away, he decided not to disturb her. He'd talk to her later.

"Might as well come in, Clay."

"I'm sorry, Nana. I didn't mean to wake you."

Nana Dot reached for her glasses on the nightstand. "I wasn't asleep. Just pondering the day."

Was this the opening he'd been hoping for? He felt it his duty to discuss his concerns, but he didn't want to offend her or create distance between them. "About that..."

Nana sat up. "You want to talk about what happened with Howard this morning."

"Don't you think we should?" Clay leaned against the door. "I'm really trying not to butt into your business."

"Then, don't."

At her sharp words, he tensed. Easy-going Nana Dot had never used that tone with him before. He experienced more than a grudging sympathy for how Kelsey must've felt earlier.

"Howard apologized to you and explained what led to his outburst."

Recalling Kelsey's complete devastation, he stiffened. "An explanation doesn't excuse what he said to her."

"No, it does not. But Howard and I talked through the situation."

"You were satisfied with his explanation?"

"I am." She pursed her lips. "Howard was having an uncharacteristically bad day. We all have them." She leveled a look at him. "Including you."

Removing his hands from his pockets, he took a step into the room. "How uncharacteristic was it, though? How well do you—do any of us—know Howard Summerfield? No one would blame you for having second thoughts. For putting the brakes on your upcoming—"

"I am not a child, Clayton."

His gut tanked. This was not going well.

"I know everything I need to know about my fiancé."

Clay raked his hand over his head. "I'm not trying to upset you, Nana, but marriage is a serious commitment."

She laughed out right. "That's rich advice coming from Mr. Don't Fence Me In. What Howard was feeling this morning is only natural. He's new to bereavement."

"Which is exactly my point, Nana. His wife has only been dead a year."

Spots of color dotted her cheeks. "Howard and I are getting married next weekend. I suggest you deal with your own commitment issues before you go handing out unsolicited and unwelcome advice."

Clay's chest heaved. "I'm sorry, Nana. It was not my intention to upset you."

She flung the coverlet aside. "Well, you have. I'm stung you have such little faith in my judgment." She shook her bony finger. "I'm not senile yet, young man." She fumbled for her shoes on the floor beside the bed.

Getting down on one knee, he scooted them to within her reach. "I love you, Nana. You deserve only the best."

Lips pressed tight, she slipped on her shoes. "For me, Howard Summerfield is the best."

What a disastrous end to a day that had begun with such promise when he'd picked up Kelsey this morning.

"Please don't be angry with me," he rasped. "I'm only trying to look out for your best interests."

She glowered. "I'm perfectly capable of looking out for my own best interests."

"Yes, ma'am."

Nana glared at him another second. "Are you aware it's nearly impossible to stay angry at a contrite cowboy on one knee with good manners?" She laid a cool, brown-spotted hand gently against his cheek.

Something coiled inside him loosened.

"No, ma'am, I was not aware of that fact. But I promise to keep that in mind next time I make somebody mad." He offered his arm as she rose from the bed.

"'Course, I won't guarantee it'll work on every woman." She arched her brow. "Kelsey

Summerfield is far more sophisticated than me. She might just laugh in your face."

"I daresay you're probably right."

"Best not tick her off, then."

"I'll try to remember that, Nana."

"See that you do." Straightening, she smoothed her slacks. "We good?"

"Yes, ma'am." He hugged her. "We're good."

Patting his shoulder, she stepped away from him. "Your father will be wanting a turkey sandwich."

He walked her downstairs. But he couldn't help reflecting it wasn't characteristic of mild-mannered Nana Dot to be so defensive. Unless deep down, she harbored her own doubts about her upcoming wedding to Howard.

A sharp sense of foreboding needled him.

It was like seeing a car stalled on the railroad tracks. A train of reckoning was coming. And he was helpless to prevent the collision.

CHAPTER TWELVE

UNLIKE EVERY OTHER Friday after Thanksgiving in her living memory, Kelsey did not spend the day shopping. With Clay and his family busy at the ranch, she decided to put together a business proposal for creating her event planning business—just for fun. With her relationship on the upswing with her father, maybe she could get him to look it over and, based on his experience running a company, offer her a few suggestions.

Not a person who thrived on silence, she took her laptop and a calculator to a corner booth at the Jar. At the register, Trudy sent her a little wave, but she and the waitresses were rushed off their feet with the breakfast crowd. Kelsey ordered a chai latte and got to work. Only when the bell above the entrance jangled with increasing frequency did she pull her head out of her notes. Blinking, she scanned the diner, filled to capacity since she'd last lifted her gaze. With a glance at the clock on the wall over the bulletin board, she realized she'd worked through breakfast and into lunch.

The petite blonde café owner, Kara MacKenzie, approached the booth.

Hastily, Kelsey gathered her materials. "I am so sorry to have taken your booth out of circulation all morning."

Smiling, Kara shrugged. "It was fine. What are you working on so intently?"

It occurred to her that the chef was a successful entrepreneur in her own right.

"I'd love your input on a plan I'm putting together for a local business start-up I'm contemplating. Perhaps I could discuss it with you when you're free."

"I'm free now." Kara sat down on the opposite bench. "Since Trudy has taken over the day-to-day management, I mainly come by in the mornings to get the lunch special going." She threw Kelsey a bittersweet smile. "Now that I've also trained Leo, our former short-order cook, in the fine art of French country cuisine, he really doesn't need me as much, either. Somehow I've worked myself out of a job."

Kelsey laughed.

"I'd like to hear about this project of yours. I'm about anything that brings more business to Truelove."

Turning the laptop around, she outlined her scheme to open an event venue. She also detailed her experience in planning various corporate events for her father's company over the last four years. "It's just an idea. Not sure I could ever come up with the capital to make it happen."

"You'll need investors. Are you thinking of building a venue or using an already existing site?"

Kelsey sighed. "Biggest line on my proposed budget is acquiring a property. Specific location yet to be determined. Although, if I had plenty of investors and dreams came true…"

"Why don't you think dreams can come true?" Kara tilted her head. "What are you dreaming of?"

An image of a certain cowboy flitted through her brain. Her cheeks warmed. No way was she admitting to that impossible dream. Dreaming of Birchfield seemed tame by comparison.

She extended her phone across the table. "Have you ever been to the top of Laurel Mountain Road?"

Kara scrolled through the photos she'd snapped of the house and grounds. "I had no idea something like this existed on the outskirts of Truelove. Like you, I'm not from around here." She glanced from the phone to Kelsey. "Tell me what you're thinking of doing here."

"Birchfield could host parties for every occasion. But primarily, we'd offer all-inclusive packages with top-notch accommodations for wedding parties. This would be a bride's one-stop shop for all things surrounding her special day."

"Food, too?" Kara scanned the photos again. "The kitchen would need updating with commercial equipment."

Kelsey nodded. "I'd offer a small preferred-vendor list for everything else, but we'd have an in-house chef. I'd want Birchfield to be renowned for its fine-dining experience."

"When you dream, girl, you dream big." Kara handed the phone back to her. "But first let's talk about the really crucial issue."

Kelsey tilted her head. "What's that?"

"Why don't you believe dreams can come true?" Kara's eyes, the color of blueberries, narrowed. "My life is living proof they can and do."

Over another round of coffee, Kara shared

her story. As a child, she'd been homeless and orphaned until adopted by a legendary queen of North Carolina barbecue fame. Her mother, Glorieta Ferguson, was the successful owner of a chain of Southern down-home cooking establishments.

Kara sipped from her coffee mug. "Now I have the most wonderful husband in the world. My son, Maddox, who is my very heart. And this dear little café." Her gaze misted. "Dreams do come true."

In spite of her humble beginnings, Kara's other passion besides creating spectacular food was giving a hand up, not a handout, to those around her. Paying it forward, Kara gave back to the surrounding community. The food bank and county homeless shelter were weekly recipients of the Jar's bounty. She'd also established a scholarship to send local youth interested in the culinary arts to the program from which Kara had graduated in Charlotte.

That generosity of spirit, Kelsey realized, was the crux of the difference between someone like Kara and her own family. Her dad was only interested in their bottom-line profit for the company. Was she any better than her father, though?

Far too often, she'd focused on her own self-interest with no thought for the larger picture. She mulled over how she might incorporate the same model of helping others into any future business of her own.

Kara insisted she join her for lunch. Over the chef's signature Madame Croquette sandwiches, they talked and laughed. Kara was especially interested in the innovative foodie scene in Asheville that Kelsey had firsthand knowledge about.

"I've been toying with the idea of concentrating my skills once again on more haute cuisine." The chef laid her hands flat on the table. "I have some capital set aside. I'd be extremely interested in becoming involved in a partnership like the one you're proposing for your event venue." She shrugged. "If you'd be interested in working with me."

Kelsey's breath caught. "I'd love to work with you, Kara." Securing a chef with her skills and business savvy would go a long way toward making her dream a reality. "It's early days yet, though. It may not ever come to anything."

"It will." Kara patted her hand. "You don't give yourself enough credit. You remind me of my mother, Glorieta. You've got everything you need to succeed."

"Except money."

"The barbecue queen started her culinary empire as a single mom with practically nothing going for her but for a belief in herself." Kara squeezed her hand. "It'll happen. She's taught me a gut instinct for this kind of thing."

Kelsey smiled. "With you in the kitchen, the sky's the limit. Care to shake on it?"

The petite chef grinned. "Sure thing, partner."

Of course right now, they were partners of exactly nothing. But with Kara's faith in her, she suddenly felt her dream might not be so impossible after all.

They talked some more, but finally Kara excused herself to discuss tomorrow's menu with Leo. Kelsey knew she'd found a friend and potential business partner in the creative Mason Jar owner.

She spent the rest of the day finalizing her business proposal, her plan now also including Kara MacKenzie. Surely her dad couldn't help but be impressed by the chef's extensive credentials. That night, she wrote a short email to her father, attaching the document and asking for his opinion. Before she lost her nerve, she quickly hit Send.

Not long after, Clay texted to see if she wanted to go to the Truelove Christmas parade on Saturday. The next morning, he came by for her. Leaving his truck at Martha Alice's, they walked the few blocks over to Truelove's downtown.

From the mounted loudspeakers at the edge of the town square, strains of "Winter Wonderland" provided a festive note. Friends called out greetings to each other. Pretty much what seemed the entire population of Truelove, North Carolina, had turned out for the annual parade. And also for the free hot apple cider, courtesy of the Mason Jar.

She was struck by Kara's giving heart. Not too shabby a business move, either, to get people in the café to order something more. After the parade, Clay spotted Sam and Lila, waiting in line with their little girl to see Santa.

Clay made a sweeping gesture. "Small-town charm at its finest." He took her arm. "Let's go see Santa on the square."

"Going to hand him your wish list, Clayton?" she teased.

"This Christmas looks like all my wishes are

already coming true." He winked. She blushed. "But seeing the matchmakers in elf costumes is worth the wait."

"GeorgeAnne Allen is in an elf costume?"

"She's surprisingly good with the kids." He grinned at Kelsey. "But it boggles the mind, doesn't it? Seeing is believing."

It was indeed worth the wait.

Emma Cate looked adorable sitting in Santa's lap in the square.

GeorgeAnne arched a look at her. "You can wipe that smirk off your face, missy. Next year, you might just find yourself taking a turn as Santa's helper. You'd prove a very believable elf."

Clay laughed.

Her denim-blue eyes crinkling, ErmaJean handed him a green-striped candy cane. "Just so you know, after this wedding we're coming for you next, McKendry."

Clay's laughter turned into a sudden fit of coughing.

Kelsey pounded him on the back. "Small-town charm at its finest, Cowboy."

Emma Cate giggled.

At the firehouse, Clay introduced her to some of his friends. Lila made sure she met other young women her age. Everywhere, children played and skipped and bounced with the joy that was Christmas.

Kelsey had a sudden vision of herself attending many Truelove Christmas parades in the future. Strolling the square on the arm of a handsome certain somebody. Maybe with a little boy or a little girl. In cowboy boots?

She darted her gaze at Clay. He and Sam were taking turns pushing Emma Cate on the swings at the school playground. As if feeling her eyes on him, breaking off midsentence, Clay lifted his head and smiled at her.

Lila nudged Kelsey. "He likes you, you know."

Her cheeks warmed. "He—we—haven't even kissed."

Lila smiled. "That's how I know he really likes you. Flirting is like breathing to Clay. In you, he's finally found his perfect partner. You give it back to him as fast as he can shovel it. You keep him in his place."

Kelsey tilted her head. "It's a sacred duty."

Lila chuckled. "I guarantee he's working up his nerve to kiss you."

Kelsey gave a very unladylike snort. "Clay

McKendry isn't exactly a shrinking violet. If he wanted to kiss me, he would have."

"He's making up his mind whether he's going to be brave or not."

Kelsey grunted. "It would not do for me to get my hands on that Angela person."

"Clay seems all fun and froth, but he's a serious guy. When he kisses you—"

"If he kisses me." Kelsey rolled her eyes.

"*When* he kisses you, he will mean it. For real and forever."

Kelsey let out a sigh. "In the meantime?"

"Pray for wisdom and patience." Lila slipped her arm around her. "Trust me, I know. For every one step forward, expect to take two steps back."

Kelsey gritted her teeth. "Greaaat…"

LATER THAT AFTERNOON, Clay brought Kelsey back to the Jar to meet up with his grandmother and Mr. Howard for the cake tasting. Owing to the festival, the diner had extended its hours just for today. Kara walked them to the corner booth where Maddie Lovett, one of Kara's scholarship recipients, had set up her wares.

Maddie was young, eager to please and extremely talented. They had a good time selecting options for Nana Dot's wedding cake. The buttercream secret family recipe was out of this world.

The apprentice baker had just packed up and left them to finish off the samples with their coffee when Kelsey's phone buzzed. She glanced at caller ID. A *V* creased the space between her brows. "It's Felicity from the resort."

Clay dabbed at the cake crumbs with his finger. "Working over a holiday weekend? That's what I call dedication."

"Excuse me." Kelsey slid out of the booth. "I should take this." She retreated to a quieter spot near an unoccupied stool at the counter. Hand over her ear, she spoke rapidly into the phone. Her features fell.

Concerned, he was about to go after her when Howard beckoned someone near the door.

"Son!" Howard slid out. "Over here. Boyd."

Clay whipped around.

His first impression of Kelsey's father was that she'd inherited her eyes and dark hair from him. The dash of silver at his temples gave him a distinguished air.

"Look, Polka Dot." Howard helped Nana

ease out of the booth. "Boyd's paid us a surprise visit to meet you."

But given the man's startled expression, Clay wondered if Boyd Howard Summerfield III wasn't the one surprised. Stock-still at the entrance, his eyes panned furtively as if seeking an escape.

Nixing any plan to flee, however, Trudy took hold of his arm. "Howie's son. We've heard so much about you."

Clay wasn't surprised his aunt had latched onto him. He could see how she would find the widower attractive. Women went gaga for the whole tall, dark and handsome if slightly brooding thing.

She tugged him over to the booth. Clay stood up.

Clearly delighted, Howard clapped his son on the back and made the introductions. "Why didn't you tell us you were coming?" Howard grinned.

"Are you able to stay in Truelove awhile?" Nana clasped his hand. "We would love for you to come out to the ranch and visit us a spell."

"How could you do this, Dad?" Kelsey growled.

Everyone turned.

Fists balled, she radiated sheer fury.

Clay took a step toward her. "What's wrong, Kelsey?"

"I'll tell you what's wrong." She jabbed her finger in the air between her and her father. "Suddenly the resort finds itself double-booked for December third."

Clay's stomach tanked. After all her hard work...

"Oh no." Howard slumped. "What happened, honeybun?"

Nana rallied. "Doesn't matter. We'll find something else. Something better."

"There isn't anything else available, much less better." She clenched her teeth. "But you knew that didn't you, Dad? And you waited deliberately, all this time, until Thanksgiving weekend when you knew it would be impossible to rebook somewhere else, to sabotage Grampy's wedding."

Howard's brow wrinkled. "Son?"

Boyd Summerfield pursed his lips. "Surely this is not the place to discuss this little misunderstanding. The inn double-booked the date."

"And how would you know that, Dad, unless you were in this up to your eyeballs?" All five foot four of her, Kelsey got in his space.

"What did you promise Randleman to insure we lost the venue?"

"I'm sure I have no idea—"

"You used me." Kelsey quivered. "When you offered me a job at Summerfield after putting on this wedding, I believed you and I were finally connecting with each other."

Clay's gaze pinged between father and daughter. "What job offer?"

Howard's son blew out an exasperated breath. "What do you need a job for, Kelsey?" He threw out his hands. "Grampy and Granna made sure you'd be well provided for, job or no job. You've got your trust fund to rely upon."

Clay went rigid. "What trust fund?"

"You were only pumping for information to destroy Grampy's wedding. How could you, Dad?" she whispered. "How could you?"

Every doubt, every insecurity, the very worst part of himself rose inside Clay.

Howard and Boyd started to argue.

"Stop it!" Nana put her hands over her ears. "Stop it right now. This isn't what a family is supposed to be. I won't be the wedge that comes between a father and son."

Her breaths becoming increasingly short, she

put out her hand to steady herself against the edge of the table.

Clay moved to her side. "Nana, what is it? What's wrong?"

She shook her head wildly. "I can't do this, Howard. I can't marry you. The wedding is off."

Howard gasped. "Dot, no. We can work this—"

"It's my heart." Chest heaving, she reached for her grandson. "Help me, Clay."

Then, her knees buckled, and she started a slow descent to the floor.

CHAPTER THIRTEEN

CATCHING HIS GRANDMOTHER in his arms, Clay eased her into a chair. Her breathing was labored. She clutched her shoulder. Her eyes behind the lens of her glasses were wide with terror.

"Aunt Trudy!" he yelled. "Call 9-1-1."

Kelsey's father shrank back. Howard staggered. A roaring filled Clay's head. Someone must have summoned Dr. Jernigan. Gripping his medical bag, he rushed into the café.

"Clay." Kara tugged at his arm. "Give the doc room to take care of her."

Sick with fear, he allowed himself to be trundled aside. The diner had gone quiet. No one moved. It felt to him as if no one breathed. At the table beneath the community bulletin board, the matchmakers prayed for his grandmother.

He put a shaky hand to his head. This

couldn't be happening. Why had this happened? His gaze landed on Boyd Summerfield.

Clay lunged. "You did this!" He jabbed his finger in the man's face, which had gone pale. "This is your fault."

The petite Kara grabbed hold of his shoulder. "This isn't the time. Nor the place."

Kelsey eased her trembling grandfather into a chair. She touched Clay's arm. "What can I do?"

"Haven't you done enough?" Scowling, he shook off her hand. "Nobody needs or wants you here."

She reeled as if he'd struck her.

As soon as the words left his mouth, he was sorry. If he lived to be a hundred, he'd never forget the look on her face. But she was a Summerfield and well-schooled by the people who inhabited her world.

Within seconds, she'd composed her features. Only her white knuckles where she clutched her purse betrayed any hint of inner turmoil. "I'll be at Martha Alice's. Please let me know how Miss Dot is doing."

Lips tight, he gave her a short, clipped nod. She left the café. Siren blaring, an ambulance arrived from the fire station across the square.

Dr. Jernigan finished checking Nana's vitals. Easing back, he reslung the stethoscope around his neck. "Frightening as it was, I believe this is a panic attack."

Trudy sagged against Clay. "Thank You, God."

"As a precaution, though, I'd prefer Dorothy go to County for a thorough assessment." Dr. Jernigan signaled Luke Morgan and another paramedic. The two men on either side helped Nana to her feet.

The panic attack must have frightened his grandmother. It had certainly terrified Clay and everyone else. She went onto the gurney without protest.

Boyd stepped forward. "Let me drive you, Dad."

Howard pushed him away. "Like you care."

Boyd's face fell.

Nana reached out her hand. "Howard?"

Kelsey's grandfather grasped hold. "I'm here, Polka Dot."

Her mouth wobbled. "I didn't mean what I said. I love you, Howard. Don't leave me."

"I love you, too." Standing by her side, Kelsey's grandfather kissed Nana's forehead. "Don't you worry. I'm not going anywhere."

Straightening, he glared at his son, Clay and then Luke. "I'm going with Dot in the ambulance."

Luke nodded. "Yes, sir, Mr. Summerfield. Of course."

Clay followed them onto the sidewalk. "I'll drive you, Aunt Trudy."

"You head on, nephew."

Trudy locked eyes with Summerfield. If looks could have killed, Boyd would have been incinerated on the spot. "Since you're so eager to drive to County, you can take me and prove you're not the total jerk I'm thinking you are." She jabbed her finger into his suit coat.

He flinched.

"Along the way, you and I are going to have a little chat."

Kelsey's father dropped his gaze to the pavement.

His aunt's mouth thinned. "And by chat, I mean I'm going to talk and you're going to listen. Got it?"

Boyd swallowed. "Yes, ma'am."

Clay wasn't sure what to make of his usually happy-go-lucky aunt. He was only glad he wasn't on the receiving end of her wrath. McKendry women didn't get riled often, but when they did? Katie, bar the door.

At the hospital, Clay sat in the waiting room, reassuring an anxious Howard. While they awaited word on Nana, he combed through every conversation he'd ever had with Kelsey, searching for clues she'd been playing him.

He'd believed he'd been betrayed by the best when Angela threw him over for the bright lights of Raleigh and the more upwardly mobile podiatrist. But he never saw Kelsey's treachery coming.

Bottom line, he was a fool for trusting someone like her. For lowering his guard. For ever falling— He gritted his teeth.

He was not in love with her.

She wasn't the woman he'd believed her to be. She'd lied. Hurt his grandmother. For the sake of winning her father's favor to get a job.

What kind of people had he and Nana Dot gotten involved with? These Summerfields had ice water running through their veins. And then there was the whole trust-fund thing.

Fear and insecurity raged inside him. What a chump he had been to have ever thought there might be a future with her. They were from two totally incompatible worlds.

Boyd and Trudy joined them in the waiting room. Based on Summerfield's shamefaced look, he suspected Trudy had had her say and then some. Fire still sparked in her eyes.

Kelsey's father touched Howard's arm. "I need to apologize. I had no right to interfere. There's no excuse for what I did, but I thought I was looking out for you."

Howard clamped his jaw. "You weren't looking out for me. You were looking out for yourself."

"I'm sorry." Boyd dropped his head. "I was afraid."

"Of what?" Howard grunted.

Boyd opened his hands. "Of losing you. I realize I've got control issues."

Trudy snorted. "Jerk issues, too."

Boyd flushed.

Howard made a noise in the back of his throat. "When will you learn that in trying to control everything, you only push people away?"

Dr. Redmayne came out through the double triage doors. After assuring them Dorothy had indeed suffered a panic attack and was being released soon, she allowed the family to see her in a curtained area off the ER.

Lying in the hospital bed, Nana Dot looked extremely fragile. Clay blinked away unwelcome tears. The panic attack had only underscored that the time he had left with his beloved grandmother was far less than the time they'd shared in the past. He wasn't ready, not by a long shot, to say goodbye to the feisty woman who'd taught him everything about life, faith and family.

Trudy rushed over. "Mama!"

Nana accepted her hug but then waved her away. "No need for the long faces. I'm as hardheaded as ever and fit enough to dance at my own wedding."

"Will there be a wedding, Mama?"

Nana Dot pleated the sheet between her gnarled fingers. "Unless Howard's changed his mind."

"My mind and heart remain firmly yours." Howard gave her a big smile. "Hello, Polka Dot." Stooping, he planted a kiss on her upturned face.

Boyd begged her forgiveness for what he'd done.

Nana looked at him a good, hard, long moment. "I'd never cut you off from your father, Boyd. That's not who I am or how I operate."

"No, ma'am." His voice choked. "I see that now. I'm sorry for misjudging you."

"Shall we start over, then? You and me?"

"I'd like that, Miss Dorothy."

She smiled.

Offering to drive her and Howard to the Bar None, Summerfield and Trudy went to collect his car from the parking deck.

"Clay, could we have a quick word?" Nana patted Howard's arm. "How about giving us a minute, dear?"

"I'll wait for you in reception." He shuffled out.

Clay swallowed past the lump in his throat. "You gave us a scare, Nana."

She held out her hand. "Sorry about that."

He took her hand. "Just don't do it again." He blinked away the moisture in his eyes. "What was it you wanted to speak to me about? The ranch? Everything's fine."

Nana frowned. "I wanted to talk about you and Kelsey."

He pinched the bridge of his nose. "There is no me and Kelsey."

"I don't for one minute believe she was know-ingly a part of what Boyd tried to pull, Clay."

He shrugged as if he didn't care one way or

the other. "We're too different, Nana. Never would've worked. Better to have found it out now before hearts were engaged." He grimaced. "Poor choice of words. I meant before hearts got broken."

She peered at him. "I've seen how you are with her."

He clenched his fists. "I'm not in love with her."

Even as he said it, though, something inside him knew he was the one lying now. But he'd get over her. Like he had with Angela.

"I've seen how she looks at you, too," his grandmother said softly. "Clayton, my darling, don't let pride rob you of the chance for something extraordinary."

His chin wobbled.

"Talk to her. Give her the opportunity to explain." Nana squeezed his hand. "You owe her that."

He jutted his jaw. "McKendrys don't owe the Summerfields anything."

Nana sighed.

"But because you asked, I'll talk to her."

An orderly transferred Nana to a wheelchair. They found Howard in the reception room. Outside, Boyd pulled up in his SUV. Once Nana, Howard and Trudy were settled, Clay headed for his own vehicle. And the reckoning with Kelsey.

Driving to Truelove, doubts surfaced about the conclusions he'd jumped to regarding Kelsey. But mentally reviewing the reasons a relationship would never work between them, he stoked the flame of his anger. *Fool me once... Fool me twice...*

At Martha Alice's, he worked to get his emotions under a tight rein. He hadn't even gotten to the porch before Kelsey rushed out of the house. She must have been watching for him.

"How's Miss Dot?" She hurtled toward him. "What did the doctor say? Is she going to be all right?"

"A panic attack." He looked past her. "Just like Doc Jernigan said."

"I'm so relieved. Marth'Alice and I have been praying." She flung her arms around his middle.

He went rigid.

She lifted her head. "What's wrong?"

He kept his arms clamped to his side. If he so much as touched her, he'd lose his resolve. "In this weather, you should have a coat on. I won't keep you."

Slowly, she unwound from him. Her heels

lowered to the frozen ground. "You were scared for Miss Dot. I get that. It's okay. I understand. That first day when Grampy hurt his—"

"Eighty years old, and she's managed to survive drought, storm, disease and widowhood without so much a flicker of concern." He glowered. "But let the Summerfields come into her life, and she has a panic attack."

Her eyes swam with unshed tears. "I love your family, Clay. I wouldn't—"

"I don't think it's a good idea for us to see each other outside of family obligations."

"You don't really think I sanctioned what my father did, do you? I would've stopped him if I'd known." She blinked rapidly. "You believe me, don't you, Clay?"

He didn't say anything.

"After everything we've shared?" She gave him a wobbly smile. "And then there's the whole Irish rock-band thingy."

"Maybe it wasn't about the job." He clenched his jaw. "But I think you'd do almost anything to win his approval."

She took hold of his arm, but he jerked out of her reach. "It isn't true. I promise you I would never—"

"Whether or not it's true is beside the point. Summerfields and McKendrys don't belong together."

"Your grandmother and my grandfather prove that isn't so."

Clay scowled. "That's different."

"How is it different?"

"Because you are the Summerfield, and I'm—" he clenched his jaw "—not."

Her eyes widened. "Is this about my trust fund? Clay, the money doesn't matter to me."

"It matters to me."

She lifted her chin. "Who's the snob now?"

He folded his arms. "Well done, by the way. When did you and your father hatch the plot? Before, during or after you had me chasing wedding venues over three counties? Got to hand it to you, babe." He sneered. "You Summerfields take the art of manipulation to a whole new level. Angela's got nothing on you."

Hurt flickered in her eyes.

"This would never have worked. A city girl like you. A country boy like me." His mouth flattened. "One day, you'll see I did us both a favor."

"Please don't do this," she whispered. "See me,

Clay. Not the money. Choose me," she pleaded. "I-I love you, Cowboy."

Clay forced himself to look at her then. "But I don't love you."

Her breath hitching, she stumbled backward. "Oh." She wrapped her arms around herself.

Clay fought a visceral urge to take her into his arms. "We've said everything that needs saying. Goodbye, Kelsey."

He turned on his heel.

A QUIET, DEVASTATING despair engulfed her.

Completely gutted, Kelsey watched—hoped—prayed—Clay would turn around, but his long stride carried him swiftly to his truck. He never looked back. Not once. He was done with her.

The red taillights of his pickup disappeared around the corner.

She let herself into Martha Alice's house. She found the older woman waiting for her, hands clasped under her chin. "You heard?"

"I didn't mean to eavesdrop, but—"

"We didn't exactly lower our voices. Just as well." Kelsey drooped. "The Truelove grape-vine will undoubtedly do the rest for us on the off-chance people in the next county didn't catch it the first time."

"He didn't mean what he said." Martha Alice enfolded her into her arms. "He was upset by what happened with his grandmother. He wasn't thinking straight."

For a second, Kelsey closed her eyes, inhaling the faint aroma of roses that clung to Granna's best friend. "I think he meant every word." With a sigh, she pulled free of the older woman's embrace. "He appeared to have thought everything through quite well. Perhaps it's time I do the same."

She laid her hand on the newel post.

"Let's have a cup of tea."

She almost smiled. In the world of the two best friends—Martha Alice and Granna—tea could fix anything. Not everything, however.

"I'm going upstairs to pack." She climbed several steps and paused. "I came to love it here, you know. Not only your wonderful house but Truelove, too. I'd actually come to see myself making Truelove my forever home. Surrounded by friends, family and faith."

Almost exactly what Clay once told her mattered most to him. She'd foolishly, as it turned out, believed she mattered to him.

"These last few weeks..." Her eyes misted. "I've had the best time of my life."

"Don't go, sweetie. Please." Martha Alice wrung her hands. "I know it seems hopeless right now, but things will get better. They always do. When he calms down—"

"It's time for me to go back h—" She swallowed, unable to call it home any longer. "To Asheville." She had to leave now before she lost her courage. "Thank you, Miss Marth'Alice. For everything."

The older woman's eyes filled with tears.

In her bedroom, she pulled out her suitcase and emptied the bureau drawers.

Home meant friends like Kara, Lila and Martha Alice. Home was Grampy, but thanks to her father's actions she'd never be welcome at the Bar None again.

Kelsey's mouth twisted. The Summerfields weren't a family. They were a corporation.

Home had come to mean Clay, but he despised her. That he could believe such lies about her robbed her of breath. She'd felt such a connection with him. Believed they understood each other so well. But for him to think her capable of sabotaging Grampy and Miss Dot's happiness? He didn't know her at all. Perhaps he wasn't the man she'd believed him to be.

Only thing she had left was her faith. Which made it sound like faith was a last-ditch effort. Not what she truly believed, she was just feeling sorry for herself.

She sank onto the bed. *Forgive me, God.*

It was Granna's faith that had made a home for seven-year-old Kelsey, who in losing her mother lost her father, too. It was Granna's faith that had given her the confidence to grow and flourish and dream. It was time to make Granna's faith her own.

When she came downstairs, Martha Alice waited for her. "What about the wedding?"

She set down the suitcase. "Supposing there will even be a wedding, they won't want me within a mile of it, much less a part of it."

"Don't be so quick to discount your grandfather or Dorothy."

But based on Grampy's reaction to the sweet potato rounds at Thanksgiving, she knew better than to expect the benefit of the doubt over something of this magnitude.

Martha Alice put her arm around Kelsey. "It would make you feel better if you'd allow yourself to cry. You never shed a tear at Joan's funeral. It's okay to cry when you're hurt."

She gently extricated herself from the old woman's hold. "No, it isn't."

At her mother's burial that long-ago day, her father had been angry at what he called her unseemly display of emotion. Summerfields must not, never should, did not cry in public. Even when her mother's coffin was being lowered into the ground. The next day, he had moved Kelsey into Granna's.

"What good would crying do?" Kelsey looked at her. "What good has it ever done?"

Martha Alice's face crumpled. "Kelsey."

She refused to give in to the tears that threatened to overwhelm her. Once she did, she wasn't sure she was going to be able to stop. Not for a long, long time. But the pressure inside her chest mounted. It was imperative to leave now before she lost it completely.

Kelsey gave Martha Alice a quick, fierce hug. Jerking open the door and gripping her suitcase, she barreled toward her car. Darkness was falling fast.

The café was closed. The end of the business day, the sidewalks had rolled up. Nothing much to do here at night except gaze at the stars. Not a bad deal if done with a particular cowboy.

No longer an option for her, of course. A sob forced its way out of her throat.

Cinching her hands in an iron grip around the steering wheel, she took a final look at the small mountain town that could have become her home. Where, for a time, she'd believed she'd finally found a place to belong. Her car rattled over the bridge. She blew past the sign.

Love had not awaited her in Truelove. Only pain and heartache.

Reaching the highway, she turned on the radio. Christmas carols rang out full blast. But it wasn't loud enough to drown out the noise in her head.

What was it about her that people found so hard to love? Her father. Clay. Why did no one but God and Granna ever choose her? She'd never been able to decide if she was just too much or maybe just not enough.

A lancing pain stabbed her chest.

In the privacy of her car, "Joy to the World" blaring, on a lonely mountain highway, she let the tears come. She hung onto the wheel as if for dear life.

Tortured sobs racked her. Stealing her breath.

Gouging her heart. For what had been—the loss of Granna and her mother. For what never was—a relationship with her father. For what never would be—with Clay.

She cried all the way to Asheville.

CHAPTER FOURTEEN

OVER THE NEXT two days, Kelsey ate a lot of ice cream out of the carton. In her pajamas.

She kept the curtains drawn. Lights off. With a tissue box handy in case she dissolved into a sudden storm of tears.

Kelsey didn't feel like talking to anyone, despite her phone practically blowing up with messages from concerned friends. All of them from Truelove.

Curling into a ball on the couch, she broke into sobs. Most of the people she loved best in the world lived in Truelove. Including Clay.

A man she'd believed would never let her down. But that's what people did. One way or the other, they always let her down.

Even Clay.

She scrolled through the texts and listened to the voice mails on her cell. It comforted her to know people cared. Martha Alice. Grampy. Trudy. Kara. Lila.

The outpouring of love and sympathy took the edge off the hurt. Not all, but some. She'd get around to thanking each and every one. Just not now. She just couldn't. Not yet.

Of course, the one person she most wanted to hear from was the one person who hadn't reached out. Clay had made his feelings—as in, lack thereof—clear. But every time the phone rang or a text dinged, she looked at the caller ID, hoping against hope.

She'd learned from Andrew there'd been a confrontation between him and their father. Her brother and Nicola were leaving the company to start a new, nonprofit venture.

Reaching the umpteenth message left by her father, she stopped scrolling. She might never be ready to talk to him. Granna had taught her to be a forgiving person, even to those who'd hurt her most. Who deserved it the least. And she would. Eventually. She was working on it.

But she was tired of begging people to love her. She was sick of making excuses for their bad behavior. People either loved you or they didn't. And if they didn't, there was no way to make them.

Her future yawned empty and bleak. She was now without a job. Without a family. Without Clay. Tears flooded her eyes. She fanned her face.

Despite the blow she'd been dealt by people who should have loved her the most, one day she'd dust herself off and get back to living life again.

As a child, she'd watched her mother battle through unimaginable pain. Kelsey had the same fire in her veins. The same indomitable spirit. She was a survivor.

God had a plan for her. She didn't know what it was right now. But Granna had taught her to trust Him with the good and the bad. He alone was the perfect Father. The One who would never let her down.

Life would go on. Her gaze strayed toward the kitchen. As soon as she finished off another carton of Rocky Road.

The cell rang in her hand.

Shrieking, she dropped it onto the cushion. It wasn't a number she immediately recognized. Voice mail kicked in.

"This is Dorothy McKendry. Your grandfather has called you five times in the last two days. He's worried about you. I'm worried about you."

She pulled a blanket over her head.

"If you don't call me in exactly thirty seconds, I'm phoning the Asheville police to do a wellness check on you. One. Two. Three—" Dorothy hung up.

What?

She scrambled out from underneath the blanket. Inadvertently, her foot kicked the phone off the couch. She grabbed for it, missed and fell onto the floor between the sofa and the coffee table with a thud. The cell scudded underneath the sofa. Arm outstretched, she scrabbled for it. When her fingers finally closed around the phone, she clambered to her knees.

Leaning against the cushions, she frantically hit redial. The cell rang. Her chest heaved.

Dorothy caught it on the first ring. "Nice to hear from you, dear. I'm handing the phone to your grandfather. I'm going to the barn to give my idiot grandson what for the second time in as many days."

She didn't envy him being on the receiving end of Dorothy's ire. If she hadn't felt so low, she would have spared him more sympathy. But she was still working through the hurt.

"I'm sorry, Miss Dot, about what my father did to you and Grampy," she rasped.

"Dear girl, your grandfather and I know you had no part in that."

Her relief was such that she sagged against the sofa. "Thank you, Miss Dot, for believing me."

"We love you, Kelsey."

She blinked rapidly. The ever-present tears lay right beneath the surface.

"Please listen to what he has to say. We want you with us at the wedding. Here's Howard."

She was so thankful her father's schemes hadn't succeeded in robbing the elderly couple of their happiness.

"Hello, honeybun."

The sound of his beloved voice undid her. "Oh, Grampy," she sobbed. The crushing weight of sadness broke through her tight control like water overwhelming a makeshift dam. "I-I'm so...sss-sorry."

"None of this is your fault, Kelsey. Over the last few days, your father and I have had a series of painful heart-to-hearts at the Bar None."

The phone pressed to her ear, she climbed

onto the sofa again. She was surprised her father was still in Truelove.

"What he did was arrogant, manipulative and wrong." Her grandfather's voice quieted. "But some of this is my fault. The result of how I raised him."

"Grampy—"

"As a parent, I failed Boyd. I put the company ahead of everything. Far too often, I left Joan to deal with him alone. I should've been there for her and for Boyd. When your mom died, he didn't have the skills to cope with his grief. He turned to the one thing I'd taught him by example would save him—work. Instead of showing him the all-sufficiency of a far better Father than I. A lesson I'm only now slowly learning, too."

His voice thick with emotion, she waited for him to regain a semblance of control over his feelings.

"You needed your dad, and what you got was two old people who loved you more than life itself. We rejoiced, despite the sorrow Boyd's neglect caused, that God had given us a second chance to do better by you than we had by him."

Tears trickled across her cheeks. "You and Granna more than made up for his absence."

"I hope you'll find it in your heart to forgive him, honeybun. The one person who could have helped him weather the storms of life was the one he lost. Although I didn't always appreciate it at the time, God has gifted me with the love, faith and strength of two incredible women. Joan and Dorothy. Not so alike on the outside. But on the inside—" his voice broke "—equally magnificent."

She took a quivery breath. "I-I'm happy you and Miss Dot are still together."

"The wedding is still on for next weekend, but we need our wedding-planner extraordinaire to make it happen."

"I love you and Miss Dot, but I'm not coming back to Truelove, Grampy."

"Summerfields don't leave a job undone." His voice warmed. "I know it's asking a lot, but we want you here to share our special day. Please, Kelsey."

Returning to Truelove meant there'd be no avoiding Clay. Yet after everything Grampy had done for her, she could no more refuse him than she could tell herself to stop breathing.

"Okay, but—"

"She said *yes!*" her grandfather hollered to someone in the background.

"Hold the tee shot, Grampy. I'll be there for the wedding, but until then I'm handling the wedding details long distance from Asheville."

"Whatever you think best. Gotta go, but we'll talk again later tonight to go over your new plan. Okay?"

New plan… Back to square one.

They said goodbye. Ready or not, it was time to dust herself off. Start planning a wedding and living life again. Even if it meant without a certain cowboy.

ALTERNATE PLANS WERE hastily made. She checked with Reverend Bryant and booked the church for the wedding. Exactly what Dorothy had wanted in the first place.

Wedding-planner lesson number one— just do what the bride wants. She could have avoided a multitude of headaches if she'd only listened. She made arrangements for the florist to deliver the flowers to the church on Saturday morning.

Trudy took charge of calling the thirty-odd guests to inform them about the change in venue. With the exception of Kelsey's family, nearly everyone else on the guest list resided in Truelove. Rebecca's family and her parents would spend the weekend at the ranch.

Andrew's family had already decamped Asheville for a long overdue ski vacation at the condo this week. Day of, they'd make the thirty-minute drive to Truelove. Martha Alice informed Kelsey her father had become a fixture around the small mountain town, especially the Jar. She continued to dodge his calls.

With the wedding less than a week away, she was unable to locate another caterer or photographer. Thank goodness she'd booked Maddie Lovett to make the wedding cake. If all else failed, the guests could eat cake.

She checked the weather forecast with increasing regularity in the final days leading to the Big Day. Snow was predicted. Forget winter wonderland, though.

It wouldn't be the gently falling snowflakes she'd envisioned, but an honest-to-goodness, no-holds-barred, road-closing, electric-grid-disrupting, polar vortex of a snowstorm, swooping down from the Arctic.

The temperatures had already dropped. Winter had arrived with a vengeance. The weather person on television was calling it *the snowstorm of the century.*

She wore a path in the carpet around her living room. Due to daily marathon calls, trying to plan for every contingency, her neck had developed a semipermanent crick from propping the phone between her ear and shoulder. Somehow she'd managed to leave her earbuds at Martha Alice's.

Kelsey stopped in her tracks. What was she trying to prove? Who was she trying to impress?

No one. Not anymore. She only wanted the day to be everything Miss Dot and Grampy deserved. Time to surrender to the inevitable.

It was time to bring in the Double Name Club.

Swallowing her pride, she called GeorgeAnne Allen. Surprisingly gracious, the matchmaker suggested they meet for lunch at the Jar to make plans. Kelsey grimaced into the phone, but there was no point in postponing the unavoidable.

Kara met her at the door of diner with a hug. "I'd be honored if you'd allow me to cater the reception."

"Thank you." Kelsey slumped against her. "That's a weight off my mind."

"I'll do my best to replicate the menu you selected at the resort."

Kelsey shook her head. "Your cooking will far exceed anything the resort could offer. I trust you to put together whatever you believe Dorothy and guests would love the most."

The petite chef squeezed her hand. "I won't let you down." She motioned to the table underneath the community bulletin board. "Your wedding elves await."

ErmaJean Hicks waved. IdaLee smiled. Martha Alice beckoned her over.

Her eyes widened. The entire contingent of the Double Name Club had shown up to help, including some of the younger women who'd befriended her over the last month.

GeorgeAnne tapped a pen against a pad of paper. "Let's get started, shall we? We've got a wedding to organize."

Over the course of lunch, a flurry of plans were made. Everyone was eager to pitch in. Callie Jackson signed on to do the photography. Lila volunteered to oversee the decoration of the church. Trudy would wrangle the groomsmen into setting up tables and chairs in the fellowship hall for the reception.

Clay had told her once Truelove was the kind

of town that would do anything for one of its own. For Dorothy's sake, the matchmakers had come to the rescue. Yet Kelsey couldn't help but bask in the reflected glow of their willingness to number her, if only temporarily, among their own.

The lunch meeting broke up.

Martha Alice pushed her chair under the table. "Are you sure I can't persuade you to have a proper catch-up at my house over tea?"

"Another time. I'm meeting Reverend Bryant at the church to scope everything out before I return to Asheville." Tea with Martha Alice would lead to probing questions regarding Kelsey's current emotional state. She wasn't ready to discuss her feelings for Clay with anyone, not even dear Martha Alice. Everyone went their separate ways.

GeorgeAnne headed toward the blonde, rather statuesque, veterinarian picking up an order. ErmaJean stopped to chat with the brunette pharmacy assistant, seated on one of the red vinyl stools at the counter. Which plus-one would Clay bring to the wedding?

Tears stinging her eyes—why had she not brought that dratted tissue box with her?—she thrust open the door to a mad jangle of bells and exited the diner.

She had a feeling the matchmakers wouldn't rest until Clay tied the knot with someone. She hunched her shoulders against the chill. What did it matter, though? He'd made it clear it wouldn't be with her.

A snowflake landed on her nose. Startled, her gaze drifted to the leaden December sky. It was already beginning to snow? This wasn't good. Not good at all.

She drove to the white-steepled church on the outskirts of town.

After the wedding, she wouldn't be making many, if any, trips to Truelove. It wasn't just the cowboy she'd fallen for. She'd also fallen for the small-town charm and caring community in Truelove.

It was going to take a long, long time to get over Clay McKendry. Seeing him eventually get married and fill the farmhouse with little cowboys and cowgirls wouldn't help. She'd need to put distance between herself and the heartache.

Asheville was too full of reminders of that glorious day with him in the city. It no longer felt like home. Home would have been wherever her cowboy called home. Except, he would never be her cowboy.

Choking off a sob, she mangled the wheel.

She really wanted to pursue event planning. She'd enjoyed picking Felicity's brains at the resort. Perhaps the wedding coordinator might have a suggestion for getting started or refer her to contacts who'd hire her and provide on-the-job training. She'd take anything, anywhere.

Moving far, far away had never sounded so attractive.

At the church, she parked beside a lone sedan. Like something out of a Currier and Ives post-card, the church was extremely picturesque. A reception in the fellowship hall wasn't anything close to what she'd hoped, but with only a few days remaining before the wedding, she was thankful for a place where Dorothy and Grampy's family and friends could celebrate with them.

Waiting for her on the steps, Reverend Bryant ushered her into the sanctuary. She made notes on her phone. Dorothy's pastor was a kind, gentle man. She found him easy to talk to. If things had worked out differently, she could have seen herself making this little country church home.

She put away her cell. "Thank you for meeting me on such short notice."

He threw her a boyish grin that belied his fifty-odd years. "I'm looking forward to joining in holy matrimony those octogenarian newlyweds of yours."

She hitched her purse onto her shoulder. "We'll see you on Saturday, Pastor." Huddling in her coat, she returned to her car.

The wind had picked up.

On the drive to Asheville, more snowflakes floated out of the sky and dusted the windshield, but the snowstorm wasn't supposed to arrive until the day after the wedding. *Please, God.* There'd already been far too many hiccups.

Yet the unsettled feeling wouldn't leave her. By the time she reached her apartment, the snowy precipitation had increased. She bounded up the stairs. An isolated snow squall, she hoped. It would soon blow over.

Reaching the third floor, she ground to an immediate halt.

Her chest tightened. Her breath hitched. Anxiety and anger warred for prominence in her heart. "Why are you here, Dad?"

"When you didn't return my calls—"

"There was a reason I didn't return your calls." Her mouth flattened. "As you well know."

"Since you wouldn't talk to me on the phone, I decided it would be better for us to talk in person."

Brushing him aside, she inserted her key into the door. "You've wasted a trip." She stepped into the apartment. "I don't want to talk to you." She started to close the door.

His gloved hand caught the door. "Are you going to leave me standing out here in the cold?"

"Kind of like you left me high and dry on Granna's doorstep?" She wrenched the door from his grasp. "Yes, Dad. I am."

His eyes cut to the apartments on either side. "Must we have this conversation out here?"

She gave him a brittle smile. "Sorry to once again sully your sterling reputation. Summer-fields prefer to let their dirty laundry molder behind closed doors."

"I'm doing it again." He sighed. "My entire life, I've cared far too much what other people thought. With the help of Reverend Bryant, it's a chain I'm working on freeing myself from."

Her dad was in counseling?

"I wasn't much of a father to you. For that, I will be forever sorry." His gaze locked onto hers. "It was my loss. I've missed so much of your life."

Taken aback, she let go of the door. It had never occurred to her he might come to apologize. Boyd Howard Summerfield III didn't do apologies.

"You might as well come in." She stalked into the living room, leaving him to follow or not. "I could've used a father then. Now we're more strangers than father and daughter."

He flinched. "I deserve that. But I'd do anything to rectify the situation between us." He followed her into the living room, but his trademark *I own the world* stride was gone.

She kept the couch between them. "Why the sudden regret?"

"For sabotaging the wedding, Trudy gave me a tongue-lashing I'll never forget."

Kelsey lifted her chin. "Good for Trudy."

He rubbed his jaw. "She also had a great deal to say about my lack of parental skills."

Kelsey turned away. Maybe she wasn't as good at hiding the hurt as she'd always supposed.

"I took a good, hard look at the man I've become." His face became bleak. "I didn't like what I saw. Nor the wrong choices I made after your mother died."

She wrapped her arms around herself. "I'm well aware how you feel about me. You blamed me for Mom's death."

"No, Kelsey. It was me I blamed. For failing her. I failed you, too."

"In a strange way, I always understood why you hated me, Dad."

He gasped. "I don't hate you, Kelsey. It's myself I've had a hard time loving."

She looked at him. "That would make two of us."

To her horror, tears rolled down his cheeks. "I'm sorry, Kelsey, for making you feel you weren't loved. For causing you to believe you weren't worth loving."

She'd never seen her father cry.

"Can you ever forgive me?" He took a deep breath. "Is it too late for us to be father and daughter? I know you don't need a father anymore—"

"No matter her age, a girl always needs her father, Dad."

"Would you…" his voice quavered "…would you give me another chance to be the father I should've been?"

Boyd Summerfield had never done anything but hurt and disappoint her.

Yet suddenly, anger and bitterness seemed such a heavy burden. Chains whose weight she was no longer willing to bear. If it were not for God's second chances, she shuddered to think where and who she might be.

"Forgiveness will be easier won than my trust, Dad."

Through the tears, his eyes shone. "Thank you."

Something clattered on the roof.

Kelsey darted to the window. "I hope that was an early visit from Santa and not what I'm afraid it is." She pulled aside the drape. Sleet littered the paved surfaces.

He checked the weather app on his phone. "It's not looking promising. The forecast has changed. The storm's arrived quicker than anticipated. Asheville is getting several inches of ice."

Kelsey's stomach twisted. A snowstorm was one thing. An ice storm quite another.

She raced toward her bedroom. "That settles it."

Her father ventured no farther than the door. "That settles what?"

"I can't run the risk of becoming stranded

in Asheville." She pulled a suitcase out and threw in everything she'd need for the wedding. "Marth'Alice will let me stay with her. Hopefully, the storm will blow itself out before Saturday, but if not?"

Arms crossed, he leaned against the doorframe. "What is that clever brain of yours concocting now?"

Her father believed her clever?

She resumed her frantic packing. "I'm going to collect the flowers from the florist and take them with me to Truelove. Kara will let me store the buckets in her cooler at the diner."

"Will they be ready this soon?"

"If not, Marth'Alice and ErmaJean will help me finish them." She fluttered her hand. "Because that's the kind of town Truelove is."

He gave her a sheepish smile. "One of the perks of Grampy marrying Dorothy, it seems the Summerfields have been welcomed into the Truelove fold by proxy."

She heaved a sigh. "I love that about Truelove."

"I love you, Kelsey."

Midmotion, she stopped and looked at him.

His mouth trembled. "I didn't say that enough to you."

Try never...

"But I do." An oft-concealed vulnerability crisscrossed his features. "Love you."

They gazed at each other across the expanse of the room and the gulf of years. Her heart pounded. Second chances came with their own sets of risks. She breathed a quick prayer for courage.

Catch me if I fall, God. Then she stepped out onto the emotional ledge with her father. "I love you, too."

He swallowed. "Could I hug you?"

She smiled. "I'd like that, Dad."

His arms went around her, and she closed her eyes. The familiar, warm, spicy notes of his signature cologne enveloped her nostrils. For a moment, she could imagine she was a child. That her mother was still alive. That she was home again. Resting his chin on her head, he wept softly. She hugged him.

After a time, he pulled away. "I don't want you driving to Truelove." He swiped at his eyes.

She opened her mouth to protest.

He held up his hand. "I'll drive you myself. My vehicle is better equipped to handle the treacherous conditions. Give the florist a call to let them know we're on our way. We'll load everything into my SUV."

CHAPTER FIFTEEN

KELSEY CALLED MARTHA ALICE, who promised she'd have a hot, hearty meal awaiting them. Granna's best friend also invited Kelsey's dad to stay in one of her guest bedrooms.

With her father's help at the florist's, they were on their way out of Asheville within the hour. They kept the radio tuned for weather updates. Already late afternoon, with the storm, darkness descended like a heavy curtain. Local forecasters were dubbing the snowstorm the Christmas Blizzard. News reports came of the city shutting down behind them. The roads were slick, but the ice changed to snow as soon as they left town.

Their progress slowed to a crawl. Just in time, they turned onto the Truelove exit. Word came the State Highway Patrol was closing the highway. Conditions continued to deteriorate. It had been hours since she talked with Martha Alice.

The older woman would be anxious, but Kelsey had lost cell service not long after they crossed the county line.

The higher the vehicle climbed into the mountains, the worse the winds became, buffeting the SUV. Whiteout conditions prevailed. Somewhere on the right edge of the asphalt lay a massive gorge. One misjudged curve, one patch of black ice...the guardrail would never save them.

"I'm sorry, Dad." A hurricane of snow obscured everything but the pavement in front of the headlights. "I shouldn't have brought you out on this foolhardy journey."

They had to be close to Truelove, though. Surely this was the last peak before the road descended into town. In the green glow cast by the instrument panel, her father's face was grim but determined.

"As if I'd let you go out by yourself on a night like this." He flicked her a glance. "You would've come with or without me." He threw her a self-deprecating smile. "For better or worse, you're like your old man. Once you get an idea in your head—"

The car lurched and slid on the pavement.

Stifling a cry, Kelsey held onto the armrests. *Please, God.* The vehicle careened.

His knuckles white, he grappled with the steering wheel. His lips moved. Was he praying? Was it possible her father had truly changed?

The tires found traction. He regained control of the car. She gave his arm a squeeze. He turned his head briefly. In his eyes, there was gratitude and love for her.

Her breath caught. Hope swelled in her heart that a future might be possible with her dad. A way forward from the pain of the past.

Descending the mountain into Truelove was worse than ascending. It was nearly seven o'clock by the time the comforting twinkle of Truelove's downtown Christmas lights came into view. She felt weak with relief. The one-hour drive between Asheville and the tiny mountain town had taken three. She was thankful her father hadn't allowed her to drive the distance alone. She would've never made it without him.

He steered the car along Main past the shuttered café. "What should we do about the flowers?"

"The flowers will do fine in Marth'Alice's

unheated garage until we can haul them to the diner."

Sheltered in the valley of Truelove, the wind no longer roared. Snow fell fast and thick, but he easily made the turn into Martha Alice's neighborhood. At least Truelove hadn't lost electricity. Which boded well for the upcoming wedding. Surely the storm would be over by then.

Martha Alice had the porch lights on. The white candles in the windows cast a welcome glow, pushing back the darkness. A phone pressed to her ear, the older woman peered out into the night. How long had Martha Alice been on the lookout for them? She must be so worried.

With a screech of metal, the garage door opened. Her dad veered into the empty bay beside Martha Alice's car. For a moment, he let the engine idle. Finally, he forced his hands to relinquish their death grip on the wheel.

Kelsey's throat clogged. "We made it."

"With God's help, we did." His gaze connected with hers. "And with God's help, I pray we will continue to do so."

She gave him a tremulous smile. "I think we just might."

Martha Alice flung open the connecting door to the house. Kelsey and her father got out of the car. Her legs felt as wobbly as a newborn calf's.

Which sounded like something a cowboy would say. *Clay McKendry, get out of my head.*

A pair of headlights swept across the open garage, and the door of a truck flew open. Outlined against the lights, a tall lean figure wearing a Stetson emerged. Clay stalked into the garage.

Bundled in his fleece-lined coat, he barreled toward her. A thunderous expression contorted his features. "Do you have a death wish, Summerfield?" He jabbed his gloved, index finger at her. "What city nitwit drives over the mountain in weather like this?"

"How did—"

"Martha Alice called and told me you were driving to Truelove." He waved his arms. "And that you should have arrived hours ago."

"I—"

"She was worried sick. I was wor—" He clenched his jaw. "I imagined you at the bottom of a gorge." A muscle pulsed in his cheek. "I was heading to the mountain to search for you when Martha Alice called again to say you were pulling into her driveway." Eyes blazing, he loomed over her. "How dare you put yourself in danger like that."

"Dad drove me here."

As if noticing for the first time they weren't alone, his gaze darted to her father, standing frozen beside Martha Alice.

Done with the emotional roller-coaster known as Clay McKendry, she drew herself up and got in his face. "What's it to you, anyway? Don't pretend you care."

The anger died in his eyes. "I…"

For a split second, she glimpsed something akin to anguish in his features. But without another word, he turned on his heel and stomped to his truck. Reversing out of the drive, he sped away.

She stared until the red glimmer of his taillights disappeared into the storm. He'd best heed his own advice. If he didn't calm down, he'd be the one driving off a cliff.

"When I called to let him know you were safe, I had no idea he'd react this way."

She cut her eyes at Martha Alice.

Knotting her hands, the older woman dropped her gaze.

Oh, she reckoned Martha Alice understood

exactly how Clay would react. Probably bargained on it. Although, what it proved she hadn't the slightest idea. Except underscoring that he was a stubborn, pigheaded idiot. Which made her even more of an idiot for loving him.

Hands stuffed in the pockets of his overcoat, her father cleared his throat. "I didn't realize about you and Clay."

A sudden weariness assailed her. "There is no Clay and me, Dad."

He stabbed his hand through his salt-and-pepper hair. "I'll tell him you had no part in the stunt I pulled. I'll fix this, CeCe."

She almost smiled. She'd forgotten once upon a time before her mother's last, fatal illness he'd had that little nickname for her. "There's no fixing I'm a Summerfield and he is not." She squared her shoulders. "There's no getting around the insurmountable curveball of my trust fund."

Her father frowned. "He took issue with your trust fund?"

"Crazy, isn't it?" She moved past him toward the steps into the kitchen. "Created at my birth, a trust fund I've yet to gain access to and I've never actually seen a penny of. His pride is the immovable obstacle here, Dad."

Her father's eyes narrowed. "Immovable objects move when confronted by irresistible forces."

Kelsey's gaze cut to the driving snow outside the safety of the garage. "Miss Marth'Alice..."

"Don't worry." The older woman touched her arm. "I'll text Dorothy to make sure he got home okay."

"Thank you."

Drooping with fatigue, Kelsey forced down a few mouthfuls of the dinner Martha Alice reheated. But she soon excused herself to go to bed. Lingering at the kitchen table, her father glanced up from scrolling through his messages. "Good night, hon."

Maybe the day hadn't been a complete disaster after all.

She gave him a tired smile. "Good night, Dad. See you in the morning."

The next day, she awoke to a bright white, reflective glow spilling into her bedroom.

Pushing off the quilted bedspread, she padded over to the window. Moving the curtain aside, she surveyed the altered landscape. Snow had transformed Truelove into a winter wonderland.

A cold, brittle sunshine beamed from a blue

sky. In the distance, she heard the sound of a snowplow. Martha Alice's street had been cleared. Dashing across the room, she tried the light switch. When the bedside table lamp sparked to life, she breathed a sigh of relief. So far, so good. As long as the streets were clear and the electricity didn't fail, the wedding could go ahead tomorrow.

The aroma of coffee wafting from the kitchen drove her downstairs. She needed a strong dose of caffeine before she tackled the remaining items on her to-do list. There were the flowers in the garage to be sorted. She needed to check in with Kara. She and Lila should start decorating the church.

She was still mentally reviewing the tasks yet to be accomplished when she ambled into the kitchen. Coffee cup on the table, her father was already at work, answering messages on his phone. He looked up. "Morning, hon."

Kelsey grabbed a mug and poured some coffee. "Hey, Dad."

"Um… There's something I'd like to discuss with you."

Her heart sank. That sounded vaguely ominous. "I'd love to talk, but I'm working against the clock today getting ready for the wedding."

"I understand. I'll be brief. I finally had a chance last night to look over your business proposal." He folded his arms across his chest. "You did a wonderful job explaining your vision regarding the company you want to establish with Kara MacKenzie. I crunched the numbers."

"Wait." She blinked at him. "You think me going into the event-venue business is a good idea?"

"It's a great idea." He nodded. "You identified a gap in the market, did your research and offered a viable solution to meet the need."

She sank into a chair opposite him. "You think my idea is doable?"

He cocked his head. "More important than doable, I believe it would be a profitable venture." He smiled. "I really think you're on to something here."

Boyd Summerfield was a shrewd, bottom-line, dollars-and-cents, profit-focused businessman. If he believed she and Kara could be successful, they would be.

She set the mug on the table before she spilled the contents.

He took her hand. "I believe in you, Kelsey. In planning Grampy's wedding, I've been impressed with how you've coped with one challenge after the other. I believe in your dreams, and I want to be a part in making them come true."

"Thank you, Dad." She swallowed. "This means the world to me."

He threw her a rueful smile. "It seems the entrepreneurial apple has not fallen far from the Summerfield tree."

"There's so much groundwork that needs to be laid in undertaking a new business. I'd want your input every step of the way. Especially in locating a site for the venue." She sat forward in the chair. "If you'd be interested, I'd love for you to mentor me."

"Of course, but I'm not sure you are fully grasping what I'm saying." He squeezed her hand. "I'm proposing a business partnership with you and Kara. I'd provide the initial financial investment. You and Kara would bring your particular areas of expertise into the operation."

Her jaw dropped. "You want to go into business with me?"

"With you and Kara." He let go of her hand and settled into the chair. "After the wedding, I'd like to meet with you both. We can talk through the particulars, and I'll have my attorney draw up the papers."

Jumping up, she threw her arms around him. "Thank you, Dad. Wait." Only then did something less pleasant occur to her. "You're not doing this out of guilt, are you?" She stepped back. "Or because you're trying to buy my affections?"

Somewhere in the house, a telephone rang. She heard Martha Alice answer it.

"I love you, Kelsey, and I look forward to us forging a stronger relationship." His forehead furrowed. "But when have you ever known me to let sentiment overrule good business sense? If it wasn't a good plan, I wouldn't sink personal capital into it." He looked mildly affronted. "Give me some credit. I'm a Summerfield."

Yes, he was. And so was she. She'd finally gotten a seat at the table. Thanks to her father's generosity, not only the seat but the table, too.

Clutching her cell phone, Martha Alice stumbled into the kitchen. "Sweetie?"

At the look in her eyes, the smile died on Kelsey's face. "What's wrong now?"

"Reverend Bryant called." Martha Alice bit her lip. "The pipes in the fellowship hall burst overnight. The entire space is flooded."

Staggering, Kelsey grabbed hold of her father's chair. For the love of Christmas weddings, would the mishaps never end?

"The good news is the sanctuary is untouched." Martha Alice placed a hand on her sleeve. "The wedding can proceed there as planned."

"But not the reception." She moaned. "What about the food and Grampy's first dance with Dorothy? And the cake... And... And..." She sucked in a breath. "Maybe you should rethink going into business with me, Dad."

Getting to his feet, he put his arm around her. "This disaster is not of your making. If I hadn't booted you out of the resort, this wouldn't be an issue. You get them married tomorrow. I'll find a place to celebrate afterward." He kissed her forehead. "Don't worry, CeCe. This time I promise I won't let you down."

LAST NIGHT WHEN Martha Alice called to tell him Kelsey had gone missing while driving over the mountain, Clay's heart had nearly stopped. Grabbing his hat, coat and gloves, he'd plunged out of the farmhouse and into his truck. Pressing the accelerator, he drove as fast as he dared toward town and the road that led over the mountain to the highway.

The entire week without her had been excruciating. Driven by thoughts of her, he hadn't slept in days. He scraped his hand across the stubble on his face. Nor shaved. He'd barely eaten.

How had a little thing like her ever managed to get past his carefully tended defenses?

At the ranch, everywhere he turned he saw her. Wearing his hat. Scooping out the cow stall. Her attempts to lasso the fence post. He ached for her so bad he began to believe he might die from missing her.

Coming down the ridge in the driving snow, images of her replayed on a continuous loop in his mind. Ice cream in the city. Dancing the two-step in her apartment. Kelsey flinging herself against the stone walls of a Scottish castle and declaring she adored it.

He adored her. Not much use in denying it. He suspected he might even love her. There was so much to love about Kelsey Summerfield.

The truck flew past the icicle-laden Welcome to Truelove sign. On the bridge, his tires skidded. Steering into the slide, he fought to regain control of the wheel. Going into the frigid, rushing waters of the river would help neither Kelsey nor himself.

It killed him to recall the accusations he'd hurled at her upon learning of her father's duplicity. Completely unfounded allegations.

Once he'd calmed down from his knee-jerk reaction, he realized she wasn't the kind of person who would have gone along with her father's attempt to ruin the wedding. That just wasn't who she was. Yet he'd allowed past issues with Angela to color his perception of the situation. It made him sick to his stomach to think how when she'd needed him the most, he'd turned his back on her.

Just like her father. She must hate him. He hated himself for hurting her.

A frightening image replaced his happier memories. A vision of her Subaru plowing through a guardrail. Of a sickening screech of metal. Of Kelsey trapped, plummeting to her death.

Of never getting to tell her how much she meant to him.

He started to shake so hard his teeth rattled. "Oh, God, please don't let me be too late. Show me where to find her."

Then Martha Alice called again. Furious with

Kelsey—furious with himself—he'd quickly detoured toward the matchmaker's house. His ginger hair had gotten the better of him, and instead of embracing her, he'd lashed out at her.

Going toe-to-toe with him, she'd given as good as she got. But when she'd given him an opportunity to tell her how he felt, he'd drawn back as if from the edge of an abyss.

Clay McKendry was barely making ends meet at the Bar None. Kelsey Summerfield was a trust-fund baby. Beyond that, there was nothing else to say.

He'd fled the scene—and her stricken face— before he lost what little remained of his pride.

Clay returned to the ranch to find a tight-lipped Howard glowering at him and Nana Dot on the phone. *Thank You, God*, at least his parents were still at Rebecca's house until Friday.

"He's just arrived, Marth'Alice." His grandmother flicked him a stormy look before giving him a nice view of her shoulder. "Yes. Please do. I'll call you tomorrow."

Great. Now everybody was mad at him.

In no mood for another lecture, he stormed off to his room. Throwing his hat on the floor, he stomped on it with the heel of his boot. And flung himself onto the bed. That night, nightmares of what could have happened to Kelsey plagued him. Three times he awoke, thrashing in the sheets, drenched in sweat.

He was out the door for morning chores well ahead of dawn and Nana Dot. Despite the rumbling of his stomach, he decided to skip breakfast and avoid his grandmother.

Clay could hide in the barn all he wanted, but he didn't manage to outrun the long arm of Nana Dot. Although, this time in the form of his Aunt Trudy.

Midmorning, she stomped into the barn. "I've got a bone to pick with you, Clayton McKendry."

He kept his head down and the shovel in motion. "No time to shoot the breeze, Trudy."

Grabbing the shovel, she wrenched it out of his hands.

"Hey!"

Clay scowled. Like all the McKendry women, she was tall and bony and stronger than she looked.

"I heard about your little temper tantrum last night at Marth'Alice's."

"From who?"

"Boyd."

Since when were she and Boyd Summerfield on speed dial?

"Stay out of it, Trudy," he growled.

His aunt tossed the shovel into a pile of hay. "I wish I could. But I refuse to stand by and watch my favorite nephew ruin his life."

"I'm your only nephew."

Hands on her hips, Aunt Trudy smiled. "Exactly."

"She could buy and sell the lot of us with the snap of her fingers. We'd never work." He shook his head. "Do you have any idea how much Kelsey Summerfield is worth?"

"Do you have any idea how much Kelsey Summerfield is truly worth, nephew?"

His heart pounded. Rubbing furiously at his eyes, he dislodged his hat. The Stetson fell onto the straw-laden floor between them.

"Looking worse for wear." She picked it up. "What happened to your hat?"

"Nothing," he mumbled. Except an encounter with his boot last night.

"I wasn't only commenting on the hat." She handed it to him. "Don't let your pride rob you of the best gift God's ever tried to give you, Clay."

He clamped the misshapen hat on his head. "It's complicated."

"Only because you're making it complicated."

For a long, long moment, she contemplated him. He squirmed under her scrutiny.

"I'm going to tell you something I've never said to another person, not even my mother, simply because it would cut her deeply." Trudy sighed. "She tried so hard to be everything for Gary and me when we were growing up."

"Trudy—"

She held up her hand. "Kelsey and I, bank accounts aside, have far more in common than you'd suppose. Both of us had emotionally unavailable fathers. We see ourselves forever and always through the prism of our fathers' neglect."

He swallowed.

"When girls like us don't receive the love we should have from our fathers, we struggle for the rest of our lives to believe anyone can ever truly love us."

His gut clenched. Was he any better than her father? His stupid pride had reinforced the already-negative self-image she had of herself. He fell against the stall.

Unlike his, Trudy's eyes remained dry. "Do

you or do you not love her, Clay?" Her gaze never wavered.

"I do," he whispered. There was a sweet freedom in finally admitting it out loud. "But it's too late. I've ruined any chance I might have had with her."

Trudy cocked her head. "It's not like a McKendry to quit so easily. Now is the time to dig in your spurs and fight for what you want most. For the person you love the most. If it's not the ending you hoped for—"

"It's not the end."

His heart swelling with hope, he straightened off the wall.

She dusted off her hands. "I think my work is done here."

And his was just beginning.

They went into the house. He grabbed a quick shower and changed into his best jeans and boots. He'd just placed his Sunday Stetson on his head when his cell buzzed with an incoming call from a number he didn't recognize.

"Hello."

"I realize you have no reason to do me any favors..."

Going rigid, he glared at the phone in his

hand. How dare Boyd Summerfield contact him? He was about to disconnect—

"There's been a situation, Clay. I've been on the phone all morning. For Kelsey's sake, I'm going to need your help."

CHAPTER SIXTEEN

IT HAD BEEN a near thing. But between Sam, the matchmakers and other Truelove friends, they'd pulled it off. Clay called dibs for the honor of watching Kelsey's face transform once she got a gander at what they'd managed to put together one day before a wedding the likes of which Truelove had never seen. A wedding no one would ever forget.

On the Big Day, he filed into the sanctuary with the other groomsmen. Reverend Bryant stood at the altar. Clay, Andrew, and Kelsey's father positioned themselves beside Mr. Howard at the front of the church. Boyd squeezed his father's shoulder. Mr. Howard flashed him a smile. Kelsey's father was doing everything he could to make amends.

Earlier today, he'd asked Clay for his forgiveness in sabotaging the wedding, and Clay had given it. Trust was entirely dependent on how Summerfield treated his daughter henceforth.

Not that Clay would likely have any firsthand knowledge of how Kelsey was doing now or in the future. But he and Andrew were becoming friends. According to Aunt Trudy, Boyd and Kelsey had forged a new bond. Yet if Clay got so much as a whiff her father was giving her anything less than the respect she deserved, Boyd Howard Summerfield III would have Clayton Joel McKendry the Only to deal with.

The processional began.

Clutching her bouquet of crimson-red and snow-white roses, Kelsey started down the aisle. His heart slammed against his ribs. Her hair had been wound into a fancy bun, revealing the smooth curve of her neck and shoulders. His hand tingled with the remembered feel of her hair sifted through his fingers. The floor-length gown with the delicate beaded sleeves brought out the blue in her cornflower-blue eyes. She was so beautiful she took his breath away.

Kelsey's eyes—those beautiful eyes—connected with his. His heart stopped. He forgot to breathe. In that moment, time itself fell away.

There was no one else. Nothing but the

music and her walking toward him. His heart welled with emotion. But just as quickly, she tore her gaze from him. He felt it like a blow.

She held her head high, the bouquet in her arms. Smile never faltering, she moved to the spot in the lineup opposite him. Rebecca and Trudy joined her. But he only had eyes for the woman who'd lassoed a don't-fence-me-in cowboy like himself.

Oh, Keltz, his heart whispered. *Please. Give me another chance to show you how much I love you.*

In a matching tux, five-year-old Peter bounded down the aisle as a fast clip, ready to be out of the limelight. He stuttered to a stop at his designated place in front of his Uncle Clay.

"Whew!" The little boy blew out an exaggerated breath. "Glad that's over."

Subdued laughter tittered among the assembled guests.

"You did great, bud," he whispered.

His nephew waggled his fingers at his mom. Smiling, Kelsey's eyes found Clay's. He found himself oddly reassured. Perhaps she wasn't as angry with him as he feared. He drank in her loveliness.

Eloise danced down the aisle, like her aunt always a bundle of energy. She scattered the petals hither and yon before sliding into place at Kelsey's elbow. Eloise grinned at him. He winked.

A rosy blush bloomed in Kelsey's cheeks. Good to know she wasn't as immune to him as she'd like him to believe. The music changed. The congregation rose.

His father appeared with a radiant Nana Dot.

For Clay, the ceremony unfolded as if in a dream. Vows were said. Rings exchanged. He never took his eyes off Kelsey. *God, help me to show her how much I care. To tell her how much I love her.*

Chomping at the bit, he became slightly desperate for the ceremony to end. Reverend Bryant declared the elderly couple Mr. and Mrs. Howard Summerfield to loud cheers from the audience. The pastor instructed Mr. Howard to kiss his bride.

"Don't have to tell me twice."

With a twinkle in his eyes, Howard bent Nana Dot backward and planted a big one on her lips amid much hooting and applause. The music started again. The newlyweds sauntered down the aisle. Eloise and Peter followed the bridal couple. Peter's sneer expressed his opinion of having to touch a girl's arm.

"That'll change, little buddy," he muttered. Especially if it was the right girl. Once he'd found the right story.

Like the story of Clay McKendry and Kelsey Summerfield. Opposites on paper. Perfect in every way that mattered.

His saucy aunt gave the distinguished Boyd Howard Summerfield III a sassy hip bump as they headed out. At first startled, Kelsey's father threw Trudy a boyish grin. Flabbergasting Clay and, from the surprise etched on Kelsey's face, his daughter as well. Leave it to Trudy. Boyd might not be as far gone from human emotion as he'd feared.

When it was their turn, he and Kelsey met in in front of the altar. Scarcely daring to breathe, he held out his arm. Her lashes flitted upward and down again as swift as a butterfly's wing.

But she took his arm. Together, they walked down the aisle. He laid his hand over hers, relishing the feel of her bare skin against his fingertips. Something sparked.

"So much static electricity today," she murmured for his ears only as they negotiated the length of the aisle.

His pulse quickened. "So much."

Once out of the church, she slipped out of

his grasp to make sure the wedding party found their rides to the reception. She was the last to leave the church. He waited for her at the bottom of the brick steps. When she finally came out and closed the doors behind her, he straightened.

She'd donned the white faux-fur stole she'd chosen for the bridesmaids to wear in case of inclement weather. Snowflakes drifted lazily from the dark December sky. It didn't get much more inclement than a blizzard a few days ago. "Why aren't you at the reception?" She cut a look at the almost-empty parking lot.

"I was waiting for you."

"You didn't have to wait for me, Clay."

Okay… She wasn't going to let him off the hook that easily. Which was as it should be. He could work with that.

"How were you planning on getting to the reception, Kelsey, if I didn't drive you?"

"I guess I hadn't thought it through." She blew out a breath. "Or maybe I was stalling. Putting off seeing the disaster that should've been Grampy and Miss Dot's wonderful night."

"It is going to be a wonderful evening." One foot on the step between them, he stuffed his hands in his trouser pockets. "Have a little faith."

She gave him a scorching look that could have melted snowdrifts.

He gulped. "I should never have doubted you. I know you would never have done anything to hurt your grandfather or Nana Dot. I'm sorry, Keltz. Forgive me. Please?"

She studied him for such a long moment he feared he'd lost her for good.

"Calling me Keltz won't always grant you a get-out-of-jail card, Cowboy."

She'd said *always*. Gratitude nearly buckled his knees. "Kelsey, I—"

"I need to supervise the reception." Moving past him, she headed for his truck. "We can meet for coffee next week."

He stared after her. Was she friend-zoning him? He settled the black, tuxedo-accessorizing Stetson firmly on his head. *Not so fast, little missy.*

They got into the truck. He veered out of the church parking lot.

"Wait." She turned in the seat. "Truelove is the other way."

He gripped the wheel. "We're not going into Truelove."

She frowned. "But the reception's at the Jar."

He drove up Laurel Mountain Road. "We're

headed to the reception. It's just not being held at the Mason Jar." He steered between the two stone pillars.

Kelsey's eyes became huge. "The reception is at Birchfield?"

The rhododendrons lining the curving drive were alight with a multitude of white twinkling fairy lights. Uplighting brought the birch trees into prominent display. He enjoyed watching the glow of wonder dawn upon her face. They crested the hill. Against the blue velvet of a mountain twilight, the house gleamed with lights, life and a party already in progress. She gasped with pleasure.

Clay bit back a smile. Nailed it. Job well done, if he did say so himself.

"How…" She flung out an arm. "Who did this?"

"It was a community effort. Martha Alice stole your sketchpad from your suitcase. Andrew cracked the password on your laptop. Lila kept you busy at the church. Your dad recruited me. Apparently, I'd listened more to your wedding ramblings than either of us imagined. I supervised the implementation of your designs." Parking beside her brother's car, he cocked his head. "What do you think?"

"I think…" she put her hand to her throat "…it's spectacular. Oh, Clay, it's everything I dreamed." Her eyes shone. "A real-life winter wonderland."

He helped her out of the truck. Golden oldies blared from within.

She clasped her hands under her chin. "But I don't understand how you were able to secure Birchfield for the reception."

Her father waited for them at the base of the sweeping stone steps.

"I don't have any details. I think that's a question best left for your dad to explain."

Boyd took her arm.

"Clay?"

Much as he longed to pour out his heart, now was not anywhere close to the moment he'd envisioned. He stuck his hands in his pockets. "We'll talk later."

Humming "Deck the Halls" under his breath, he went into the house to congratulate the happy couple.

"DAD? WHAT'S GOING ON? How did we manage to rent Birchfield for Grampy's wedding reception?"

He smiled. "I didn't rent it. I bought it."

She sucked in a breath. "You what?"

"Actually, MacKenzie, Summerfield and Summerfield are buying the property. Mary Sue's letting us use the space on spec tonight." He lifted his chin. "I can be very persuasive when I put my mind to it."

She threw open her hands. "MacKenzie and Summerfield Squared could never afford a place like this."

"It's been on the market five years with nary a bite." He fingered his chin. "Did I mention Martha Alice is on the board of governors at Ashmont College? Talk about the art of negotiation. Granna's best friend talked them down a mil. We got the place for a song. We'll earn it back and then some, just like that." He snapped his fingers.

She gaped at him. "Dad…"

"Your grandfather and I are turning your trust fund over to you, effective immediately. Not that there'll be much left after renovations. Good bones, but the house will need updating."

A sudden terror seized her. "Suppose we fail?"

He put his arm around her. "The best investment I could ever make is making your dreams come true. And it won't fail. I know a good opportunity when I see it. Speaking of a good opportunity..." He glanced at the house.

She spotted Clay through the floor-length window.

Her father chuckled. "I think there's a young man who wants to talk to you. Badly."

"I'm still not sure how you roped Clay into this."

"Do you like what we did, Kelsey?"

She flung out her arms. "I love it."

"As for that immovable cowboy of yours..." he tapped his finger against the side of his nose "...never forget when we put our minds to something, Summerfields are an irresistible force."

The front door swung open. "Dad?" Andrew appeared, backlighted against the chandelier. "Sis?"

She caught her father's sleeve. "What about you and Andrew, Dad?"

"We're good. I've decided to invest in both my children's dreams." He patted her arm. "Try not to torture the cowboy any longer than absolutely necessary. He's a keeper, CeCe."

Racing down the steps, Eloise tugged them inside. After that, Kelsey was a veritable whirlwind of activity. And she loved it. Every minute of it. Almost as much as she loved a certain cowboy.

All through the sit-down buffet, she could feel his probing gaze upon her. No matter where she was or what she happened to be doing, his eyes followed her. But she had no time to talk. There was so much to oversee. The cake cutting. Toasts by the best man and maid of honor. Finally, the bride and groom's first dance.

"Polka Dot." Grampy smiled at his bride. "Shall we show 'em how it's done?"

Dorothy placed her hand on his arm. "Let's."

Unabashedly romantic, strains of "When I Fall in Love" filled the makeshift ballroom.

Across the crowded room, Kelsey locked eyes with Clay. A lump settled in her throat. Forever. That's what she wanted. Forever with him.

But what did he want? He'd denied loving her. Suppose he never did?

He said they needed to talk. What if he really just wanted to let her down gently for the sake of their families? What if he'd decided there was no room in his heart for her?

Choking back a sob, her hand to her mouth, she rushed out of the ballroom.

Looking for a place to hide. Anywhere but here. Before she completely humiliated herself.

Again.

Brow constricting, as soon as Clay saw her features crumple, he made to go after her. But the song ended, and Nana Dot stepped in front of him. Kelsey disappeared into the crowd.

"I won't keep you, but I wanted you to be the first to hear that as soon as we return from our honeymoon—"

"Don't say *honeymoon* to me, Nana." He scanned the room, searching for a glimpse of Kelsey.

His grandmother rolled her eyes. "Once we return from our honeymoon, Howard and I have decided to move to a retirement community near Asheville."

That got his attention.

He frowned. "But the ranch…"

"I'm leaving it in your capable hands. We'll visit from time to time, but we want a place of our own where you won't cramp our style."

Clay made a face. *TMI, Nana Dot. TMI.*

"Howard is going to teach me to play golf. I'm going to teach him to enjoy life. Besides, I have a feeling you'll be needing the extra space sooner than later." She smiled. "Thank you for making this the happiest day of my life, Clayton." She gave him a small shove. "Go get your girl, honey."

Clay kissed her cheek. "Yes, ma'am."

Birchfield was enormous, but eventually he tracked down his favorite wedding planner.

He found her staring out at the night through a pair of French doors, which looked over a stone terrace.

"Kelsey?"

Her shoulder blades stiffened.

"Can we talk now?"

"I should see if Kara needs anything in the kitchen." She wrung her hands. "Make sure the getaway limousine has arrived." She made as if to move past him. "Or—"

"For the love of Christmas, Keltz."

He scooped her into his arms.

Flailing, she beat at his back. "What are you doing?"

Such a little thing. Light as a feather. Striding toward the French doors, he shifted her in his arms. Unbalanced, she squealed and clamped her arms around his neck, hanging on for dear life.

That was better. He grinned. Finding the handle, he threw open the doors and carried her outside. A scent of evergreen permeated the air.

"Put me down this instant, Clayton McKendry."

"Only if you promise not to run away again."

"I'm not—" She pursed her lips. "Fine. Let's get this over with, shall we?"

Without further ado, he set her on her feet. She wobbled.

He put out a hand to steady her. "One thing I should have told you at the church."

She looked at him.

"You are the most beautiful woman, inside and out, I've ever known."

Her posture relaxed a tad. "You don't clean up so bad yourself, Cowboy."

She shivered.

Clay took off his tuxedo coat and handed it to her. "Why is it in every big moment of your life you always lack proper outerwear?"

She pulled the jacket around her. "It's a gift." She raised her chin. "What do you want from me, Clay?"

He scrubbed his hand over his face. "I want to be in your life."

Kelsey's eyes narrowed. "What about City Girl versus Cowboy? Never the two shall meet, remember? Least of all, be friends."

"I don't want to be your friend."

She blinked. "Oh." She turned, but he caught hold of her arm.

"I told you I'm not good with words. I meant to say *just*."

She bit her lip. "You don't want to be *just* friends?"

He ran his fingertip over her mouth. "Stop with the lip-biting. You're killing me."

She looked at him like he'd lost his mind. "Why does my lip kill you?"

He slid his arm around her waist. "Because it reminds me how much I want to kiss you."

"Since when?"

Clay pulled her closer. "Since forever."

Her eyebrow lifted. "So what's stopping you?"

Clay examined her features. "You?"

She smiled. "A dilemma easily solved." Rising onto her tiptoes, she tilted her head. He lowered his.

Her lips parted. "Kiss me, Cowboy." Only a whisper of a breath separated them.

Clay's heart seized. She brushed her lips against his mouth. Then pulling away a fraction, she winked.

"Absolutely killing me," he grunted.

One hand around the back of her neck, he pulled her mouth to his again. In no hurry, he took his time. Kissing her until he believed his heart might beat out of his chest. Until they were both breathless.

She twined her hands into his. "I thought you didn't want to be a *you two*."

"No one I'd rather be a *you two* with than you." He pressed his forehead against hers. "We go together, you and me. Like mistletoe and holly. Peanut butter and jelly."

"Just so you know, I actually prefer Nutella and jelly."

He sighed. "Of course you do."

"But I'm a Summerfield, and you're a McKendry. A kiss doesn't sweep those issues away."

"I said a lot of stupid things."

She smirked. "Nothing new there."

"I'm serious, Kelsey. I don't care about how much money you have. I just want you."

"And I don't care how little money you have, Clay." She cradled his face in her palms. "I just want you."

"We'll make Asheville and Truelove work. If I have to hire another operations manager and relocate, or travel the distance multiple times a week, I don't ever want to live a day without you in my life."

"Me either, Cowboy." She pressed her cheek against his pleated shirtfront. "I missed you, too.

But you won't have to let go of your dreams for the Bar None."

He shook his head. "I won't let you sacrifice yours, either. You're in your element as an event coordinator, utilizing those oft-touted leadership skills."

"Glad you've finally come around to my way of thinking." She grinned. "But I won't be calling Asheville home much longer. I'm moving."

He tightened his arm around her. "You've taken a job somewhere?"

"I'm moving here to manage Birchfield, Truelove's newest entrepreneurial venture. And the trust fund won't be an issue much longer."

She gave him the thumbnail version of her partnership with Kara and her dad. "He's loaned us the money to cover the sale price. Kara and I will repay the loan as the business turns a profit."

"Knowing your father, I'm guessing it was a loan plus interest."

"Exactly." She smiled. "Stick with me, and I'll make a business tycoon out of you yet."

"I intend to do just that." He wrapped his arms around her. "Stick to you. Though, I have to warn you, I can be a lot sometimes."

Her lips quirked. "I think I can manage."

Music floated out to the terrace.

She cocked her head, listening to the romantic ballad. "I love this song."

"What it says is true. I really couldn't help falling in love with you."

Taking her into his arms, they danced. "I love you, Kelsey Summerfield."

Her breath hitched. "I love you, Clay McKendry."

Snowflakes drifted from the darkened sky.

Kelsey was an extraordinary woman. And his life with her promised to be extraordinary, too. Lifting her hand, he kissed her fingers.

The music changed, becoming more up-tempo.

Grinning, he tangled her fingers through his. "How about we go show 'em, darlin', how it's done?"

CHAPTER SEVENTEEN

Ten Months Later

"WHERE ARE YOU?"

"Hi, Dad." Kelsey pressed the phone to her ear. "I'm headed to the Mason Jar for a cinnamon latte."

"No time for that."

Okay...

Her relationship with her father had come a long way since Grampy's wedding. He'd taken to spending weekends at the ski-resort condo. They had dinner together at least once a week. He'd been a great support and mentor over the last year as she and Kara opened their new business venture.

"I've been talking to a guy who's interested in doing a prospective wedding with you. He wants to meet you at Birchfield."

"Sure." Coming into town, her car rattled over the bridge. "What day is he free to come by?"

"Today."

She'd gone to the Bar None to surprise Clay, but he hadn't been around. Maybe he'd gone to the agri-supply store. She'd drive around the town square and see if she spotted his truck. Driving along Main, her gaze flitted past the Allen's Hardware store, the bank and post office—Wait.

Was that her dad's luxury SUV parked outside the Jar? Not many of those around Truelove, where residents favored trucks. On Wednesdays, he was usually at his office in Asheville.

But over the last year, he and Clay's Aunt Trudy had been spending increasing amounts of time together. On the surface, the two couldn't have been a more unlikely pair, but Trudy made him laugh.

"What time today does he want to meet, Dad?"

"In fifteen minutes."

Whoa… Definitely no time for a coffee. But a prospective booking was a future moneymaker.

Her gaze scanned both sides of Main Street. No sign of Clay's truck. Giving the Jar and a cinnamon latte a last, longing glance, she by-passed the café. "I'm on my way there now."

Once out of the town limits, she veered onto the mountain road. At their peak this week, the trees were awash with color. The Blue Ridge glowed with the red, orange and yellow foliage of autumn.

Hard to believe it had almost been a year since Grampy and Miss Dot's wedding. The newlyweds had settled into life at the retirement community. Dorothy had taken up golf. On Sunday evenings, Kelsey, Clay and her father often went over to eat dinner with them. They glowed with happiness.

"So what's the story with this guy I'm meeting, Dad?"

Her car wound up the mountain.

"I've had a chance to talk with him extensively. He's a good guy. I'm praying this will work out for you."

She steered around a curve. It still took her aback to hear her dad refer to matters of faith. He'd made so many changes to his life. For the first time, she felt she really had a father. And she was grateful. So grateful for their improved relationship. Something she'd never dreamed possible.

Brown leaves littered the pavement, swirling under the tires of her car. "You think he could potentially prove to be an important account? For other events in the future?"

"Sky's the limit." Her father chuckled. "This could be a real game changer."

That sounded promising. Exactly what the fledgling event venue and catering establishment needed. She sneaked a glance in the mirror.

If she'd had more of a heads-up, she would have taken greater pains with her attire to present a more businesslike image. Truelove had mellowed her. The client would have to take her—jeans, ankle boots and red buffalo-check shirt—just as she was.

"What's the man's name? Any details I should—"

"Um…" In the background, she heard voices and what sounded like rattling crockery. "Got to go."

"But, Dad—"

"Just one more thing."

She approached the stone pillars, marking the entrance to the property. "What's that?" She steered up the winding drive, lined with rhododendrons and birch. The morning mist highly atmospheric, the stone mansion loomed around the bend.

"You deserve all the happiness in the world." He cleared his throat. "I love you, CeCe."

She blinked at the still-unaccustomed endearment from her usually brusque father. "I love you, too. Is everything all——?"

"We'll talk more later. Bye, now." He hung up.

Okay... That had been odd.

She pulled to a stop in front of the mansion. She'd beat the client here. Great.

At the bottom of the stone steps, she took a moment to appreciate what she and Kara had accomplished. She loved this house even more than she had the first time she saw it. Kara had overseen the installation of a state-of-the-art commercial kitchen and also updated the expansive dining room. Kelsey had undertaken the refurbishment of the upstairs suites. They hired landscape architects to restore the overgrown gardens.

By spring, the venue had welcomed its first guests—a small, intimate family wedding party from Maryland.

Since then, Birchfield had hosted bridal and baby showers, girls' weekends and family reunions. Thanks to her father's influence, they'd hosted several Asheville corporate events. Birchfield was booked solid for parties during the busy, upcoming holiday season. Word had spread, and they were preparing for Thanksgiving nuptials involving a Michigan couple.

Kelsey loved what she did. In helping others celebrate the best moment of their lives, she'd found her passion. She rested her hand on the brickwork of the house. She loved bringing this house to life.

She could have never imagined a big-city girl like herself would be so content in tiny little Truelove. But it wasn't just Birchfield she had to thank for that. She and Clay had grown closer than she could ever have dared dream.

Her fondness for pickup trucks and cowboys had increased immeasurably.

When not working, they spent most of their time together. Which made it weird she couldn't locate him this morning.

Kelsey peered down the driveway. The guest was still a no-show. She hoped she hadn't come up the mountain for nothing. Might as well finish some paperwork while she waited. It was then she heard it.

She cocked her head, listening. Was that—no, it couldn't be. Bagpipes?

Out of the mist, a bearded older man appeared. Blowing into the mouthpiece, he played a rousing rendition of "Scotland the Brave." Behind him, another man stepped out of the trees. Her eyes widened. Was that Clay?

The piper led the procession toward where she stood, frozen on the steps. Arms at his side, Clay marched solemnly behind him.

In full Highland dress.

She gasped. Her cowboy wore a blue-green tartan kilt. An Argyll jacket with a matching formal bow tie. Sporran. And traditional Scottish brogues.

Reaching the base of the steps, the piper did a snappy about-face, returning in the direction in which he'd appeared. Clay stopped in front of her. The droning of the bagpipes continued long after the piper had been enveloped once again by the mist. The droning sounds echoed against the mountains.

"Clay, what's going on?" She propped her hands on her hips. "My dad said he wanted me to meet with a guy—"

"That guy would be me." He broadened his chest. "A guy interested in doing a prospective wedding with you."

She swallowed. "With me?"

"Definitely with you. Your father and I have spent a great deal of time talking this week. He, Aunt Trudy and the rest of the matchmaker gang are waiting at the Jar for a full report on how the next few minutes play out." His gaze dropped to the ground. "On how I pray the next few minutes play out."

The next few minutes... Was this what she thought—hoped—it was?

"Just so we're clear, why exactly are you wearing a kilt?"

"Last year, you wanted me to wear a kilt for the whole medieval-Scottish-wedding theme you had in mind, but I refused." He looked at her. "I've changed my mind. About a lot of things, since getting to know you better. Since falling in love with you."

He went down on one knee and opened a small jewelry box. Inside the black velvet lining, the Art Deco sapphire and diamond ring—from the jewelry store that long-ago November day—gleamed.

She covered her mouth with her hand. "Oh, Clay."

"Kelsey Summerfield, I love you." He threw her the lopsided smile that made her insides quiver. "Though it wasn't love at first sight, I soon tumbled fast and hard."

Tears pricked her eyelids. "I love you, too."

He tilted his head. "You're not going to cry on me, are you? If you cry, I'll never get through this, and I've got important things I want to say to you."

"I won't cry." She fanned her face with her hand. "I'm not crying."

"That's better." He nodded. "I didn't realize it at the time, but I think I fell in love with you when I saw your gentleness with Nana Dot at the bridal boutique in Asheville. And seeing you in your bridesmaid dress that day…" For a second, he fell silent as if struggling to rein in his emotions. "I've cherished these months with you in Truelove."

She put her hand to her throat.

"Darlin', you are the song I've always wanted to sing. The dream I'd didn't dare dream. The gift I never deserved—"

"The home I always longed for," she whispered.

His Adam's apple bobbed in his throat. "You are the perfect combination of sassy and sweet."

She smiled through her tears.

"You are funny and smart, and you could do way better than a poor ol' cowboy like me."

She shook her head. "You're the best."

He held out the ring. "Would you do me the honor of becoming my bride, Mrs. Clay McKendry?"

"Don't you mean, Mrs. Clayton McKendry?"

His lips twitched. "Don't push it, Keltz." He shifted. "Please say you'll marry me." He grimaced. "'Cause in this kilt, the gravel on my bare knee is killing me."

"I will. I accept. I do." She bounded down the steps. "I love you, Clay." She held out her hand. He put the ring on her finger.

Standing with a slight groan, he kissed the back of her hand. They shared a long look. Bright and full of hope for all the happily-ever-after possibilities tomorrow would bring.

Rising on tiptoe, she draped her arms around his neck. "You look mighty fine—just as I knew you would—in that kilt."

He laughed.

She cupped his cheek. "But don't go losing the Stetson just yet."

Giving her a cheeky grin, he wrapped his arms around her. "You like cowboys, do you?"

She smiled at him. "Who doesn't love a cowboy?"

★ ★ ★ ★ ★

WESTERN

Rugged men looking for love...

Available Next Month

Sweet-Talkin' Maverick Christy Jeffries
The Cowboy's Second Chance Cheryl Harper

....

Fortune's Baby Claim Michelle Major
The Cowgirl's Homecoming Jeannie Watt

....

 LOVE INSPIRED

A Valentine's Day Return Brenda Minton
Their Inseparable Bond Jill Weatherholt

Larger Print

Keep reading for an excerpt of a new title
from the Western Romance series,
HILL COUNTRY HOME by Kit Hawthorne

CHAPTER ONE

LALO'S KITCHEN WAS really hopping tonight, with every booth and table full and the back patio crammed to capacity. A crowd stood closely packed just inside the glass front of the old downtown building, waiting to be seated. Seemed as though the entire town of Limestone Springs had unanimously selected that evening to dine at Lalo's. Beyond the pass-through, Tito's Bar was doing a brisk business as well.

Jenna Hamlin balanced a loaded tray high above her head as she threaded her way through the crowded room. One of her servers had called in sick that afternoon. Luke, the other manager, had come in on his evening off to pitch in and was now busily bussing tables, but the wait staff was still spread way too thin.

She reached the guy sitting alone at the two-top over by the exposed brick wall and brought her tray down to waist level.

"Here you are, sir," she said, setting the glass in front of him. "One sweet tea. And your loaded nachos should be out in a few minutes."

Her mind was already racing two or three steps ahead. She had two entrées and a basket of cheese curds to deliver to the couple at the next table, and drink orders to take from the party of four that had just been seated in the corner booth. So when the guy asked her a question, it threw her off her rhythm.

She stopped in midstep and turned back around. "I'm sorry?" she asked.

He spoke up, louder this time. "I said, *did you stick your finger in my tea?*"

Then he sat back and smirked.

Slowly his meaning broke over her. He looked so pleased with himself, with his round blue eyes and toothy grin—as if he'd said something clever, as if Jenna ought to be flattered by the suggestion that she could sweeten tea with the touch of her finger.

Jenna had seen this guy before in Lalo's Kitchen. He had one of those names made of initials—C.J. or T.J. or something. He liked to talk, especially to the female wait staff. Only a few days earlier, Jenna had watched Veronica, one of her part-timers, trying desperately to get away from him, a forced smile pasted on her face, as he droned on and on.

I didn't want to be rude, Veronica had told Jenna after finally making her escape. *He is a customer, after all.*

That's why he thinks he can get away with it, Jenna had replied. *He's taking advantage of that customer-is-always-right crap and using the power imbalance to gratify his ego. Don't let him get away with that. Be polite but firm, and if that doesn't work, come get me or Luke, or even Tito from next door. We'll back you up.*

Veronica had looked doubtful. She was young yet, only a senior in high school. Jenna was thirty-two, with years of experience waiting tables and tending bar during college, as well as other experience with men who abused power.

Now was her time to shine, to put all that wisdom into practice.

She gave Sweet Tea Guy a quick, cool smile, just enough to show that she got the joke without implying that she thought it was funny. "No, sir," she said. "Our sweet tea is sweetened with a simple syrup made from cane sugar."

His grin widened. "But why go to all that trouble when you can sweeten it yourself?" He waited a beat, then added, "You know. Because you're so sweet."

Either he was too obtuse to take a hint, or he simply didn't care. It amounted to the same thing.

Jenna pushed down the rising wave of annoyance. She didn't want to appease the guy, but she also didn't want to lose her cool. Getting mad would just give him power over her. She would be polite, unruffled, firm.

"No, sir," she said again. "That wouldn't work, and it wouldn't be sanitary. Is there anything else I can do for you?"

"Well, you can sit down here with me, and smile at me while I drink it," said Sweet Tea Guy. "Make it go down easier."

Jenna didn't dignify this with a reply.

"Enjoy your drink," she said, then turned and walked away.

She delivered the entrées and cheese curds to the other table, took the drink orders at the booth, cleared some dirty dishes and took them to the washing station, narrowly avoiding a collision with Lalo Mendoza, the restaurant's owner. Lalo was the cousin of Tito Mendoza, who owned the bar next door. Like Luke, Lalo had come in this evening to help, but unlike Luke, he was merely getting in the way without contributing anything, standing around with his hands on his hips and a worried expression on his face. Jenna finessed her way past him, then headed back to the break room to check on Halley.

Any time Jenna was at Lalo's Kitchen, Halley was there too—which meant Halley was there for roughly half her waking hours in any given week. Between rush times, when the dining room was mostly empty, Halley sat out front, reading, doing her schoolwork, wiping down tables, wrapping silverware. But whenever the dining room started to fill up, Jenna sent her to the break room, which not only freed up valuable table space but also kept Halley away from obnoxious customers like Sweet Tea Guy.

The situation wasn't ideal, but there were worse alternatives. At age twelve, Halley was legally old enough to stay home by herself while Jenna worked, but there was no way on God's green earth that Jenna was letting Halley get farther away from her than sprinting distance. That was how it had been for the past year and a half, and how it would continue for the foreseeable future.

The building that now housed Lalo's Kitchen had once been a law office, but that had been eight years ago, well before Jenna's time. She'd only ever known it in its present form, beautifully renovated in a pleasant blend of modern comfort and retro style. The exposed brick wall on the left side of the big open dining room continued down a long hallway that made a straight shot to the back of the building, with doorways on the right. Jenna went down the hallway, backing against the wall to make way for Clint, another part-time server, who was carrying a loaded tray to the dining room. She passed the kitchen, where Abel, the cook, was lifting a metal basket of fragrant, glistening sweet potato fries out of the deep fryer. Next came the two restrooms, followed by a third door, topped by a sign that said Employees Only. This led to a passageway connecting Lalo's Kitchen to Tito's Bar, with access to two break rooms, two offices, and a closet of cleaning supplies shared by both businesses.

Jenna entered the passageway, then opened the door to the break room belonging to Lalo's Kitchen.

It was a small but comfortable space, with a narrow

fridge shoehorned in at the end of a wall of efficient cab-
inetry. Leftover cake from Clint's birthday stood on the
counter next to a stack of disposable plates. Another wall
was taken up by two rows of cubbies with employees'
names written on labels in Veronica's pretty hand-letter-
ing script. There was even a cubby for Halley, filled with
schoolbooks, notebooks, sketchbooks and leisure reading.

But Halley herself was nowhere in sight.

Jenna backed up through the Employees Only door,
which hadn't yet shut behind her. The restroom doors were
both slightly ajar, and the lights were off.

She turned the other way, looking down the remainder
of the hallway to the glass back door. She'd never liked that
door. It led to the patio, the space of which was divided by
vine-covered columns and trellises into lots of cozy little
room-like areas. Anyone could slip in from there while
Jenna was occupied in the front and reach the break room
without her ever knowing.

A sound from the passageway made her jump. There
was Halley, coming out of the break room of Tito's Bar,
holding a canned soda in one hand and a paperback book
in the other, with one finger marking her place.

Jenna hadn't had time to build up much of a panic,
but her knees went weak with relief and she had to lean
against a wall.

"What were you doing in there?" she asked, fear sharp-
ening her voice.

Halley tossed back her straight blond hair. "Tito told
me he got me some of those sodas I like, so I went to his
break room to get one."

A quiver of irritation ran down Jenna's spine. She didn't
like for Halley to go into areas that properly belonged to
the bar, at least during business hours. Besides the safety

issues, she felt sensitive about bringing up a child so close to a bar.

Of course, Tito's wasn't really a *bar* bar. Yes, it did have the word *bar* right there in the name—Tito's Bar. But it stood right next to Lalo's Kitchen, with a big pass-through doorway connecting the two businesses about halfway down the connecting wall, which gave it the vibe of a bar and grill, or even a European tavern, rather than a straight-up bar. You could bring your craft beer from Tito's over to your table at Lalo's, or take your burger from Lalo's to your spot at Tito's, and pay for your purchases at either cash register. And as Tito himself often said, people who were willing to pay eight dollars for a beer generally weren't looking to get drunk. Still, the place did sell hard liquor, and have the occasional three-sheets-to-the-wind customer.

"You know, we have a full selection of craft sodas on tap right here in the restaurant that you can drink for free," Jenna said.

Halley shrugged. "I like these ones from H-E-B. Tito got them just for me. But the box they come in is too deep to fit in our break room fridge. So he put them in *his* break room fridge and said I could come get one anytime I want."

"Take a few out at a time and keep them in our fridge," said Jenna. "I don't want you going back and forth between the restaurant and the bar."

"But Tito's fridge is, like, twelve feet away from ours!"

"It's in a different building. Anyway, I don't want you leaving the break room at all without asking me first."

They were rash words, and she knew she'd made a mistake the instant she heard them coming out of her mouth. Halley stared at her in disbelief. "Seriously? You want me to ask permission every time I go to the restroom? That doesn't even make sense. I'd have to leave the break room to begin with before I could find you in the dining room to ask permission. And that's if you're even *in* the dining room. Sometimes you fill in at bartending, which means I'd have to go to the bar to track you down—and you don't want me to go into the bar."

Jenna's head swam. She didn't have time to quibble over semantics; she had to get back to work. But she couldn't walk away without fixing this.

"You don't have to ask permission to go to the restroom," she said. "But for everything else, find me and ask first."

"What do you mean, *everything else*? You just told me to stay out of Tito's break room. Where else am I going to go?"

Jenna sighed. "Look, I know it doesn't seem fair for you to be stuck in the break room for hours on end. But that's how it has to be right now."

"Why?" Halley asked.

"What do you mean, why? You know why. You can't be too careful."

"Yes, you can."

Halley wasn't whining or cajoling. She was as cool and composed as Jenna had been with Sweet Tea Guy.

"*What* did you say?" Jenna asked, putting some starch in her tone, in a last-ditch hope that Halley would back down.

Halley did not back down.

"I said yes, you can. You *can* be too careful. If you're so afraid of crowds that you never leave your house, or so scared of doctors that you refuse to go to the hospital when you're hurt, or so worried about food poisoning that you never eat food and end up starving to death, then you're too careful. I'm just saying."

She was right, of course. It was exactly the sort of thing

Jenna would have said to her own mother at that age, in pretty much the exact same words.

Jenna stared at Halley, and Halley stared right back. When had Halley gotten so *tall*? She was almost eye to eye with Jenna now. It was almost like looking in a mirror. That hair, those cheekbones, that hard set to her chin, were eerily like Jenna's own.

The unflinching gaze of the bright blue eyes, though— that was all Chase.

Jenna drew herself up as tall as she could. "This isn't that and you know it. I just want you safe, Kara. Okay?"

"Halley."

"What?"

"I'm not Kara, I'm Halley."

Jenna shut her eyes. She wanted to scream. What was happening? How had this situation gotten so far outside of her control?

"I know," she said. "I'm sorry. Just be safe, okay, Halley?"

"Okay, Mother," Halley said with a tiny sigh.

She managed to pack a lot of subtext into that sentence, foremost of which was, *You're not my mother.* Halley had never said those words to Jenna, not out loud, but Jenna could feel them in the air.

Halley had started calling Jenna Mother when she was four years old, long before either of them could have possibly suspected that Jenna would one day be her legal guardian. Halley had gone on calling Kara Mom, but by some odd child logic, she'd found this other word that meant the same thing and decided to use it for Jenna. Kara hadn't liked it much, but she hadn't been able to stop Halley from doing it, and eight years later Halley was still calling Jenna Mother. Sometimes the name had a warm, affectionate feel to it. Other times, like now, it sounded formal and stiff.

Halley went to the correct, Jenna-approved break room and closed the door behind her. The whole thing was surreal, as if Jenna were watching herself at that age, shutting her bedroom door in her own mother's face.

Somehow she'd never envisioned Halley going through a back-talking, authority-challenging stage. Halley was supposed to be immune to all that. She'd seen so many ugly things at such an early age that she was supposed to be grateful just to be in a stable environment, and happy to follow the rules because they were there for her protection.

She used to cling to Jenna whenever Kara came to pick her up, her voice shrill with desperation. *No, please! Don't let her take me away. I want to stay with you!*

It had been like ripping her heart out to let Kara pry off those clinging little arms and take Halley back to the house the two of them had shared with Chase—a dank, disorderly, comfortless house full of brooding silences and ugly outbursts.

Halley didn't cling to Jenna anymore. There was no need now that the two of them were together all the time. The stable, peaceful home life with a predictable schedule, no yelling and plenty of food in the fridge was now the everyday life. Maybe it had lost its value now that there was no horrible alternative to compare it to. Maybe it was confining and dull.

That could spell trouble. Halley wasn't even a teenager yet, but she would be soon. And sometimes teenagers did terrible things.

Jenna shook her head hard. What mattered was that she'd gotten Halley far away from the bad stuff. She'd changed their names, covered their tracks and started a whole new life for them several states away. If Halley started giving her a little lip, well, Jenna could deal with that.

She got back to the dining room just in time to see Clint bring Sweet Tea Guy his order of nachos. Sweet Tea Guy didn't look pleased about exchanging Jenna with Clint, but there was nothing he could do about it. In another twenty minutes—half an hour, tops—he'd be gone.

But he didn't leave. And as the evening passed and the crowd thinned, he moved on from sweet tea to beer.

Never mind, Jenna thought as she served and bussed tables. *You can't stay here forever. I can wait you out.*

One of the big TVs was rebroadcasting the Monaco Grand Prix. Jenna's dad used to watch Formula 1 racing, and when she was little she'd watch with him sometimes, curled up next to him in his big armchair. The Monaco Grand Prix was a notorious street circuit race, with very little room for passing, and no room at all for driver error. Jenna watched a red Alfa Romeo careening through the streets, skimming walls and buildings with mere millimeters to spare.

The sight flooded her with memories of another Alfa Romeo, also red, driven by a broodingly handsome boy with his left hand resting carelessly on the steering wheel and his right arm stretched out along the seat back, warm against Jenna's shoulders. That one had been a street car, not a race car, but with enough power in its engine to reach glorious adrenaline-spiking speeds with no trouble at all, hugging the turns of narrow country roads through the Blue Ridge foothills. She'd loved those drives—windows down, music cranked up, the world rushing by as the boy at the wheel gave her that heart-melting James Dean smile. Now the memory made her sick.

She closed out a party of seven, and after they left she saw Luke wiping down Sweet Tea Guy's table. Yay! Gone at last.

"Looks like things are finally calming down," Luke

told her. He was tough-looking, with his strong build and full beard, but with the kindest eyes Jenna had ever seen. "I'm going to head home."

"Okay. Thanks for coming in."

"No problem. Have you finished making out next week's schedule?"

"Not yet. I'll get it sent out tomorrow."

"All right." He started to go, then turned back. "Almost forgot. The chalkboard got messed up tonight. I think someone spilled a beer on it. I know Veronica usually does the chalkboard art, but she's gone home. Do you think Halley might want to give it a go? She's always drawing, and she's really good."

Jenna smiled. "I'll ask her. I'm sure she'll be happy to try her hand."

"Great. See you next week."

As she watched him leave, she sent up a quick prayer of thanksgiving that this most excellent of bosses was back on the job. Some months earlier, Luke had gotten fed up with Lalo's constant micromanaging and undermining and had actually quit without notice, just taken off his apron and walked out the door, right in the middle of a dinner rush. It had been a pretty dramatic thing for mild-mannered Luke to do, but as it turned out, he'd also been dumped by his girl and was at the end of his rope.

That had been the beginning of a busy and stressful time in Jenna's work life. To Lalo's credit, he'd pitched in, doing his best to take over Luke's duties, but he hadn't done them very well. He'd have done better to give Jenna more responsibility to help, which as it turned out was one of the many things Luke had wanted him to do all along, but he hadn't. It was as if Lalo had to prove that he knew best.

Lalo did not know best.

It was sorely trying for Jenna, being lectured on how

to do her job by someone who knew far less than she did about what that job actually entailed. The part-time employees weren't being managed properly; they slacked off, playing fast and loose with the schedule. Afraid to hold them accountable, Lalo tried instead to make them all happy by demanding more from his reliable employees. It was a case of the squeaky wheels getting all the grease, and the smooth-running, reliable wheels having their bearings ground down under excess strain.

Lalo's Kitchen had gone noticeably downhill. Food quality suffered, service got slower and sloppier, and the place always seemed to look dirty. Every day, Jenna heard from longtime customers complaining about the decline. They missed Luke, and his dog, Porter, and the way things had been under his management, and they weren't shy about saying so. Slowly, those longtime customers started dropping away.

Jenna liked to think that the final straw had been when she'd given Lalo her two weeks' notice. She hadn't wanted to leave the place that had been a major factor in bringing her to Limestone Springs to begin with, but it wasn't the same place anymore, and she'd said so. Lalo had replied, *Hold that thought*, and taken out his cell phone and called Luke right then and there, and begged him to come back. Luke had agreed to return only if certain demands were met, one of which was that Jenna get moved up to management. Lalo had complied. Since then, he'd mostly kept out of the way and let his managers manage. The customers had come back as well, revenue went up, and everything was better.

By closing time, Lalo's Kitchen had cleared out completely, and Tito's Bar was mostly empty. Standard policy for both restaurant and bar was to not rush customers out right at closing time. As long as they were behaving themselves, they could stay while the workers cleaned around them, and as long as they weren't drunk, Tito would go on serving them.

Jenna stood in the pass-through between the bar and the restaurant, leaning her shoulder against the casing as she faced the bar. It was quieter now, quiet enough to hear the music being piped into both spaces—a carefully crafted mix of hits and lesser-known favorites from the past few decades. Tito was in charge of playlists, and he took the responsibility very seriously. He knew exactly what to play to foster whichever mood he wanted to cultivate in the customers.

He was standing behind the bar now, slender and straight in his snowy white shirt and black vest, his perfect posture making him appear taller than he was. He always wore black and white at work. Jenna didn't know if he even had any other clothes. Light from the overhead pendant fixture shone on his hair, making it look impossibly glossy, like polished ebony.

His dark eyes swept over his domain. Long tables and benches ran almost the full length of the room. They were empty now except for one stein of beer on the table closest to the pass-through.

Jenna liked Tito's face, with its high forehead and cheekbones tapering to a long chin covered by a neatly trimmed beard, its thick black eyebrows and deep-set dark eyes, its wide, sensitive mouth. It was a thoughtful, intelligent, inquisitive face, with a look of query and searching about it—a responsive, mobile face, capable of being quirked into a rich variety of comical expressions. He was graceful and deliberate in movement, whether pouring a drink or running a damp cloth across the sparkling-clean surface of the bar top. At the end of the night, when he was counting money, he always put on a pair of old-fashioned gold-rimmed spectacles that perched unevenly on the end of his long bony nose, and looked at Jenna over the tops of them with his forehead all wrinkled up.

Everyone liked and trusted Tito. Customers confided in him, spilling out their troubles over their drinks. It was a stereotype, the sympathetic bartender, but justified in his case. There was something about him that inspired confidence, something deeply compassionate but also thoroughly rational, a razor-sharp intellect softened by self-deprecating humor and a sincere interest in other people.

Jenna understood the draw. She felt it herself. It would be so easy to confide in Tito, pouring out the whole messy history of how she and Halley had come to Limestone Springs, sharing the doubts that wracked her day and night, appealing to him for the wisdom and insight she knew he'd be happy to share, if only she'd ask.

But that could never happen. Her secrets had to stay secrets. She had to keep her new life, and Halley's, airtight. She couldn't afford to slip up.

Tito's eyes met Jenna's, and he smiled at her. It was the easy, casual smile of a good friend, but it sent a peculiar flutter through her heart. She smiled back.

She was about to turn around and head back to her own duties when someone appeared just beyond Tito, out of the hallway that ran along the far wall to the restrooms. It was Sweet Tea Guy. He crossed in front of the bar to the table closest to where Jenna was standing, picked up the beer stein and raised it to her, his grin as goofy as ever.

Jenna felt her own smile wilt.

Ordinarily, Jenna liked working closing shifts. She and Halley were both night owls, and homeschooling gave them the freedom to set their own hours. Her favorite time of day was after the last customer had left and the doors had been locked—especially on nights when Tito was closing, too.

And now here was Sweet Tea Guy, refusing to leave, ruining everything, the way inebriated guys always did.

Minutes passed. The part-timers did their end-of-shift cleaning tasks and went home. Luke left for the night, and so did Lalo. And still Sweet Tea Guy sat stubbornly in his spot, clutching his drink, refusing to budge.

Jenna went back to the break room. Halley was sitting on the tiny sofa with a book, her coltish legs bent at sharp angles. She looked up expectantly as the door opened.

"Sorry, you can't come out yet," Jenna said. "Some die-hard is out here taking his time. He got a little inappropriate with me earlier, and I don't want you in the dining room until he leaves."

Halley scowled. "Can't you throw him out?"

"Not yet. We'll clean around him for as long as we can and hope he takes the hint and leaves on his own before it comes to that."

Halley let out a long, exasperated sigh—whether at Sweet Tea Guy for being so inconsiderate, or at Jenna for not throwing him out, or at Jenna for being so protective, was impossible to tell.

"It shouldn't be much longer," Jenna said with an optimism she did not feel. "Tito just switched the playlist over to indie pop."

Indie pop, according to Tito, was the genre to play when you wanted lingering customers to wind down and clear out. Ordinarily it worked like a charm, but Jenna suspected Sweet Tea Guy might be a tougher nut to crack.

"Lock the door behind me," she said.

Halley gave her an incredulous look.

"Do it," said Jenna. "I'll come get you when he's gone."

Halley clomped over to the door and pushed it shut.

As soon as she heard the dry click of the lock, Jenna shut her eyes and leaned her forehead against the door, suddenly exhausted.

Then she opened the door to the supply closet and started loading her cleaning cart. A clipboard hung from a hook on the side, with a checklist for all the tasks to be done at closing, and spaces for the closer to initial as each item was completed. Everything was right there, perfectly spelled out with no ambiguity. Luke had designed those checklists, and Jenna loved them.

Her back was to the doorway, but she saw the shadow fall from behind her. She turned. There was Sweet Tea Guy, blocking the exit. His grin was as wide as ever, but its goofiness had been replaced by something else.

"There you are, sweet thing," he said softly. "Let's have a little alone time, you and me."

As come-ons went, this one was pretty bald. It was insulting that he could possibly believe that Jenna or any other woman would take him up on it.

Her heart pounded hard, not with fear but with anger—against him and every other man who'd ever tried to take what wasn't his.

Jenna grabbed the push broom. She was ready to rumble. Sweet Tea Guy was messing with the wrong woman. He had no idea how thrilled she would be to take out her frustrations on someone who so thoroughly deserved it.

But before either of them could make a move, a calm voice spoke from the passageway.

"Sir, this is an employees-only area. We don't allow customers back here."

Jenna couldn't see who'd spoken, but she didn't have to. She would know that voice anywhere. It was rich in timbre, with a smooth, rolling cadence—the kind of voice used by advertisers to sell fine wines or luxury cars.

Sweet Tea Guy didn't even turn his head, just waved a dismissive hand. "It's all right, Tito," he said. "I know this girl. We're having us a little visit. Go on back behind your bar."

"No," Tito said. His voice was still calm, but the pitch had deepened, and he'd dropped the *sir*. "Come on, R.J. We're closed for business now. It's time for you to go home."

R.J. did turn then, shooting a scowl in Tito's direction. He was a big, tall man, probably a good fifty pounds heavier than Tito.

"I'll leave when I'm good and ready," he said. "Now go back to the bar and mind your own business."

"You'll leave now," said Tito.

R.J.'s hands curled into fists, and he lumbered off to the left, out of Jenna's field of vision. She heard the sound of a scuffle, followed by a yelp of surprise. She hurried through the doorway of the closet in time to see R.J. with his arm bent behind him, being frog-marched by the bartender down the passageway and around the corner.

"Hey!" R.J. barked. "What do you think you're doing?"

The break room door opened, and Halley's shocked face peeked out.

"Close the door!" Jenna shouted. "I told you to stay put and keep the door locked!"

Halley did not shut the door. She came out and crept close to Jenna, almost touching but not quite. Together, they followed Tito into the dining room.

"Get your hands off me!" said R.J. "Who do you think you are? Let go!"

He kept hurling abuse at Tito all the way across the dining room to the glass door, finishing up with how he was never going to spend another dime in Tito's Bar or Lalo's Kitchen again.

"Funny, I was just about to suggest that very thing myself," Tito said.

He tossed R.J. outside, shut the door behind him and turned the bolt.

R.J. stood on the sidewalk, rumpled and indignant, glaring at Tito through the glass. There was no trace of a grin now, goofy or otherwise. His face was red and twisted with rage.

Unfazed, Tito took out his phone and snapped R.J.'s picture, then tapped his screen a few times. "I'm adding R.J. to the *do not serve* group text," he said.

He didn't look the least bit rattled or shaken. He certainly didn't look as if he'd just bounced a much larger man out of a bar. He didn't even appear capable of doing such a thing, which was probably part of the reason why he was so successful at it. Customers at Tito's Bar were generally well-behaved, but whenever one of them did need to be removed from the premises, Tito was up to the task. People underestimated him at their peril.

R.J. straightened his shirt in an exaggerated way and walked off down the sidewalk, his steps weaving a bit from side to side.

Tito flipped the sign on the door to the Closed side and turned to face Jenna and Halley. "Sorry about all that," he said, picking up the abandoned beer stein and carrying it behind the bar. "R.J.'s always been a little on the obnoxious side, but tonight's the first time I've seen him cross the line. You all right?"

"I'm fine," said Jenna, but her voice shook a little, and a wave of weakness washed over her. She was still clutching the push broom. She leaned it against the back of a booth, steadied herself and said, "You didn't have to do that, you know. I could have handled it."

The words sounded ungracious in her own ears, but Tito

didn't seem to mind. He glanced at her over the bar top as he poured out the last of R.J.'s drink and said, "Okay."

Then he picked up the dedicated cell phone used for streaming music and started tapping. The strains of indie pop that had been coming through the speakers instantly ceased.

Tito looked at Jenna and smiled. "It's closing time," he said. "And you know what that means."

Jenna knew, all right. The best part of the night was about to begin.

NEW SERIES COMING!

RELEASING JANUARY

Special EDITION

Believe in love.

Overcome obstacles.

Find happiness.

For fans of Virgin River, Sweet Magnolias or Grace & Frankie you'll love this new series line. Stories with strong romantic tropes and hooks told in a modern and complex way.